HOSTILE TERRITORY

LINDSAY MCKENNA

Blue Turtle Publishing

Hostile Territory
First edition 2024
Original Copyright © 2015, R. Eileen Nauman
ISBN Print Edition: 978-1-951236-51-9

Excerpt from *Shadow Target*
Original Copyright © 2015, R. Eileen Nauman

This is a work of fiction. Names, characters, places, and incidents are either the product of the author's imagination or are used fictitiously, and any resemblance to actual persons, living or dead, business establishments, events or locales is entirely coincidental.

This edition is published by arrangement with Blue Turtle Publishing Company.

Dear Readers,

Now, book 5, Hostile Territory, features Special Forces Army Sergeant Mace Kilmer and Sierra Chastain, sniper. The last thing he wants in this hellhole of this Peruvian jungle where he hunts down drug lords, is to see a woman backing up his team. They are a hunter-killer team sent under top secret orders to stop the incursion of Russian drug teams pushing into the Highlands of Peru, near Machu Picchu, a World Heritage site and Cusco, a major city. His three-man team operates in the dark, along with three other teams. Together, they are hunting down the murderous Russians who take no prisoners. The other two Latino drug lords are outgunned by these ex-Spetsnaz storm troopers who rape, kill and plunder the innocent villagers to get more cocaine out of them, than ever before.

Sierra Chastain works for Shield Security, a global security company run by an ex-US Navy SEAL. Because she speaks Spanish, she is being sent under-cover to link up with Kilmer's team to hunt down a lethal Russian drug ringleader. When Kilmer sees what he thinks is a man leaping off the lip of a Blackhawk helicopter, he's more than shocked to see a woman staring back at him. They are like two territorial dogs in a fight. Sierra is a seasoned sniper and isn't going to take Patriarchal male B.S. from him. It's not a match made in heaven, but in hell.

Mace doesn't want to like Sierra, even though she's a vaunted Marine Corps trained sniper. She's a team member, gets along well with his other two sergeants, who adore her. Bringing goodies from the U.S. like hot sauce, candy, and junk food galore, the three of them have no quarrel with one another. Except Kilmer, who runs the team. His snarly attitude doesn't get far with Sierra. She's not afraid to stand up to male who has misplaced his authority, and he is caught off guard by her confidence…never mind he's drawn to her, man-to-woman. That is the thorn in his side, but he hides it, not sure what to do about it. How to treat her like any other military person and ignore her sex. He's been out in this green hell far too long.

There's no "handling" Chastain. Mace knows he has to somehow make amends and peace with her because she has an important job to do, and they can't do it without her. His ugly family past and destroyed marriage get in the way of seeing her skills and abilities. All his life he has worked with men, not women. Somehow, she gets inside his gruffness and snarly nature and over time and danger, knowing they will only survive if they are a team, Sierra quells his distrust and gains it, instead. And worse, they both know they are powerfully drawn to one another and can't do one damn thing about it. Not in this high-octane lethal environment. Will they survive?

Warmly,
Lindsay McKenna aka Eileen Nauman

Dedication

To all the readers who love romantic military suspense!

CHAPTER 1

S IERRA NEEDED HELP. She tried not to limp into the Shield Security facility where she worked. Hefting her black, nylon weapons bag over her left shoulder, she headed straight for the basement where the men's and women's locker rooms were located. Damn, but her right calf ached like a sonofabitch. Every bone in her body was stiff.

The flight out of Nairobi, Africa, had been long, and she'd slept most of the way back, until the landing gear thudding into place had awoken her on the approach into Reagan International Airport, Washington D.C. She had slept deeply, thankful that Shield always paid for business class tickets for their security contractors. If she'd been stuffed back in the cattle car of coach, she probably would have needed a pry bar to get her out of the seat with her leg in its current condition.

It was late afternoon at Shield Security. She passed by a couple of contractors she knew as she walked to the stairs leading to the basement.

"Hey, Chastain, good to see you back," one man called, lifting his hand in hello to her. "Good hunting?"

Sierra wearily raised her own hand back. "Yeah, we nailed that bastard in Somalia. Hey, is Alex Kazak around? Have you seen him?"

"Yeah, he's in a brief with Jack Driscoll on an upcoming mission to South America. Want me to send him down to the women's locker room?" and he grinned.

"Yeah, do that," she said in all seriousness. Gripping the oak rail on one side of the wide stairs that led down into the well-lit locker area, all Sierra wanted to do was get her weapons to the Weapons Room armorer down there. The sniper rifle she'd used, an XP, had handled the sand, heat and wind that Somalia was infamous for. Damn, her leg hurt.

Sierra dropped off her weapons bag to the woman manning the Armory. Freed of the seventy-pound load, her calf felt better. She wanted to get out of her civilian clothes and yearned for a long, hot, hot shower. She'd been able to clean up at a top-secret SEAL facility across the Somali border, in Kenya, and throw on her scruffy jeans, a red long-sleeved tee, plus a denim jacket for the trip home to the headquarters of Shield Security here in Alexandria, Virginia. Outside, it was snowing, building into a blizzard, late December as it was.

Halting at her locker, she shed her clothes, not looking too closely at her handiwork on her wounded right calf. She'd adhered the six-inch-long knife cut back together with green duct tape. It was an old SEAL fix for any wound when one didn't have the time to tend to it properly. Grimacing, she decided to leave the tape on while showering. Quickly unbraiding her black hair, feeling the sand and grit on her scalp, she yearned for real shampoo and conditioner. Hobbling into the shower area, Sierra hoped by the time she was done, that Alex would come down and help her.

Alex Kazak stuck his head around the corner of the women's entry point to their locker area, knocking on the wooden frame. "Sierra?" he called, his low voice echoing through the utility. He knew better than to enter unannounced. Half of Shield's security contractors were women, and he had no wish to run into a naked one of them by accident. The door was as far as he'd go.

"Yeah! Alex?"

"It's me. You need my medical services, Sierra?"

"I do," she hollered back. "Hold on one sec…"

Alex stepped away from the door, holding it open. He saw tall, curvy Sierra, her long black hair damp around her proud shoulders, come limping out. She was wearing a long red t-shirt that hung to her knees. Instantly, his gaze moved to her right leg. "What happened?" he demanded, pointing toward it.

Mouth quirking, Sierra limped out of the bathroom utility and pulled the white towel around her shoulders. "Last-minute knife fight with some Somalis who were a little pissed we shot their leader." She grinned up at the tall Ukrainian ex-Spetsnaz operator. "Let's go to the dispensary?" and she pointed to the right.

"Yes," he murmured, worried. "You wrapped it in duct tape?"

Scrubbing her damp hair with the towel as they walked down the tiled hall toward the medical facility, she said, "Yeah. Old SEAL trick."

"You were with SEALs?"

"This time around, yes." She smiled up at the broad-shouldered Ukrainian, huge in comparison to her. Sierra was five foot ten inches tall and weighed one-hundred and sixty pounds. She came from medium-boned stock via her Eastern Cherokee mother and was not a little thing at all. But, against Alex, she looked it. The big Ukrainian had married Lauren Parker, Chief Sniper Instructor at Shield. It had been a beautiful Autumn wedding. Sierra counted herself lucky to have been able to attend their small but warm ceremony before leaving for her sniper assignment in Somalia.

"Did you get the HVT?" Alex asked, opening the dispensary door for her.

Inside, there was a small waiting room and reception desk. Alex was one of two combat medics at Shield and, whenever he was on duty, he handled minor medical issues for the contractors. If it was serious, they were taken to the nearby hospital for treatment. Motioning toward the opened door on the left side of reception, he said, "Take room number one. No one is around. It is near quitting time on a Friday night." He smiled down at her. "You know how everyone leaves early on Friday afternoon?"

Sierra pushed room number one's door open. Inside was a gurney covered with paper and a medical room filled with everything that Alex would need to sew her up. "Yes. And there's a blizzard coming in."

"First of the season, they say," Alex said. He quietly closed the door behind him and set his medical bag on the counter. Going over to the examination table, he pulled out the bottom ramp for her. "Why don't you lay on your left side and expose that wounded right leg for me?" He helped Sierra up the step. She was fully capable of doing so herself, of course, but in Alex's eyes and world, she was a woman and therefore deserved respect. He watched Sierra closely, careful that she wasn't putting too much weight on her wounded calf. Releasing her elbow, he went to the cabinet and pulled out two warm light-blue blankets. Once she'd gotten settled and had tugged the hem of her nightie t-shirt down to her knees, he made sure she was comfy, and covered her with the blankets so that only the leg with the green duct tape on it was available to him from beneath them.

Pulling on a pair of latex gloves, he took a pair of blunt-nosed scissors and then gently felt around the wound with them. "Tell me about this?" he asked. He saw Sierra snuggle into the pillow, knowing she was exhausted. Her skin was golden-colored because she was half-Cherokee and half-Caucasian. Her black hair was still slightly damp and lay around her head and shoulders.

"Not much to tell," she murmured, closing her eyes. "I nailed the HVT and we were on the roof of a building across from where the tangos were at. They were like a hive of angry hornets and they came boiling out of every damned entrance of that building afterward."

Alex gently pushed and prodded here and there, watching her expression. "You had egress points? Yes?"

"Of course. It's just that it took a few seconds for me to break down my XP, get it in its sheath, and strap it onto my ruck before ex-filling." She let out a huff of air. "By that time, the tangos had spotted us on the roof and came over to say hello."

Alex grinned. "Okay, I am going to cut this tape off your calf. You know it will hurt."

"I know," Sierra muttered, steeling herself. Duct tape was great to stop bleeding, close a wound, and give it support, but it was hell peeling it off the skin around the wound later.

Alex carefully cut away the tape. As he did, blood leaked out all over his gloved hands and onto the paper beneath her leg. "When did this happen?"

"Yesterday," Sierra admitted. "And don't start ragging on me, Alex. I wasn't anywhere that I could get it looked at."

"Surely, you could have stopped at a hospital before taking the flight home?"

"I just wanted to come home," Sierra muttered, tensing as he began to pull the tape off her flesh. Her fist curved tight, and she forced herself to breathe through the red-hot pain.

"Okay," Alex murmured, removing the tape. "It is over. You can relax now, Sierra."

"How bad is it?"

Alex studied the six-inch knife wound, looking closely at the swollen, bloody area. "It is clean. No infection. Yet. Did you take antibiotics as soon as you could?"

"Yes. The max load prescribed. I know what infection in Africa can do."

"Good," he praised quietly, gently moving his long, large fingers along parallel to the deep cut. "Do you know if the man had a rusty knife? Did you see?"

She snorted. "Oh, come on, Alex! Like I was looking to see if the blade was clean steel or rusted? In the middle of a knife fight for our lives? Hell, I don't know."

"But you did give yourself a tetanus shot as soon after was you could?" and he lifted his chin, looking up at her. Sierra was laying with her eyes tightly shut, her wide, expressive mouth thinned. Her hand was still in a fist, telling him she was feeling quite a bit of pain from the wound. He daubed the area with lidocaine to reduce the pain. Instantly, her mouth relaxed.

"Of course, I gave myself that tetanus shot. You make sure our blowout kit has one of everything in it," she said, barley opening one eye and giving him a half grin.

"You are a model patient, Sierra."

"I was going to try and stitch it up, Alex, but I almost missed my flight. There was nowhere in business class that I could do it." She laughed. "If I had, the people around me would probably have fainted from all the blood."

He laughed along with her, nodding. "Okay, I am going to put some lidocaine into a syringe. You know the drill. I'll put it outside and around the wound, and then I will wait until the numbness takes hold. After it's numb I'll put some in the wound and you won't feel a thing."

"Then," Sierra said wryly, "you're going to scrub the shit out of it and disinfect it and then tape me up so there won't be a scar or, worse, an infection. Right?" and she raised one arched, black eyebrow, giving him a demanding stare.

Alex's mouth moved into a sour smile. "Yes. You should have become a combat medic, Sierra. You are good at this." He continued to numb the wound site. Sierra didn't move, didn't jerk her leg out of his hands. She lay still and tolerated the pain as it lessened.

"No thanks. I like being a sniper. Not as messy."

"Okay, this stage is done." He dropped the syringe into the sharps container on the wall and said, "let me examine the rest of you while that lidocaine takes hold, and I can brush the area?" That was protocol. He didn't trust Sierra not to have other cuts. And when in Africa, or any other jungle environment, infection could blow up on a person in a matter of hours and kill them if they didn't get medical help right away.

Sierra groaned. "I'm fine, Alex. I'm just exhausted. Can't I just lay here under these nice warm blankets?"

"No," he murmured. "You know the drill. You are supposed to be getting an exam after every mission is complete." He peeled off the blanket from her shoulders and patted it around her waist. "This will not hurt," he promised, moving her damp hair aside, critically examining her skull, face, ears, hairline and neck.

Making an unhappy sound, Sierra muttered, "You're too damned good, Alex." She relaxed as the Ukrainian lifted her shoulder to make sure it worked, pushed up the material, examining her arm on all sides, and then laid it back down gently against her body. "Really. I'm okay, Alex."

"Mmm," was all he said, using his hands to check her ribcage by gently pressing inward to test each bone. Sierra flinched.

"Just bruises, Alex. That's all."

He stood there, watching her forest-green eyes narrow a little as he pressed her lower ribs a bit more firmly. She winced again. "Want to tell me about this, Sierra?" he asked in a casual manner. Alex had found all operators tended to let bruises, and even fractures, go if they could get away with it. They all said the same thing: they were okay. Nothing was wrong. *Right.*

"During our exfil, we got into a fight with five Somalis who were supposed to protect the warlord of theirs. The one I'd killed. They all had machetes and knives on them."

"How many SEALs in your team?"

"Four, plus me, the non-SEAL." She grinned a little. "It was a fair fight. Five against five."

He placed his large hand gently against her cranky ribs. "And how did you get this?"

"I was pushed into a palm tree," she admitted. "Hit here," and she took her right hand and pointed to her tender ribs. "Just bruises Alex. Honest to God, just bruises."

"Any broken skin?"

"No. I looked all over my torso when I showered at the SEAL facility afterward."

"Hmmm, okay, I'm going to poke and prod a little more to make sure there is no fractures, Sierra."

"I knew you'd say that," she grumped, scowling.

A slight smile hovered around Alex's mouth as he examined her ribs through the t-shirt. Watching Sierra's expression closely, her mouth thinned a little, but she didn't try and move away from his fingers as he pushed a little more here and there. "Okay, I believe you. But you have three bruised ribs, Sierra."

"They'll be fine in a couple of days," she assured him brightly, grinning.

"Good thing you have the next month off." Alex knew that Jack Driscoll, owner of Shield and an ex-SEAL himself, always slated a month break between ops this intense. Driscoll fully realized the brutality of such missions and wanted his people to rest up and come down from the dangerous situations they were constantly placed in.

"Tell me about it. I intend to just stay in my cabin outside of Alexandria, read my paperback books, enjoy really good hot coffee, and sleep a lot."

"Sounds like a good prescription to me," he murmured. Alex worked her hip, moving it slowly to see if she reacted. She did. "Same reason? You were shoved into that palm tree?"

"Yeah," she grunted.

"Stiff?"

"Very."

"Nothing broken though," Alex assured her. "Bruises there, too?"

"Yes. No skin is broken. Move on."

He chuckled. Operators knew that any abraded skin or open wound could become quickly infected. He knew Sierra would not risk that and lie to him. "Well, I'm going to give you a shot of antibiotic in your butt. You knew that was coming."

"I'd feel left out if you didn't, Alex."

"Your black humor always is refreshing, Sierra."

"It's all I got left in my tank right now."

He laughed quietly and finished his examination of her. "Okay, time to scrub out that knife cut. It should be painless for you." He took off his gloves, dropped them in a wastebasket, and pulled on a new pair after getting the items he'd need to clean out the wound.

"Did you and Lauren have a nice Christmas together?"

"Very," Alex assured her, testing the flesh to make sure it was numbed. Sierra didn't flinch, so he went to work on it. "It was my first Christmas with her. I helped her bake a goose. She made the stuffing. It was very good."

"Is Lauren happy staying at Shield and not going out on missions anymore?" Sierra asked.

"Yes. And I am very happy about it, too."

"How was the Shield Christmas party? I missed that, too."

"Very funny. Some of the operators got together and put on a skit. Of course, there was wine, beer and plenty of good food, too." Once he'd scrubbed out the wound, placed antibiotic into it, Alex went to work taping it closed so that Sierra would only have a very thin scar. Because she was young, only twenty-eight, that slight scar would disappear over time.

"I joined two years ago," Sierra told him, "And I had a great time at their Christmas party that first year." She snorted. "I was sitting on a hot rooftop for weeks with my XP, waiting for that Somali warlord to appear. I was bitching to the SEALs that last year I was with Shield employees having a great time and this year, I'm frying in the heat and sand of Mogadishu. They had no pity for me," and she laughed.

"I think," Alex said, nearly finished up, "that Jack has your Christmas gift in his office. You might drop by and pick it up on your way out. Is your car in the long-term parking lot behind the building?"

"Yes." Sierra made a face. "I think I'm going straight home, Alex. I'm whipped. He's closing down the office for this coming week, right? With New Year's and all?"

"Yes. Starting tomorrow, Saturday, the office is closed.

"Where's the New Year's Party going to be held this year?"

"Up at Cal and Sky's home. They have volunteered to put it on."

"Oh, that's great! She just had a baby. I want to see their little girl!"

Alex smiled. Their baby is beautiful," he said warmly. "And they are so happy with her."

"That's good," Sierra murmured, feeling tiredness wash through her. The blankets were warm. She was safe and could let down. Alex, being the gentle giant he was, was soothing with his bedside manner. She'd never seen the man angry or upset. It was as if he were a healing energy, wherever he went. Maybe it was his combat medic personality.

She said, "That's in five days. I'll be able to attend. I'll call Sky and let her know I'm coming. See if she wants me to bring something up for the casserole dinner that we always have."

"That would be good," Alex agreed. "There, you are finished, Sierra." He looked proudly at his handiwork. "It looks very good. I'm going to dress it and then place a waterproof bandage over it. I will need to see you in three days. We can meet here at Shield. Okay?"

"Okay. Thanks, pardoner. You're the best."

"I am sure Jack will expect a sit rep, situation report, on your mission, but I will tell him I'm giving you five days off due to the wound before it is to be handed into him. Okay?"

Sierra reached out and touched Alex's thick forearm sprinkled with its dark hair. "You're the best. You're SUCH a hen mother, Kazak."

Alex grinned and said, "It is 'mother hen', Sierra."

"Somehow," she said, sitting up, smiling, "some of your converted slang has taken hold around here and now everyone is slaying our slang. This is all your fault, you know?"

Chuckling, he nodded, placing items in an organized way back into his medical kit. "I am trying very hard not to slay the slang, but every day, someone will drop by my office and give me a new saying to see what I do with it."

"In hopes that you'll say it backwards?" she chuckled. The humor in Alex's hazel gaze made her feel good. He had a good touch with people and everyone at Shield loved him dearly because he could take a joke and laugh with them.

"I suppose so," he said, grinning. "Did you pick up any Somali language? Some of their slang to share with me?"

Easing off the table, she said, "No, unfortunately I didn't. But," she gave him an evil look, "one of the SEALs knows the language and he put a few down on paper and gave it to me. It's in my rifle bag. I'll get them to you when I see you later this week."

"Right now," he said, patting her shoulder gently, "I require you to go home and rest and sleep. Do a lot of both. Okay? You're still up on that cortisol cliff."

She tested her leg and it felt so much better. "I can't fool you, can I, Alex?"

"No, not when it comes to anything having to do with combat. Come, I will walk you to your car."

Sierra sat up, gasping. She was covered with sweat, the flannel nightgown she wore soaked through. Wildly looking around the bedroom of her cabin, she saw that it was barely light outside the curtained window. Rubbing her face, her heart pounding so hard she thought it would leap out of her chest, she muffled a frustrated sound. The nightmare had been the Somalis chasing the HVT team through the city. They were racing for their rally point when they were jumped by a group of machete-wielding attackers just outside the city.

Making another sound, Sierra pushed the covers aside. As she lifted her legs across her queen-sized bed, pain rippled up her right calf. Dammit! She'd been back five days and every night this same scenario stalked her dreams. Her feet hit the cool cedar floor. It was stabilizing. Looking at the clock on the bed stand, she pushed her thick hair away from her face, some stray strands sticking in rivulets of sweat. It was nearly 0800, eight a.m. Helluva way to celebrate the New Year's party. She'd stayed overnight at Sky and Cal's home, driving back to her place the next morning. The same nightmare had occurred at their home, too.

Pushing out of bed, ignoring the pain that came when she put her full weight down on her right leg, Sierra headed for the bathroom. She had to get out of her fear-drenched, smelly nightgown, and wash her hair. Desperate to be rid of the sour odor off her skin and clothing, she muttered a curse. Wrinkling her nose, she entered the tiled bathroom, feeling the electrically heated floor beneath the bare soles of her feet. They warmed. Shutting the door, Sierra pulled the bamboo curtains aside and looked outside at the coming dawn. Her cabin sat on a hill, ensconced with bare, deciduous trees, their gray limbs lifting skyward. She saw a cloudless sky. An oak tree, one that sat near the north side of the cabin, had its branches covered in ice and layers of snow. It looked beautiful to her. Turning, Sierra knew the drill. This wasn't the first time, and it wasn't going to be the last time, she had nightmares. It was part of her business. As her mother had told her, dreams were the way people worked through their emotions about something that had happened to them.

She pulled the glass door open, wanting so badly to get beneath the double rain sprinklers located on either side of the huge room. There was a tiled bench as well, and she gratefully sat down, double-checking the waterproof bandage on her calf. Her knife-wound was healing quickly, and she appreciated how good Alex was. The scar was just a thin red line now under the surgical tape holding it together.

As she showered, the warming droplets soaking into the hair running half-way down her back, the water in streams across her face, Sierra tried to put out of her mind what Jack Driscoll had told her at the New Year's party. He'd said an urgent South American mission had just been handed to them by the CIA. There was an immediate need for a sniper to join a three-man hunter-killer Special Forces team in the highlands of Peru. Jack had said he was targeting her for the mission. Was her leg healed-up enough to take the assignment?

Sierra washed her face with her favorite bath gel. The one scented with a Plumaria fragrance. Inhaling that wonderful fragrance, she quickly washed the fear-sweat away, luxuriating in the steam, humidity and heat around her body.

Did she want to take that mission? Jack had said that no other sniper was available. They were all out on other assignments. She was the only one left. Grimacing, she didn't feel good about it. Her gut had never led her wrong. Jack seemed to think it was a straightforward op. One certainly well within her skillset to handle. Best of all, she was fluent in Spanish, the language of Peru. She was the perfect operator for the mission.

Washing away the bubbles from her face, Sierra quickly scrubbed the rest of her body. Her ribs were still sore but improving. The bruises along her ribcage were turning from blue and purple to green and yellow. Alex had looked at them approvingly, satisfied that, in another week, she'd be fine. Frowning, Sierra realized she'd been dragging her feet about the up-and-coming mission. Why? Whenever she got a bad vibe on a mission, it usually went to hell in a handbasket sooner or later. Or worse, a busted op.

She'd had a bad feeling about the Somali mission, too, and look what had happened. Her mother was very psychic, and Sierra had her DNA. She could sense things when others could not. Feel things, and yet not be able to interpret exactly what she was sensing. As a sniper in the Marine Corps for many years, her intuition had saved her life far too many times to be mere fantasy. Her full mouth thinned as she reached for the shampoo that was also scented with Plumaria. Whenever she ignored her intuition, things didn't go well. Her heart squeezed with guilt and anguish as she began to wash her long, thick black hair.

The last time she hadn't listened to her intuition, it had gotten Jeb killed on a mountain in the Hindu Kush. Sierra should have said something sooner. Should have… he died because she'd ignored her sense of danger nearby. Why? Why had she done that? Jeb had died in her arms, and she'd been unable to save him. The man she'd loved for five years, had worked with as a sniper and spotter team all that time, had bled out in her arms. And there'd been nothing Sierra could do to halt the bleeding or save his life. Even now, her heart wrenched in her chest, reliving that event.

That had happened several years ago. And, on some days, Sierra almost forgot about it, about losing the man she'd loved. And, on other days, like right now, the grief of the loss of Jeb brought her to her knees. She missed him so much. Missed his Tennessee laid-back southern-boy way of talking and outlook on life. His easy-going sense of humor. The kindness and love he always bestowed upon her. The only reason they hadn't married was that the Marine Corps would have separated them. Forced them apart. Because husband-wife sniper teams were not allowed.

Tears formed in her eyes. She missed Jeb. His deep love for her, his gentleness, his respect for her as an equal, all mixed with the soothing water from the shower heads above.

At times like this, when a mission had gone sideways and her life had been in danger, Sierra found that the nightmares always brought back memories of Jeb. When he'd been alive, he would hold her, murmur soft words against her hair, give her a sense of safety in their dangerous world. Because he'd loved her with all his life. And he'd given his life so that she could live.

CHAPTER 2

S IERRA WIPED GRITTY grains of sleep still pricking her eyes from their corners while she sat waiting in the briefing room of Shield Security. It now was day seven since her return from Somalia. Jack Driscoll, the big boss, wandered in, looking sharp in his black chinos and his crisp, white collegiate shirt, open at the neck. Alex followed in next, looking like he'd only just awakened about as recently as she had. He was in a pair of Levi's and a red cowboy shirt with the sleeves rolled up to just below his elbows. And then, she was surprised to see Lauren, Alex's wife, walk right in behind him. She wore a soft-lavender corduroy set of pants and a pale-pink long-sleeved sweater. Her red hair was tamed up into a knot on the top of her head. Usually, briefings only included people who knew something about the area, land or mission. They would fill her in on all the need-to-know intel that would help her during the op. But Lauren? Sierra nodded and smiled as her sniper sister sat down across opposite from her at the long, tiger-maple table.

Jack took the head of the table, Sierra on his right, and Alex on his left. Someone shut the door, and it grew quiet in the room. Jack provided the mission brief to all of them by clicking the 'Send' icon on his screen. The brief came up on the monitors of the computer desktops at each chair. He picked up the remote from the tabletop and clicked it toward the laptop set up on another small table to his left. The screen at the end of the room lit up with the power-point briefing he had put together for them.

"Okay," he said, looking over at Sierra, "here's the story. The CIA is asking for another of our snipers down in Peru." He flashed the map of the country on the screen. "That red circle is where you're going to be operating out of Sierra. It's called the Highlands, which sit anywhere between eight to fourteen thousand feet on the slopes of the Andes mountains." He picked up the laser pointer. He spun its beam tightly in such a way that the blurred, red dot encircled the area. "Your base of operation is going to be Cusco, which sits at nearly twelve thousand feet. It's closest to the Highlands. Your other base is going to be Aguas Calientes, a small tourist town at the foot of the world heritage site, Machu Picchu."

Sierra made notes on the separate, lined, yellow legal pad she always carried with her during a briefing. She never typed anything into her laptop.

Jack continued, "There are three US Army Special Forces hunter-killer teams, three men in each, assigned to this same area. They are under CIA directive. Over the last seven years, the Russian mafia, via a power base in New York City, has aggressively been entering this area. The Russians are the new players in this war, sparring with two drug lords who have controlled the growing of coca for the last twenty years, harvesting the leaves, and cooking them into cocaine. One of the old-school drug lords is Diego Valdez, out of Boliva, and the other is Marcos Suero, from Lima, Peru. The Latino leaders had a good, working relationship with the Q'ero Indians who live throughout this entire region. They are a tribe that was pre-Incan. And when the Incans took over to rule South America until the mid-1500's that lasted one-hundred years. Then, the Spanish came in and destroyed their empire but the Q'ero people, because they lived in such remote areas in the Highlands, had little contact with the Spaniards. Now, the Russians, who we all know are not very kind or generous, are constantly battling the Latinos and taking over their cocaine territory. And they aren't nice about it. And what is worse? The Q'ero people have been more or less pushed into or enslaved by the Russians to make and carry their cocaine up to an area where it can be transported by Russian helicopter out of the region."

On the screen, Sierra saw the photo of a hard-faced white man with a scar along his jaw, bald-headed, his large nose crooked severely to one side from an old break, his dark brown eyes glaring out at whoever had taken the picture. She got a chill down her spine, warning her that this man was evil personified. His mouth was thin, just a tight line, his jaw clenched, chin thrust out, as if he dared anyone to take him on. Apart from the startling one on his jaw, she saw a lot of other old scars here and there across his face. Flinching inwardly, she saw the top half of his right ear was missing. He was wearing military camos that she realized were Spetsnaz in origin.

"Who's this?" she asked Jack, glancing up at her boss.

"Your nemesis. Ex-Spetsnaz Captain, Olezka Volkov. He's forty years old, six foot three inches tall and two-hundred and twenty pounds of raw, hard muscle. His best friend, Petrov, who used to be the leader of Vlad Alexandrov's drug team, was killed by Sergeant Mace Kilmer. Mace is the head of one of these three-man spec force teams. After Pavlovitch was killed in a firefight at the village of Orilla, in the Peruvian jungle, a new Russian mafia leader in New York City, Rurik Burgov, chose Volkov to head up this team. I think Alex might have something to add?" and Jack looked over at the Ukrainian operator.

Sierra saw Alex's brows move downward, felt a shift of energy around him, saw the banked anger in his hazel eyes. "Who is this Volkov, Alex?" she asked.

"Someone you need to be very, very careful of ever meeting, Sierra. The only way you want to meet this cold-blooded bastard is to site him through your scope and pull the trigger."

Her nostrils flared. Volkov looked like an evil menace to her. "Okay, give me background on him?"

"I was with Vlad Alexandrov's team," he told her. "Me and Nik Morozov both: another combat medic. When we were in Spetsnaz, we were like long-lost brothers. When we left the military and came over to South America, I needed a lot of money to help my sister, Kira. Nik was in a similar situation, with his brother Dan, who had a TBI, traumatic brain injury. We joined Vlad's group. There are five Russian teams in that area. Volkov ran one of them. He used harsh methods to force the men of these Q'ero Indian villages to work for them, growing and making cocaine so it could be exported." Alex grimaced and rubbed his large hands together, scowling. "Worse? Volkov would have his second-in-command choose a young girl or teen daughter from the chief of the village's family. He would rape her in front of them, to force them to grow, gather and produce cocaine for them. Instead of for the Latin drug lords."

"Vlad Alexandrov and Volkov both employed rape as a weapon. I and Nik tried to stop it in our group. Alexandrov threatened to put a bullet in our head if we tried to stop the rapes by him and several other men on his team, including Petrov. We had to walk away," Alex went on, sadness in his tone. "I'll never get the screams of those poor, innocent women… the ones they raped, out of my head."

"Those bastards," Sierra hissed. She knew Alex and his friend, Nik, had come out of a drug team in South America. Knew that he had saved Sky's life after Vlad had captured her, and Cal's along with it. If not for Alex turning traitor on his drug team, the both of them wouldn't be alive today.

"Volkov," Alex warned her heavily, "is ten times worse. He will not only drag out the wife of the chief, but he will take every daughter as well, no matter what their age. He'll have his men rape them in front of the terrified villagers. And then, he will shoot the oldest son of the chief in the head to bring home his point that he should work for the team or else."

"No…," Sierra whispered, feeling her stomach clench. She looked up and saw the rage in Lauren's eyes. She sat tense, her hands gripped together, her knuckles white.

"Volkov is willing to do whatever it takes to claim the territory," Alex said unhappily. "He has enslaved men from the ten Q'ero villages that comprise his territory in the Highlands all the way down to the jungle area near Aguas

Calientes."

"But," Sierra said, consulting her hand written notes, "Nik Morozov is now with us."

"Yes," Jack said. "He'd been a CIA mole working for the US government."

Alex snorted. "Volkov is a monster. You must be very careful."

More cold chills ran down through Sierra's spine.

"A fitting word, Alex," Jack said, "they are indeed all of them monsters. Look at this new photo, Sierra," and he flicked the remote.

Sierra turned her attention to the wall at the end of the table. The man who appeared was obviously American. He was wearing US Army jungle cammies. Her heart lurched. It surprised the hell out of her. Why? What was this reaction all about? She unconsciously rubbed her white sweater where her heart lay beneath it. The man had a hard face, straight black eyebrows over large, intelligent gray eyes. His hair was military short. The look in his eyes was flat, and she could tell he took no prisoners. Sierra saw no life in them. Just... grimness. His nose was long and had been broken, a bump at the root of it. He was a warrior who had led a rough life, she thought. And if his mouth had been a thin line, she'd have said that he was Volkov's cousin. But it wasn't. His mouth was humane looking to her. Even the corners of his mouth naturally lifted upward. It was his saving grace, Sierra thought. Still, her body responded to his man who wore a black baseball cap, sunglasses perched on its brim, his shoulders so damn wide that he looked like a football player, not the spec force operative she guessed he was. "Who am I looking at now?"

"Sergeant Mace Kilmer," Jack said. "There's a lot of intel on him in your mission brief. He's thirty years old, six foot three inches tall, two-hundred and ten pounds of mean muscle. This guy is a weapon's specialist and runs a team of two other men, Sergeants Caleb Merrill and Nate Cunningham. The first is a communications specialist and the latter is an 18-delta combat medic. They've been fighting and taking down HVTs the last two years in the area. No one knows this region better than Kilmer."

Lauren stirred. "I was assigned to Kilmer's team, Sierra. And Jack is right. This guy is a gruff, hard, son-of-a-bitch, but he's the right man for the task." She shook her head. "And he doesn't sit well with a woman in the team, believe me. A real patriarchal bastard."

Groaning, Sierra cut Driscoll a glance. "So, why not pick one of the male operators to go down there with him?"

"Because none of them speak Spanish, and you do."

"Gimme a break," Sierra groaned. "I don't need that shit, Jack. I really don't. It's a damned distraction of the worst sort."

Lauren smiled a little. "Kilmer grows on you after a while. Sorta like a friendly fungus. At first, he's snarly and growly, but after you show him, you know what you're doing, he backs off and supports you one-hundred percent. He's old school chauvinist until you prove to him differently."

Rubbing her brow, Sierra muttered, "This is a pain in the ass to deal with, Jack. It really is."

Jack flashed another picture. "Then get your reason for going right here."

Sierra suddenly shut her mouth as she saw three women laid out in front of a village, their clothes ripped off, lying naked. And dead. "What the hell," she whispered, her fingers curving into her palms.

"Volkov's calling card," Jack said grimly, holding her widening eyes. "Nik Morozov took these photos when no one was looking. That's the chief's wife and her two daughters, ages thirty, sixteen and fourteen."

Sierra choked up, tears rushing to her eyes. She turned her head away. "Get that photo off there," she whispered, her hand touching her throat. Feeling as if she were going to throw up, she quickly stood and rushed out of the room.

Lauren glared at Driscoll. "Dammit, Jack, you shouldn't have done that! You know Sierra's younger sister was raped and murdered. You didn't have to go that far."

Driscoll sat back, his mouth hardening. "She wouldn't take this mission otherwise."

Cursing softly, Lauren glared at her boss. "You're about as hard as Volkov."

Alex gave his wife a gentle look. "Perhaps you need to see how Sierra is? She is probably in the women's bathroom?"

Glaring at Driscoll, Lauren angrily stood up, shoving her chair back, her lips curling away from her teeth. "You're a son-of-a-bitch, Driscoll." And she stalked out, heading hurriedly down the tiled hall.

Lauren swung into the women's bathroom, hearing Sierra in one of the stalls, sobbing. "Sierra?"

Sierra was hugging the toilet, having just flushed it. She barely turned her head as Lauren came in. "It... was too much... God, Lauren. It was too much..." and she buried her face in her hands.

"I know," Lauren said, coming in and placing her hands over Sierra's hunched shoulders. She handed her some wet paper towels. "Here, wipe your mouth and nose?"

Hand trembling, Sierra took them, and did just that. "I have to get up. I have to wash this crap out of my mouth," and she struggled to stand. Her knees felt weak. Lauren put her hands beneath Sierra's armpits and easily hauled her to her feet.

"Come on," she coaxed, "let me help you."

Sierra felt like someone had gut punched her. She couldn't rid herself of those horrifying images. They were innocent Indian women. Like her. Being abused. Terrified. Murdered by these Russian men. By Volkov. Lauren aimed her to the wash basin. She planted her hands on either side of it while Lauren filled a paper cup with water and handed it to her.

Sierra gratefully took it, sloshing the water around in her mouth, her hand trembling badly. She spat it out. After three times, her mouth finally felt clean once more. Head hanging, her hands planted on the sides of the wash basin, she whispered brokenly, "Driscoll, damn him, he didn't have to do that to me, Lauren."

Lauren moved her hand gently across Sierra's hunched, tense shoulder. "I told him he was a first-class bastard. He knew your sister was raped and murdered. Damn him," she seethed. "Men are such overwhelming jerks sometimes."

Wiping her nose with the back of her hand, Sierra muttered, "Jack knew I was backing out of the mission. That's why he did it. He knew I wouldn't let other Indian women suffer that fate, if I could help it." Twisting a look up at Lauren, she said, "And I won't, Lauren. I'll take the mission, Kilmer's attitude be damned. I have my priorities straight. I'm going to take great pleasure shooting Volkov, taking that cold, heartless monster out of the human race." She gave Lauren a cutting smile, her eyes dark and narrowed. "He's mine. And I'm going to take him down."

Mace Kilmer remained hidden just inside the Highlands tree line, waiting for the Night Stalker Black Hawk helo bearing his new sniper to arrive. *New year, new sniper.* They were in the dry season of Peru and, even at nine thousand feet, it was cold an hour before sunset. A hundred yards either side of his position were his other two special forces sergeants, their M4's at the ready with bullets chambered, watching, keeping eyes out for Volkov and his band of killers. They had run hard through the jungle, climbing from seven thousand feet to their present elevation, keeping the local Russian team at a distance. Volkov had no idea they were in the area, stalking them, and Kilmer wanted to keep it that way. Still, he was uneasy about the ex-Spetsnaz Russian who was known as 'The Butcher'. The Russian team had five fellow ex-Spetsnaz soldier in it. His team only had three.

It was always a cat-and-mouse game that Kilmer had to play with these Russian mafia drug teams. A radio call came in and he pressed the mic once, letting the pilot know he was in position at the correct GPS location in order to land. His gray gaze swept out across the open area. To his right sat La Paloma, a village, a mile away. He saw the Q'ero men slowly moving around in that village, getting ready to end the day's work. Thin flames and wisps of smoke rose from beneath the tripod kettles here and there, the cluster of thatched huts surrounding the food area. The smoke from the fires spiraled into the air for a few dozen meters, but then slewed down the slope toward lower altitude far below them.

He heard the thunking blades of the Black Hawk. Lifting his spotter scope, he saw the dark-green, unmarked Black Hawk, climbing up the cliff faces of the Highlands. The altitude they flew in made it tough on the machine. Restless, he stood up, remaining hidden for the most part behind the wide trunk of the hundred-foot Dragon's blood tree towering above him. He and his men had cleared the landing area of any loose rocks and twigs so that any such litter wouldn't be swooped up by the blades as the Hawk landed.

His CIA handler, Tad Jorgensen, had spoken highly of the sniper from Shield Security that was coming in to assist them to find and kill Volkov. He snorted. The last damned sniper sent down to them had been a woman. Lauren Parker had promptly gotten herself kidnapped by Petrov, which had thrown their entire team into chaos. Instead of going after Petrov, they'd needed to search for and find her before she was killed. Luckily, they'd managed to locate and rescue both her and Nik Morozov, the medic who'd helped her escape. Rubbing his stubbled jaw, Kilmer scowled heavily. He'd told his handler he wanted no more women snipers. He didn't give a damn how good they were. One was fucking enough for a lifetime.

The outline of the Black Hawk became more and more sharpened and crisp the closer it got. Mace called to his men, letting them know the Hawk was landing. The sniper on board had orders to clear the helo and head directly into the tree line. There was no way Mace, and his men were going to stroll out into the open. Not with Russian mafia teams around. And those bastards knew, without any doubt, that Army Special Forces teams were on the ground, in their back yard and hunting their asses. They were very watchful, more so than usual.

Mace slipped his M4 off his shoulder, snapping off the safety, holding it tensely, his gaze ranging around widely. He wanted no surprises when this Hawk landed. He needed that damned sniper alive and hungry for a kill. He watched the Hawk lower quickly, the Night Stalker pilots bringing the bird in fast. They were most vulnerable at take-off and landing, so it was going to be a swift egress. He'd been told by his handler that S. Chastain was a Marine Corps trained sniper. That was good. They were the best-trained in the world. Bar none. He might be Army, but he would at least acknowledge that the Marine Corps did SOME things right.

The gusts of downwash as the Black Hawk's nose came up sent ninety-mile-an-hour gusts in all directions. Mace told the helo to land. The copilot acknowledged his order and he saw the nose level out, the tricycle wheels touching the earth. Huge clouds of dirt rose around the bird. Mace crouched, rifle in place, watching to the right and left, seeing his men doing the same. It was their responsibility to keep that Black Hawk and its pilots safe.

The noise was deafening, the whine of the engines on top of the helicopter familiar to Mace's ears. He couldn't see the bird as it touched down, his view of it swallowed up by the thick, roiling dust blown twenty to thirty feet outward and skyward. The percussion of the blades buffeted his body. He leaned into the side of a tree for balance, so that the blast wouldn't send him ass-end over teakettle. It had happened more than once.

The copilot notified him that the passenger had egressed, and they were now lifting off. Mace rogered the radio transmission. The Black Hawk went straight up like an arrow shot out of a bow. It banked, starting to tip away down over the side of the same harsh, rugged cliff face it had come up over. The underside of its rotors was inclined toward him, the wash from them tearing into the bare ground and blasting it into the air. Mace drew in a breath of relief as he stood to his full height, watching the clouds of billowing dirt intently. Any moment now, their sniper would appear out of that brown out area.

His gray eyes narrowed as he saw someone with a rifle in one hand and a heavy ruck on their back trotting out through the airborne storm of dust. He saw the long legs, the cammos the sniper wore, the face and shoulders of their guy still hidden by the granular clouds. Mace was pleased to note that the dude was humping his gear without a problem, heading straight for where he was standing. As the figure drew clear of the bulk of the roiling dust, Mace's black eyebrows dove downward. *WTF?* His eyes still stung from the blasts of grit being sent like a storm surge into the tree line as the helo dropped out of view below the rim of the cliff. Wiping his watering eyes, he blinked several times. He HAD to be seeing things!

Mace's mouth started to drop open, but he promptly snapped it shut again, rage tunneling through him. The figure materializing out of the dust was a woman! He clearly saw her face and the long, black braids hanging down the front of her cammie jacket. She was tall and medium-boned, her shoulders wide and capable. She was carrying her ruck. He knew it weighed easily around sixty pounds. She was in good shape.

Mace didn't want to stare at her, but he did. Her face was wide and oval, its skin a golden color. She had high cheekbones, her brow broad. He swore she was Native American because the black hair framing her fearless-looking green eyes reminded him of the color of the swamp oaks back where he grew up in North Carolina. And, damned if his lower body didn't take off like it had smelled a woman in heat! Damn it! Grimly, he moved out and just in front of the tree so she could spot him. And spot him she did, making a quick, trotting correction toward him.

Mace didn't want to be influenced by the fact that he thought she was a damned hot-looking woman. She couldn't be more than in her late twenties. It was her wide green eyes, framed by thick black lashes, that grabbed his immediate attention. Big black pupils surrounded by that rich green color, a thin black ring around her iris. The look of an eagle. She didn't miss a thing, Mace saw, as she aimed herself at a steady jog right up to where he was standing.

He saw the calm look in her face, and he couldn't tell what the hell she was thinking as they silently sized one another up. She moved her XP sniper rifle, enclosed in its rainproof sheath, over to her left hand. Thrusting out her right hand toward him, he heard her say, "I'm Chastain. Sergeant Kilmer?"

Mace stared down at her offered hand. She had long, tapered fingers. A graceful womanly hand. He quickly observed a number of old, white scars across the back of it. A part of him wanted to grip her hand and feel her flesh, feel her feminine fingers. Another part reared back in anger. He refused to take her hand, glaring down at her. Mace saw her full lips purse, her eyes hardening as she dropped her offer of a handshake.

"Yeah, I'm Kilmer. Shield was supposed to send a man," he snarled. "What the hell happened?"

"They decided a man couldn't handle this assignment, Sergeant. So, they sent a woman instead."

He reared back at her droll reply, her gaze unwavering and never leaving his, challenging him. Mace would have respected her if she'd been a man. Never mind that he could see the soft fullness of her breasts even beneath the thick cammie jacket she wore. Chastain was tall. Maybe five ten or five eleven. And she sure as hell wasn't afraid of HIM, her face giving nothing away except the fact she was pissed off at his poor manners.

"This is a mistake," he growled. He called in his men. They had to make tracks, or they could run into Volkov and his blood-thirsty team.

"Sure is," she said, in a growl that matched his own. "Let's get this show on the road. I want Volkov sooner, not later." And then she added acidly, "So I can get the hell away from the likes of you as soon as possible."

Mace almost laughed. Almost. Well, he could see she was nothing like Lauren Parker insofar as personality went. "What'd you do, Sugar? Drink a quart of vinegar this morning for breakfast?"

Her fine nostrils quivered, and her eyes narrowed as she considered his gruff reply. "I don't like bullies, Sergeant." She jammed her index finger down, pointed at the damp jungle floor between them. "Let's settle this right now because I don't want to spend one more minute in this team of yours with your attitude. I'M NOT YOUR ENEMY. Volkov is. So, get your head screwed on straight about this op and stop this sniping at me because I'm sure as hell not taking it from anyone. Especially you."

CHAPTER 3

W HY WAS HER body quivering inwardly like it was aching and yearning? Sierra couldn't believe the rudeness this Special Forces sergeant gave her. She knew her body and knew when a man turned her on. And, dammit it all, Kilmer was a helluva ruggedly good-looking specimen of a man. There was a powerful, sensual aura around him. Nothing obvious, for sure, but she was picking up on it like he was the other half of her or something. *No way.* Sierra was shocked by her body responding like that, at his angry gaze sweeping across her face and torso. Her body reacting so blatantly to those eyes of his looking her up and down. His arms were sprinkled with dark hair, the cuffs of his cammies rolled up to just below his elbows. She caught herself almost about to become mesmerized by the play of muscles as he flexed his hands. The man was built. Tight, and in superb physical condition. Too bad his sour personality sucked in comparison.

Kilmer's gray eyes were almost colorless, like ice. Like him. Her fingers flexed around the XP sheath in her left hand. He looked gut-shot when she took him to ground with her sharply worded comeback. What? He wasn't used to dealing with a woman in a confrontation? Her lips twitched, but Sierra decided not to smile because he was clearly upset. His nicely shaped mouth was bowed into a downward curve. His glare did nothing to her. She'd been hazed, unmercifully razzed, and bullied by Marines a helluva lot tougher and bigger than he was. And she'd taken their shit and thrown it back at them. Still, she liked the way the man stood, his wide shoulders proud and thrown back with natural ease. He wasn't pretty boy looking at all. But he had a darkly tanned face, three days' worth of scruff on it, making him look dangerous.

She saw all the crow's feet at the corners of his large, wide-spaced eyes, saw the intelligence in the man, despite his obvious prejudice against women. And, as her gaze drifted downward, across that magnificently sprung chest of his, her fingers itched to explore beneath his cammie to find out more. Where was her brain? Now, she was acting like a man: thinking between her legs! Sierra had never had this happen in her life, and it threw her completely off balance. Not about to go there, having a job to do, she lifted her eyes again, meeting his.

"Where's your men?"

"Coming. Are you going to take over my team, too?"

For an instant, she saw a gleam of amusement in his eyes, and then it was gone.

"Tell you what, Sergeant. You stay on YOUR turf, and I'LL stay on mine. Don't try to tell me what to do and I won't do it back. Deal?" Again, Sierra saw that brief laughter in his eyes. She wondered if he was laughing at her. Most likely.

"You got a deal, Sweetheart."

Sierra almost snapped at him to not call her by that nickname, but the southern drawl this man had was as if he'd reached out and stroked her flesh with that whiskey tone of his. Her skin DID react! She got gooseflesh up and down her arms, as if in reaction to the caressing quality of his low, sensual male voice. Instead, she gave him an irritated look.

Kilmer stood with one hand around his M-4, the other hanging loosely at his side, a man completely comfortable with himself. Sierra liked the way his damp cammies hung on his male frame. He wore a knife on his left, down on his hip. A .45 pistol in a drop holster was strapped to one of his thick, oak-like thighs. Like her, he wore a large ruck on his back. The man positively oozed sex. She licked her lips, an almost unconscious reaction, and quickly jerked her gaze away, focusing instead on the man coming in from Kilmer's right.

The soldier was a few inches taller than she was, with short brown hair, a scruff beard, and eagle-focused blue eyes. He was dressed like Kilmer. The look in his gaze as he drew closer, and got a bead on her face, was one of shock. Yeah, they must have been expecting a man, not her. Sierra had no idea how the communications had gotten screwed up, but she didn't care. The soldier halted, throwing out his hand to her.

"Chastain? I'm Cale Merrill. Glad you made it here safely."

Sierra instantly like the warmth in the man's eyes. "Thanks, Sergeant Merrill."

"Call me Cale," he said, shouldering the strap on his M-4 over his shoulder. "We don't stand on much protocol around here."

The third soldier arrived. He slowed, his green eyes going large as he looked Sierra over, surprise in his expression.

She gave him her hand. "Sierra Chastain," she told him.

"Nate Cunningham. Just call me Nate. Glad to have you aboard."

"Thanks," Sierra said, giving Kilmer a dirty look. His men were a helluva lot nicer than he was. He merely gave her a bored look back, as if waiting for introductions to be waded through so he could get on to more important business.

"Sierra," Nate said, shouldering his rifle. "An unusual name."

She smiled a little, shrugging out of her ruck. Laying it down on the damp floor of the jungle, she knelt and secured her XP sniper rifle to the back on it, barrel down, with the Velcro bindings on its straps. "My mother is Eastern Cherokee and she wanted to name her children after natural things. She'd gone to the Sierra Mountains as a young woman and fell in love with them." Sierra hitched the seventy-pound pack back onto her shoulders, belting it up and snugging the shoulder straps.

Nate grinned. "Wow, great story." He took off his black baseball cap and wiped the sweat off his brow.

"Saddle up," Kilmer growled.

"Where we heading?" Merrill asked.

"To our six-day vacation retreat," he said dryly.

Sierra frowned and then looked to Nate, who seemed the most open and friendly toward her, for an explanation. A vacation retreat? *Out here?* She doubted that, wondering if Kilmer was ragging on her already. *More than likely.* Damn the man was so charismatic. Her body was still responding to his nearness. She felt like exploring him with her hands, wondering what he looked like naked. Sierra was shocked at where her thoughts were going. WHAT the hell was going on with her? Worse, she recognized male interest when she saw it. Kilmer had made no bones about physically appreciating her. Her flesh skittered with eagerness. Damn. That's all she needed!

"Where do you want me?" Sierra demanded of him. She was used to being on trails, in a single line with her team. And then, she realized her poor choice of words, and the slight, very sensual crook of Kilmer's mouth as he regarded her question. Rolling her eyes, Sierra wanted to let him know, in no uncertain terms, that she wasn't going to stand for sexual harassment in either looks or innuendos. Those days were long over.

"Take my question at face value, Sergeant," she snapped. "Don't embellish it with your own private thoughts." Instantly, she saw Merrill and Cunningham's eyebrows fly up at her warning growl to Kilmer. The soldiers looked at one another, confused. *Great.* She saw Kilmer give her a slight nod, a tiny bit of apology briefly in his eyes.

"Cale, I'll take the lead. Chastain, you're behind me. And don't you lag behind because, if you do, I'll have your ass out of here by tomorrow morning. Are we clear?" Kilmer growled as he leered down at her, grim.

"Crystal clear," Sierra said, grinning, slipping her thumbs beneath the shoulder straps of her ruck. She saw Kilmer's eyes go to slits for a moment. What? Did this over-testosterone-ladened male think she couldn't keep up on a column? Keep pace? If that's what he thought, then he had another think coming. And, even though her right calf was only seven days into recovery, so long as she didn't slip and fall, tear it open again, she'd be okay and easily be able to keep up. And Sierra knew Kilmer was going to set a blistering pace just to try and run her into the ground. Newbies were always challenged to see if they could take the heat in the kitchen.

"Nate, bring up the rear," Kilmer snapped, turning on his heel and moving instantly into a ground-eating trot down a thin trail through the jungle.

"Got it," Nate said, nodding.

Sierra moved out quickly. She was five ten and had long, long legs. And she'd just come off an op, so she was in top physical condition. The sergeant moved out at a steady, trot. He had long legs, too. She had no idea how long they would be humping through the jungle paths but forced herself to relax and let her body move into the rhythm it needed to be in to work for her and not against it. Her hearing was acute. She heard howler monkeys echoing cries throughout the jungle as they moved silently, like ghosts, through the darkening jungle. There wasn't much brush on the ground, but Sierra was well aware of the roots sticking up here and there. Many were covered by leaf and limb debris. She had to keep her feet high enough, so she didn't accidentally trip on one of the hidden roots. That could spell disaster for her healing calf.

A good infantry trot with a sixty-pound pack was fifteen minutes. She was carrying eighty-five with her XP sniper rifle. Sierra knew just how important it was to have a correctly-fitting ruck. Shield Security had had one made exactly for her body specifications. Unlike in the military, where one size fits all, and blisters, strains and aches were the norm. She trotted along, balanced, but still feeling the tenderness of the recent knife wound to her calf. Before she'd left, Alex had used surgical tape to give the scar support so it wouldn't tear open. Neither he nor her had wanted anything of the sort to happen, and Sierra wasn't about to tell Kilmer she had been wounded recently. He'd probably make a call to his CIA handler by sat phone on the spot, telling him he wanted her out of here right now.

She had no problem following Kilmer. It was darker in the jungle, the triple canopy above them blocking out the sun as it creeped overhead. Her vision was sharp, alerting her of many a hidden root. The trail started down a steeper descent, and it was muddy. Kilmer slowed his pace as well he should. Sierra was glad to see that, even if she pissed him off because she was a woman, he still wasn't going to risk any member of his team injury by running too fast down a muddy decline. Maybe there was hope after all.

Her olive-green cotton t-shirt was sticking to her body. She wore a green cotton bra, and it was soaked, too. Sierra wanted to rest to take off her cammie jacket, but she wasn't about to ask Kilmer to stop for a minute so she could shrug out of it and pack it into her ruck. She wasn't about to give the grizzled sergeant any reason to call her weak. She'd sweat through her clothing like she always had in Somalia. But the humidity was a helluva lot higher here, and sweat was trickling freely down her temples. The inside band on her black baseball cap had been specifically designed to absorb sweat from the brow and keep the wearer's eyes clear and able to focus on what they needed to see. Another little invention by Jack Driscoll. The man was a genius at making small and large design changes to what they wore a carried, making everything easier on them, making it all take less energy out of them, so that they could throw all that back into a firefight, instead.

Drinking out of her Camelbak, Sierra knew the rules on hydration. She was losing a lot of fluids via sweat. And they had to be equally replaced. She sipped constantly as Kilmer trotted slowly down the descent. Always looking around, her hearing keyed, she saw him doing the same thing. They weren't in a safe place at all. She could feel the danger around them. No one's ruck or rifle made a single noise. Operators knew how to make the gear they carried as quiet as possible. To have some metal clinking could draw the enemy to them in a heartbeat.

The trail evened out into a long, straight run between the trees. Despite Kilmer's size, and he was a damned giant compared to the rest of his team, he ran bonelessly, a honed Olympic athlete of another kind. Kilmer would never win a medal, but Sierra appreciated his silent running despite the weight he carried and his height. She didn't have a radio on, so when Kilmer came to a halt, she saw Nate and Cale come up to them. They were all breathing hard, but out of wide-open mouths to quieten their breath. All the men had sweat gleaming on their skin. Sierra took off her cap and wiped her brow. She looked up to see Kilmer critically studying her. Did he think her a shrinking violet? She had been a Marine. No one was tougher than them. She stared belligerently back at him, just daring him to make some snarky comment.

But he didn't. Instead, he said in a low voice, "We have about a mile to go. This is hostile territory, so keep your eyes and ears open. If you hear anything, give a click on the radio."

Sierra looked pointedly at him. "If you'd given me one? I'd have turned it on."

"We'll get you set up with one once we make camp," he told her gruffly. "I doubt you'll spot anything, but it if you do, hit me on the arm or shoulder once to let me know."

"With pleasure," and she gave him a challenging look.

Kilmer's strong, chiseled mouth barely hooked faintly upward in one corner, but said nothing. He lifted his hand, a signal for them to fall into a single line once again.

They reached the camp without incident. Sierra watched Kilmer slow and saw what looked like an opening in the jungle ahead. She was breathing hard, but her legs felt good and strong. She figured he was probably wondering why she hadn't cried out for help from a big, strong man yet to save her. Laughing to herself, she paid attention to the meadow opening up before them. There were four thatched huts, small ones, about ten feet from one another. They were built up along the tree line, facing inward on the meadow. She saw a fresh-water collection station between two of the huts, large five-gallon drums lined up to hold any rain.

Kilmer turned to her as they approached the huts. "Chastain, you take that one," and he pointed to the second hut along the row. "I'll be over here, then Merrill and Cunningham are the tail of this donkey."

Nate snorted. "We could always look at it in reverse, Mace. I'm the head and you're the ass."

"That fits," Sierra murmured, grinning broadly as she turned and walked away from Kilmer's overpowering masculine presence. She heard him snort.

"In your dreams, Merrill. How about some breakfast grub?"

"Coming up," Cale said with a chuckle, heading for his hut.

Sierra found the hut an amazing place to call home. It was made from palm leaves, branches and grass. It smelled slightly damp within, but the earth was dry. That was a good sign. Someone had done some excellent work on the roof to stop the rain from entering the hut.

"Hey, Sierra?"

She turned, twisting toward the entrance. It was Nate leaning in.

"Yeah?"

"Did you bring a poncho liner? Rains a lot around here. Thunderstorms nearly every night."

"Yes, I think I have everything." And then she shrugged. "I hope I did."

"Well, no worries," Nate assured her. "Between the three of us, if you're missing some gear or whatever, I'm sure we'll have some kind of backup to share with you."

Sierra felt warm inside. Despite all of Kilmer's gruffness and dislike for her, the other two soldiers seemed sincerely welcoming. "Thanks. I tried to think of everything, but most of my missions were in the Middle East or Africa. So, I may not have some jungle gear. If I don't, I'll come to you?"

Nate gave her a grin. "Sure. You know where to find me."

Some of her worry melted away. Cale and Nate were good men. Professionals. They didn't knee jerk like Kilmer. They simply accepted her. But Sierra also knew she had to pull her fair share of the weight, too. She quickly got her poncho liner down in case rain came in and wet her lightweight sleeping bag. Much of what was in her ruck were items she'd need, such as rifle and pistol cleaning kits, matches, MREs and some of her favorite junk foods. She had brought along several large bottles of Tabasco sauce. MRE food was so damned bland that it needed some heavy spicing-up until her tastebuds felt satisfied.

By the time she was done, long rays of sunlight were slanting through the triple canopy of the jungle. Sierra crawled outside through the door of her hut, pulled down the plastic tarp over the entrance behind her, and stood up. She wore her drop holster with her SIG sauer pistol in it. On her other hip, she carried, as always, a SEAL SOG seven-inch knife in a black nylon sheath. She'd taken off her jacket, paring herself down to a clean, dry, muscle shirt because it was just that hot and humid. Her boots were waterproofed so at least her feet were dry. Her cammy trousers remained damp from the run and Sierra doubted that they would be dry ever again in this climate, and figured she'd just have to get used to it.

She spotted Kilmer sitting out near the fire pit area. There were three long logs in a triangle around it. He had his ruck open at his side and had some gear from it in his hands. She wandered over.

"Can I help with anything?" she asked him, hands on her hips, standing before him.

Kilmer looked up. "Sit down."

Man of few words. Okay… Sierra headed for the next log over from his.

"No. Here," and he jabbed his long index finger down at the same side of the log where he sat.

Swallowing, her mouth going a little dry, Sierra hesitated. There was just such animal, primal energy around the man. It excited her. It made her yearn for sex when she hadn't even thought about it over the last two years. Sierra gently shut the door on her past. On her love of Jeb. For whatever reason, and she wasn't sure what was happening or why, Kilmer turned her on, made her salivate. He made her remember what good sex, good loving, could be all about. As she slowly turned and walked toward him, she focused on his large, square hands. Beautiful hands with long fingers. She saw so many scars across them. His hands worked, gracefully for a man, as he untangled some black, plastic cords between them.

Sierra chose the far end of the log, where a good six feet stood between them.

His head snapped up. Eyes narrowing on her, he said, "I don't bite. Get over here."

Coulda fooled her. Was this his pleasant side? Sierra reluctantly stood up and moved three feet closer. She saw the exasperation in his eyes. Okay, then… She moved within two feet of him. And she could smell the sweat on him, his unique male odor that sent her into a gnawing ache and felt his power as a man. She was in such trouble. Thank goodness, he couldn't read minds, and she primly folded her hands on her lap, keeping her thighs pressed together.

"Turn toward me."

Her eyes widened as she blinked at him. "Why?"

Kilmer gave her an impatient look. "Jesus. You act like I'm gonna haul off and hit you."

She raised her brows. "Well, that wouldn't happen. I'd react. You wouldn't get near me," and she held his measured gaze.

"Didn't your mother ever teach you how to be social?"

"Didn't your mother ever tell you women are EQUALS to any man and to quit treating me like a second-class citizen?"

"Obviously not. Now hold still. I've got this headband put together. I need to see if it fits you or not. We wear headbands with radio mic near our lips. The radio itself stays up on your shoulder, protected in a waterproof bag."

Sierra wasn't expecting him to touch her. Her breath hitched and she froze for a moment as his huge hands seem to encapsulate her entire head. She saw something… an unknown emotion… fleetingly, in his eyes. Maybe a thawing as he worked the elastic headband over her head and then got his fingers tangled in her long hair. She usually had straight hair but, in this humidity, it curled here and there.

"Hold on," she murmured, her hands flying up to his, untangling the strands of hair that had gotten trapped among his fingers. The utter pleasure of touching this man, his skin tough but warm, strong and yet surprisingly gentle, caught her completely off guard. Sierra felt like her fingers were burning from where they'd made brief contact with his. The strands released. She instantly jerked her hands away, gripping them in her lap. Her heart was doing funny things inside her chest. Racing. Heat was stabbing down from her breasts all the way to her lower body, and she felt like the downstairs staff were whining and wanting far more attention than they had gotten in a long, long time. Gulping, she closed her eyes, refusing to look up into Mace's face. If he was shaken by their contact, he didn't show it. In fact, his face had drawn into a grimace as if she was the last person on Earth he'd ever want to touch.

Her heart sank a little. but her skin skittered with heat and pleasure wherever his fingers brushed against her scalp. Her heart wouldn't settle. She inhaled his scent like it was some wonderful fragrance. Was she finally awakening from the grief and loss of Jeb? It had been a long, hard two-year slog. Suddenly, Sierra was shaky inwardly, feeling horny as hell. If anyone had told her she'd feel like this out on an op, she'd have had a damn good uproarious laugh over it. She'd been out on dozens of ops and, with the exceptions of the ones she'd been on with Jeb, had never felt any kind of sexual magnetism between herself and her partner. Until now. Until sourpuss Kilmer. *Geeze.* Was she drawing in patriarchal men like him to her now? That thought made her eyes open wider. Terrible thought, really. Kilmer was the exact opposite of Jeb. He was a snarly Type-A leader who couldn't even be nice if he tried. Jeb had been so kind and forgiving of others. He had been easy to live with and be around, unlike Kilmer. While Jeb was like a beautiful, polished diamond, Kilmer reminded her of an ugly, rough-cut lump of coal.

He stopped fiddling with the headband. "How's that feel?"

Sierra opened her eyes, touching the band, repositioning it slightly. To her surprise, it wasn't too tight or too loose. Kilmer was pretty good at judging the size of her head and that band. Swallowing, she croaked, "Okay. It feels fine. Thanks."

He brought down his hand.

Instantly, Sierra jerked away from it as it approached her cheek.

"What the hell," he snapped. He glared at her. "You're acting like I'm go-ing to hit you. I would never hit a woman."

The fierceness of his low snarl hit her hard. She felt suddenly ashamed and tried to relax. "I just came out of an op in Somalia. Things went to hell," she choked out, holding his angry glare. Sierra saw that she'd hurt his fragile male ego with her swift reaction. The moment she'd told him that, he'd scowled and dropped his hand away.

In a low growl, he said, "You should have said something."

"Like you were all ears?" Sierra charged hotly beneath her breath so the others couldn't hear her. "You haven't exactly been the Welcome Wagon here, Sergeant." She saw Kilmer grimace and then look away for a moment, his Adam's apple bobbing several times. There were a lot of emotions swirling around inside him and she'd been too shaken by the unexpected appearance of his hand going for her cheek, to try and untangle and interpret them. Some were regret. Others, anger. And something else… something… something that Sierra couldn't translate. He twisted his head in her direction, his gray eyes narrowed and stormy looking. His long hands were tense on his thick, curved thighs and she swore he was about to kiss her senseless.

Kiss her?

What the hell was going on here? Taken aback by what she saw in his eyes, in his expression, thawing as it had for a split second, she knew he wanted to kiss her! WTF? It wasn't as if she also hadn't been secretly wondering what it would be like to press her lips up against that strong, beautiful mouth of his. She wasn't exactly blameless in this moment, either. Sierra felt shaken doubly so. She'd thought all this was only one way. Did Kilmer want her? Man to woman? Impossible! He hated the very earth she walked on. He didn't want her here with him. He didn't trust her. And she was sure he didn't think she could shoot and hit the broad side of a barn. She must be suffering from jet lag. And Sierra was sure that the cause of her confusion was because she hadn't gotten the rest and down time she needed between missions. That her mind was wobbling all over the damn map with this prickly soldier. She was imagining things that weren't there. Truly, she was sleep deprived. Maybe all of that was crashing down on her right now, distorting her perspective, making her jumpy and distrustful of this man's intentions. It had to be her fault. He was looking at her right now like she was an alien that had just landed from another galaxy far, far away.

"You need to see if the mic is long enough to reach your mouth," he grunted, waving a finger in her direction, making sure to get it nowhere near her face this time.

Fingers trembling, Sierra was more than a little aware of how to handle a headband mic. Why the hell didn't he just hand the whole apparatus to her? Why did he WANT to put it on her? Touch her? It made no sense. The mic was too short, so she quickly lengthened it and locked it in place. He handed her the small radio in a case. She quickly plugged the jack from the headset into it and then looked back at him for approval. Damn, the look in his eyes… Her heartbeat increased. The man could strip her with those pale, narrowed eyes of his. The heat in his stare didn't threaten Sierra. Rather, it made her feel suddenly warm and achy.

"Looks fine," he grunted. He turned away and zipped his ruck closed by his muddy boots.

Her throat was dry. "Do you want me to wear it around camp here?"

"No. Just when we're out hunting. Stow it in a plastic bag to keep it dry and together in one place."

"I figured that much out." She saw him scowl and turn, giving her a raking look.

"Tell me about your op in Somalia. What happened? You're jumpy as hell."

She pulled off the head band and stood up, stuffing the mic rig all down in the thigh pocket of her Cammy trousers. Sierra didn't want to be this close to Mace. He unsettled the hell out of her, made her defensive and wary of him. Not that he'd given her a reason for any of those reactions. Licking her lower lip, she wanted more distance between them. It was better that way. At least, for her. Sitting at the end of another log, she said, "I was embedded in a SEAL team. We had orders to take out an HVT in Mogidishu."

"And you were their sniper?"

"Actually," she said, her voice becoming less strident, "there were two of us. Me and another SEAL. If one of us missed, the other wouldn't." She hitched one shoulder and managed a strained, quick, one-cornered smile. "You know their saying? One is none and two is one? I was number two." She saw his face relax as he considered her story.

"The SEALs have their own sniper school now. Different from the Marine Corps school, though." Mace Kilmer said.

Sierra replied, "Yes, their school is more SEAL specific to the types of ops they pull."

"Then why didn't they have a second SEAL instead of you?" he asked.

She saw his blunt stare and felt heat bolting down through her breasts, warming her as a woman. There was no anger in his eyes now. Just – curiosity and a teaspoon of interest. Interest in her story? Or interest in her? Shakily, Sierra sensed that Kilmer's focus was directly on her. Maybe as a bug under his patriarchal male microscope? Certainly not a man interested in her as a woman, sexually speaking. "I don't know. I don't ask questions like that. I go where I'm assigned." she said.

Mace rubbed his stubbled jaw, thinking for a bit. "You must be pretty damned good for those SEALs to have wanted you along in that hellhole. And you must have had a sniper history that made them want you on that op."

Her brow dropped. "You been in Somalia?"

"Yeah. Nothing pretty to write home about, believe me."

"Oh," she laughed a little nervously, "that's one thing you and I can agree on."

He studied her, the silence lengthening between them. Finally, he said, "So what happened to you over there? Something did. You're too fresh from it, and too reactive."

CHAPTER 4

M ACE HAD TO get a hold of himself. When Chastain came out of her hut wearing only a muscle shirt and cammies, he felt like his world suddenly changed. He had no explanation for it. She walked tall and proud with her shoulders back, the sleek feminine muscling of hers showing clearly, in every inch of exposed skin, that she was all athlete. He saw the hog's tooth on a leather thong around her neck. Every Marine who graduated from sniper school was given one. It just made her look all that wilder. A woman of nature. In tune with everything around her. Sierra was damned buff, no fat on her. He couldn't keep from staring at her breasts beneath that shirt, the lush curves of them straining against the material. Her hair was long and loose, a thick, black cloak flowing over her shoulders and down her upper body, the tips slightly curled inward just above her breasts. The way she walked, with her casual cat-like grace, told him plenty about why she'd been able to keep up the demanding five-mile trot. She'd handled the run like a pro.

Why the hell should he be so drawn to her? She was smart-mouthed, in-your-face, and intolerant of anything remotely prejudicial toward her as a woman. Mace believed in women. He just didn't want them out here in this unforgiving jungle. The Russians had captured Lauren Parker. Thank God, Nik Morozov had been there when all that went down and had, later on, helped rescue her from being raped and then killed by those degenerates. Scowling, Mace sat on a log, waiting for her to answer his question. He saw the stubborn set of her jaw. Those damned lush lips that he wanted to kiss, were compressed. Those cypress-green eyes of hers were wary-looking. He could smell her scent. A female fragrance that set his entire lower body on high alert. Damn, the last thing he needed was a hard-on to top off his discomfort with this whole deal. That would be more than embarrassing. It was unprofessional and something she didn't deserve.

When he'd placed the elastic radio band around her head, he'd enjoyed touching her silky, slightly-frizzy hair. Sierra had been so close, and he'd deeply inhaled her woman's scent like the starved predator he felt he was. She had been tense, not trusting of him. Worse, when he'd lifted his hand to adjust her

mouth mic, she'd all but bolted, jerking back from his hands. That had startled
Mace. The terror he saw, for just that moment, in her eyes had tunneled
through his chest, slammed into his heart, and squeezed it. He couldn't explain
why she had such a hold on him. All they did was fight and snipe at one
another. And he knew he was at fault. He's the one who had refused to
welcome her or shake her hand. Was it any wonder she didn't trust him? No.

The very instant she could, Sierra had butt-shuffled away from him, putting more space between him and her on the damp log. Now, he lamented that
teenager-level knee-jerk behavior of his earlier. A good leader made the people
he worked with feel welcomed. Like they were a part of the team. And Mace
was, if nothing else, a team man. He had a lot of pride. Maybe too much. It
wasn't like him to tell her he was sorry. It just didn't come easy to him. Never
had. He cast around for a way to apologize without saying it right out loud.
Bothered by Sierra's reaction, he asked about her op in Somalia. Mace saw her
eyes go dark with pain. She hunched forward, elbows on her thighs, hands
clasped tightly between them.

"I was over there for three months," she began in a low, clipped tone. "Me
and the SEAL team were on the rooftop of a three-story home, camouflaged,
waiting for an HVT to go to the building where he gave his pep talks to his
murdering thugs."

"That was a damned dangerous situation," Mace said, catching and holding
her gaze. Sierra looked exhausted. He hadn't realized so until this moment. Her
skin was a beautiful gold color, natural, and it had hid the smudges beneath her
eyes. Guilt ate at Mace. He'd deliberately set a blistering pace to wear her
down, to prove to her that she couldn't handle being an operator on an A-
team. She'd handled it without a problem. Why was he doing this? The intel
from his CIA handler, Jorgensen, said that S. Chastain had ranked in the top
ten percent of snipers in the Marine Corps. She knew her business. And there
was no question, she was a professional and he'd been an absolute jerk.

"Yeah," she muttered, rubbing her brow for a moment, "but it was what it
was. Then again, all ops are." She shot him a wry look. "You know that better
than most. Right? Hunter-killer teams do the dirty work behind the scenes. It's
the most dangerous kind of work."

Her huskily spoken words made him feel good. She had such a sensuous,
low voice. Purely feminine, smoky, setting him on fire. And if Mace didn't
know better, he swore he'd seen yearning in her eyes earlier—for him. The
WAY she looked at him whenever he caught her glancing in his direction, felt
purely like a woman-to-man gaze, reflecting his own appreciation and connection with him. It took everything he had to not respond to that heated look
she'd just given him. Mace didn't think for a moment she was flirting. He knew

how women flirted, and what Sierra was doing certainly wasn't that. Maybe he was just wishing that it was. Hell, he was so damned horny. It had been three months, way past time, for him and his team to land in Cusco for a week. There, they could get real food, hot showers, shave, find a woman who wanted to have sex with an American, and enjoy some downtime from the tension that always lorded over them.

He needed a woman so fucking bad. And maybe, because of his own state, he was misreading Sierra's look. He had to be.

"Did you tail your target?"

Sierra nodded, rubbing her face. "Yeah, but things went sideways after we ex-filled off the house roof. Our car broke down halfway out of town. A group of thugs came at us with machetes and knives." Lifting her chin, she muttered, "Go figure. We'd made good our escape from the area of the HVT take-down. Only to have the car engine blow, leaving us in a very bad situation with a local gang. They saw us and came in after us. They didn't know who we really were."

Grimacing, Mace growled, "You're lucky to be alive." He found his heart pounding with dread for her. She was incredibly confident, naturally beautiful in a way he'd found very, very few women to be. Sierra wore no makeup. An operator wouldn't. The odor would tip off tangos that she was in the area. A single scent or fragrance could get her killed. There was something about Sierra that Mace couldn't quite define. All he wanted to do was stare at her, lose himself in her, and that was the craziest reaction he'd ever had to any woman. *Ever.*

"We got into a skirmish, found another vehicle, a beat-up truck, got it going and got the hell out of there. THAT was a nightmare." She snorted softly. "Sitting up on a rooftop was a piece of cake in comparison."

Mace nodded and saw the pensive look in her face. "Look, Merrill is going to make us some breakfast and then I want you to sack out for a while. We aren't going anywhere for a few days. Things are pretty up in the air right now and this is one of the safest places I know of, except to sit in a bar in Cusco drinking pisco sours," and he gave her a grizzled smile. Instantly, he saw her eyes lighten, and he groaned inwardly as her full lips parted. The way her slender neck curved into her shoulders made Mace ache to reach out and stroke it, feel her pulse beneath his fingertips.

"That sounds great. If there's anything I can do to fit in? Take up some task that needs doing?"

He liked her team spirit. "I'll think about it," was all he said. "Just keep your weapons oiled daily. This high humidity will start rusting out a gun barrel in a day if you don't pay attention."

"Not to worry. In my book, cleanliness is next to godliness." She stood up, rubbed her palms against her thighs. "In fact, I think I'll do that right now, give the weapons an oil protection."

"Good, because you can count on thunderstorms and rain nearly every night."

Grimacing, Sierra walked away. Just the sway of her hips and that fine butt of hers made his hands itchy to cup those firm cheeks. He had it bad! What he should be doing is setting out a watch schedule. The Russians were always around. There was only one real way in and out of this place, save for that one rally point the men had built a year earlier. The one they had then hidden and camouflaged. But he still needed a man on guard on that trail a mile out of the meadow.

Sierra gathered up her hair into a ponytail with a thick rubber band. The thickness of it loose was too heavy. It made her feel overheated to wear her it all down. She brought out a bottle of Tabasco sauce, a jar of Bacon Bits, and a package of fresh, shredded cheese. She took it all over to Cale, who had the cooking duties. He was squatted down, a big black iron skillet on the metal grill in one hand, pushing at least a dozen eggs around in it.

"Could you use any of these in all that?" she asked, showing her treasure of condiments to the soldier. Instantly, she saw Cale's eyes light up.

"All of it. Put a bunch in? We like Tabasco sauce. And we're all out."

Sierra got busy sprinkling a handful of Bacon Bits, some shredded cheese, and the sauce into the eggs. Cale quickly folded them in with a spatula. "I brought some perishables along with me. I was told you've been out here three months without a break?" and she looked into the sergeant's square face.

"What did you bring?" he asked, holding the skillet just above the flames of the small fire that flamed away below in the pit.

Sierra saw Kilmer and Nate wandering out, as if on cue. They could probably smell the food on the air and she smiled to herself. "I brought a ton of Baby Wipes with me.

Cale groaned. "Really?"

She knew how important they were out in a hostile climate. Toilet paper wasn't exactly handy. "Yeah. I brought a dozen boxes. I can share them between all of us."

"You're an angel," Cale said fervently, standing, the eggs ready to portion out. "Yeah, we'd all appreciate that, Sierra. Thank you."

She'd forgotten her kit. As she turned, Kilmer held out his own to her. "Take mine."

Stunned at his suddenly being nice, she gaped for a moment. "No… thanks… I have a kit. I just need to go get it. I'll be right back. You guys go ahead. I'll catch up."

By the time she returned with her kit that served both as a plate, and also contained the necessary metal utensils within it, she saw that none of them had started eating yet. They'd been waiting for her. Touched, she scraped out the last of the eggs from the pan, seeing that they had fairly divided them among the four of them. The soldiers were sitting on all three logs and she hesitated, not wanting to sit next to Kilmer on his.

"Sit here," Mace said, to her dismay, patting his log.

Her stomach knotted. *Great.* She couldn't very well say no, so she sat at the end of the log, a good three feet between her and him. "Chow down," she urged them.

"Cale told me you brought the good stuff," Kilmer said, pointing his fork down at the eggs.

Sierra felt heat flying up her throat and into her face. She rarely blushed. "I knew you guys had been out here for three months. I thought it might be nice to bring in some perishables to give to you. I know how much it means to me to get real food while out on an op."

Nate spoke up. "Sierra? How long were you in the Corps?"

"I went in when I was eighteen and left when I was twenty-six." She grew uncomfortable, hoping they wouldn't ask her too many personal questions. But she also knew these soldiers saw her as an unknown quantity. Someone they didn't know and hadn't trained with. And they were going to feel her out. It was natural in a situation like this where every person on the team was essential. To be someone who could be trusted in a firefight.

"What made you go in?" Cale asked, savoring his eggs.

"No one made me go in," Sierra told him. "My father, Hank, was in the Marine Corps. He was a sniper. I wanted to follow in his footsteps." She saw Kilmer was slowly eating his food, seeming to savor every last bite of it, satisfaction showing in his face. It made her feel good to bring these gifts to them. They worked hard and their lives were on the line every day.

"I imagine," Kilmer said, "that your father taught you to shoot, hunt and track at an early age?"

Sierra met his interested gaze. The man could melt rocks with that smoldering look in his gray eyes. "Yes, starting at six."

"Are you Native American?" Nate asked. "You sure look like it."

"I'm half Eastern Cherokee through my mother," Sierra told them. "My father is white. He owns a garage on the reservation in North Carolina."

"Did you pick up mechanical skills from him, too?" Cale wanted to know.

"I did. He taught me a lot of car mechanics. It was easy to transfer those skills to pistols and rifles."

"I would imagine," Kilmer said, "that Marine bootcamp was pretty easy for you?"

"My father had warned me about it," Sierra said, smiling a little. "He worked with me for a year, preparing me physically for all the PT." Shrugging, she said, "It was easy in some ways. In others, it wasn't. But I graduated and that's all I cared about."

"How many brothers and sisters do you have, Sierra?"

Her stomach tightened and she stopped eating over Nate's friendly, curious question. "I have a younger sister, Dawn."

"Pretty name," Nate said, finishing off his vittles. He set the kit aside and picked up a cup of coffee. "Is she gung-ho like you?"

Shaking her head, she said, "No. Dawn is nothing like me. She stays at home. She likes it there." Because of the brain damage done by her rapist, Dawn now had the personality of a five-year-old and would never get better. It broke her heart. She lifted her eyes and met Kilmer's hooded gaze. It was as if he sensed her being upset. This time though, his gray gaze didn't feel like it was ripping into her. This time... it felt as if he cared. How could that be? Quickly finishing off her breakfast, she got up and excused herself. She was going to take Kilmer's advice and hit the sack. She desperately needed some sleep.

"What do you think?" Cale asked Nate and Kilmer after Sierra had left them.

Nate shrugged and sipped his coffee, keeping his voice low so it didn't carry. "I think she's the real deal. What about you, Mace?"

Two sets of eyes settled on him. "I think she's a team player. It was damn nice of her to bring this stuff for our eggs."

"She brought a dozen Baby Wipes to divide between us, too," Cale said.

Mace's eyebrows rose momentarily. "She did?" He knew the ruck she'd had on her shoulders was a big one. And heavy.

"Yeah. Pretty damn thoughtful if you ask me."

Nate nodded. "The woman has a head on her shoulders. I like her style."

"Well," Mace grumbled, "let's hold off on giving her sainthood status, shall we? Right now, she's tired. She just came in off a three-month op in Somalia with a SEAL team. She's whipped. I think if we take the next three days and rest up, it will be good for all of us. Then, we'll start testing her out on the trails and see how she fits in or not."

"I think she will," Cale confidently told them. And then he grinned. "Not only is she one hot babe, she's intelligent and she's kind. Nice combination if you ask me."

"Hands off," Nate warned him good naturedly.

Shrugging, Cale said, "She's certifiably hot. She'd stand out no matter where she was. Most likely has a dude in her life, for sure. It doesn't hurt to appreciate her attributes."

Mace scowled. He said nothing. It wasn't lost on his men, who he'd worked with for four years, that Sierra Chastain was like a beautiful goddess out here in this godforsaken, toxic Peruvian jungle. He worried over her safety. He'd worried over Lauren Parker being assigned to them for the exact same reason: a female operative could be captured, tortured, and raped. The Russians would have their way with any woman, no question, and then kill her. It made his gut clench when he thought about any of that happening to Sierra. She was tougher than Lauren Parker had been. They both had the same level of confidence, but there was just something rare about Sierra. Mace couldn't put his finger on it. *Yet.* But he would, sooner or later. He had to know what made Sierra tick. He had to know she was someone they could utterly trust when the shit hit the fan. With the Russians around, Sierra was a liability because she was female. And he worried a lot about that angle of this dangerous dance with the Russian drug runners.

Igor Belov glared at his ten-man team. They were in the village of Tuyur and had pushed three families out of three huts and moved right in. These Indians lived in province of Paucartambo, the Highlands, only a handful of villages strung out along the cliffs at nine to twelve thousand feet of altitude. The Q'ero women knew what was expected. They would feed his team, bring food to them. He sat outside the largest hut where he and his second-in-command were staying, along with their medic, Sacha Pavlov.

Igor's thick, black eyebrows drew downward as he sat on a tree stump out in front of the thatched hut. *Pavlov.* The man was a pain in the ass. Yet, they didn't dare be in a jungle and not have a competent medic among them. Scowling, Igor watched the annoying medic, who had gone down halfway through the hundred-person village to set up a medical clinic. Rubbing his stubbled jaw, Belov supposed it was because of the breed, the medic service desire to help the sick and all that shit, that he set up these clinics. The ex-Spetsnaz medic had been the lone survivor of the old drug team in which his best friend, Petrov, had run. They'd mixed it up with one of those US Special Forces hunter-killer teams that had been dropped into Peru to take them out.

He idly watched the children and mothers lining up to be cared for by Pavlov. The man knew Quechua, the language of the Q'ero and Spanish, which were good things to have picked up. What Belov didn't like was the Russian's squeamishness when it came to raping a woman or two in order to bring a village around. It was necessary. Not that Belov didn't enjoy the demonstration. Scratching his crotch idly, he smiled a little, gazing around the village. The sun was up over the eastern horizon and the morning was just beginning. The steaming cooking pots of littered the village that curved around a small nearby stream. The black iron tripods all had fat kettles suspended over small fires with couscous, a grain that had thirty percent protein in it, their thin smoke rising languidly into thick clouds hovering all above at treetop level.

After having grown accustomed to the damned noisy howler monkeys that infested the jungle outside the haven of the village meadow, the peaceful morning calls of birds sounded a helluva lot better to Igor's ears. Much nicer than those screeching bastards swinging all around overhead. He glanced around and saw his men outside their huts, tarps spread on the ground, oiling their rifles and pistols. It was a daily ritual. Or rust would leap at the chance to corrode the barrels and could make them miss a shot.

Pavlov. Something bothered Belov about the medic. He didn't know what, but his warrior's instincts told him the man was not to be trusted. His scowl deepened as he thought back to when Vlad Alexandrov headed this team. Some other medics, Alex Kazak and Nik Morozov in particular, knew Pavlov. The three of them had been best friends from what Belov understood. Their teams had been working together in ops in and out of Russia at that time. Those three has been like brothers. And then Kazak had turned traitor on Alexandrov and fled. Belov idly wondered if Pavlov missed his brothers-in-arms. Combat medics were a breed apart from the regular Spetsnaz teams. Now, Pavlov was close to no one in the team and that irritated the hell out of Igor.

He watched as Pavlov, who was sitting on a wooden bench, brought a little five-year-old girl with tiny black braids onto his lap. He saw the mother, who was also smiling, standing nearby as the medic gently looked in the child's ears, checked her eyes and then asked her to open her tiny mouth. There were seven other mothers lined up, with children ranging in age from newborn to, perhaps, ten years old. Belov knew that Pavlov was well-known among the Q'ero villages. Wherever he went, he held medical clinics. And out in this green hell of unrelenting jungle, there was no other medical help available to these Indians. They were, for the most part, cut off from the rest of the world.

And that was good. Belov needed to keep the Peruvian policia out of the area. Right now, the ruthless Russian teams were winning the war against the Latin drug lords who had once ruled this region. And Lima's officials were hard pressed budget-wise to bring enough policia into the area to get rid of them. Slowly, they were taking over and pushing the other drug lords out of business. He smiled. Lima, the capitol of Peru, sat on the coast of the Pacific Ocean. Those rich enough to live in the capitol held the power and purse strings. And they could care less about the areas where the struggling Q'ero Indians, the remnants before the great Incan empire arrived, still outlived them and the Spaniards. These people were farmers. They had no voice in the government. They were the descendants of pre-Incan people. And then, the Spanish assault came in the 1500's. And they escaped the murderous soldiers of Spain, as well. Their lives had all worked out well until Igor Belov and the other Russian teams, took over.

But it was a worry. And he knew that the Peruvian government had granted permission to the US to help undercover operatives down here. Bankrolling them with stateside government funds. Belov estimated that at least three black ops US Army hunter-killer teams were on the ground in their area. He was in touch with the other Russian team leaders. And in the last six months, the six Russian teams had lost three of their leaders to the stealthy Army Special Forces soldiers. There was a price on his head, and he knew it. And he understood these black ops teams were as good as Spetsnaz. Belov trusted no one. Especially Pavlov, although he couldn't pinpoint why. Maybe because his best friend, Kazak and Morozov had turned yellow and run. Would Pavlov, someday, do the same?

Belov grimaced and considered the question. He spread a cloth across his thick thighs and picked up his pistol. Beginning to quickly disassemble the weapon in order to oil it, he considered Pavlov once again. It was hard to get a medic for each Russian team. But down here in this fucking green hell of a jungle where, if a man scratched his hand, he could die twenty-four hours later of some damn bacteria, a medic was essential. He wished he could trade Pavlov off for another medic. A more trustworthy one. This one refused to join the rest of his men when they took young women from a village to satisfy their sexual appetites. The coward always turned away and left, anger in his eyes. Belov wondered if Pavlov, if he ever had the chance, wouldn't maybe shoot all of them in the head as his judgement for all the rapes he had walked away from.

Of course, Pavlov was a medic. His whole life, his passion, was saving lives, not taking them. Igor had never seen the medic fail to return fire in a firefight, however. He was a deadly accurate shooter as they were, no question. It's just that the medic lacked a set of balls when it came to taking a woman. *The pussy.* Still, Pavlov was important because clearly, the villagers were not afraid of him. They loved and eagerly welcomed him. When they saw the medic come into the village the children, who were always frightened of the rest of the team, were not afraid of Pavlov. The children surrounded him like he was St. Nicholas, and it was Christmas. He always carried candy in his cammo pockets for them, without fail.

Maybe it was good that Pavlov was there. The villagers, once his soldiers raped a few of their women right in front of them, usually fell into line quickly. The men would take time out of their farming practices and tend the coca fields for them. If they didn't get the point the first time around, Belov would grab a few more women out of the village and rape them too. Those that survived, well, Pavlov had to take care of them. Growling a curse, Belov continued to clean his pistol, oiling it well. There wasn't a Q'ero village who didn't see Pavlov like some saint to be worshipped, while being scared as hell of the rest of the team.

Maybe it was just as well. Igor knew from his decades as a Spetsnaz officer, that they all feared him and his team. He knew from long experience, that fear was the greatest controller of people. And it was fine by him that this village, like all the rest, were terrified of him and his men. They damn well better be. Let Pavlov be seen as the good guy. Sometimes he was able to get intel out of the local Indians about the Special Forces teams operating in the area. They too, visited these villages. And they had a medic with them also, from what he understood. And sometimes, children talked, and Igor would find out when one of these Army teams had come through or even stayed overnight in one of these villages. That was useful intel because, like a player in an invisible chess game, Igor was making moves in hopes of finding the Americanos and killing them first.

CHAPTER 5

S IERRA SLOWLY WOKE up. She rubbed her eyes, feeling drowsy. Light peeked around the plastic doorway of her hut. Slowly sitting up, she heard the low voices of the Special Forces team nearby. Her hair had come partly loose from her ponytail as she'd slept. She fumbled behind her head with the twisted band, eventually freeing her black hair to tumble across her shoulders. Trying to tame down the strands, she slowly moved around. What time was it? Looking down at the watch on her wrist, she saw it was 1600 or four p.m. She'd slept a long time! Sierra knew she'd been tired.

Her mind and her heart turned to Mace Kilmer. He was a confusing man in her life. As she searched for her brush and comb among the toiletries she kept in a small plastic bag, Sierra didn't want to be drawn to him. But damn, she was. And why? Why him of all men? He didn't want her in his life. Well, okay, he'd seemed a little less abrasive earlier when she'd connected with them and they'd asked her questions, probing her, finding out more about her. She knew this was part of the evaluation. It was the same with any team she'd worked with. Being an unknown in a tight team could disrupt the flow between the members of it. Sierra got that. She knew what teamwork was. As she slowly pulled the brush through her hair, she thought that the last thing she wanted to become was a bump in their daily grind. Something that threw the team out of rhythm, that destabilized them. That was a no go. No one understood that better than her. And she knew part of Kilmer's growliness was due to his unspoken worry that she'd be a problem child, gumming up the fluid mechanics of his band. Sierra knew, if that happened, it could get someone killed. And she had no desire to be that person.

Part of her job as a security contractor was to fit seamlessly into any group, and not stir up a bunch of turbulence across her incoming wake as she did so. But Kilmer didn't know how good she was at doing so, and that she wouldn't ruffle the heart of the crew's unified performance. And he was more than aggressive about protecting his men as a whole. That wasn't a bad thing in her book. A good leader looked after her or his soldiers. And Mace was an alpha-wolf leader, no question.

Her fingers moved through her long hair, separating and weaving it. Quickly, she tamed the wild strands into one united braid, and snapped a rubber band around the end to stop it from fraying apart again. She flipped the braid over one shoulder, so that it hung between her shoulder blades. It was simply too humid and hot to wear her hair down. And a braid, or braids, always kept it out of her way when she was in stalking mode as a sniper. Right now, Kilmer was standing down the men for three days. It wasn't a bad idea because it would allow Sierra to move into the group during a less stressful and dangerous time. Her appreciation of Kilmer's wisdom as a leader impacted her. She just wished he'd stop hating her because she was a woman, instead of the male soldier he'd expected. What the hell had happened to him previously to make him so distrusting and wary of military women? Or was he a patriarchal male, harking back to the days when women in combat just hadn't even been imagined as a possibility or, much less, tolerated? Mouth quirking, Sierra got to her hands and knees, took a deep breath, and crawled out of her hut.

She saw the three Army soldiers sitting together in front of Kilmer's hut. They had a waterproof tarp spread out between them and the men were oiling their weapons and other equipment in order to protect them against the humidity and the ever-present possibility of rust. As she rose to her feet, scrubbing her face, trying to wake up, she automatically keyed her hearing, tuning it to the baseline sounds of the jungle surrounding them. Mostly, she heard birds calling, and she relaxed a little.

Moving over to the group, she saw Mace lift his head. The men all wore baseball caps, and each had a holster with a .45 in it around their waists. They remained armed at all times. She'd left her own hut without a pistol.

"Hey, guys, can you tell me where your latrine facilities are around here?"

Kilmer hitched a thumb to his right and said, "Over there. There's a small trail. You'll see it. And Chastain? Wear a pistol on you at all times."

She knew that was coming. "Right," she murmured, nodding. Kilmer was just doing his job. Letting her know the lay of the land. Turning, she walked back to her hut, crawled inside, and grabbed the green nylon web belt and holster. She stuffed some toilet paper into the large thigh pockets of her cammies. Re-emerging, she headed toward the eastern edge of the meadow. Spotting the trail entrance, she walked down the damp, muddy path, surrounded by trees, darkness falling as their canopy of leaves cut the sunlight off from reaching the earth.

The path emerged into an area that was about one third the size of the meadow back where the huts were located. Looking around, she saw that a lot of holes had been dug here, and then filled in. It was an Army latrine thing. In other areas, there was nothing but litter and a lot of toilet paper rotting in the jungle. Getting her business done, Sierra had questions for Kilmer when she walked back into the village meadow.

"Get a good nap?" Nate asked her.

Sierra halted. "Yes. Thanks for letting me catch up." Her gaze drifted to Kilmer. He was frowning, his attention on the pistol in his hands. She felt her lower body stir, completely taken aback by it. The man was undeniably male. A beautiful specimen, in fact. Sierra took in a deep breath. "Is there anything I can do around here to help out?"

"Yeah," Cale spoke up, looking at her. "We're going to give you the wood-collecting patrol." He grinned. "Might sound easy, but it's not. All the wood is wet and damned hard to get to burn." He pointed to the last hut. "We usually find and stack wood in there. Not a lot, but enough for three fires a day. When we get here to what we term our 'safe place', we try to cook some local food we've bought from the villagers along our route instead of eating MREs."

"That's a great idea," Sierra said. "Is there any particular place you want me to go fetch the wood? Length? Size?"

"I'd go up the path we came in on," Cale advised. "But keep your hearing keyed. It's the only way in and out of this place and Igor Belov is always around."

"Understood. Should I take my M-4 rifle?" She saw Kilmer shove his pistol into his holster and stand up.

"I'll take you out and show you," he grunted. "Get a pair of gloves and then all you need is your pistol."

Sierra didn't know whether to be happy or sad Kilmer volunteered to come along. She saw Cale give Nate a grin. What was that about? No one was talking. "Yeah... okay," she muttered, turning, and heading to her hut. *Gloves and hat.* She was already wearing her sidearm. Above them the sky was a druzy blue, the sun hot as she hurried from her hut to where Kilmer was standing, looking bored.

Falling into step with him, the path just wide enough for both of them but only barely, Sierra wanted to make sure their hands didn't accidentally brush against one another's. The path led up a slight incline. Mace seemed to check his stride for her. She could feel the tension around him, wondering what was going on inside that head of his. Even with the black baseball cap drawn low over his eyes, she felt him invisibly sensing the area. All operators did, more or less. She fell into step with him.

Once the meadow drew out of view behind them, he seemed to relax a little. It wasn't anything obvious. There was jungle on either side of them and she saw it looked like fairly easy going between the spindly trees that grew everywhere through it. In some places, there were huge Flying Buttress trees, their roots looked like massive wings expanding out from the trunks of them.

"You ever been in jungle before?" Mace asked her.

"African. Does that count?" and she looked up and grinned at him. He scowled. Damn, didn't this man have a sense of humor? He was all business all the time? Didn't he ever let down?

"Yeah." He waved his hand off to the right in front of her. "Peruvian jungle is different. It changes. There're some spots where the woody vines are so thick, twisted and huge, that you can't get through the area. You never want to be caught in a situation like that. It's like a box canyon, strategy-wise."

"No place to hide or run there? Confined to the trail only?" Sierra guessed. She thought she saw some of the hardness in his face ease a tiny bit. When he cut her a glance, she saw respect in his eyes.

"Right. Accurate assessment, Chastain. Here though, we can get through the jungle. Tomorrow, I'm going to sit down with you, and we'll go over the trail maps we've made of our territory. I've been trying to get satellite infrared flyovers to take photos so we can continue to map the area, and as you can see, we have cloud-cover almost twenty-four hours a day. Infrared can pierce it, but the problem is they don't have any extras they can sit on station and help us."

Frowning, Sierra looked up. She could see the blue sky, but it was as if there was some semi-opaque gauze between it and them. "That sucks."

"Tell me about it."

She smiled a little, starting to relax because he wasn't being so growly. "So, in those areas where the jungle is like a Chinese puzzle, it's more dangerous for us? We don't know if Belov is coming our way?"

"Right."

"What about a Raven drone? They're small and light. They could fly just above the triple canopy?" Again, she saw him give her an approving glance. Had Kilmer thought her an empty-headed doll with no military and tactical experience? *Must have.* She kept her bile to herself. She was going to have to work with this hard, rugged soldier until she brought down Belov through her crosshairs. Maybe he was testing her, probing, finding out what she did and did not know. Just because she was a civilian security contractor didn't mean she didn't interface regularly with the military. Maybe he wasn't sent her personnel record to know about her? That was S.O.P., standard operating procedure. She knew her boss would make damn sure it had been sent to Kilmer. So? He hadn't gotten it yet? Sierra thought it was the better part of valor NOT to bring this up to him right now. He was growly enough without being brought to task for not reading her file before she started this op.

"We have two Ravens," he muttered, "but the problem is the triple canopy itself. The camera it carries can't look down between the leaves to see what's on a path a hundred feet below it. And," Mace shook his head, "you're going to find out pronto how the thunderstorms roll around this jungle. They pop up from mid-afternoon onward and all through the night. The winds, as you probably know, are variable, and a small drone like that can be pushed off course by the winds that accompany those storms, so we lose our acquired target."

Rubbing her brow, she grimaced. "No eyes in the sky for us, then."

"Ninety percent of the time, that's right. It all comes down to us knowing the trails, knowing infil and exfil points. And when we get into those walled-off paths in the vine jungle, it gets dicey. For everyone. I don't want the four of us meeting the ten men of Belov's team in one of those alleyways. There's no place to take cover and dodge bullets."

"But it would be the same for him and his team."

"Yes, but they have superior firepower. It's ten against three." He halted in a slight swale, throwing his hands on his hips, looking down at her. "The paths are only wide enough for one man. They were created over thousands of years by the wild pigs that made them. Pigs aren't very wide, so the trails are narrow. And in some places, as you'll find pretty soon, the walls of the jungle are hemming you in."

"Crap," she muttered. "That means if we met Belov in the vine jungle area, then it's an old-fashion shoot-out and only one man, the guy at the front of the line, can fire his weapon at us."

"Yeah, until we drop 'em and then the next Russian in line starts opening up on us. Whac-A-Mole. Plus, these trails twist and wind. There're not any quarter mile straight lengths of path." He angled his gaze at her. "Which means, for a sniper, it's so damned hard to find a hide, sit in it, wait to acquire your HVT. Because, even if you did, you might have a hundred yards line of sight at the most, and that's it."

Her eyes widened as she considered the information. "That means if I take down the HVT, there's nine other tangos who are a hundred yards away from me? And they're going to open up with everything they have." She saw concern and worry in his hard expression.

"Yeah. This isn't going to be a picnic for you, Chastain. There's only so many hide areas where you MIGHT have two to three hundred yards between you and him. Even then, egressing the hell out of there is going to be dicey at best."

Her mouth compressed. "Makes a rooftop position in Mogidishu look easy."

He grinned a little, one side of his mouth lifting. "Yeah, that's the idea. No roof tops here."

"What about hills? A cliff area? Something high so I could do a look-down-shoot down?"

"No cliffs around here, unless we're up in the Highland area where you flew in." He waved his arm around. "This is jungle. It's got nobs or little hills here and there but nothing like what you're wanting from a sniper standpoint."

"Crap."

"Shit is more like it."

Snorting, she spotted some smaller branches off the trail and went over and started collecting them into the curve of her arm. "Really," she said, agreeing with him.

Kilmer moved ahead and picked up more of the branches that had come down during a recent thunderstorm. "Part of our mission is just mapping all the primary and feeder trails in the area," he told her. "The feeder trails are small tributary paths off the main ones. Sometimes, it's smarter to take a feeder than the primary. The pigs are always creating new trails as they push through, rooting out grubs, worms, and other stuff from beneath the soil."

In no time, Sierra had an armful of smaller twigs and larger branches in her arms. Kilmer had gotten an armload, too. "But those feeder trails could be a dead end. That wouldn't be good if we're trying to exfil." She saw him give her a pleased look.

"Bingo," he said, heading out onto the trail and gesturing for her to walk with him back toward the meadow. "That's why mapping the feeder trails is so damned important."

"So, you're doing all that, plus trying to pick off the leaders of each of the Russian mafia teams in your territory?" Sierra guessed. The wood was damp and heavy, having absorbed the constant rain in the area.

"Correct. It's whac-a-mole, all over, again. You kill one of those bastards and the New York City mafia sends in a new leader to take over. And then it's the same game, just with fresh players, all over again."

"How much time do you parcel out for trail mapping?" she wondered. Sierra found herself not wanting to go back to the meadow just yet. She saw that Kilmer was being less abrasive with her the more he realized she was a damned good strategist and tactician. She had a good mind for the geography and topography of an area. As a sniper, that was of key importance to her being able to complete her mission.

"Fifty percent."

"Do you set up traps for Belov?"

"Yeah," Killmer grumped, unhappy. "But it's always a guess. Without sat-ellite imaging or being able to use a Raven to spot him and his team, it's always second guessing. What we've tried to do is establish his route. Every Russian team in this area has to go to ten different locations that have an Indian village each. They run a circuit. With Alexandrov, he was predictable. Petrov, who took over for him, was less so. And Belov is completely unpredictable. So, trying to establish a hide for you to sit in and wait him out is going to be near impossible unless he stops being erratic in his routes."

"I was briefed by the big guy at Shield Security, Jack Driscoll, that there's a mole in Belov's team. Sasha Pavlov? He's a combat medic and ex-Spetsnaz operator." She twisted a look up at Mace. "Do you know about him?"

"Yes. He has certain Indians in each village that he trusts, that will give us any messages from him when we arrive in their particular village. He's a good man," Kilmer said. "And if we didn't have Pavlov feeding us intelligence, we'd be totally screwed. We'd never be able to meet Belov on a trail. There're over twenty-five trails, and three times that of feeder trails in our area of operation."

Sierra took in a deep breath, beginning to grasp how tough an assignment this was going to be. "What does Pavlov pass on to you?"

"Usually, the lowdown on when the Indians of the village have to hump out the cocaine in sacks to carry it into the Highlands area." Mace breasted the small hill, the meadow not far ahead. "He'll let us know the time when it's to be picked up, or the trail they're taking. We try not to make Belov suspect someone on his teams knows the schedule. So, we hit them at different points and areas, but not consistently. We let some of the coke get through in order to keep Pavlov protected."

"Both the CIA," she told him, "and Jack are worried about Sasha. Jack said he's a good man, with good moral fiber. That he hates being with the mafia, but he doesn't have a choice."

Mace shrugged. "Then he can leave. I don't see the issue here. It's good pay to be a drug soldier."

Sierra shook her head as they walked down the incline. "It's not so black-and-white, Sergeant."

"Call me Kilmer, or Mace," he grunted, giving her a dark look.

That was a nice surprise. "Okay," she said. Sierra knew, in the military, everyone went by their last names or by their nicknames. She had no idea if this team did as well but would find out sooner or later. "Jack told us that Pavlov's family had been massacred by Russian separatists. He comes from dairy farm people. He has a younger brother who survived the raid, the only one left alive. Pavlov used to have four sisters and two brothers." Her voice dropped into a sad tone. "It's hell having a sibling who's too injured to live on his own…"

Mace looked down at her. But he didn't say anything. They carried the branches and twigs over to the hut that served as the camp's makeshift woodhouse, stowing them one by one inside, where they could slowly start drying out.

Sierra enjoyed this time working with Mace. She would hand him the branches, and, with his long arms, he'd take them and reach inside the hut to stack them neatly. Every once in a while, their fingers would briefly touch. And every time, Sierra felt a spark of warmth on her skin wherever they made accidental contact. She looked at the way his collar pulled away from his thick, muscular neck, and appreciated the muscles and masculine power of him. And both sweating profusely as they were in the high humidity, she unconsciously inhaled his male scent. It made her want to unbutton his shirt and run her hands in exploration over that massive chest of his. She knew he would look incredible naked. Why, oh why, was her mind going THERE? Flustered, Sierra forced herself to finish off the task and then get up, rubbing her dirty palms down her cammie trousers.

She saw that Cale was busy cutting up a chicken he'd just plucked the feathers from. Going over, she asked him, "Can you use some help? I'm a great sous-chef."

Cale grinned, quickly butchering the chicken. "Sure. I've got some lard in that tin by the log. Drop a couple of tablespoons into the skillet there and get it melted over the fire?"

Sierra was happy to help. Nate came by with a gallon-sized Ziploc bag of what looked like yellow cornmeal in it. He washed the chicken parts off in a bowl of clean rainwater and crouched next to Cale, handing them to him. In no time, the chicken was coated in cornmeal, and Nate gently put each piece into the skillet, being careful not to splash up the melted lard in the bottom of it. Sierra placed the huge skillet over the grate across the fire.

"Fried chicken tonight!" Cale called, washing his hands off in the water, and then throwing it out on the grass.

"You guys live high on the hog out here," Sierra teased, moving the skillet a bit. Cale handed her a fork so she could turn the meat when needed.

Nate put water and then coffee grounds into the percolator, setting it on one edge of the grate. "The Q'ero people of the villages are always happy to have US dollars instead of Peruvian soles. There's about a three-to-one ratio, with Uncle Sam returning three times the price for the food they purchase down in Cusco. They're happy to share fresh eggs, chickens, fruit and vegetables, when they're in season, with us."

"Yeah," Cale said. "Sometimes we meet a big boar on one of the trails. We shoot it, field dress it, and then put it on a long pole and carry it into the nearest village."

Nate grinned and sat down on one of the logs. "Yeah, Sierra, you oughta see the villagers celebrate. They dig a huge hole, start a big fire, and make a lot of coals. Then they wrap the pig in some kind of large jungle leaves and bury it all. The next day, that pig is done, and it can feed everyone in some of the smaller villages. And us, too."

She smiled and said softly, "You guys are more like Indians, not whites. In my culture, the hunters go out and hunt deer and bring it back field dressed. They then give the heart and liver to the elderly, plus the best meat. They take only enough of that deer for their own family and distribute the rest to the tribe."

"These villages do the same thing. By bringing in a boar to them, it gets us a lot of intel," Cale told her. He got up and peered at the chicken frying and popping in the skillet, looking satisfied. "When we first got here, they feared us just as much as they did the Russians. When they found out we were going to medically care for them, give them food and dollars, then, they adopted us. It's been a good relationship between us. They always let us know when Belov and his men have come through. They'll tell us which way he left so we can follow his trail and, hopefully, catch him."

Sierra saw Mace wander over. For whatever reason, he looked more relaxed. Had their talk done it? Had she convinced him she wasn't some female airhead? That she was a worthy candidate to be in his team's midst? Sierra had worked with Special Forces teams before. One thing they had in common was the Sergeant, the leader, was damned protective of his men, of their care and safety. She couldn't blame Kilmer for being threatened by her entrance into their team. He came and sat down, saying nothing, on the same log where Nate was sitting.

"Cale?"

"Yeah."

"I brought a box of Potato Buds with me. Would you guys like some real mashed potatoes to go with this chicken?" Sierra instantly saw all three men's faces light up. She laughed to herself: a way to a man's heart was through his stomach. For a moment, a thread of sadness wound through her own heart. Jeb had loved her cooking. She'd often brought US food in boxes and jars out on their missions. Just getting a little home-cooked food every once in a while, was a treat. And no less there than it was here.

"Damn, you're mighty handy to have around, Chastain," Nate said. "You wouldn't, by any chance, have some butter with you?"

Giving him a wry look, Sierra said, as she turned the chicken over in the skillet, "I do, but by now, in this tropical heat, it's melted in the bottom of the jar I put it in."

Rubbing his hands, Cale said, "Mashed potatoes with real butter AND fried chicken tonight." He looked at his buddies. "Does it get any better than this, dudes?"

Sierra chuckled. "Cale? Come take over for a minute? I'll get the plastic bag of flakes and the jar of butter from my ruck."

Nate got to his feet. "I got a small saucepan in my pack. We'll use it to make the mashed potatoes."

Sierra turned and saw Kilmer looking at her. His mouth was relaxed. The color of his eyes was a stormy gray, and she had no idea what that meant. Automatically, her body went hot, reacting to the burning look he was giving her. It was as if she had caught him without his tough soldier's mask in place. As if this was the real Mace Kilmer. She rose on shaky knees, still under his intense perusal. Quickly looking away, she forced herself to leave the circle and go to her hut.

Her pulse was amping up. There was no mistaking the look in his eyes this time, though. He damn well desired her. It was a naked, scorching look and she was old enough to know when a man was hungry for a woman. Her fingers trembled as she pushed into her hut on her hands and knees. Dragging over her ruck where she kept her stash, she opened it. Mouth dry, she licked her lower lip, unable to explain fully why her body was blazing like a three-alarm fire. The fire's flashover consumed her lower body, and she felt the gnawing ache of wanting a man who really knew how to love his woman. All the way. She sensed Mace would be a skillful lover. Her skin skittered as she visualized his long, calloused hands moving across it. Closing her eyes for a moment, Sierra told herself to get it together.

There was no WAY she was going to let Mace's naked, hungry look dismantle or distract her. He hadn't expected her to turn around like that. He'd been staring at her backside. Sierra knew she had a nice butt. Jeb had told her that it was one of her finer attributes. Pulling out the gallon Ziploc full of Potato Buds and locating the small pint jar with the melted butter, Sierra tried to settle down her suddenly riled body.

Kilmer was like a flame. And she was the hapless moth. Sierra knew she wasn't helpless in this unexpected development. He had never made any move toward her in any way to suggest he wanted her sexually. But she knew these teams stayed out three months at a time. And not having sex for three months was a pressing detail. She laughed to herself, closing her ruck. She hadn't had sex in nearly two years, not since Jeb had died. But Kilmer seemed to fan the flames of her traitorous body like a blowtorch. What was she going to do?

CHAPTER 6

M ACE SAT ALONE on his log, fried chicken, mash potatoes and melted butter in his kit. Cale had invited Sierra to sit with him and Nate. The three of them looked cozy on the same log together and he felt a frisson of envy. She had a quick smile for his two men. Given that he'd been a bastard to her since she arrived, Kilmer couldn't fault her on not wanting to get anywhere near him unless she had to. But damn, the woman's natural good looks, her wide, lush mouth drawing into a smile, her teasing and giving as good as she got from Cale and Nate back, made him damned jealous. Okay, so he admitted it. He wanted that curvy, firm, tall body of hers parallel to his. He was already fantasizing about it, which pissed the hell out of him. He'd been doing ops in Peru for three years, out in the bush three months at a time, and he'd NEVER been so damned sexually hungry as he was right now. Worse, he was partly erect, which really made him irate. He couldn't even taste the wonderful chicken, it was that bad.

It would be easy to blame Sierra, but he was old enough, mature enough, to take responsibility for his thoughts and actions. That long, thick braid of hers swinging gently between her shoulder blades as she turned her head right and left to talk with Nate or Cale, sent a yearning through him. What would it be like to loosen her hair? Thread his fingers through it? Feel how cool and silky it felt? His men had lit up like Christmas tree light bulbs when they invited her to sit between them and she did. He was shocked, grumbling to himself that he should have invited her to sit by him. If only he had any social skills left. But hell, he knew she wouldn't have. The golden sparkle in her cypress-green eyes made him ache. And her laughter was low and husky to his ears what mellow whiskey felt like flowing down his gullet, warming his entire body. Sierra was easy-going, jabbing Nate in the ribs with her elbow when he mercilessly teased her. The three of them laughed quietly, keeping their voices down. In the jungle, noise was swallowed up by all the nearby vegetation. Still, they knew they were in hostile territory.

The slope of her cheeks was high, her eyes slightly tilted. Mace decided she probably took after her Cherokee mother in spades. Her black hair had a reddish tint. It was thick, slightly curled around her temples, giving her a wholesome look. Mace had a helluva time reconciling her young, fresh college-aged face with the fact she was a deadly sniper. Reminding himself she'd been a Marine; he was amazed at her ability to unwind and relax. He wished he had that ability, but he didn't. The fact that he was team leader was a burden he bore willingly, but it also didn't allow him to let down that much, either. He felt himself longing for a different connection with her when she tipped back her head, exposing her long, slender throat, her hand against her mouth, laughing hard over one of Cale's comments.

He'd never seen his team this loose or this happy. Hell, with a good-looking woman around, he was happy too. Still, he wished Sierra was with HIM and not THEM. How juvenile could he get? Apparently, very much, Mace admitted sourly. One thing age and maturity gave him was the power to be brutally honest with himself. That way, people didn't disappoint him. Nor did he project his personal shit on them, either. Or… he tried not to, and he hadn't done well with Sierra in that regard at all. He'd projected a lot of unfair judgements on her, none of which she deserved. His conscience smarted mightily over it and he wished he could somehow fix all that. He watched as Cale wiped tears out of his eyes, the three of them laughing so hard they all had one hand across their mouths to mute the sounds, and the other against their bellies. Grinning sourly, he tasted his chicken, tasted the cornmeal with its hint of thyme, salt and pepper combined. The fact that Sierra had personally made his next forkful of mashed potatoes, had poured the liquid-gold butter over every man's kit, just made them seem to taste all the better to Mace. Damn, having a woman around as a teammate wasn't such a bad thing in some respects. It brought a sense of the feminine into their harsh, dangerous lives. Sierra brought softness. A maternal touch. He saw both his guys blushing like school kids whenever she reached out spontaneously and touched one of their arms over some comment. Yeah, his men deserved this, and he felt warmth crawling through his chest and then making a dive south.

He didn't see Sierra as motherly at all. She was hot. Damned hot. And that muscle shirt she wore, although loose, clung damply to her flesh, around those small breasts of hers, and Mace just about lost it, starting in on a visualization of his large hands slowly grazing their curves, feeling the fullness of them under his palms. He scowled, forcing himself to look down at the last leg of chicken on his kit. He grabbed it, biting into it like he was a wolf biting into a recently killed carcass. But he listened. He WANTED to hear her low, smokey voice, the natural warmth that was in it. And all he could think about was how her voice made his flesh riffle with need, imagining her lips, her teeth nipping and tongue licking him here and there. Mace decided that whatever else he did when they went into Cusco in a week's time, he was going to find a willing woman to bed and take the edge off this ridiculous situation.

"What do you do in your down time?" Sierra asked Nate.

He shrugged. "Sleep. Because we don't get a lot of it out on the trails. Humping a one-hundred-and-twenty-pound ruck. Our weapons. We're drinking a couple gallons of water a day. Mace, here, relents every once in a while, and gives us two or three days of downtime after a hard push," and Nate grinned over at Kilmer. "But he's such a hard ass that we usually don't get time outs like we're getting now that you're here." Nate blinked and teased, "You're special, Chastain."

"Yeah," Cale chuckled, "and we're damned glad you are. We get three days to rest up."

Sierra gave Mace a quick glance. He was slowly chewing his food, staring into the fire pit. Her heart squeezed. He looked so alone. Sad and alone. There was no other way to couch it. She felt it, intuitively. Even though the corners of his strong, well-shaped mouth curved naturally upward, there was a heaviness he carried that she couldn't define. And he didn't seem the type to dump anything on anyone. Well, except on her at first. And he seemed to have realized he'd been doing that, and reined in his prejudice, and even seemed a little grateful that they were on a more equal footing with one another. That was the problem with operators: they buried their feelings until they'd never see the light of day again. Her heart wanted her to get up and move over and sit with Mace. To excuse herself from the pleasant company of Nate and Cale. She felt kind of uncomfortable that the three of them were behaving like old friends on an overdue meetup, while Kilmer sat there alone. Really alone. And sometimes, she would feel his gaze on her. It felt like his hand was lightly skimming her body whenever he was trying to secretly look at her. And when she would look up and see him studying her, it triggered her all over again. This time, Mace's gray eyes were not hard. Nor was there anger in them. Just— yearning. Need.

Swallowing against a dry throat, Sierra kept her gaze on her kit, finishing up the mash potatoes and butter. Did Mace need her? In what way? She allowed herself to remember the burning hunger in his eyes as they'd gathered wood earlier and had her answer. And instantly, she felt her lower body clench in its own kind of hunger. Sierra hadn't known a sex drive could die, but hers had when Jeb did. Her body had gone dormant. And never once, not until just now, had it stirred and began to awaken. It was a hungry beast, not polite and not subtle. Sierra wasn't going to lie to herself. The man was pure sex and so damned charismatic in his stony, silent way. It just rippled off his powerful, muscular body like heat waves and she felt every wave, silently lapping them up like the starving animal she had become. No question, Sierra sensed Mace Kilmer could satisfy her completely. All she had to do was remember how his big hands were when he had slid that radio band around her head, her scalp taking off like wildfire, and how she'd known then that, despite his size, he could be gentle. And most of all, because she'd been around big men in the military, and she'd always been shorter and leaner than them. Neither their height nor weight had ever intimidated her.

As she scraped up every last bit of the mash potatoes left in her kit with her spoon, she literally ached to feel Kilmer's mouth upon hers. There was something so terribly lonely about him and it felt like a knife slicing at her heart. Sierra wondered if he would open up to her in the future. Would he trust her enough to do that? To lower those tough shields, he wore around himself? Maybe Cale or Nate could fill her in on his private life? They were treating her like a kid sister, Cale even tugging once on her braid. She liked these two men. They had the capacity for childlike play, like she did. And Sierra knew how important it was to let down and relax out on an op. It wasn't always tense. It wasn't always dangerous. There were long periods of boredom, and then there were these kinds of playful moments to balance out the intensity of an op.

"What do you do," Cale asked, "when you're slumming on an op, Sierra?"

She gave them a wicked grin. "I'm usually out with a sniper partner, my spotter. And if I'm not, like when I'm assigned to a larger team, I like to grab sleep. But when I wake up, I like to challenge the guys to a game of Scrabble."

Nate laughed.

Cale gave her a confused look.

"What?" she demanded, giving them a dirty look.

"A board game?" Cale drawled, rolling his eyes. "On an op where you could get your ass shot off?"

Nate giggled and put his hand over his mouth, giving Sierra an apologetic look. "Seriously?" he choked.

Sierra felt heat rising in her neck, groaning because she was blushing. "Yes, seriously. What's wrong with a game like that? It sure beats the horrible boredom we go through. As long as my spotter is on watch, I can play against myself." And then she added defiantly, squaring her shoulders, giving them an imperious look, "I like expanding my word vocabulary."

Nate and Cale just about fell off the log, laughing hysterically.

Sierra scowled, settling her elbows on her thighs. She happened to glance over at Mace. He had a thoughtful look on his face. At least he wasn't laughing at her like these two dudes were.

Nate finally stopped giggling, both his arms around his belly. "I suppose… I suppose you're a writer. Is that why you like Scrabble?"

Snorting, Sierra said, "No, I'm not a writer. But I do like crossword puzzles."

Cale wiped the tears out of his eyes and kept chuckling. "A sniper who plays scrabble out on an op. Oh, Gawd, I am NOT EVER gonna forget this one!" He cut Sierra an amused glance. "I'm so glad you're here. You have entertained me more in the last hour than the last three years I've been out in this hellish place." He reached out, gripping her shoulder, trying not to laugh. "Thank you…"

Sierra didn't know whether he was being sincere or not. Or just ragging on her, which military men and women tended to do mercilessly with one another.

"Give her some breathing room," Mace ordered in a growl, giving his men a look of warning. "Nothing wrong with Scrabble."

Instantly, Cale's eyebrows flew upward. "Not you, too?" He looked around Sierra and grinned at Nate. "You think Kilmer plays Scrabble?" and he started giggling again.

Nate's mouth dropped open as he considered Cale's accusation. "No… you don't, Kilmer. You have NEVER brought up Scrabble and we've been out here for three years with your sorry ass."

Shrugging casually, Mace growled darkly, "Like you know everything about me?"

"Yeah," Merrill answered with a huge grin, "even down to how many pieces of toilet paper you use when you shit."

Sierra clapped her hand over her mouth, trying to stifle a huge laugh.

Nate laughed uproariously, tipped his head back, lost his balance and fell off the log.

All Sierra saw was a tangle of long legs and arms up in the air like a dead bug as she turned and failed to try and stop his fall. Nate was on the ground, rolling around, laughing himself silly. She turned and gazed across the fire pit at Kilmer. He had that dark look in his eyes, watching Nate rolling around on the damp ground.

"Really? You play Scrabble?" she asked him, hope in her voice.

Cale shook his head. "Oh, this should be good. Okay, Kilmer, tell us the truth. In your deep, dark little box of treasured secrets you hide from everyone, do you honestly play Scrabble?"

He shrugged, his face remaining unreadable. "Unlike you two assholes, I have one helluva word vocabulary, even if I don't waste it on the likes of you two birds."

Nate went into more spasms of laughter, rolling and holding his belly, tears running out of his shut eyes. "Oh, sure, Sarge. Let's see," he giggled, "your vocabulary consists of about ten words and we hear 'em all the time. All swear words!" and he went into another paroxysm. "That's a helluva BIG vocabulary!"

Sierra couldn't help but smile as she watched Nate with his legs up in the air, reminding her of a little boy playing and having fun. It struck her that, because of the nature of their mission here in Peru, it was dangerous all the time. There was no safe place to really let down. Even here in this meadow, it wasn't a hundred-percent safe. And a warm bubble of happiness burbled up through her chest as she realized she was helping these men to let down and truly relax. Laughter, she knew, was always healing.

"My heart be still," Cale said, dramatically clapping his hands dramatically to his chest as he looked over at Kilmer. "You really DO play Scrabble?"

"Yeah. What of it?"

Nate kept giggling, helpless to stop.

Sierra grinned at Mace. "Better watch it, or you're going to be put in the same box with me," she teased. She watched his gray eyes thaw, a slight hitch of one corner of his mouth flex upward for a faint moment.

"I've been in worse places," he said, holding her gaze.

Cale tried to take several deep breaths and calm himself.

Nate finally got on his hands and knees, crawling back up on the log. His palms were muddy, so he wiped them down the length of his thighs. Giving Sierra a warm look, he said, "Thanks. We REALLY needed this."

Chuckling, she murmured, "Yeah, I got it. You're welcome."

Cale wiped his face and shook his head. He pinned Sierra with his gaze. "Honest? You brought a Scrabble game along with you?"

"Yeah," she said, pointing toward her hut. "It's in my ruck. Why?"

"What's this world coming too?" Cale asked all of them, rolling his eyes again, snickering.

"At least it's a healthy board game," Sierra defended archly. "You sharpen your mind with it."

Cale gave her a smirk. "I can think of all kinds of games, Chastain, but they sure don't include a board game."

"You're not going there," Kilmer growled. "Keep it above the belt, Merrill."

Cale turned ten shades of red. He turned, giving Sierra a sincere look. "Hey, I'm sorry. Really. It just escaped outta my mouth."

"No worries," Sierra said, putting her hand on his broad shoulder patting it like a sister would a brother. "You guys have been out here for three months with no civilization to tame you down a little," and she squeezed his shoulder and released, more than understanding.

"You've been out on ops that long before?" Nate asked, finally becoming like his old self.

Grimacing, she nodded. "Yeah. It sucks, big time." She gave them all an understanding look. "I do know what you go through, guys. I really do."

"And that's why you bring the Scrabble along?" Nate asked.

"Better than the boredom. You can only sleep so much, you know? At least with Scrabble, even playing against myself, it's interesting. I learn something new every time. I have a very low boredom point and this keeps me sane."

The men nodded, becoming serious once again. Cale studied Kilmer. "So? Do you carry a Scrabble board around in your ruck? I ain't ever seen one."

He grinned sourly. "No, I don't."

"Well," Sierra said, giving them all a hopeful look, "maybe tomorrow? If it works out after we've done with all our daily tasks, maybe a round of Scrabble? I've got room for three players," and her lips curved away from her teeth as she watched Cale shake his head.

"I dunno," Nate said, hesitant.

"Sarge oughta take her on," Cale goaded. "He says he knows how to play. We ought to make bets. See who wins. Put money on the table. I'd like to win that pot."

Now it was Sierra's turn to roll her eyes. "You guys... no betting! I play because I love creating words. I even brought along a Scrabble dictionary. The damned thing weighs four pounds!"

Kilmer shook his head, "You're serious about that game, aren't you?"

Sierra was to take the 0300 to 0800 watch a mile from the meadow. Mace had volunteered to be the one to get her in the swing of guarding the only entrance to and from the village clearing. He'd come to her hut, lifted the plastic tarp, and gave a low growl, telling her to get up. Instantly, Sierra had jerked out of a deep sleep. Momentarily confused, she quickly got her gear together, grabbed her cammo jacket, her M-4, holstered her .45 and crawled out. She had her NVGs on and saw Kilmer in shades of green standing casually by the fire pit, the still-glowing coals in it casting its walls almost white.

She looked around, everything a grainy green and two dimensional. Above, it looked like low clouds hung barely above the tops of the trees. Every sound felt like it was coming through cotton, the calls of frogs muted and far away. There was lightning off in the distance, part of the fog lighting up for a moment like a soft, sputtering green-white neon sign. It must have rained because the grass was wet, the ground muddy beneath her boots. Sierra had her shooting gloves on, fingers free so she could feel that trigger pressure. Mace stood with the M-4 across his powerful chest, NVGs in place, baseball cap low over his eyes. He was a big man, tall, constantly reminding Sierra of the lethal jaguars that roamed these jungles.

She joined him. Having put on her radio headset, she spoke quietly, "Test."

"Roger. We're good to go. Let's saddle up."

This time, Sierra followed him. This time, he wasn't cutting his stride for her. A mile later, up and over the incline and down a fairly long, flat path, they relieved Nate from his guard post. He told them goodnight and trotted back, eager to grab some sleep. His cammos were soaked.

Mace led her off the path, taking her into the jungle tree line. Following him, she saw a thick log on the ground about eight feet inside the line. He gestured toward it.

"Have a seat."

Her pants were going to get wet, but hell, she was discovering everything was always damp around here anyway. The log was about six feet long and she sat at one end of it.

Kilmer came over and sat about a foot away from her.

Sierra was glad to have his bulk nearby. He towered over her. She felt that male warmth pouring off his body. They'd walked very fast. She wasn't out of breath, but it had been a good warm-up. Taking her M-4, she placed it across her lap, the safety off, the muzzle pointed away from them.

"When we're out here," Mace told her in a low tone, "you can sit here if you want. Or you can wander around. The intersecting trail there," and he lifted his hand and pointed to the T-intersection, "is a main trail. This is a feeder trail that leads to the meadow."

"Does Belov move his men at night?"

"Hardly ever," Mace said. He turned off his NVGs and pulled them down, so they hung around his neck. "You won't need these unless you hear something. Then flick them on. Saves batteries that way."

Sierra followed suit. Her eyes quickly adjusted to the night. There had to be a fairly full moon phase somewhere over above the western horizon because she was able to barely start to make out the dark shapes around her.

"Did you bring an extra lithium battery for your NVGs in case you need to replace it?"

She patted her top pocket on the right side, "Yes. I've worked with SEALs too much in the past to forget something basic like that," she told him wryly. "They have a saying: One is none, two is one."

"It's a good saying," Mace agreed. "Murphy's Law sure as hell is alive and well in the black ops community."

She laughed softly. "No joke." If something could go faulty on an op, it would. Sierra knew from way too much experience that, no matter how well a mission was planned, something always went wrong. Always. And it was up to the operators to be flexible and figure out a fix to keep the mission from going sideways.

"Did you bring a protein bar and gallon of water in your ruck?"

"Yes." Mace had given her a list of things he wanted the guard to place at the entrance. He was meticulous, but Sierra found a sense of protection in the sergeant's experience and knowledge of the territory.

"Scrabble game?"

She slapped a hand against her mouth, muffling the laugh. Twisting her head, she looked up in his direction, seeing his eyes gleam in the very low light. His face was harsh and rugged looking, but she felt his smile even though she couldn't see it. She wished she could. She thought it would change Mace's whole face. Make him look less harsh. Less intimidating. "That was the best laugh I had in a long time," she admitted, grinning broadly at him. "Your guys… they really needed that release. So did I."

"Yeah," he muttered, looking around. "It was good for all of us."

"I needed it badly," she admitted more softly. "I saw so much in Somalia. It's got to be the most toxic human waste dump on this planet. I swear to God it is."

"Not high on my vacation list of places to go, either," he agreed drily.

Sierra said nothing for a moment, trying to take in the night sounds: any noise that was out there that told her no humans were coming. If anyone was, the night sounds would suddenly halt. And if they did, that's when she'd go on alert. She felt companionable with Mace close to her right now. This time, he didn't intimidate her, for whatever reason. Finally, she got up enough courage to ask, "Do you really play Scrabble?" She heard him chuckle: a deep, rolling sound in his chest.

"Yeah. When I was a kid. I never played it once I joined the Army, but Ana Beth loved the game."

Sierra heard his voice suddenly go off-key, barely hidden emotion behind it. She felt her heart thump once to underscore the sudden vulnerability she heard in his normally hard, emotionless tone. "Who is Ana Beth?" She felt him tense for a moment. He moved his M-4 around on his lap, as if thinking before he answered. Had she overstepped her bounds with him? It had been a personal question after all, and normally, asking about that kind of stuff, about anything not directly related to the op, was off limits.

"I fell in love with Ana Beth when I was eight years old," he told her. "We went to the same grade school. I thought she was the most beautiful, most lively, smiling girl in my class."

"Your childhood sweetheart?" Sierra probed gently, hearing his low voice go warm with memories.

"Yeah. When I was in the sixth grade, I told her I was going to marry her after I joined the Army. She believed me. And so did I." Mace moved his hand lightly across the stock of his weapon, good memories surfacing. "Then I was twenty and so was she. She became an Army wife. And she put up with me. She was a little thing; barely five foot six, thin as a rail and delicate." His voice fell. "Ana Beth was fragile…"

Sierra said nothing, sensing that Kilmer had slipped into the past, recaptured by it. She understood. She had been through loving Jeb and losing him. Sensing the same bad vibe now in Mace's voice, she remained silent. Mace lifted his hand, trailing his fingers slowly back and forth across the weapon on his lap, as if in deep thought.

"Ana Beth did a lot of good wherever she went." He laughed a little. "She was a charity hound. Always doing something for others. Always taking care of those who had less than us. Who were suffering… She used to knit caps and mufflers for children for Christmas presents. She was a sewing queen and she loved to quilt. She was always making charity quilts for folks who lost their homes to fire, or flood or whatever. She made beautiful baby quilt blankets for newborns for the local hospital."

"She sounds like a wonderful, caring person," Sierra said quietly, feeling a terrible sadness settle around Mace. Almost literally, she could feel the heavy blanket of it embrace him. It brought tears to her eyes, and she blinked rapidly, forcing them back.

"She contracted breast cancer when she was twenty-five. I was on a four-month deployment to Afghanistan. She told my commander not to tell me. She knew it would distract me. That I'd want to be home to support her." He shook his head, his voice ragged. "When I got off deployment, she was near death. I walked into our house, and she was there, on the couch, covered in some of her quilts she made, so cold. So cold…"

Sierra's heart froze with anguish. Closing her eyes, she suddenly wanted to cry for him. There was nothing she could say. Nothing. Steeling herself, feeling the scabbed-over grief and loss of Jeb ripping off from its most tender edges, she wanted to reach out and slide her arms around him. Just hold and protect him. Against the pain he must have walked into. The shock of finding his wife like that. Thinking she was well but finding her dying.

Mace sighed heavily. "You know, she loved Scrabble. She taught me how to play it. I didn't often have much time with her, always training, always getting called away on missions. But sometimes… sometimes, when I had a night at home, she'd plead with me to play. She'd put that damn game up on the dining room table, get it all set up, give me the word dictionary because she knew I'd need it," and he laughed a little.

"Did she live?"

"No. There were—complications." His hands stilled on the M-4 and he stared into the night. The words came out quietly, through barely held emotions. "Ana Beth got pregnant. Three months into it, and I didn't know anything about it, the doctor found a tumor in her breast. It was the most aggressive kind of cancer. The doc told her to have an abortion so she could take the chemo and radiation to try and save her life. She refused. Ana Beth was born to have children. She loved them. And we'd been trying for some time to get her pregnant." Mace shook his head. "She was trying to avoid chemo or radiation to get our baby viable so it could be taken from her and still live."

"Oh, no," Sierra whispered, shaken.

"She died two weeks after I got home. Her and our baby."

Sierra reached out, sliding her hand across his back, resting her head against his sagging shoulder, closing her eyes. "I'm so sorry, Mace... so sorry for all of you," and whether he wanted it or not, she hugged him with all her strength. They were bound by grief.

CHAPTER 7

M ACE ABRUPTLY STOOD up. He had to. His heart felt like it was getting ripped out of his chest. All that grief he'd sat on for so long was tearing up through the center of him, squeezing his heart until he thought he was going to have a cardiac arrest. He moved swiftly, silently, out of the tree line, turning to the right, M-4 in his hands, unsafed, his hearing keyed. If he'd remained next to Sierra one more second, he knew he would have made the biggest screw-up of his whole career. He had almost been about to turn and sweep her into his arms, crush her against him, and cry until the tears over his loss ran dry.

What the hell was the matter with him? Why was he so damned reactive to Sierra? Pulling up his NVGs, he flicked them on, heading for the main trail ahead. Lightning flashed in the distance, illuminating the cottony puff-ball clouds hanging silently overhead. His heart felt like it was going to leap out of his body. Rubbing his chest, he slowed and then halted at the intersection. Breathing hard, raggedly, Mace was barely aware of the night noises around him, his whole focus on the loss of his wife and baby so long ago. He couldn't remember feeling this torn up before. But in truth, he'd savagely sat on all his emotions after he buried Ana Beth. And their baby. Tears leaked out of his eyes, running down the sides of his face. He didn't try and stop them.

The wind picked up, desultory, the leaves of the trees swatting against one another, the outflow of some thunderstorm miles away. The cool, heavy, and humid air felt good. He wiped his face. His flood of tears mixed with his sweat. Freezing for a moment, Mace felt strung between the past and the present. What was the magic that Sierra brought with her? Clearly, something was there. He wiped his face again, forcing the tears back, taking several gulps to tame his rampant emotions screaming to be released. Men didn't cry. HE didn't cry. More tears fell.

Half turning, he worried about Sierra. He could barely see her grainy, green form still sitting on that log. Relief poured through Mace. He didn't want her coming after him. He hoped she was old enough, mature enough, to under-stand he needed to be alone. If she walked up to him right now, he wasn't sure he could control himself. Grab her, hold her. Just feel her woman's body against his own. Wanting her arms around him as he sobbed out his heartache. Mouthing a curse, Mace turned his back on her. He had no way to comfort her, to tell her he was sorry, or apologize for his abrupt departure after she'd given him that tender hug that had conveyed so much to him. Her arm had been strong, caring. And he'd damned near fractured and broke into a million pieces right there. *With her.* Somehow, Mace sensed just how strong Sierra really was. He gulped, trying to stop crying, his mouth contorted, and he wanted to scream out all the unfairness that life had dealt him. Strapping the M-4 over his shoulder, he pulled out his canteen and slugged down half of it, the tepid water feeling good to his twisted insides.

Capping the canteen, Mace felt steadier. A little less out of control. He looked up and down the trail, finding nothing. There wouldn't be, most likely. His mind was churning with so many memories, remembering Sierra's husky words, her voice so damned gentle as if she knew something terrible had happened to him in his life. Bitterly, Kilmer turned and slowly walked across the feeder path and down the main trail, keeping his ears tuned in. His tears abated, and he took swipes at his cheeks to get rid of them. His mind was on Sierra. So was his heart, but he damn well didn't want to go there. She was on this mission for a real-world reason. Not just as someone for him to yearn for, to fantasize about. He was so fucked.

Lightning zigzagged closer, illuminating the cottony-white clouds hovering over the muted jungle. Mace jerked the NVGs down, flicking them off. His night vision was ruined. He'd have to wait until his eyes adjusted. The roll of nearby thunder told him a storm was headed their way. The wind had picked up in warning gusts, too. Turning, he walked back to where Sierra was sitting. He could barely see her face, only the shine in her eyes and he felt as if she were sad for him. Few people knew what had happened to him.

He sat down, leaving another foot between them. "There's a storm coming," he said in his roughened, low voice. "If you're on guard duty, stay here. The tree canopy is going to stop most of the deluge."

"I'll still get wet? But not as wet?"

He grinned tightly, hearing the amusement in her husky voice. He ached to tunnel his fingers through the thick mass of her black hair, unbraid those strands, run them through his hands, spread them like a halo around her golden face, and watch her eyes grow drowsy with arousal. He wanted her arms around him again. They took his pain away. "Yeah, we're going to get wet. It's just a little more protected in here, is all."

"I can handle that."

She sounded low-key, unperturbed. How badly Mace wanted to look into

Sierra's eyes, read her, see the emotion in her face and see how she was feeling. Right now, she was the cool, calm professional. No feelings in her voice. Just clear clipped sentences, short and concise. He inhaled deeply, grateful for her maturity and understanding, somehow, that he'd needed to be alone for a while.

The rain started almost immediately. First it was plopping sounds, like small bombs, huge drops detonating far above them in the large treetop leaves. And then it began to sound like someone had opened up with a nonstop machine gun, the rain coming faster and faster. Mace felt his shoulders becoming wet, and he lowered his head a bit so the rain coming down would wash over the bill of his cap, leaving his eyes dry so he could see. There could be no more talking. Suddenly, the whole jungle around them sounded like marbles in a glass box being shaken, the clatter ramping up until the deafening noise made any verbal communication impossible. Lightning flashed above them. Crackling thunder followed seconds later. And every time, it seemed like the bolt tore open the belly of the unseen storm anew, dumping more water on them. The wind whipped around, frenzied, and chaotic, tearing at their faces and clothes.

Mace turned to check on Sierra. She was sitting stoically, head bowed, her gloved hands across the M-4 in her lap. Yeah, he was sure she'd handled all kinds of weather as a sniper. Hours of it. Suffering in heat or bone-chilling cold. Or leg-numbing snow. A sniper didn't budge when out on a stalk. No matter what kind of weather was thrown at them. They just took it. Dealt with it. Part of a sniper's trade. Yet, dammit, he WANTED to slide his arm around her hunched shoulders. He could see she was wet and shivering. Most people thought it never got cold in a jungle, but a thunderstorm could drop the temperature from eighty to forty in a heartbeat. And most people just weren't prepared for it. Just like she wasn't.

"Come here," he growled, hooking his arm around her, drawing her against him, bringing her head in beneath his chin so he could warm her a little. Sierra was trembling badly. He could hear her teeth chattering uncontrollably. Her hand gripped her rifle hard to herself, keeping the barrel away from them. At first, she tried to draw away, but he used his strength to keep her against him. And Mace wouldn't let her go. He opened up his cammy coat, twice the size of hers, drawing both sides of it around her head, shoulders and back, as far as they would reach. She'd drawn up her knees, clinging to him, pressing against his huge, warm body. He was used to this weather. She'd come out of hot, arid desert terrain where constant hundred-degree Fahrenheit peaks had thinned her blood for three months. After going through that, being thrown into this kind of humid, hot and cold climate, would take any man or woman down.

"It's all right," he told her gruffly, her hair piled up over his stubbled chin, tickling his cheek and nose. Sierra smelled so good. Part sweet, part musky, rich earth. All in the silky strands of her thick hair. Closing his eyes, Mace knew no Russians were going to be out on this night. They never were. But that didn't mean that danger wasn't all around as he held her, warming her against his body and the dry layer of his inner clothing barely separating his skin from hers. Nature had stepped in with its own threats. The lightning was frequent, the thunder over the jungle quaking and trembling the mud underfoot. The powerful downbeats of the rolling roar surrounded them. The ground shook whenever bolts hit nearby.

As the storm rolled over them, deluging them with rain, rivulets running like small torrents around a log that had come to rest slightly higher up the slope, Mace felt Sierra slowly stop trembling. One slipping step at a time, he got her to the log and managed to sit both of them down on it, his coat still wrapped around her. Little by little, he was sheltering her against the storm, warming her with the natural heat radiating off his tightly muscled body, holding her safe. Protecting her. Mace didn't give a shit about women being strong or not. Sierra *was* strong. She was just adjusting to an opposite climate that was going to stress her to the nth degree. And he wasn't going to abandon her. He wasn't going to shove her off to sit alone on the other end of the log, her fingers turning numb, her teeth chattering nonstop, just to be tough. That was a bridge too far for Mace. He'd already screwed up by forcing her to jog six miles right after she'd just got off the Blackhawk. It had been small of him to do that. He should have welcomed her, treated her like an equal, instead of acting like a snarky patriarchal bastard. He'd delighted in hurting a woman. Was that who he was?! He hoped not. Maybe this humane gesture would partly cleanse what he'd done earlier. To somehow, forgive him. He hoped so.

He didn't want to care about Sierra. But he did. And Mace was confounded by this. Sierra was the antithesis of Ana Beth. She was strong where his wife had been like a waif, barely here, barely alive in some ways. Sierra had come to him when he'd asked her to. Ana Beth had fought that when he'd asked the same of her, proclaimed herself strong, and gutted it out without his help or support. And to what end? As Mace sat there huddled with Sierra in his arms, his mind roiled. What was real strength? Was it being physically tough? Mentally tough? Knowing when to surrender? When to ask for shelter or help? How often had he, through the first two years after he became a widower, asked himself these questions over and over again? What could he have done different to keep Ana Beth alive?

If Ana Beth had taken the life of the three-month-old fetus to save herself, she might still be alive. The doctors he'd talked to had said she had a chance to survive with aggressive chemo and radiation treatments. Yet, she gave HER life in the hope her baby would live. And in the end, because of her choices, her stubbornness, they'd both died. He ended up with nothing. Mace wondered why Sierra had capitulated to him. Had, after he insisted, surrendered to his superior strength, to his experience in this situation she knew little about. Who was smarter here? Who was more survival-oriented? So many questions he'd asked over the years. And he'd never found an answer. Not one damn answer.

The storm was slowly letting up, the flashes of lightning lessening by the minute, the thunder rolling past them, booming and striking the earth and making it shudder far away from them. Sierra had stayed snuggled beneath his jaw, relaxing into him, no longer trembling, just a small shiver every now and then. Inhaling her scent, Mace closed his eyes and thought he'd died and gone to heaven. Sierra was not weak. She didn't whine. She didn't complain. But she knew enough about real survival to trust him. And it was trust.

Tears stung Mace's closed eyes. The word 'TRUST' hung like the Sword of Damocles over him. Ana Beth had NEVER trusted him. She had told him repeatedly that he was a man. How could he know what a woman wanted or needed? She would tell him what she needed from him. Yet, Mace had recognized Sierra's stress. She hadn't asked for help. But she hadn't refused his embrace and help when he offered it, either. Sierra had trusted him. A cold, hard knot deep inside him, released. A knot that Mace had felt for years tied around his heart. He felt it unknot, relax, and then dissolve in a sudden heat that suffused his entire chest. He felt the heat of that release. He felt freed from the prison of his grief and anger over Ana Beth's decision to give up her life for the baby she carried.

There wasn't any right or wrong in this. Mace had cried so much after their deaths. He'd cried until his heart felt torn in half. What he did realize, out of that whole mess of his feelings, was that Ana Beth had never trusted him. Mace had never been able to figure out why. He'd always loved her, treated her as an equal, respected her. He just couldn't figure it out. And all the anguish of that had turned into a hard rock in his heart. A rock that had suddenly just dissolved the moment Sierra came willingly into his arms. Trusting him.

Sierra slowly stirred. She was damp but warm from of Mace Kilmer's furnace-like body heat. The feeling of his arm sheltering her, holding her close, his cammy jacket spread across her upper body, made her sigh with relief. And gratefulness. The rain had finally quit and no one was gladder than she was. Licking her lips, she whispered, "Mace?"

"Yeah?"

His chin was resting lightly on the top of her hair. She smiled a little. "I think I'm okay now."

"Sure?"

No. But Sierra knew if she stayed, she couldn't trust herself to remain professional. She was afraid she'd lift her left hand and slip it up beneath his damp t-shirt, feeling his slab-hard belly, feeling the power of his chest, the silky hair across it tangling through her fingertips. The man was so damned sexy. She swallowed, not wanting to leave. "How did you know?"

"Know what?"

"… That I was shivering?"

"Saw it."

She felt the deep heartbeat in his chest, closed her eyes and pressed her ear against him, greedily sponging the sound of him into herself. With a ragged sigh, Sierra pulled away. She blinked several times, lifting the hat off her head, realizing she saw grayness on the eastern horizon. Looking at her watch, it was nearly 0700. Where had the night gone? Had she slept against Mace and not realized it? It was only an hour until their watch was over. Rubbing her eyes, she lifted her chin, staring up into his hooded gray eyes that silently regarded her. She saw amusement in them. And something else. Something that Sierra couldn't translate. But she felt Mace wanting her, man to woman. That, she was clear on. But not here. Not now. Probably never. She had a job to do.

Giving him an apologetic look, Sierra pulled free of his arm and out of his jacket. Instantly, she missed his body warmth. Missed him. "Do you do this with all the newbies?" she asked, managing a small smile of thanks.

"You're the first." He smiled a little, looking at her hard, as if memorizing her.

"Now Cale and Nate will really have something to laugh about," she said, moving away from him, standing, her knee joints stiff. The cammie trousers were still wet, clinging to her legs.

"It's none of their business, Sierra. What happened is between you and me. It stays here, with us."

It was the first time he'd ever called her by her first name. When he said "Sierra" it had felt like a soft, tender brush of his hand across her skin. He hadn't touched her but Sierra's goose-pimpled skin still felt like he had. Turning, she frowned, staring down into his deeply shadowed face. It had to be her imagination. It was what she wanted from him. Her lower body flamed to life. Wanting him. Wanting all of him. "You're sure?" she demanded, her voice dropping with concern. The look in his gray eyes was clear. She felt no manipulation. Just the honesty gleaming in his narrowed gaze, making her feel like she had a stove turned up to high deep inside of her.

"One hundred percent." Mace looked her over. "Remember? You came out of Somalia a week or so ago? You were there for three months? Blood turns thin in a high-temperature, low-humidity climate, Sweetheart." He gestured toward the low-hanging clouds over the jungle. "Out here, it can be ninety degrees and ninety-nine percent humidity, but when one of those storms roll by, it can drop the temp to forty degrees just like that," and he snapped his fingers to emphasize his point. "You were in a mildly hypothermic state. No need to go there. And you were smart enough not to fight me but came into my arms so I could warm you up." He smiled thoughtfully. "It comes down to survival, Sierra. And you're a smart woman. You're a survivalist at heart."

She looked around, hearing the birds begin to chirp and welcome the coming day hidden in the clouds. The howler monkeys were starting with soft hoots. In a few minutes, it would escalate into a crazy cacophony. Pushing her hair away from her face, she ran her fingers downward, pulling her thick, damp braid over her shoulder. Shaking her head, she held his gaze. "How do you stand this?"

"What?"

"This… awful weather." Touching her crinkled cammies clinging to her legs, she muttered distastefully, "I hate this. I love to see the sun. See blue sky. I don't like getting wet like this."

Mace chuckled and rubbed his stubbled jaw. "You picked a helluva MOS to be a sniper then. I'm sure you've had ops where you got good and wet and stayed wet for hours? Days?"

Shrugging, she quickly loosened the braid, rewinding it with quick, knowing twists, wrapping the rubber band around the end of it. Pushing it across her shoulder she saw Mace's expression falter for a moment. That hungry look for her had returned. And then, in just one blink of her eyes, it was gone. "Yes, but it was always over in Iraq, Afghanistan or Africa." She scowled as she looked around through the moist, laden air, the denseness of the humidity painting everything with a gauzy cotton veil. Nothing seemed what it really was out here in this jungle, she realized.

The moment she had untangled her braid, allowing her thick, rich hair to fall across her shoulder, Sierra had seen Mace's expression change. It wasn't lost on her that most men like a woman's hair. For many sensual reasons. If she'd been thinking, she wouldn't have done it. Sierra didn't want to look like she was teasing or flirting with Mace. She was afraid to lose her professionalism. She never had, in all the years she'd been in the military, and she wasn't about to start now. She had an unblemished record that she was proud of. A love affair was not on her to-do list of things she wanted to immerse herself in.

Mace slowly rose to his full height, stretching, putting his arms over his head, his M-4 in his left hand. "You never got to rest up between ops," he said.

"If you'd had a month in Virginia, your blood would have thickened. You wouldn't be so sensitized to being wet and cold."

She nodded. "No question." And then she gave him a slight smile. "You weren't cold or shivering at all."

He lowered his arms, twisting and moving his broad shoulders. "I've been out here for three years. I'm acclimated."

"That's a long time," she said softly. *Too long.* She had never heard of a Special Forces team being put into a mission phase for three years like this. "You could have had other assignments, Mace. Why did you stay down here?"

He moved around the log, stretching his legs, getting the circulation going. "Between you and me?" and he held her gaze.

"Yes?" Sierra saw the sudden sadness come to his eyes along with a flash of anger in their depths. She yearned for this kind of intimate, personal talk between them. And for whatever reason, Mace had opened up to her. He trusted her. She trusted him.

"I had two younger brothers, Caleb and Joseph. Caleb died at twelve years old of a drug overdose." Mace frowned, looking down at the ground. "I was sixteen when that happened. He was just a kid. Some dirtbag of a drug dealer handed him some fentanyl-laced heroin on the street. Caleb died of an overdose."

Sucking in a deep breath, Sierra stared into his hard, fixed face. She felt the anger radiating around Kilmer. "I'm so sorry…"

He glanced at her, pulling the strap of the M-4 across his chest, settling the dull-black rifle against his back. "There's more. Joe, the middle son, ran away and went to Charleston where he got mixed up in a drug gang. Later, he became a dope dealer." Mace shook his head. "I guess he's still alive. I don't really know. He never came home, and he never called my father. Or me. He's lost to our family…"

Sierra felt her heart open with such agony for Mace. "That's why you're down here. That's why you keep coming back. You want to stop the flow of drugs into the States."

"Yeah, once you know my history," Mace said wryly, "I'm pretty easy to figure out. I want to take these vermin down. I want to take every last one of them off this earth. If I can take them out here, that's one less kid that's going to die from an overdose." He settled his hands on his narrow hips, looking around, his voice low. "Or tear a kid out of a good family, a loving family, and become lost for the rest of their life… gutting his entire family in the process…"

Sierra stood there feeling tears burn in her eyes. Feeling how much Mace Kilmer had gone through. "There's nothing I can say that will fix this or help you," she said quietly.

Mace turned, looking at her. His mouth had thinned, and he gave her nod. "No, there's nothing."

She wanted to close the distance between them, throw her arms around this man's thick neck, draw him against her and simply hold him. Just for a little while. Mace had been given no reprieve in life. No love. That had been torn away from him. And the loss of both his younger brothers had to be a constant reminder, like salt in the open wound of his heart, of what drugs had done to him and his family. No wonder she had felt that heavy blanket of sadness around him. Aching to hold him, despite knowing she had the strength to do so, Sierra forced herself to stand exactly where she was.

"I wish," she offered, choking up, "I wish there was something I could say… to help you…" and she offered her hand and a helpless shrug. Sierra saw the hardness in his gray eyes melt as he regarded her. The silence strung out gently between them.

"You're doing it," he said gruffly.

Confused, her brows drew downward. "I—don't understand, Mace." And she didn't, giving him a quizzical look. She saw one corner of that hard, chiseled mouth of his briefly move up.

"Someday you will." And then, his voice softened to a low growl. "Anyway, for whatever reason, you sure as hell know how to pull secrets out of a man. I don't know how you do it, but I was flapping my jaw last night about personal things I've never shared with anyone."

Swallowing, her heart in her throat, yearning so damn badly to hold and kiss this scarred warrior, Sierra gave a slight shrug. "I don't know, Mace. I usually have a good bond with the men I work with. Like Cale and Nate. They're like older brothers to me."

Nodding, Mace said, "Yeah, I saw that. You're good with people, Sierra." And then he said, "Maybe you missed your calling. Maybe you're a shrink in disguise. Or a social worker?"

She gave an abrupt but quiet laugh over that one. "Me? No way! I prefer to get along with my team rather than be a burr under someone's saddle, that's all."

Grunting, Kilmer studied her. "Well, my men are happy you're here. I haven't seen them let their hair down and have so much fun, laugh so hard, as they did yesterday evening with you. Whatever you have in you, Sierra, it's a special magic."

Her? A special magic? Her flesh became heated and inwardly Sierra groaned because she was blushing once again. She liked the way Mace regarded her. "I'm just the salt of the earth," she assured him. "Nothing more."

Lifting the baseball cap off his head, Mace said, "Not from where I'm standing, Sweetheart. You're something else and I haven't yet figured out how the hell you got through all my walls, walked into my secrets, my personal life, and just opened up the door and let them fly free."

She felt his quandary. "Whatever you share with me, Mace, is going nowhere. I promise you that." Sierra knew how important it was in the healing process to let old grief go. And last night, maybe for the first time, Mace had talked about his marriage. His wife. His lost baby. Her heart winced and felt such anguish for him. The lines in his face were deep, telling her of the weight and responsibility he'd carried as an operator. There was no question he was a responsible leader. He cared fiercely for his team. And all these years, Kilmer had carried such raw grief for all his losses. There had been so many.

"Thank you," he replied gruffly. Looking down at his watch, the time had flown. It was 0800. Their guard duty was over. "Come on, I'm going to show you how we set up two of the motion sensors we have nearby. If anyone, man or animal, comes down our trail, the two sensors will notify us back at camp."

"Why don't you use them 24/7?" she wondered out loud, walking with him out of the tree line.

"Because they run on batteries. A helluva lot of batteries. We can't keep enough of a supply in to keep them operational. So, we use them when we're here at our base camp and turn them off, cover them in plastic and camouflage them until we need them again. The rest of the time," he said, sloshing through the mud and water on the trail, "we set out night watches."

"Probably don't work because of all the rain and high humidity?" Sierra asked, walking at his side.

"Yeah. Trust me," Mace said with derision in his voice, "there's no manufacturer on this planet that can make something waterproof for a jungle climate like this."

Sierra believed him, her trousers stiff and chaffing at her thighs. She knew she would have abraded skin by the time they arrived back at camp. And yet, she was sorry that their time together was at an end. Mace had trusted her with his most precious and painful memories. Unsure of what that even meant, or of what was even happening between them, Sierra let it all go. Maybe she was just at the right place and right time. Maybe if it had been someone else, Mace would have unloaded all of this on them instead.

All Sierra did know was that Mace intrigued her on every level. He was a man carrying a lot of secrets. And her intuition told her, none of them were good.

CHAPTER 8

S IERRA FOUND HERSELF without even a single moment of spare time to feel her way through that night she'd stood guard with Mace. He'd sheltered her through one of the daily downpours she'd almost gotten used to since. That night he'd shown her the ropes of protecting their safe place from potential drug team incursion into the team's campground. Ever since she'd flown in, their numbers increasing by one, from three to all four of them, the time of each member's watch on their night guard rounds had decreased. She missed Mace being at her side, but that was a purely selfish feeling. And nearly every night, it rained down buckets. Mace had told her to wear her poncho; that it would protect her from the worst of the cold and she wouldn't get as wet as before. But nothing stayed dry. Ever. Sierra yearned for a hot, dry summer. She still had desert-thin blood in her veins.

When she came back at 0800 on the last day, they were making camp in the meadow, she saw excitement in Cale's and Nate's faces. They were hopping around like energized bunnies, their rucks out and they were rapidly packing them up. Sierra looked toward Mace, who was standing near the fire grate, cooking their breakfast of the last hens' eggs they'd bought days earlier. She saw him lift his chin; his gray gaze settling on her as she approached. Her whole body went hot, and she felt that gnawing sensation. Damn, the man could turn a rock on with just one heated look!

"Go get some drier clothes on," he told her. "And then pack everything up. We're meeting a Hawk up on the Highlands area in four hours."

Frowning, she halted. "Why?"

Mace stirred the dozen eggs in the skillet. "Because the US Army, in all its wisdom, is getting us out of this green hell for a week off in Cusco." He studied her. "You interested?"

"Oh, yes!" she blurted, thrilled.

Nate and Cale snickered, both of them on their knees, happily packing their rucks.

"She learns fast," Nate said, laughing.

"REAL fast," she told them with a grin. She glanced down at Mace as he squatted over the grate. "Honest? Seven days? In Cusco? In a dry place? And I can use a dryer on my hair?"

Cale howled. "Oh, for a hair dryer!"

"Oh, stuff it, Merrill," she muttered darkly, shaking a finger in his direction.

He beamed, a silly-assed grin spread across his face.

"Yeah," Mace grunted. "We each have rooms at a Swiss-owned hotel in Cusco. Nice digs. Hot water, a bath with a shower, hot, good food and dry sheets."

"It sounds like heaven," she whispered dreamily, hitching up her M-4 and heading for her hut.

By the time they left their digs, it looked as if they'd never been there. Sierra had found out from Nate on the second day that drug runners used this feeder trail, hauling heavy sacks of cocaine on their backs from here all the way to Bolivia. It was like a rest stop, she supposed. Mace's team made damn sure any indication they'd even been here was erased into non-existence. The Special Forces team had several of the enslaved Indians' schedules down pat. Belov and his men took Indians and their donkeys ladened with cocaine through this area once every two weeks. And Mace always made sure they left two days early in case there was a change in Belov's schedule. No one wanted to meet them here. It was too enclosed. Only one exfil route.

The team hoofed up to the Highlands in record time, the promise of the first decent night's sleep in seven days pushing them on. Sierra took her spot behind Mace. He led the group at a blistering trot up the trails that were constantly inclining ever-steeper. The Army Night Stalker pilots would meet them in a Black Hawk at nine thousand feet, just outside the jungle's tree line. On the bare cliffs of the Highlands. She was breathing hard by the time they summited the rocky area scattered here and there with low, hardy bushes. It was nearly noon, the sky a light blue above them, the air chilly. And, with her clothes damp, she felt as cold as always. The guys seemed to realize this and encircled her, shielding her from the gusting wind off the high, snow-covered Andes mountains in the distance. She was grateful for their thoughtfulness and care.

"Really, Sierra," Nate told her while they waited for the helicopter to arrive, "you need to buy a couple of vicuna or alpaca sweaters when you're in Cusco. Wear them beneath your armored vest and they won't get wet and they'll sure as hell keep you warmer."

"Good idea," Sierra noted, wrapping her arms around herself, seriously feeling the cold now. The guys heard her teeth chattering and pushed their bodies up against her. "Thanks," she muttered. "I'm really not a wuss."

Cale chuckled, pulling the brim of his hat a little lower over his sunglasses. "We'd NEVER call you that, Sierra."

"Better not," she chattered, grateful that they encircled her tightly, all their bodies pressed to her front and sides. "You guys are like furnaces! You're so warm!"

"Three years out here," Cale drawled, "will do it. Feeling better now?" and he smiled down into her eyes.

"Much better, thanks." She had all her gear on, her vest and H-gear filled with mags of cartridges across her chest. Even above and beyond that barrier of armor between herself and the men, she felt not even the slightest hint of unwanted intimacy from any of them. Right now, Sierra thought that they were so damned happy to get a break from their dangerous routine that their minds were on something other than sex. But maybe not all of them. She saw the heat banked up in Mace's eyes as he put his long arms around the two men standing either side of him. They made a human triangle around her, shielding her from the wind chill and gusts. He said nothing, but the heat coming off his body always amazed her. She looked up at him and gave him a silly grin.

"You know what, Mace? You could rent yourself out as a cosmic heater. I can literally feel it rolling off you."

Cale and Nate chuckled. "We'll just call him 'Heater Boy'."

"Like hell you will," Mace growled, giving them dark, warning looks. And then he settled his narrow gaze on Sierra. "I'll deal with *you* later."

The men hooted, jeered and giggled.

Sierra scowled at Mace. "Is that a threat?" she demanded, unsure if he was teasing her or not. Sometimes, she couldn't tell. At least, not yet. Mace didn't exactly have a revolving door on his feelings and often reverted to clipped, few-word sentences. Those were tough to glean anything from, and Sierra was always having to switch to the sensing equipment inside her sniper-trained mind to pinpoint his feelings.

"Let's put it this way," Mace drawled, giving her a very intense look, "it's a promise. Not a threat."

Well, that's fine. Before Sierra could rebut his cryptic comment, she heard and then saw the olive-green Black Hawk climbing the cliff, heading up toward them. The men broke away from her. She saw Mace throw a canister of green smoke out to the landing area, a clean patch of earth they'd cleared earlier of rocks and debris so the downwash from the blades wouldn't kick them up and cause anyone injury before they even got on board.

Sierra had never felt so happy as when she leaped onto the deck of the Hawk, one of the air crewmen helping her with a hand, hoisting her on board. She balanced her heavy ruck, got in and then took it off, carefully placing it beside her on the deck. The crew chief motioned for her to sit in one of the two jump seats at the rear of the helo and strap in. She hesitated until Mace made a sharp gesture for her to get her butt into one of the seats. Wanting to pout, but choosing not to, Sierra went and strapped in. The head crew chief strapped in next to her, handing her a helmet to put on. As she did so, the other crewman slid and locked the door, turning and speaking to the two Night Stalker pilots up front. In no time, they were lifting off and sliding in a long, long bank down toward the green jungle below them at six thousand feet.

She always liked riding in a Hawk, the familiar vibration, the noise blunted through her helmet, the continuous shaking, soothing to her. Nate and Cale sat with their own backs up against the rears of the pilots' seats, eyes closed, arms hanging loosely off their drawn-up knees. Realizing they all looked grubby, muddy, and wet, Sierra yearned for a hot shower, a chance to get her hair washed and actually dried. Soon…

MACE GESTURED FOR Sierra to follow him after he signed in at the Swiss hotel for both of them under other names. There was an elevator at the rear of the cheery-yellow reception area. The white tiles gleamed, clean and highly waxed. The windows welcomed in the warm sunlight. They'd left their weapons at a hangar at the Cusco airport that was guarded by US Army personnel. A small contingent of men and women mechanics, plus two Night Stalker pilots, had welcomed them there and allowed to be within Peru's borders with the country's blessing. Peru lacked the manpower and money to put boots on the ground to go after all the druggies up in the jungle and highlands areas. They eagerly welcomed certain types of help from the U.S. military.

Sierra still had her ruck on. It barely allowed her to squeeze into the small brass elevator with Mace. Nate and Cale had taken the white marble staircase with its teak rail, first teasing them that they'd get up faster than they would in that slug of an elevator. She looked up at Mace. He looked more relaxed.

"What are you going to do first?" she wondered.

"Sit in the hottest damn bath I can make. Drink a cold beer and just sit and relax in it. How about you?"

"Hot shower and then," she picked up one of her long, damp braids in her fingers, "wash my hair. REALLY wash it," and she grinned.

"Tonight, we'll meet down in the lobby at 1800," he told her. "We'll take you to our favorite restaurant, La Ratama, on Plazas de Armas, the main square in Cusco. "We'll buy you dinner and get you drunk on pisco sours," and he grinned.

Mace's face changed remarkably whenever he smiled just a little. Sierra was amazed at the change in his face. He always looked so hard and intense, but when the corners of his mouth curved upward, Sierra swore he looked ten years younger. But Mace hadn't had a lot to be happy about in his younger years. She figured he was in his early thirties, judging by the deep crow's feet at the corners of his eyes, the slashes on either side of his mouth. He was a hard man who regularly challenged hard weather conditions and dangerous Russian teams—and won. Handily.

"Pisco sours?"

"Yeah, national drink of Peru. It's a brandy. And it's good. You'll like it. I'm buying us the first round."

Wrinkling her nose, she muttered, "My Native American DNA has no gene to break down alcohol in my bloodstream, Mace. I stay away from the stuff. But I'll drink some good, iced water with you. Maybe a slice of lime in it?"

Nodding, he said, "Fair enough. But we'll buy you the best damn dinner in this town. Argentine T-bone with all the trimmings." He rubbed his flat, hard belly. "I'm salivating already for it."

She smiled softly. "Steak sounds really good. I could use some serious protein."

"Over the next seven days, me and my men will be tanking up on all the protein we can stuff into our bellies. You should too. When we return, we're going to be balls to the wall."

"Well," she said drily, "maybe three sets of balls and a pair of ovaries?"

He chuckled as the elevator door slid open into a hallway. "Yeah, something like that. Turn left. Your room is two doors down."

The hollow thunk of her combat boots on the teak floor shining with polish made Sierra wince. They sounded so loud that she tried to lighten her step. She pushed her card into the slot and the green light came on. Mace brushed by her. "Where will you be?" she asked.

"Right next door to you," he said. "Nate and Cale are back across the other side of the elevator, same side of the hall."

She opened the door and hesitated. "Who can I call if I have questions? Or get hungry before 1800 tonight?"

Mace turned. "Me. If you get an itch in your feet to go play tourist, just knock on my door, or dial my room number."

She gave him a worried look. "But wouldn't you rather sleep after that hot bath and beer?"

"Yes," he said patiently, opening his own door and pushing it wide, "but I also don't want you wandering around by yourself in this town, either. There're safe places and some that aren't. And it's not smart for a lone woman to be walking around unescorted."

She snorted. "Great. Patriarchy strikes again."

"Look at it this way, Sierra. I can't afford to have you deck some amorous dude who thinks he's going to hit on you in one of these plazas. I do NOT want to have to find myself down at the policia station. Got it?"

She heard the grim warning in his growly voice. "Yeah. I got it," she replied just as grumpily. "I hate patriarchal chauvinism."

SIERRA FELT GLAD she'd set the alarm on the bedside clock of her hotel room as she stepped out from under the hot shower. Finally getting the chance to wash her hair felt like heaven. The knock at her door at exactly 1800 sent her heart racing a little. Smoothing down her clean, dry jeans and making sure her pink tank top with cap sleeves set perfectly, she opened the door. Three pair of eyes gawked at her. She smiled a little nervously. "Wow, you dudes clean up pretty darned well."

Nate cleared his throat. "Might say the same of you. You give new meaning to that pair of jeans you're wearing."

Giving Mace a nervous look because his eyes had instantly narrowed on her, never leaving her chest, her breasts, she supposed, made her really nervous. "I… uh, hold on a minute. I'll grab my purse."

"You got a jacket?" Mace spoke up.

Turning, she nodded. *Jacket. Okay.*

"It gets cold up here at nearly twelve thousand feet at night," Cale called after her.

"Yeah, if you got a sweater," Nate added, "better wear it, too."

Great. She wasn't at all prepared for Cusco. Digging through the few civilian clothes she had folded in the dresser, she called back over her shoulder, "I don't have much…"

It seemed at first all she had was that one heavy, denim western-style jacket that she loved. Until, under it, she discovered an equally-denim vest that had three silver conches embedded with turquoise centers and pulled that on first. Hurrying, shrugging on the jacket, she grabbed the strap of her black leather purse and headed out to where the three men stood casually in the hall.

Closing the door, she turned.

"Man, you look beautiful with your hair down," Cale whistled. He grinned.

Oh, no, she was going to blush. Again. She saw Nate bob his head in agreement. Only Mace, that silent mountain of a man, said nothing. But damn, Sierra sure as hell felt his minute inspection of her. She nervously touched her long black hair, the tips of it curling in just above her breasts. "It's clean. And it's so nice that it's laying down and not all frizzed up."

Mace moved forward, tucking his large hand against the small of her back.

"You sure as hell don't look like a Marine Corps sniper, that's for sure. Come on, we're going to buy you the best Argentine steak Cusco has to offer."

His hand felt warm against her skin beneath the denim jacket that hung down just below her hips. Guiding. Without being controlling. Sierra relaxed as Mace walked her down the hall to the white marble stairs.

"We're going to La Retama," Nate told her from behind. "The Broom. Best steaks in Peru. You'll like it."

"Have you ever been in Peru?" Cale wondered.

"No, first time," Sierra said over her shoulder.

Mace had led her past the reception area. Nate and Cale opened the doors for them, and they took the steps down to the sidewalk. It was evening and the lamps along the street, reminding her of yellow, flickering candles, glowed through the falling dusk. Nate was in front, Cale in back. Sierra truly felt like she was being escorted, sensing that they were all fiercely protective of her. She saw men and women strolling around, mothers with children in hand, old women with heavy sacks in their hands wearing brown bowler hats. It felt like a modern-day city to her in most ways, but the architecture was distinctly ancient. Either Spanish or Incan, difficult to tell, given that the Spanish had built upon the many Incan temples they'd found throughout the city when they'd conquered it in the 1500's.

Plazas de Armas was a big rectangle with major traffic around it. Sierra saw many older couples sitting on the dark-green-painted iron benches along the X pathways connecting the four corners of the plaza. Bright flowerbeds bloomed along the fringes of each sidewalk. It was a tranquil scene. When they came to a traffic-signaled cross walk, Mace shifted his hand from the small of her back and, instead, curved it around her waist, drawing her in closer to him.

"Crazy drivers," he offered as she tilted her chin to look up into his face through this new and completely unexpected move of his.

He wasn't wrong though, Sierra discovered. There were scooters and a lot of European makes of cars ripping by. They raced around the roads bordering the plaza like it was the Indy 500. Once they'd crossed the road and were in the plaza proper, Mace released her. He still kept his hand hovering lightly on the small of her back, however. She could feel the three operators always alert and watchful. They led her diagonally down the sidewalk, crossed another street and then went through a small, Spanish-looking entrance. The place was nearly dark, and she slowed, unable to see.

"I have you," Mace said, curving his arm around her waist once again. He took her forward, guiding her toward a set of concrete stairs that went up to a second floor.

His voice rippled through her, making her excruciatingly aware of him as a man. She felt him monitoring the amount of strength he used, not hauling her about, allowing her to dictate the distance between them. Mace Kilmer was a lot more sensitive and aware than she'd given him credit for. And, if Cale and Nate saw his possessive claiming of her, they said nothing, one out in front of them and the other behind.

Sierra heard the throaty Andean flute music combined with guitar playing as they entered the spacious restaurant. There were black leather booths on one side of the huge room, curved, hinting at privacy. She was glad the *maître d'* led them with a flourish to the one in the corner. Smiling to herself, she knew the operators had chosen it with good reason. It was near an exit point plus they could look out over the entire room, all its occupants, and see who was coming and going through the main archway entrance. Young Peruvian waiters, some copper-faced, others with golden flesh tones like her own, came and went dressed in starched white tuxedo shirts, black bow ties and black trousers. She saw very few other customers in the establishment.

"Are you sure this place is popular?" she asked Mace.

Nate chuckled. He slid into one side of the booth. "Peruvians and all South Americanos don't start eating dinner until about nine p.m. through midnight." He butt-shuffled over into one corner of the booth.

Mace halted and gestured for her to slide in at the other end. "Take the middle", he told her. And then, he slid in next to her, about a foot separating them. Cale took the other end of the U-shaped booth. The room was chilly, but Sierra didn't say anything. And Mace kept a comfortable distance from her. Even their elbows wouldn't accidentally touch while eating. Sierra lamented the change but understood why. The incredible sense of protection from Mace cosseted her and, even these bare few feet away from him, could feel the heat rolling off his body, as if he were, indeed, sunlight.

"I couldn't eat that late," Sierra admitted to them. "Thanks for choosing 1800." She saw the three of them nod and give her sage-like looks.

Mace ordered three bottles of local beer from the waiter and asked in Spanish for a glass of gas water.

"Gas water?" Sierra said, frowning over at him. "What's that?"

"Carbonated water," Mace told her. "You can't trust water here. And if it's got gas and bubbles in it, you know it's good water. Never order water without gas in it."

"Yeah," Nate chuckled. "Diarrhea special."

"We're having dinner," Mace reminded him archly, giving him a dark look. Toilet talk was off the table.

Nate gave a good-natured shrug. "Hey, Bro, I'm a medic. What do you expect? Do I want to treat... well... you know what, while we're here for R and R?"

Grinning, Sierra took the pristine white linen napkin and spread it across her lap beneath the tablecloth. It was wonderful to be back in civilization once more. "I get the drift, Nate. No worries." And she was sure they had all suffered dysentery from drinking bad water at some point. It was an operator's karma. She watched the waiter hurry back with the cold beers on a tray. He served her gas water first, pouring it with a flourish into a tall glass that held a slice of lime in it. The look on the men's faces, the longing for a tall, cold beer, was heartwarming to her. Without a word, they tipped them back, their Adam's apples bobbing, as they chugged down the icy-cold brew. She delicately sipped her gas water.

And then another round of beer was ordered. She watched in amazement as they each drank down three beers a piece before their thirsts were finally sated. Amazed, Sierra understood how the heavy sweating, the loss of electrolytes for three months, would make these men crave that beer with a passion. And a passion it was. Each man looked relaxed, or as relaxed as any operator ever got, silly-assed grins on their faces, feeling good.

CHAPTER 9

THERE WAS A soft knock on Mace's hotel room door. He'd just gotten out of a hot shower and was heading to bed. The team had gotten back from another glorious dinner an hour ago and the days were moving too swiftly for him. They always did. This was day three of their downtime and he wished it was not. Frowning, the towel wrapped around his waist, he looked through the peep hole. It was Sierra. The frown remaining on his face, he opened the door and stood there. She was still in her clothes from dinner.

"What's wrong?" he asked.

"Oh, nothing." She gave him a nervous smile. "I was trying to coerce the guys to come and play some Scrabble with me. You know? Just something to do? I wasn't sleepy."

"What did Nate and Cale say?"

"They'd had too many beers," she said, wrinkling her nose. Giving him a hopeful look, she asked, "Would you? I love the game and I'd really like to play with someone."

He rubbed his damp-haired chest. "Where you setting it up?" Mace instantly saw her brighten. And damn, his heart swelled. And his lower body stirred.

"My room. I can lay it out on the desk in there."

"Okay, give me ten minutes? I'll come over and clean you out."

She gave him a happy grin. "We'll see about that!" and turned on her heel, walking down the hallway to the opened door of her room.

Mace grinned sourly and shut the door. Well, hell. It was killing him after four days to keep his hands off Sierra. The team had gelled with one another, and she was like a kid sister to everyone except him. Mace couldn't think of Sierra except in terms of the woman he wanted in his bed, wanted to love, to share that heat he saw burning sometimes in her eyes.

He'd thrown on a black t-shirt and a pair of jeans but had remained barefoot as he wandered into her room. Good to her word, Sierra had pulled out the small, rectangular mahogany desk. She had set the two chairs on either side of it. The board fit perfectly. He saw the excitement in her eyes, that look of challenge he always saw in a sniper's expression. "You're out for blood," he drawled, sitting down.

"Does it show?" and she laughed and sat opposite him. "Here, pick one tile. Whoever has the letter closest to Z, gets to go first."

"Are there any rules?" he asked, taking the black fabric bag from her.

"Well, the normal ones that come with Scrabble. Why?"

"Because when I played, we always had pennies on the side and for whatever the person named their price, we could buy a tile."

She gave him a horrified look. "Oh, no. No, we play by official Scrabble rules."

He chuckled and put the tile he'd drawn from the bag on the board. "Well, well," he murmured. "I got a Z. How about that?"

"Geeze," Sierra muttered darkly, "I can see where the energy on this round is going. You must have Irish luck, Kilmer."

"Hasn't Nate or Cale told you yet never to play poker with me?" he inquired mildly, blindly selecting seven tiles from the pouch. He handed it back to her. She dove her hand into the bag and drew her own seven tiles. They both started to switch around their tiles on the wooden racks in front of them into an order known only to themselves.

"No," she grumped, giving him a worried look.

"Do you play poker?"

"No."

"Do you want to bet money on this game?" he asked, watching Sierra closely.

"No way."

"Okay," he said as he watched her daintily rearrange the tiles on the rack, "I have to bet something." He saw her eyes widen. And he also saw how happy she was. It made him feel good inside.

"Why do you have to bet, Kilmer? Why can't you just enjoy the challenge of the game? Isn't that enough?"

"No," he said, his grin tugging at the corners of his mouth. "Okay, so you don't like to bet with money. How about we bet on some THING?"

Frowning, she stared at him. "Like what?"

"Oh," he murmured, giving a lazy shrug, "how about something like the winner gets to kiss the other person?"

Shocked, she stared at him, her lips parting. "Mace!"

"What?" he asked innocently. His grin grew and he saw her cheeks flame a deep pink. "I'd like that bet."

Nervously, she moved around in the chair, her scowl deepening. "Well…," and she chewed on her lower lip. Her arms wrapped around her chest, and she stared hard at him. "You can't be serious."

"As a heart attack," he said, keeping his voice little more than a growl. Mace had seen her wanting to kiss him a number of times. Now, this was a way to strategically get her in a corner and have her do just that. It gave Sierra a reason that she could live with.

"It would be just one kiss," he said, trying to look innocent.

"That's if YOU win," she accused.

"Right. What do you want if you win?" She looked like she was about to come out of her skin, and he laughed inwardly. The constantly, cool, calm Sierra *could* be shaken up. And he saw her thinking about it.

"*Not* to kiss you," she said defiantly. "And I WILL win."

He chuckled indulgently. "Okay, then it should be easy for you to make that kind of deal with me." He thrust his hand out to her. "Deal?" He saw Sierra freeze for a moment. One way or another, he was going to kiss her. Mace felt he knew her well enough by now that, out on duty, Sierra would be fine.

Sierra grabbed his hand and shook it. "Okay," she muttered darkly, "deal."

Mace released her hand, his grin broad. "You'd better be thinking of what kind of kiss I'm going to give you when I win, Sierra."

"Humph! That will NEVER happen!"

Mace shrugged easily. He said, "Well, since it's my turn to start," and he laid out all of his seven tiles, spelling 'LOOSENS'.

"No!" Sierra wailed, standing up, tipping her chair back. She stared at the word he'd placed on the board.

"What?" Mace teased mercilessly. "You think I cheated?" He saw the sudden panic in her eyes, her cheeks a ruddy red color. He'd just pretty much straight-up won the game. He'd been able to lay out all seven tiles and they had made an acceptable, dictionary word. He'd gotten the fifty-point bonus on top of the double multiplier for the middle square. Sierra made a mewling sound, staring at him in disbelief, and then back down at the board.

"I've NEVER had this happen! I've never seen anyone be able to put down all their first seven tiles at once!"

Chuckling, Mace gave her a smile. "Time to pay up, Sweetheart. I won fair and square. Now," he said, slowly standing, pulling his chair aside, "you owe me that kiss you just shook hands on…"

Sierra felt suddenly naked. She wasn't, but that's what it felt like. Mace came around the table, heading her direction. Her mouth went dry. She shot out her hand, her palm encountering his hard, male chest, feeling the warmth of his flesh beneath her fingertips. "We can't!" she whispered frantically. "We can't do this!" Mace stood there, hands on his hips, grinning down at her, heat and promise in his gray eyes.

"You shook on it, Chastain. Are you telling me you're going to back out? That your word isn't your bond?"

Gulping, she shook her head. "N-no... I mean... Mace, we can't do this!"

"You've been wanting to kiss me for a while," he noted, arching one eyebrow.

Sierra was breathing raggedly. Her heart was skipping beats. Oh, what had she done? "I've always been a woman of my word," she shot back. "It's just that—well—we WORK together, Mace! We can't mix business with personal. You know that." He didn't look convinced at all. Her hand fluttered. "You know this is WRONG."

"Then why did you agree to it?"

"B-because I thought for sure I'd win, that's why. I-I was just humoring you, is all."

Giving a shrug, he said, "That was nice of you."

She glared at him. "Damn you, Kilmer!" She squared off at him, lifting her chin, planting her hands on her hips. "You did this on purpose!"

"What? Win?" He opened his hands and chuckled. "I DID want to win, there's no denying that."

"You made that bet *after* you saw your tiles!"

"Yes," he admitted gravely, "I did."

"You KNEW from the get-go that you'd win!"

"Yes, I did."

Her nostrils flared. "That wasn't fair, Mace! It would be one thing if you'd made the bet BEFORE seeing the tiles you drew from the pouch!"

"You didn't set down any rules about bets, did you?"

"No," she sputtered angrily, "I didn't!" She could barely breath, her gaze always moving back to his mouth. A mouth she had wanted to kiss since she'd met Mace. Damn, the man was infuriating! She saw the gleam in his eyes, his real smile changing his hard face, taking her breath away. He looked so much younger when he smiled. Her heart screamed at her to step forward and let him kiss her. Her mind was howling that she was nuts. She didn't DARE cross that line with Mace. He was enjoying this way too much. The glitter in his eyes was one she recognized only too well: operators were all so friggin' competitive. And why would Mace be any different? Damn!

"It will be all right," he said, trying to calm her down.

She stared at him. "No... it won't," Sierra said brokenly, giving him a stressed look.

"Why not?" he demanded. "We're both adults. We can handle this appropriately."

Rubbing her brow, Sierra shook her head. "Dammit, you don't understand, Mace!"

"Enlighten me?"

Her fear and yearning warred with one another. How she wanted to kiss this man! Sierra knew how good it would be. How melting... how... oh, she was in such trouble. Choking, she whispered, "I'm not afraid of you. I'm afraid of myself. All right?" She saw him give her a confused look. Compressing her lips, she stood there, arms crossed, body rigid, as if preparing for a blow to come her way. Certainly not a kiss.

Scratching his head, he muttered, "You're afraid of yourself? I don't get it, Sierra."

Groaning, she snapped, "Men are so damned thick-headed sometimes!" She saw him suddenly get it. And then he gave her a megawatt smile that avalanched her body, her pounding heart, and pummeled away all that fear before it.

"So?" he said in a low growl, slowly walking toward her, "you like me? That's it. Isn't it? You're afraid if I kiss you, you'll want more."

Giving him a mutinous glare, she held her ground. "Don't come one inch closer to me, Mace."

He halted, grinning like he'd won a helluva lot more than just a kiss. "I didn't know that. I mean," and he opened his hands, "I was HOPING. I thought that night I held you and tried to keep you dry, that I saw something in your eyes. I was afraid to interpret it, Sierra." He rubbed his jaw, shaking his head. "I'll be damned. Then? It's mutual."

Growling, Sierra said, "... I guess... maybe..."

"Then," he said, taking the victory out of his voice, "I'm going to let you decide what to do, Sierra." And he held her gaze. "And I'm okay either way. All right?"

Some relief filtered through her. But her heart and body were screaming for some other kind of relief, for him to touch her, love her. Sierra knew without a doubt, this man would kiss her into the sweetest kind of oblivion. "I can't do it, Mace. I just—can't."

"But," he cast around, "if we weren't in the situation we're in now, you'd be okay with it?"

Lifting her head, she knew she owed Mace her honesty and her courage. "Yes..."

Nodding, he smiled a little. "That's good to know."

Sierra didn't think so. "Maybe," she whispered unsteadily, "this is for the best."

"I hadn't thought you were a one-night kind of gal."

She gave him a miserable look. "No… I'm not. I just don't have it in me, Mace." And this was one time Sierra was sorry she wasn't emotionally built for that kind of fling.

"You play for keeps. I understand."

Never had she felt so damned miserable. Her gut clenched. She gave a helpless shrug. "I'm sorry."

"I'm not."

"You're not?" She saw a glimmer of amusement come to his eyes. The man had relaxed tonight, and he'd smiled so often that she was blinded by how handsome he really was. Sierra couldn't help but be drawn to Mace when he was not in threat mode. The difference was breathtaking to her.

"No. Well," he hedged, "I am, but I understand where you're coming from. Okay?"

"Okay." She swallowed, her throat tight. Starving for him. Just a taste. A touch. "I-I'm afraid, Mace. Afraid that it would distract us."

"Yeah, I get that too. I don't think it would, but I respect what you're feeling."

He stepped forward, grabbed her hand and tugged on it. "Come on, let's play some more Scrabble? I promise I won't make any more bets with you."

Her fingers curled around his strong, warm ones. "Are you sure?" and she searched his stormy gray eyes.

"Very sure," he rasped her, his voice low with feeling. "Come on. Beat the pants off me?"

She laughed a little. "Well, not that… no… but I will beat you, Kilmer."

He released her hand and pulled the chair out for her to sit on. "It's not a bad way to get to know a person," he said, walking around to his side of the table.

Giving him a wary look, Sierra collected all the tiles, dropping them into the pouch and shaking it between her hands. "Are you seriously old fashion?"

"Maybe a guy with a few morals in place?" he teased her. "Does that surprise you?"

A hesitant smile came to her lips. "I know guys who, if they were in your position, would have done a lot differently. They would have, for sure, taken advantage of the situation."

"I'm not one those men, Sweetheart." And he became very serious, holding her gaze. "I play for keeps, too, Sierra. Just remember that…"

Sierra didn't know what to do with herself when she awoke on day five. She lay in bed appreciating the clean, fragrant air-dried sheets. Being dry was something she'd never take for granted again. Pushing her fingers through her loose hair, she closed her eyes, her body remembering last night. Remembering

Mace. So strong. So damned honorable. If he hadn't done what he did, Sierra wasn't sure she wouldn't have stepped forward and right into his arms. The man was a throwback to the Age of Chivalry, and she felt only admiration and respect for his honoring of her and the circumstance. For what he *didn't* do. There was such electricity between them. It had been palpable. And how badly Sierra wanted to go all the way with Mace. But to what end? Even if they could balance the personal and professional between them out there in that green hell, it wasn't something that would last. Mace was committed down here in Peru. He wanted to extract vengeance against the drug runners.

Turning onto her belly, she pushed her face into the soft goose-down pillow, her arms hugging it. That look in Mace's gray eyes when he'd said, *"I play for keeps, too, Sierra. Just remember that…"* made her skin yearn for his large, rough hand skimming its surface. Maybe she was finally over losing Jeb. It was clear her body was coming back online. It was healthy. So was she. But her mind stood in the way and so did her values. Sierra had never played around. Oh, she'd had two love affairs before meeting Jeb, but they too, had been long-termed.

Desperately, she tried to imagine a way to make something work with Mace, but all she saw were dead ends. She would be sent on another mission to another part of the world when this one was completed. They'd not only be separated by distance but, most likely, given the type of ops they pulled, there would be no sat phone calls, no Skype or Zoom, no emails. No… nothing. And for how long? This one right now she was out on was for a minimum of three months and maybe much more if the HVT hadn't been killed yet by that time. There was just no way.

She yearned for her cabin, for her quiet, nature-filled life. To go see a movie every now and again. To get a dog, one of those doggies she loved so much, and take it out on hikes with her. She wanted to get a horse as well. The cabin she'd bought had five acres of land, had a barn on it, and she'd already put in a decent corral for her dream horse. And she wanted a huge garden, just like the one her mother had had. It was all waiting there for her. But she always came home to an empty house. No dog. No horse. No garden. No man. Groaning into the pillow, Sierra flopped over, staring up at the white ceiling. The clock on the dresser read seven a.m. Her stomach growled. She wondered if Mace was down in the restaurant having breakfast.

Something made her quickly get up, go through her toilette routine, and get dressed. She left her hair down because she always saw Mace's gaze go soft when she did so. Not much got past her. She was a sniper. She saw all the tiny details. And she always saw pleasure come to his face anytime she pushed her fingers through her black hair, taming it in place. She knew he wanted to tunnel his fingers through the luxuriant mass of it. And worse, Sierra wanted him to.

SURE ENOUGH, SIERRA found Mace eating alone at a corner table where he could see everyone. Smiling to herself, she watched him pick up on her presence. The man had powerful intuition. As she approached his table, he rose and drew out a chair opposite him for her.

"You're up early," he noted.

"I guess I'm catching up on sleep. Thank you." She scooted the chair in and looked up at him. Today, he wore a lightweight charcoal alpaca long-sleeved sweater. It highlighted the color of his eyes. And she saw he looked pleased. Because she was here with him? His black slacks outlined his lower body and long, powerful legs. His hair was recently washed, his jaw shaved free of stubble. He looked delicious to Sierra.

"Hungry?"

"Yes. What are you eating?"

"Five eggs, hash and plenty of the best potatoes in the world."

Everyone ate heavy. They burned it off so quickly in the jungle. "Sounds good."

Mace got a waiter's attention and ordered her the breakfast with two eggs instead of five. He had a pot of coffee on the table and the waiter brought over a second cup. He poured some for Sierra. Their fingers met as she took the cup from his hand.

Grateful, she sipped it eagerly, watching him over the rim of the cup. If he was upset over last night, she didn't see or sense it this morning. They'd played Scrabble until midnight, and she'd won three to two. He'd been a graceful loser. "What's on the agenda today?"

"Not much. Three years ago, I started a small charity fund for one of the orphanages here in Cusco. We have clothes, shoes and toys brought in and kept at our hangar at the airport, and when we get some R&R, we take it all over to the kids. Would you like to come along?"

"I'd love too." Her heart swelled with some powerful emotion. Sierra felt afraid to name it. As hard and as tough-as-nails as Mace was on the outside, the man was showing her he had a heart of gold hidden beneath that facade. That he thought of others, not just himself. That he cared. She wondered, after having lost his own baby, if he might be turning all that grief around and pouring his love of children into another way to cope. Deeply touched by that realization, she blinked back sudden, unexpected tears. She would never broach this sudden understanding of him, realizing how tender still his grief and heart were over that tragic time in his life. It brought back something that had happened to her shortly after Jeb's death. Her throat tightened. Only her parents knew. No one else. And Sierra couldn't even begin to think she could ever give it voice again. It was just too overwhelming to her. But if anyone could understand that person might be Mace.

"Good," he murmured, cleaning up what was left on his plate between his toast and fork. "When we're done here, I'm going to kick the boys out of bed."

"They're party animals," she said wryly.

"Yeah, young and full of themselves."

"I was never like them," she observed. "Probably because I couldn't drink alcohol."

"You missed a lot of hangovers, then," he said, grinning.

The waiter swooped in and took the plate away.

She smiled a little, moving her finger in senseless patterns over the white linen tablecloth. "So how big is this orphanage?"

"Two hundred kids. Cute little rug rats, all of 'em. A Catholic charity takes them in. Sometimes, Indian parents dump them off. The kids are on the verge of starvation. They can't feed even one more mouth."

"That's so sad…"

"Yeah, there's a lot of people that would give their right arm to have a child." He grimaced.

"I know," she said softly, feeling his unspoken pain, seeing the loss in his eyes. Just knowing about Mace's past helped her get over that one last hurdle of him being a hardcase all the time. "Has anyone ever told you lately that you're a genuine hero, Mace?"

He stared at her. "No way," he growled. "Keep your starry-eyed look for someone else, not me."

"No," she said, holding his narrowing gaze, "you're a bonafied hero. And I don't care whether you agree with me or not."

CHAPTER 10

M ACE WAS SITTING in the restaurant the next morning having just ordered an 'American Breakfast' from the menu when he saw Sierra come down the stairs. Day four. His heart pounded once off its usual beat, surprised at how beautiful she looked with her hair down, dark, shining and swaying gracefully with every step she took. She was yawning, hand across her mouth, her eyes still drowsy. He smiled to himself, feeling his lower body turn to fire by the way her hips swayed. Mace was having a tough time reconciling the fact that she was a military sniper. She looked like a young college-aged woman. This morning, she wore a bright-red long-sleeved shirt, a denim vest over it, and jeans.

Mace stood and met her at the entrance. They'd had one hell of a good day at the orphanage. And the children had fallen in love with Sierra. Who wouldn't?

"Come on over," he said, gesturing to the table.

"Hi, Mace. Thanks. I'm so tired! I feel like I can't wake up."

He slipped his hand around her elbow, guiding her between the tables filled with patrons. "Coffee will fix that," he said, pulling out the chair for her.

A waiter came over and Mace told him in Spanish to give Sierra a cup of coffee. The man nodded and hurried away.

Rubbing her face, she muttered, "Where's the other guys?"

"After we got done at the orphanage at 1600, they took off to see who could drink the most pisco sours. They're sleeping off a serious drunk this morning."

She grinned and shook her head, "Those guys have got their throttles to the firewall." Last night, Mace had taken her to a nice Peruvian cafe where they'd had a delicious meal of vegetables and the best of Argentinian beef.

"You sleep well?" he asked. Because there were no longer smudges beneath her eyes.

"Wonderfully," Sierra said wistfully, unrolling the linen napkin and placing it across her lap. The waiter brought her coffee, and she thanked him, sliding her hands around the delicate China cup. Picking it up, she inhaled the fragrance, closing her eyes, a soft smile hovering on her lips. "Mmmm, I am going to miss this. I know I will." She ordered her breakfast from the waiter.

Mace felt himself stir. The look on her face damn near unstrung him. He harshly reminded himself she was enjoying the fragrance of the coffee. Not him. Her hands were slender, graceful as she held the cup. "It's nearly 1000."

"I know. I can't believe I overslept."

"We worked hard all day yesterday at the orphanage. Plus, I think you're still coming down off that Somalia op."

"Wouldn't disagree. It was a ball-buster…"

"Why did Driscoll choose you to come down here on our op?"

Shrugging, Sierra said, "I was the only one available. We have five snipers, all women, available through Shield, but they were all out on missions. I just happened to get my HVT and came walking in the door of the office when he buttonholed me on this up-and-coming mission."

Scowling, Mace said, "He should have given you a longer turnaround time. Given you a rest." And he said it from a protective standpoint, not meaning that he didn't want her on the op, although she looked a bit surprised over his statement. "It's just a comment, not an indictment on you," he added wryly, sipping his coffee. She sat there, a faint smile tugging at her lips and enjoying the coffee. He wondered what it would be like to wake up with her in his arms. The thought was heated. Charged with possibility. Mace instantly clamped a vise down on the idea. Sierra had been right: to mix business with pleasure would be foolhardy. It would leave them open to distraction, which was deadly.

"What do you feel like doing today?" he wondered.

"I'd love to just be a tourist today," she sighed, giving him a warm look.

Mace nodded, his hands itching to tunnel his fingers through that black, shining hair of hers. Here in Cusco, the humidity was way down compared to the jungles up at sixty-five hundred feet. "Mind if I be your guide?"

"No, not at all." She wrinkled her nose. "I'm definitely going to take you up on buying some sweaters, though. Even last night, I was cold. It was so nice of you to take off your sport coat and put it around my shoulders."

"Glad to do it." Hell, he wanted even now to put his arm around her, tuck her in against him like he had that night they'd stood duty out in the jungle. Mace wasn't ever going to forget that night, or the way her body had fit against his, so soft and curvy. Or how good it had felt to have her in his arms. It made him feel good that he could do something positive for Sierra. His heart swelled silently with happiness, in a way that he hadn't felt for such a long time that he'd almost forgotten the sensation. It sent a keening ache through Mace. After Ana Beth died, he'd died. His emotions, except for the loneliness, were put in a deep, dark place. Watching the way Sierra's hair slipped and slid over her capable shoulders as she moved, made him poignantly aware of just how damn lonely he was for a woman in his life again. A home, again. A family…

"Do you know of a store where we can buy some?"

"The Q'ero Indian women are selling them on some of the plazas. Some have stalls. Some sit on the ground and sell them. You won't have a problem finding any."

She smiled. "This was such a vibrant city last night. I really am anxious to explore it today."

"If you like history, you'll always like coming to Cusco."

She frowned. "Is there a chance we could run into Belov or other Russian mafia men here?"

"Yeah, there is," Mace said. "That's why I don't want you out wandering around alone. If I can't take you, Nate or Cale will. The Russians always have an eye for young, beautiful women and I don't want them to even see you, much less give you any problems." He saw her cheeks go a pink color, realizing she was blushing.

"I thought I'd fit in by putting my hair in a set of braids." She held out her one hand. "My skin is gold-colored, not white. They'll probably think I'm a local, not a tourist."

Grunting, he said, "Wouldn't matter. You're beautiful, Sierra. And those mercs, when they get time off to come here, are ready for drink and womanize. There's no way I'm putting you in their path." Her cheeks went a deeper pink. Wasn't she used to being complimented? That she was a damn good-looking woman? And she was avoiding his eyes. Luckily, their breakfast came.

Sierra sat on the stone steps that led up to the beautiful Spanish architecture of one of the Catholic churches in Cusco. Mace had stuffed her purchases into her day pack and zipped it closed. The sun was warm and welcoming near noon as they sat there watching Indians and Peruvians of Spanish cast begin to walk into the church for the noontime Mass. The wind was playful, tugging at the strands of hair at her temples. She'd plaited her hair into two long braids. The women who'd sold her the colorful Alpaca sweaters she'd bought had thought she was Q'ero; many of them spoke only broken Spanish. So, Mace, who spoke their indigenous language, had translated for her. The women in black or brown felt bowler hats, swathed in bright cotton shawls, and long, full skirts sat constantly knitting one after another alpaca sweaters, their wares displayed on a blanket in front of them. Sierra loved those moments, seeing the women doing what they did. And, although Mace was an intimidating size, whenever he spoke Quechua, their faces always glowed and smiled with approval.

Sierra gave Mace a warm look as he sat down next to her. She said, "I love this place. It feels like a second home to me."

Mace kept an eye on all the tourists and native people that flowed in and around them. They sat on the lower steps, off to one side to stay out of the way of most of the traffic. "If you're up to it, I'll take you over to the market of theirs they have near Plaza de Armas. It's really something."

"This is so nice to really relax and let down," she murmured, giving him a look of thanks. Mace wore civilian clothes, trying to appear a tourist. But he still didn't really fit in. He was so damn tall and stood out. Trying to emulate him, Sierra wore nothing on her head and hoped she fit in a degree. Her head felt bare without her baseball cap on it though.

"Yeah, it is." Mace said.

"Do you guys get a week off every three months?"

"Usually two weeks."

"Why only one week this time, Mace?" Sierra found herself wishing she could spend two weeks in this city with him, just exploring its Incan history.

"Because the CIA wants Belov taken out."

Snorting, Sierra said, "You guys bust your humps out there. No one gets any decent sleep. Aren't they concerned about your team? Sleep deprivation?"

He watched a group of policia coming up and moving quietly through the gathering crowds that traversed the steps. "No. They could care less." Straightening, he asked, "Want lunch? I know a nice little hole in the wall that has the best Peruvian food you'll ever taste."

Perking up, she said, "I'm starving." Grinning, Sierra touched her stomach for a moment above the vest she wore. "I loved overeating on our first night out and finishing off that twelve-ounce steak."

Unwinding up, Mace offered her his hand. "Was I right? Best steak you've ever eaten?"

She gripped his large, scarred hand, taking secret pleasure in sliding her fingers into his, feeling the thick, hard callouses on his palm. "Absolutely right. That was an amazing meal." Reluctantly, Sierra started to release his hand but felt his fingertips hooking hers back into a palm-against-palm clasp.

"Just play along for a bit?" he asked, keeping her hand firmly in his. "We want to appear to be an American tourist couple."

"Okay," she said, looking around. Sierra noticed a lot of policia in the plaza. She glanced up at him. His face was unreadable as he perused the area. "Is something up?"

"No," he murmured, tugging on her hand, leading her down to the sidewalk. "Usually, midday until dark, the policia are a heavy presence in the squares. There's a lot of pickpocketing that goes on from the young boys. They target foreigners."

Mace led her down a side street, a narrow alley. Large gray blocks that had been cut and fashioned by ancient pre-Incan stoneworkers sat as the foundations for the 15th century buildings above them. The streets were all cobblestone pavement. As she walked on them, Sierra wondered about the men who had slaved and worked over placing each single rounded rock into the earth to make this roadway. Every stone of Cusco was an amazing page of history to her, even the ones under her very feet.

She liked holding Mace's hand. There was something protective about it. But her body was tightening with need of him—as usual. Sierra still had no idea what was going on between them. She liked being in Mace's company. He was a man versed in history. He pointed out Inca temples, showing her how tight the fit between the huge gray blocks of stone that made up their foundations were. It was like listening to her mother tell her stories about the Cherokee people, their myths, their feats.

Mace led her into a very narrow alley. Halfway down, on the right, was a bright red door that stood open. Inside, it was semi-dark, no windows, but the smell of spices and food made her stomach growl with anticipation. The owner, a short, balding Spaniard, knew Mace by name, heartily welcoming him into the tiny restaurant. The tables were round, the chairs looking hand-hewn and simple. There were three other couples eating. The owner led them to a table against one wall made of Incan, hand-carved stone. With a flourish and a big smile, he pulled out the chair for Sierra. She smiled back and thanked him, sitting down. Mace took his own chair across from her where his back was against the stone wall so he could see who was coming and going through the only entrance/exit point.

"Let me order for you?" Mace asked.

She grinned. "Sure. Just make sure it doesn't move, all right?" She saw a faint smile touch that wonderfully shaped mouth of his. How she ached to kiss this man! Sierra knew he would be a good lover.

"You got a deal," Mace rumbled, switching to Spanish to order their lunch from the owner. "You want gas water to drink?"

"Yep. Thank you."

A bowl of tortilla chips and three small dishes filled with sauces, were placed between them. Mace pointed to the green one on the end.

"Unless you want to rip the skin off your tongue, I'd advise you to try it last or leave it where it's sitting."

She grinned and scooped up the red sauce on her chip, carefully tasting it. She saw Mace pitch his chip into that green sauce.

"You must have a cast iron stomach, Kilmer." she said, leering up at him.

"Listen," he said, munching on the chip, "it's the only thing that kills the parasites and bacteria we pick up out here."

"I think I'll pass," Sierra said dryly, liking the piquant and slightly spicy red sauce.

A waiter brought over his ice-cold beer and her gas water with its lime slice.

"Who's the lucky man in your life?" Mace asked, holding her startled gaze. He assumed that she had someone. She was too damn beautiful and smart not to have men who, at the very least, lusted after her.

"No one," Sierra said. She saw surprise in Mace's gray eyes.

"Why so sad?" he asked.

Her heart twinged. She saw that Mace was sincere. It wasn't a flippant question. He genuinely was trying to get to know her. And last night, she'd almost let him kiss her. She wanted to know everything about him. In the jungle, in the darkness, he'd shared his life with her, about Ana Beth, his baby, both of whom were gone. There was no guile in Mace's eyes as he sat there, elbows on the table, one hand around his beer, watching her. Waiting.

Taking a deep breath, she said, "I was never married. I mean, I wanted to be, but circumstances prevented it." her voice quiet. She wanted no one to overhear them. "I met Sergeant Jeb Cantrell, a Marine Corps sniper, when I was twenty-two. We got put out on a two-month op together in Afghanistan." Sierra smiled softly in memory. "He was a Kentucky boy, grew up barefoot and hated going to school because he had to wear shoes…"

"You fell in love?"

"Yeah, we did, over that year. We were so good together, as a sniper-spotter team, that the Corps kept us together."

"Good sniping teams are hard to come by," Mace agreed.

"We were good for one another," she admitted. "I tried to ignore what was going on between us. I knew it was wrong. I was afraid that how I felt toward Jeb would become a deadly distraction. But he called my hand on it. Told me he loved me after we'd been together for nine months."

"But you loved him, too?"

"I did." Quirking her mouth, Sierra admitted, "I was afraid to tell him. Afraid of so much because we were an active military sniper team. And if anyone got wind of it," and she brushed her wrinkled brow, "It wouldn't have been good. We'd have been split up and assigned to other teams. I didn't want that, so I sat on how I felt toward Jeb."

"I'm sure that was a special hell."

Giving Mace a quick glance, Sierra saw he understood. "It was… awful. But when he called my hand, I fessed up. After a lot of serious discussion, we felt we were professional enough to work together despite how we felt personally about one another."

"Did it work?" he wondered.

"Yeah, it did. But we kept it a secret."

"How long did it last?"

"Four years." She sat up, pushing back in her chair, staring at the shadowed stone wall. "It was the best years of my life, Mace. I really loved Jeb. He was funny, easy-going, never getting too serious about anything except us. We were good as a team and we were on deployment assignments every six months, and then we'd come Stateside for another six, and go rotate back out. We had an apartment in Oceanside, not far from Camp Pendleton. And we kept how we felt for one another a secret."

"Didn't you want to marry?" Mace asked.

"Yes." Sierra cast her gaze over at his serious-looking face. "But we had another year on our contract. We decided to wait, get out of the Corps, and go on and get married and lead our lives as civilians." She closed her eyes for a moment and folded her hands on the table, staring down at them. "We had one more deployment... just one more... and he got killed." She tucked her lower lip between her teeth for a moment, feeling all the old grief come flowing up through her. It didn't have the raw intensity it used to. All she felt now was a sadness, instead. For what might have been. Pushing through her desire to stop the story right there, Sierra felt Mace deserved to hear all of it.

"We were on a mountain slope waiting for an Al-Qaeda HVT to cross the border from Pakistan into Afghanistan. "Somehow... and I still don't know how to this day, we got jumped by a small group of Taliban. They were damned good at finding us. Jeb took a hit to his chest. I killed the four of them, but he was mortally wounded." Closing her eyes, Sierra could still see him bleeding out in her arms. She was sobbing, trying to stop him from dying. She would never forget the moment he'd lifted his hand, gripped her forearm, and looked into her eyes. The moment she'd seen the life go out of his eyes. A lump formed in her tightening throat, and she shook her head. "I-I couldn't save him."

Mace reached out, gripping her tightly clasped hands for a moment. "I'm sorry, Sierra. He sounds like he was a damned fine man."

Just the warmth and strength of his hand over hers, helped her stabilize the emotions flowing, grief-stricken, through her. Opening her eyes, she lifted her chin and held his dark, gray gaze. Sierra saw he meant it, heard the heaviness in his low voice. "Sorry... I didn't mean to go into it in such detail." She gave him a slight, one-cornered smile that didn't quite work. "Seems like we share some things in common."

Mace lifted his hand from hers. "Not anything to write home about."

"No," she whispered, her voice strained, "it's not. On most days, it doesn't bother me. I'm twenty-eight now and I'm pretty much over the worst of the grief… the loss of Jeb. But at times like this…"

"It all comes back," Mace agreed heavily. "It took me years to get out from under the grief I had over my wife and baby dying."

"That was no picnic," Sierra agreed, giving him a gentle look. Mace still held so much pain from that time. He'd never gotten it out, discharged it. She, on the other hand, had cried so much, so often that in the first six months after Jeb's death, Sierra wondered if she'd ever stop crying. But at least, she did grieve for him, for what she'd lost.

"What about you?" she asked, her voice scratchy as she took a sip of water.

"What about me?"

"Is there someone special in your life now?" She set the glass down on the table, watching amusement come to his eyes.

"Doing what we do? There isn't a woman in the world that would wait on any of the three of us, considering we're gone nine months out of every year. No, there's no one special in my life, Sierra. It just wouldn't work."

She felt her heart squeeze for Mace. "I guess we're just destined to be lonely," she admitted, moving the glass slowly around in her hands.

"In our line of work, that pretty much says it all."

"On some days, I find myself wishing…"

"For what?"

She gave Mace a wry look. "Oh, you'll laugh, Kilmer."

He shook his head. "Try me?"

"If you laugh—"

"I won't."

She regarded him for a moment. "Okay, so here goes. Of late, I've found myself wanting to just have a real life. I'm twenty-eight. I love children. I want a family someday. My biological clock is ticking. My mother is ruthless about reminding me she'd like grandchildren," and she grinned a little over that thought.

"So? You want to settle down. Get married. Have kids. That's nothing to laugh at, Sierra."

It felt good to hear the low growl in Mace's voice, hear the honesty in it. "Thanks for not laughing."

"You'll never find someone. Not doing this job."

She laughed a little. "I found Jeb."

"True," Mace said.

Sierra thought about Mace. Thought about how she felt toward him, the tendrils of needing him growing daily more and more strongly in her heart for the grizzled, scarred warrior. He was a good man. But he was on a mission. A mission of revenge, to account for how drugs had torn up his family. And she knew him well enough, she thought, to know he was like a pit bull. Once Mace decided to do something, he did it. He never let go until it was complete. "I don't see how you can handle being out here for three years in a row, Mace. It has to be wearing on you. On Cale and Nate."

He shrugged. "We got three months back in the States. It works for us."

"But... aren't your lonely? I mean, is it so wrong to have a real life?" and she searched his hard face.

He finished off his beer and set it aside. "There's days," he admitted hesitantly, "that I ask myself what the hell I'm doing out here in this green hell. On other days, I know I'm needed, and I can't tear myself away from it. Our three teams stand between the Indians and those Russian bastards. If we left, Sierra, they'd be completely at their mercy. At least we do some good down here and that counts in my book."

"And Cale and Nate have always been with you?"

"Yeah, we're a team."

"Don't they want a life?"

"I don't know. We've never discussed it."

Snorting, Sierra said, "Men! You guys are so afraid of touchy-feely emotional subjects. It kills me."

He grinned a little and shrugged his broad shoulders. "It just isn't in us, Sweetheart. That's all."

Sierra gave him a dirty look, her heart swelling over his endearment. Every time he called her that, his voice became warmer, as if he were physically caressing her. "That's not true. I've been saving most of the money I've earned. I've bought a nice cabin in the woods outside of Alexandria, Virginia. The rest is in savings." And then she added, "I don't like being alone. I had a taste of what it could be with the right man. I guess... I guess I'm thinking that I don't want to live the rest of my life being a sniper..."

And now, Mace knew why she stepped away from him. Her heart couldn't take the loss of someone she'd fallen in love with again. She could see him almost thinking about the Scrabble game, the wager of a kiss. Sierra wasn't sure about anything with him right now. There was just so much to lose. Surely, he saw that. She did. Jeb had worn her down over time. Like all snipers, he'd been patient, and he hadn't pushed her.

Last night, Mace had controlled himself. He'd respected her needs. But his warning rang in her head and heart. He was just like Jeb. Even though he might not be a sniper, he had the patience of one. She'd seen that trait in him from the gitgo. And, from the way he'd studied her in the thickening silence stringing out between them last night, Sierra knew that he wasn't going to give up. He wanted her.

But at what price to her? To him?

SIERRA DIDN'T WANT to go back into the jungle. The seven days in Cusco had fled by like a wild mustang galloping across the plains. She'd goaded Nate and Cale into afternoon games of Scrabble. They'd come less eager than whipped dogs to the table. Mace was also there, and she'd found out very quickly he had a damned sharp mind and a helluva vocabulary too. But so did Nate and Cale. Their afternoon games had consisted of cold beers for the two men, water for her, and Mace bringing over trays laden with appetizers from the restaurant every now and then.

A warm feeling threaded through her breast as she sat strapped into the jump seat at the rear of the Black Hawk, the bird vibrating soothingly around her as they headed for the Highlands at 1500, 3 p.m., on the seventh day.

Her gaze wandered over to Mace, who sat flat on the deck. The crew chief had taken the other jump seat beside her. Mace had slumped against the back of the pilot's seat and pulled his baseball cap down over his face, grabbing a nap. So had Nate and Cale. They were laying on the deck, arms beneath their heads, eyes closed. Those three could sleep anywhere, Sierra knew. Her heart softly turned every time her gaze swept across Mace's long, hard body now in his jungle cammies once again.

He'd never made a move to try and kiss her after the night of the Scrabble game. Why couldn't she just have a one-night fling? It would have been wonderful. Sierra knew it would. Her lips tingled, imagining what it would be like to have his mouth glide against hers, open her, taste her. Groaning to herself, she wrapped her arms around her torso, closed her eyes and tipped her head back against the seat.

Too soon, they were going back in that green hell. And Belov was out there… somewhere…

CHAPTER 11

A FTER BEING DROPPED off, Mace led his team into the jungle for cover. The winds along the highland area were brisk. He made sure Sierra was second in line as he chose the well-worn path that would take them even higher, up to the Q'ero village of Caverna. The village was in the Highlands, in a godforsaken rocky, cliff area. He often wondered how the people survived up there. They had terraces of farmland, built hundreds of years earlier, down below the lofty village, where they grew corn, potatoes, quinoa and beans, staples of their diet.

He always worried when getting dropped off during daylight hours by the Night Stalkers, but to try and fly up into this area in the dark was too danger-ous. The winds shifted and flowed down off the mighty Andes toward the ocean where the city of Lima, the Night Stalkers' base of operations, sat at sea level below. No commercial flights within Peru ever flew in this region in the darkness because of the possibility of a crash, due to the powerful winds. So, they were now stuck, unless it was one of those life-and-death emergency situations. Being picked up and dropped off during daylight hours, when the winds came back in off the Pacific and flowed upward into the mountains would be their only option. They were a lot tamer in comparison and didn't tear wings or rotors off aircraft. But daylight pick-ups and drop-offs were risky as the Night Stalkers well knew, hence their moniker.

Mace's senses were on full alert as he trotted through the jungle. Within a mile, they'd broach the Highlands, and the jungle would thin out, its lush tropical plants fading to rough, bare ground due to the high altitude. Nine thousand plus feet of altitude, along with the winds from the snowclad Andes, slashed the timberline short like a cold saber. The trail was muddy as usual. His heart, dammit, was squarely on Sierra. Mace felt the impasse with her. Under-stood it, now. She'd already fallen in love once with a Marine sniper she'd been teamed with. Sierra didn't want to repeat that mistake. The man had died out on an op with her. Was she worried that would happen again if she capitulated? If she took the risk to have a personal relationship with him? Mace thought so, feeling as if he'd lost something of such great value before he'd even had it.

As he moved fluidly up the inclining trail, the heavy ruck on his back, rifle in his right hand, Mace felt his heart tearing open. It was damned painful. He'd seen the fear in Sierra's eyes, heard it in the slight tremble of her voice, as she'd told him about Jeb being killed by the Taliban in the surprise trap they'd sprung. His mouth thinned. Why would she ever want to have a relationship with him? Yet, that night he'd gathered her into his arms, slipping his cammo jacket over her to give her some protection from the pouring rain, Mace had felt himself come alive.

He thought he'd died when Ana Beth had died. But as he'd sat there on that log, sheltering Sierra, felt her shaking with cold, he'd felt his heart crack open. It had been torturous for him as he'd felt himself awakening as if from some deep, long sleep. Back in the present, his emotions were bubbling and clamoring inside his chest, wanting that unexpected intimacy between them once again. He was so powerfully drawn to Sierra that he felt nearly possessed by the feeling. No woman had ever filled his life, his body, his heart and head, like she did. And all she'd had to do all of that was just show up for this op.

Mace felt the sweat running down between his shoulder blades as he pushed up the trail. He kept an ear keyed to his team behind him, hearing their soft footfalls, the cadence of them, knowing they were remaining in line, about twenty feet between each of them in case bullets started flying. To be bunched up in a tight group would guarantee they'd all be gunned down quickly in an ambush. This way, strung out, they'd have a chance at least to dive into the jungle, hide, and return fire.

Where was Belov? Mace didn't sense him and his team around. He was hoping that their contact in Caverna had received some word from Sacha Pavlov. One of those sparse bits of intel he relayed whenever he could take the risk. In every village, he had a contact, someone he trusted, memorize his message to pass on to Mace and his team once they visited. Sometimes, if it was overly technical, Pavlov would write it down. The trusted Indian, always a woman, and usually a mother, would then slip Mace the paper. They could not read what was on it since it was in English. Most Q'ero Indians knew a smattering of Spanish, but no English. He was hoping and praying Pavlov would give him intel on where Belov and his team were heading. Then they could set up a hide and Sierra could nail the bastard once and for all.

As they breasted the hill, leaving the mud of the jungle behind, bare rock riddled with fissures and holes met their footfalls. They had been trotting for five miles when Mace held up his arm, his hand in a fist, a silent signal to stop. His team halted immediately. Mace chose a huge area of massive rocks, a hodgepodge of them, thirty feet high and at least a football field in length. It was a good place to hide, catch their breath, hydrate, and rest for a moment.

Mace first took a walk along the fading tree line of the jungle, alert and watchful. There was nothing beyond it but the gray, black and white granite escarpment that reminded him of a loaf of bread, smooth and curving upward. Above that granite cliff, sitting up there at nine thousand feet, was the village of Caverna.

As his team followed him into the rocky fortress of towering boulders, Mace found a niche and squatted down. He got rid of his ruck, setting it aside. His gaze swept over his sweaty team. Their cammos were soaked with sweat. Their green t-shirts clung to them. His gaze moved to Sierra. She had her hair in two long braids, her t-shirt clinging damply to her, the bullet proof vest over it. Her face was glistening with sweat. She came over near him, shrugged out of her own ruck and squatted down, drinking deeply from her Camelbak. Mace found himself wanting to smooth back some of those frizzy tendrils of hair clinging to her damp cheeks from behind her ear but resisted. His gaze moved to Nate and Cale. They came over shortly. Everyone looked fit and not stressed.

"Wish I was back in Cusco," Nate said with a grin as he sat down opposite Kilmer.

"Makes two of us," Cale growled, joining them.

"I'm already soaking wet," Sierra whined, picking at her t-shirt, pulling it off her skin, wrinkling her nose.

Bitching was healthy. Mace pulled a waterproof map from his thigh pocket and spread it out so Sierra could look at it. She needed to know the layout of these villages as they visited them. "Focus on this," he told her gruffly, smoothing it out on the smooth, granite surface.

Sierra knelt. "What am I looking at?"

"Caverna," he told her, sliding his finger along the map's surface. "Q'ero village, a hundred and fifty people."

"And we're going there why?" she asked, twisting a look up at him.

"Need to connect with Pavlov's contact there," Mace said, resting his arm against his knee. "What I'm hoping is he's going to tell us where Belov is headed to. And if we can get there ahead of him in time to set up an ambush."

"Interesting name for a village," she said. "It means cave in English. Are there caves in that area?"

Nodding, Mace said, "A hell of a lot of them. Frequently, Belov stashes the cocaine he's manufactured in them."

"How does he transport it all out of here?" Sierra wondered. She wiped her forehead, the humidity high even though it wasn't at all what she'd call warm up here at this altitude.

"There's two old Russian transport helos run by undercover Spetsnaz and

KGB Russian pilots out of Aguas Caliente," he said. "They pay them to transport the drug shipments out."

"To where?"

"Across the border to Bolivia, around the Lake Titicaca area."

"So," Sierra murmured, thinking aloud, "Caverna is an important choke point. A place where he's forced to come with his bags?"

"Exactly."

Nate spoke up. "Sierra, what you don't know is that Belov has those poor people in that village terrified. He needs their cave systems. A place to stash the drugs. And he terrorizes them all the time, in order to keep them in line. He's threatened them with death if any of them tell an outsider that he's hiding his drug haul in their area."

"I get it," she said, shaking her head. She turned to Mace. "Does your contact always get a message from Pavlov?"

"No," Mace said. "Just depends upon many fluid situations with Belov. Sacha has to be very, very careful about his movements in any given village. But he's set up medical clinics in all of them and that's when his contact gets to him, and they exchange messages. He can't just go to the woman's hut and speak with her. Belov watches his men. His second-in-command Milova Kushnir is charged with watching all of them." Frowning, he added, "Kushnir is worse than Belov and there's word on the street that he wants to replace Belov and become the leader, instead."

"So, Belov can't trust his own team?" she demanded.

"Not at all. Pavlov has to be extra careful with the situation. If too many suspicious events occur in a row, Belov may suspect a mole. There're times when Sacha gives us intel, but we don't act on it because it might place him into jeopardy."

Shaking her head, Sierra said, "That guy has a big set of balls to do that under Belov's nose. If he found out, he'd kill him in a heartbeat."

Cale said, "Oh, Belov would take his time torturing Sacha, believe me. He used to be an interrogator and his methods are straight out of the Middle Ages. He'd make an example of him, believe me. And it wouldn't be pretty, Sierra. The man is evil."

"All the more reason I want to take him out," Sierra muttered. She'd heard enough about Belov to make her want to vomit. The man was a sociopath, pure and simple. He had no morals or values. Greed was his god. That and power.

Mace felt his stomach clench. He said nothing, but if Belov ever captured Sierra… Instantly, he shut off. She had no idea what would happen to her as a woman. And that made him even more protective of her. "Okay," he said, glancing up at his team, "we go in careful, as always."

"Meaning?" Sierra prompted.

"Meaning Belov could be hiding anywhere around here. We have to fade into the cave area, wait, watch and listen. The Indians can't give us a high sign. If Belov is in the vicinity, waiting, that'd mean they wouldn't dare try to warn us off. He'd kill anyone who tried to alert us."

"Do we use the night, then?" Sierra asked.

"Better believe it," Mace said. He pointed to the thinning line of jungle behind them. "We're going to wait it out here, hide, rest up, grab some sleep if we can. At nightfall, we'll use the edge of the jungle and move toward the village."

"Don't they have dogs?" she asked.

"They eat them," Cale told her. "No dogs at most of these villages."

Nate added, "Just dozens of guinea pigs in every hut. That's their main meat source. They have those little critters living, breeding, birthing, and growing up in their huts. There's very little other protein around, except for a grain called quinoa. It's thirty-percent protein but they can grow it down in their fields below. This village has to go to Sacred Valley, down below, and buy any other vegetables they might want, from them."

"Yeah," Cale said, making himself comfortable by laying on his back and using his ruck as a pillow, "think about carrying sacks of vegetables from six thousand to back up here? Ball-busting if you ask me."

Sierra nodded. "No question."

Mace turned to Sierra. "Make yourself comfortable. Try to sleep." He wished like hell they were back in Cusco. Every night he'd spent there in his bed, alone, fantasizing that Sierra was there beside him, had eaten away at him. He'd seen the longing in her eyes for him as their gazes had briefly met. Literally, Mace could still feel that connection between them. Unrequited. Strong. Needy. He turned, getting up and hauling his ruck off to where two rocks met. He looked up at at the sky. It was cloudy, but it didn't look like rain. It rained a lot less up in the Highlands, unlike down in the jungle. It was a reprieve from always being damp, and having their flesh chaffed by their thick, heavy cammies. He saw Sierra lay down on her side in the dusk, still unacclimatised to the cold, head on her ruck. She tucked one hand against her breast and an ache filled Mace. He pictured himself curving along the back side of her, sliding one arm beneath her slender neck, the other across her body, his hand splayed out across her belly, holding her close. Holding her tight, inhaling the fragrance of her silky black hair and skin.

Mace snapped himself back from daydreams, "Cale? You got the watch for the next two hours," he told him. "Nate? You're next. Then Sierra and then myself."

"Roger that," Cale said, moving to his feet. He would stand watch, be their eyes and ears so that the rest of the team could grab rest and, hopefully, some sleep.

Someone squeezed Sierra's arm gently. Instantly, she woke up. Mace was leaning over her, watching her. Blinking, she sat up, rubbing her face. "I'm up," she said thickly, sleep torn from her.

"Your turn for sentry duty," he said quietly, looking around. Glancing at his watch, he said, "The sun just set."

Looking up, Sierra saw the sky had turned darker, the clouds drifting off the Andes in the distance growing gray. "Two hours?"

"Yeah, then wake everyone."

"Okay. I'm on it." Mace studied her intently for a moment and Sierra felt his warmth, his care. Her heart opened and she wanted so badly to lift her hand, slide it against his stubbled jaw, caress him. Kiss him. She'd had the chance but didn't take it. That was on her. Sadness moved through Sierra. There was no way a relationship with Mace would ever work. Despite how badly she wanted it to. Getting to her feet, she hauled her cammo jacket from her ruck along with two of her sweaters. She pulled the sweaters on and then the jacket, feeling warmer. Taking the M-4 rifle from the Velcro straps on her ruck, Sierra chambered a round, leaving the safety off. She pulled a warm alpaca knit hat from her ruck and settled it on her head. She settled the NVGs around her neck. Soon enough, she'd need them.

Stepping quietly, knowing how to walk without making a sound, Sierra left the bedded-down team, and moved out from the formation of rocks. The wind was sharp and gusting, having reversed direction to now flow down strongly off the Andes toward the Pacific Ocean far away beyond her sight. The wind slapped her with powerful gusts, whistling across the rounded, smooth escarpment, heading downward over its lip. Halting halfway around the perimeter of the massive rock fortress, she set her rifle down, quickly unbraiding her hair to let it flow free. The hair on the back of her neck would keep her warmer from the temperature she knew was about to drop sharply. Picking up the rifle again, she pulled its strap across her shoulder and continued to move, keeping alert.

The two hours of her watch crawled by. By the time she gently nudged each team member awake with the toe of her boot, her fingers were numb with cold. Once everyone was up and preparing to get into their gear, Sierra went back to her ruck. She silently thanked Mace for making her get several pairs of warm gloves. His experience operating out here on the Highlands was proving invaluable. Tugging on a pair, she saddled up and was ready with the rest of the team when Mace led them back into the sparse tree line of the jungle, heading toward the village of Caverna. He'd told her it was six miles away, set out in a rocky area.

As they approached the village, NVGs on, Sierra couldn't see anything. The wind was howling off and on like a mean banshee. She was freezing, her teeth chattering. Wishing she'd bought more alpaca sweaters; she was relieved when Mace gave them the signal to halt near another group of rocks that had been dumped indiscriminately by volcanic action maybe eons ago. She felt slightly warmer. How she wished she could be embraced by Mace, absorbing the heat from his male body, feeling the safety she automatically felt in his arms. The tension of the team amped up. She could sense it, although no one was speaking. They wore their radio headbands, in constant touch with one another. Mace had ordered them not to speak. Clicks on a radio would do, instead. Voices carried. Clicks did not.

Her neck prickled. It was a warning. She saw Mace down on one knee, M-4 in his hands, watching something in the distance. Narrowing her eyes, Sierra thought she saw movement far ahead of them. In the area of the caves. Was it an animal? A human? She couldn't make it out. Whatever it was, it wasn't good because she was getting a red flag warning. She felt more than saw Nate come up beside her. His attention was on the same area. She wanted to ask what it was but remained silent. Mace turned, telling her to get the sniper rifle out and ready.

Pulling the AW Super Magnum rifle, Sierra was now in sniper mode. Mace had gotten them all from the edge of the jungle to a stone fortress of rocks almost three-quarters of a mile from the cave entrances. It was still dark, the stars seeming so close, winking in the black velvet sky. She had the .338 Lapua bullets loaded into her mag cartridge and slapped it into the the AW. Having been trained well on the Lapua rounds during Marine Corps school, Sierra was comfortable with the AW even using the specialized bullet. Each mag held five of them. Setting the rifle up up on the bipods sticking out a third of the way down from the end of its barrel, she adjusted her 32X Night Force scope, laying on her belly on the hard ground, the barrel covered in its camouflage netting, matching the terrain. She felt Mace come and lay down next to her as she set up. Right now, as she glanced through her scope, she saw no movement whatsoever. It was 0500 and soon, dawn would crawl up over the eastern horizon.

"How's the set up going?" he asked. "Do you need help with anything?"

She felt the warmth of his bulk about six inches from her. It felt comforting to her, reminding her of how she and Jeb had worked as a sniper/spotter team. Mace had the spotting scope in his hands. "Okay. Just cross-checking everything, making sure it's online and working properly." she said softly.

"Want some spotter help?" he whispered back.

"Always." Her hands flew over the rifle, intimately familiar with it in every respect. The AW was used by the British SAS as a primary sniper rifle. She had switched to it as soon as Accuracy International had created the weapon. It withstood any extremes of temperature and climate challenges. She settled in, left arm across her body, right hand on the stock. She adjusted the cheek piece, making sure the contact of her face with it was complete. Sighting down the scope, she saw a lot of movement. The scope brought everything up close and clear. "I worry about this wind. It's a bitch."

"Yeah," Mace grunted, "a sniper's nightmare."

"Will it stop soon?"

"The gusts get less and less as it gets toward dawn. Doesn't help you dial in very much, but it's just something you have to contend with. A gust could knock off a good shot and it's a miss, not a hit."

She began to dial in, taking into consideration the temperature, the wind direction, how strong it was, clicking her long, nimble fingers over the rifle's three drums incrementally. "I've got a target." She grimaced. "Damn, there's another man right next to Belov.... They're talking, he's whispering something into his ear..."

Mace rasped, "We had no idea Belov would be here. If I had options, I'd want the bastard down in the jungle. The only problem with that is, we'd be too close and with few escape routes. At least up here, if you can drop him, we can make a run for it. He's got at least six or seven men with him, and we're outnumbered. We want to hit him and then fade into the jungle. We don't want a firefight."

"I hear you." She raised up enough to grab push the knit cap further off her brow. She didn't want it to get in the way of sighting through her scope. She settled back down; she'd already tamed her air into the pony tail that lay out of the way between her shoulder blades. Watching through the scope, she said, "Belov is out in front of the cave, now, and he's waving his arms, looks like he's yelling at the Indians bringing in the sacks of cocaine leaves. That other man is right beside him. He keeps whispering something that he doesn't want overhead, into Belov's ear... Acquiring target..."

"Take him out," Mace ground out.

If she shot and nailed Belov, his men would figure out which way the shot had come from. Even though she had the rifle's muzzle suppressor screwed on the front of its barrel, Belov would be lifted off his feet and flung backward. And, from that one motion, his men would know the direction the shot had been fired from. And then come after them like a nest of angry hornets. Sierra felt the urgency, the danger, and the slim chance she had to nail the bastard. There! He'd moved slightly and was now in the open. No Indian would be harmed. Her finger caressed the trigger.

"Target acquired….", and she squeezed off the shot.

The AW rifle jerked once, the recoil jamming deeply into her shoulder. The power of the bullet being sent to take out Belov, nearly a mile away, the energy of it, rippled through her entire body like ripples on the surface of water. Her body took a huge amount of energy from the shot. Mace pulled his night-vision spotter scope away from his eye.

"Belov's down," he confirmed. "He's dead."

"I saw one of his men with an RPG," she warned.

Instantly, they leapt into motion. Mace helped her put the AW back into its sheath, helping her get the ruck over her shoulders, the weapon snapped into place on the back of it.

Suddenly, several shots in a row rang out, echoing across the escarpment toward their position. Sparks flew as the rounds struck nearby rocks as the pair scrambled to bug out and disappear back into the jungle.

Mace snapped orders. "Nate, Cale, take the lead. Sierra, follow them. I'm going to hang back to make sure they don't get onto us or the trail we're taking."

Nate tapped Sierra's shoulder sharply. He made a gesture for her to follow him. Instantly, she was moving like a shadow into the cold night. She followed the combat medic until they were fading like ghosts back into the scraggly refuge of the clinging timberline of the jungle. The trail canted downward. Nate ran hard. She was stumbling here and there. Both wanted to put as much distance between them and Belov's team as possible. She continued to run in second position, Cale a good twenty feet behind her. Once in the jungle, they started a fast trot down the little-used feeder trail. Wordlessly, she followed, soaring with the knowledge she'd taken out Belov. Her job was done. They must have trotted a half mile up and down hills before Nate held up his fist, signaling her to halt. She skidded to a stop, nearly falling as the mud slid her forward. Cale's hand shot out and he grabbed onto her left arm, bringing her to a stop, keeping her on her feet.

"Hurry!" Cale rasped, breathing hard. "We're still in range of the RPG they've got."

Fear shot through Sierra. In her earpiece she heard Mace order Cale to come back and join him; that the crew from the cave was heading their way at top speed. He'd need help.

Cale said, "Keep up with Nate," and he sprinted along the trail, disappearing quickly, heading back to where Mace was holding rear-guard position.

Errantly fired weapons roared, shattering the area, their bullets whizzing wildly around as they ripped by her and Nate. Fear was an old friend; an emotion she never allowed to control or overwhelm her. Now, as never before, Sierra had to run for her life. Literally.

CHAPTER 12

M ACE HAD A bad feeling as he watched nine men rushing toward them. There was a mile between them. The team had swiftly moved away from the rock fortress, still in the grayness of dawn, crouched, running like shadows toward the jungle. He scoured the area. Every shadow became a person as he watched for movement, ones that might indicate a Russian operator sneaking up on them. He had no idea why his internal alarm was sounding. But he knew from long experience in the field that it was a warning klaxon and he damned well better listen to it. Cale appeared at a hard run, rifle up, alert and scanning ahead. Belov's team always carried RPG weapons with them and Mace knew that. RPGs reached a helluva lot further than a bullet and sprayed jagged shrapnel damage upon impact. Never mind the deadly pressure waves that came with it. Cale was hauling hard, the rocks slippery, and he was slowing down as he hit the muddy trail that led to the edge of the jungle. Kilmer waived him to stop when he heard the whoosh of the RPG being fired.

Sonofabitch!

Mace grunted, flinging himself forward, diving for the ground. He could barely see anything in the darkness of the jungle, but he did catch a glimpse of Cale also lunging for the ground instantly.

How close was it going to hit to them? Mace slammed into the mud, skidding on his chest, his arms flung outward, holding his rifle up. Mud spattered across his face as he slowed. Dropping the M-4 nearby, he clapped his hands over his ears and opened his mouth. If he didn't equalize the pressure between the outside air and that in his lungs, the explosion could turn his lungs to jelly in seconds, and he'd die instantly. His last thought was of Sierra and Nate. At least they were well ahead of them.

A bare instant later, the RPG detonated hundreds of yards ahead of them. The concussion wave throwing along mud, huge tree limbs and other debris, flew out in every direction from where the weapon had hit high up on the trail. The pressure waves pounded against Mace's body. He kept his mouth open, kept breathing through it as mud, water, rocks and the broken-off branches from trees rained down upon them. Covering his head with his hands, he and

Cale tucked, making themselves less of a target.

Within moments, it was over, and he leaped to his feet, grabbing his muddied rifle in his slippery hand.

"Check!" he snapped into his mic. He needed to ensure his team was safe and unhurt.

"Clear," Nate gasped.

"Clear," Cale huffed.

Mace waited. Sierra?"

Damn! He jerked around, expecting to see Russians heading in, AK-47s ready to use against them. Nothing! Whipping around, he narrowed his eyes, glaring into the darkness, trying to catch sight of Sierra. Cale was slowly getting to his feet, grabbing his rifle, heading in his direction.

Nate! Where's Sierra!" he rasped.

"She was ahead of me by at least a hundred yards," Nate rasped, breathing hard.

"Sierra isn't answering anyone," Mace said to Cale. "Nate? Stay where you are. We're comin' your way pronto!" Digging the toes of his boots into the mud, he hurtled deep into the underbrush, swallowed up by the lush vegetation, Cale hot on his heels. They ran for nearly half a mile and linked up with Nate, who was covered in mud. He looked grim.

"She went around that curve," Nate told them. "I lost sight of her."

Mace nodded. "Let's go. We've got to find her."

They spotted her on the trail a quarter mile further down the slippery path. She was sitting up. The RPG had hit nearest her position, a huge hole nearby that had blasted the jungle and trees out of the area. His heart pounded with terror as he rushed to her side and saw her hair and half her face plastered with mud. She was dazed. Gripping her by the arm, he knelt at her side.

"Sierra, are you wounded?" he demanded harshly, turning, watching their six as Cale and Nate slid to a halt, covering the trail they'd just come down.

"N-no," she managed, gripping her sniper rifle. "I'm okay... that RPG... it hit close... threw me off my feet..."

"Any wounds?" he demanded.

She was breathing hard and gasped, "N-no..."

She didn't sound good. Mace's mind churned at the speed of light. He knew the second-in-command, Milova Kushnir, would come after them. But Mace had an exfil plan in mind. Gripping her arm, hauling her to her feet, holding her still because she was unsteady and weaving, her eyes telling him she'd probably suffered a mild concussion from the shock waves, he growled into his mic, "Nate, Cale, you take trail two. We're taking three. Rally point. Confirm."

"Confirmed," they chimed in immediately.

"Roger. See you at the rally point."

Instantly, the two men ran down the fork in the trail, disappearing quickly.

Mace pointed at a small trail to their left. "Start running down that trail. I'll be right behind you. Okay?" He looked hard into her clouded eyes, felt her struggling to get her bearings. There was no way he could carry Sierra. Looking over his shoulder, the trail was clear.

Not for long.

Urgency thrummed through him. "Sierra! Are you alright? Can you hear me? Can you run?"

She jerkily nodded. "I'll – Yes… I'll do it." Turning, she pulled her arm out of his hand, heading down the narrow trail that quickly engulfed her with wet, swatting leaves.

Mace had seen blood coming out of her nostrils. She had a concussion, for sure. There had been no time to give Sierra a rest or even treat her injuries. Digging into the slippery mud, Mace catapulted his tall body forward, gripping the M-4 as he raced down the trail behind her.

He knew that Kushnir's men would trail them. But, by making his decision to split up, their enemy would see the footprints in the mud and had to follow one trail or another, or split up themselves. And Kushnir might worry, while making that choice, that one of his divided forces might be ambushed. Mace hoped that such an indecisive moment might stop the Russians in their tracks, confused and uncertain which direction to go. What he worried about most though was Kushnir dividing his team, five men each, and coming after them anyway. *Two against five.* It wasn't the worst of odds he thought, as he ran, leaping over exposed roots, the wind tearing past him. They had the element of surprise on their side.

SIERRA FOUGHT DIZZINESS, wobbling like a drunk, sometimes, along the narrow trail. She could barely see anything, everything grayish and dark along the trail. Adrenaline was spurting through her bloodstream. They'd been compromised! Kushnir had found them! And he was after them. Urgency roared through her, and she clenched her teeth, focusing on the trail as it twisted and descended, sometimes sharply, leading her to lower altitudes and into a thicker and more humid jungle. Mace's heavy footfalls were right on her heels. She tried to run as hard as she could, but dizziness came and went. And, when those spells of vertigo hit her, she began to weave, struggling to right herself and stay on the path and not stray off into the surrounding jungle to trip over tangled roots and uneven ground, and fall, unable to get up.

Sweat was running down her temples, her breath tearing in and out of her mouth as they pushed hard. Constantly afraid to hear gunfire. That would mean that Kushnir's men had closed in within striking range. She longed for her M-4. It was back in her weapons bag, hidden up near the landing zone where the Night Stalkers had dropped them off. All she had was her .45 pistol and the sniper rifle that would be useless in this kind of environment. Mace not only had her back, but also an M-4 of his own that was perfect for just these kinds of close quarter combat situations.

Her legs were beginning to cramp. She grabbed her Camelbak hose, pulling water into her mouth, trying to run and drink at the same time. Now, with two sweaters on under her cammy jacket, she was getting hot, sweat pouring out of her skin beneath the three heavy layers of clothing. If she didn't drink enough water to stave off dehydration, those cramps starting in her calves would knot and cause horrific pain, crippling her and slowing them to a crawl. They had to outrun Kushnir and his jackals!

Mace reached out, grabbing her shoulder, nearly throwing her off stride. Sierra slowed, breathing roughly, looking up at him. He was muddy like her. But his eyes were hard, flat, and narrowed. She was seeing the hunter in him now. The warrior.

"Follow me," he urged in a rasp.

Grateful to stop running for a moment, she walked about fifty feet off the trail with him. And then, she saw a small stream running down a cut between two small hills. She understood what he was going to do. Mace jumped into the ankle-deep shallow water, turning, and gripping her hand, tugging her along with him. They were going to move down the stream and there would no longer be any footprints for Kushnir's men to follow.

"As fast as you can," he rasped into his mic, his breath coming in gulps.

"Right," she whispered raggedly, also sobbing for breath, pushing herself into a slow trot. The bed of the stream consisted of granular black sand and small many colored gravel. She found her rhythm, following the stream, trying not to make too much noise. The stream twisted and turned, leading them deep into the thickest jungle she'd ever encountered. Soon, Sierra found the canopy far overhead cutting out all but a fraction of the sunlight she needed to see by.

"Get your NVGs on," Mace ordered.

Situating the goggles over her eyes, their muddy, gritty rims cutting into her flesh where they pressed against her face, Sierra saw the whole landscape in front of her light up. The stream widened to six feet across. It got deeper in the center, knee deep, so she remained near the bank where it was shallower. Fear kept pushing her hard, even though her calves were continuing to knot up in unrelenting pain. Mace kept right on her heels, silently willing her to move faster. But she couldn't, the dizziness assailing her more often and making her stumble at times. But Mace kept gripping her upper arm to keep her moving straight whenever she faltered, until she could get her balance back again.

Exhaustion was clawing at Sierra. She had no grasp on time. She was soaked, both with the water from the clear stream and from her own sweat. As the stream made another turn, it suddenly tumbled over a drop, becoming a small but impassable waterfall, and she jerked to a halt. She felt Mace move close and he slipped his hand beneath her elbow.

"Can you make it up and out of the stream?" he asked, breathing hard.

"Yes..."

Mace hauled her up to the muddy bank as if she weighed next to nothing. It felt as if the sixty-pound pack she wore was driving her heels deep into the ground. He stopped and turned her, taking off his NVGs, staring hard at her.

"Dizzy?"

"A little," she admitted, trying to steady her breathing as she pulled her own NVGs off her eyes. All around her, there was now more gray light. Enough to see where they were at.

"You've still got blood running out both your nostrils. Headache?"

"No, I'm okay, Mace. Let's just get going." She saw him give her a slight grin, his teeth starkly white against his muddy face.

"Hold my hand. We're going down beside this waterfall. We've got a secret hiding place nearby. The enemy won't find us."

Confused, Sierra gripped his hand. She was grateful for his strength as the dizziness suddenly hit her hard. She crashed into him. Mace halted, steadying her. For a moment, she closed her eyes, her hand pressed against his chest.

"Just a little further and I'll take care of you," he urged gruffly, holding her.

Sierra knew they had to move. She pulled away, stumbling, her dizziness worse with her eyes open. Pain was now throbbing through her head, and she compressed her lips, not wanting to groan or cry out. Mace guided her down the steep slope beside the noisy, white curtain of the waterfall. He halted by the frothing water at the base of it. She looked up, staring at the cascade.

"Behind the falls is a cave," he told her. "That's where we're going. Come on..."

Sierra pushed herself. She forced her wet boots one in front of the other. Dizziness nearly made her fall sideways. If it hadn't been for Mace's strong hand around her upper arm, she'd have face planted. By the time he got her into the cave behind the falls, the spray had washed off the mud from her face and water dripped through her wet hair. She was soaked. All she wanted to do right now was lie down and be still. Biting back a groan, Mace led her into the darkness. He kept his stride short, walking much slower. She was being led blindly, no longer able to see anything in the growing darkness.

And then, suddenly, she saw light above her: a huge, jagged, oval hole in the rock ceiling. There were several spindly trees growing around the hole above out from among some bushes. Probably no one on the ground above would notice the fissure, but it allowed in enough light for Sierra to see that they were in a squarish cave, its floor a flat, smooth rock surface beneath their feet.

"What is this place?" she mumbled.

"This is where Alice went down the rabbit hole," he rasped. Mace helped her sit down, not letting go of her until he was sure she was sitting and stable, not falling.

Sierra crossed her legs, fingers trembling as she started to undo the straps of her ruck. If she didn't get it off her back, it was going to pull her over backward.

Mace was there, kneeling, his face inches from her own, his hands moving quickly, releasing other straps, gently removing the ruck from her shoulders.

She groaned softly, and slowly laid down on her side, head cradled in the crook of one arm, her free hand gripped tight over her closed eyes.

Mace hauled off his pack. He went to her side, kneeling over her, hand on her shoulder. "Talk to me. What are your symptoms?"

With an effort, she whispered, "Horrible dizziness. It's getting worse. I can't stand... walk... my ears are ringing. I can barely hear you. I have a headache," and she pointed to the side of her head.

"Okay, sounds like a level two concussion," Mace grunted. He pulled the tube of her Camelbak out over her shoulder, placing it in her fingers. "Drink. A lot. I'm going to take care of you. We're staying here for a while."

It was the last thing Sierra remembered for a long while.

Mace heard Sierra groan. He had just returned from reconnoitering the area surrounding the falls, M-4 in hand. Before heading out, he had cleaned her up, finding a huge, laceration and swollen bump on the side of her head, caked blood, and embedded stony fragments around it. His best educated guess was that a rock that had been hurled out of the jungle by the RPG's explosion had impacted on her head, concussing her. He'd placed her on a waterproof tarp, laid his dry wool blanket over her, and placed her head on her wet ruck.

He moved quietly. The midday light illuminated the cave well enough for him to see that the IV he'd put in her left arm was still in place, its bag hanging off an outcropping above her head. His gaze went to her face, which was pale and strained-looking as she flexed her hand slowly. She was probably feeling stiff and sore all over and, more than likely, going through one hell of a headache from where the rock had struck her.

Mace knelt, placing his hand on her shoulder. He'd stripped her out of her jacket and the two soaked alpaca sweaters under it, down to her t-shirt and cammo pants. He'd pulled off her wet boots and had taken off her socks so her feet could breathe and not become waterlogged. Because of the cave's constant seventy-five degrees temperature, he hadn't felt the need to cover her with anything.

"Sierra?" he called, her eyes still shut. "You're safe. It's Mace." He watched her lips part and she frowned. Earlier, he'd taken her hair out of their muddy braids, and now it all lay like a black halo around her head. And he'd done his best to wash the mud out of the strands and dry them somewhat with the small towel he carried in his ruck. And, just as he'd thought, those strands were thick and strong, like her.

Her eyes barely opened.

He peered down at her so she could lock onto his gaze. Did she recognize him? See him at all? Her eyes were cloudy-looking, unfocused. "How are you doing, Sweetheart?" Given a level-two concussion, Mace knew the drill: She'd lost consciousness and then had fallen into an exhausted sleep.

Sierra would have moments of clarity, maybe even not remember anything about how she'd been injured, and then come back to clarity. Mace hoped the whole cycle lasted for under twenty-four hours. Otherwise, she would slide into a level-three concussion, which could include aphasia, speech-slurring, forgetfulness, and potential blood-clotting in her brain. If she went there, he'd have to get her out of here. Get her to medical help as soon as possible. That would be life-threatening. Even right now, she would be unable to function in the most vital ways.

Weakly, Sierra lifted her right hand, rubbing her eyes. "W-what...?"

Her speech sounded slow, but clear. Mace squeezed her shoulder, wanting her to focus on his gaze. "We're safe. We got attacked by Belov's men near dawn this morning after you took him out. Belov is dead. Do you remember that?"

She blinked and stared up at Mace. "Attack?"

"Yeah," Mace said. "Do you recall any of it?" He couldn't help himself and lightly smoothed thick strands of hair away from her face. It gave him a feeling of almost shameful, stolen pleasure to thread his fingers through them. It was an unwanted pleasure, but one that he was unable to deny. He saw the wrinkles across her brow ease as he did so. There was such a powerful, unspoken bond between them. And it was a good one. And alive. And he'd never been so scared as when she'd lost consciousness shortly after he'd gotten her into the cave. That had scared the hell out of him. It was then in that moment that Mace had realized how deeply he 'liked' her. He didn't want to use the word 'love'. That scared him even more.

"N-no, I don't remember… what happened?" she whispered, her voice wobbly and unsure. Looking up and to her left, she stared at the IV bag hanging above her head.

"You were dehydrated," Mace told her. He sat down, facing her, picking up her right hand and holding it gently between his. When he touched her, some of the tension left her face. Even if her brain was still scrambled from the concussive pressure waves that had slammed into her, some part of it remembered him. And wanted his contact. He ached to hold her. Never let her go. Protect her. Glancing up at the bag, he saw that it was nearly empty. "In about ten minutes I'll get that IV out of your arm. Are you thirsty, Sierra?"

She closed her eyes. "I'm dizzy. Thirsty. Where are we?"

He watched her struggling to remember. "In a cave behind a waterfall."

"Ohh… yeah… I remember the falls." She opened her eyes to slits, looking at him. "Things are starting to come back. Bits and pieces…"

"I think when the RPG exploded, one of the rocks hurled up in the air by it, impacted on your head, giving you this concussion. Do you recall that?" Slowly, Mace was seeing life come back into Sierra's cypress-green eyes. Never had he wanted anyone to recover from their wounding more than he did right now. He'd been hiding how he really felt toward her. It had all happened so damned fast. Mace knew he was still reeling from it, his riled-up emotions, his desire for her, the fact that he'd damned near lost her early this morning. And they still weren't safe by a long shot. He'd been making regular rounds, keeping watches for the Russians. So far, no one had shown up, and he hoped they'd lost their trail at the point he and Sierra had taken the stream to make the final dash for their safe place.

"Ohhhhhh," she muttered, "I remember now." She pulled her hand from his, touching the side of her head. "There's a goose egg here…"

"Yeah, you got hit with a pretty big rock when that RPG exploded right near you."

"I don't remember…"

"Don't worry about it." He slid his fingers across her hair, smoothing down some of its frizzy strands, watching how her eyes opened wider, changed, became softer, filled with some unknown emotion. "Do you remember me? My name?"

Her lips curved slightly. "Sure, I do, Mace. How could I not?"

He grinned a little. Sierra was slowly returning to him. Brain trauma was serious business, and he knew they weren't out of the woods yet. "Thirsty?"

"Terribly," she admitted.

Mace wanted to keep lightly stroking her hair but eased to his knee. He snapped on a pair of latex gloves and removed her IV, and then reached across her. He Swabbed around the red puncture welt with an alcohol wipe, then placed a protective bandage across it and then took down the IV bag from the rock he'd hooked it over.

"Hang on," he told her, getting up. "I'll bring you over some water." He tucked the used IV kit back into a special compartment in his ruck. Mace always carried bottled water that had been purified with tablets to take out the parasites and bacteria. When he returned, he saw Sierra had closed her eyes once more.

"I'm going to ease you into a sitting position and hold you in my arms while you drink this," he warned her. He sat down by her shoulder and eased his arm beneath hers. Sierra made a soft sound as he gathered her against his body, her head resting against his upper arm. When she opened her eyes, his heart took off at a hard beat. Her eyes were clearer and even in the half-light in the cave, he saw the depth of the layered green colors within them. Pressing the bottle to her lips, she drank thirstily, gulping it down, showing him just how dehydrated she'd become.

When she finished off the pint, he set it aside. Water had escaped down either side of her mouth and he wiped each corner of it with his thumb. It felt like a moment of intimacy, and he thought he saw her eyes change, grow heavy-lidded. Shaking off what he probably had only wished he'd seen, Mace held her gently. "Better?" he asked.

"Much," she whispered, pressing her cheek into the hollow of his shoulder. "Thank you…"

He sat there, feeling like a man who had just been pulled out of hell. Sierra was soft and warm in all the right places. She nuzzled against his damp t-shirt, her hair falling across her shoulder and down across her breast, a silky waterfall of another kind. Inhaling, Mace smelled her fear-sweat but, above that, her special womanly scent. Pulling her a little more firmly against him, she offered no resistance, which surprised him. Given both of their past histories, Mace understood clearly why Sierra wasn't even about to think about a relationship with him. Mace was sure those gutting memories of Jeb were yanking Sierra's heart away from him, even though he felt she was just as attracted to him as he was to her.

Sierra sighed and whispered, "This is wonderful… thank you, Mace. It makes my head pain lessen."

He smiled a little, moving his stubbled cheek against her hair, its strands sleek. Without thinking, he placed a light kiss upon her hair. "What? I'm better than taking an Ibuprofen?" he teased. She lay fully relaxed against him, one hand resting against his chest. His flesh tightened beneath it, and he wanted desperately to love this woman. He knew Sierra would be wild and willful in his arms, lush and hot.

"You're like a big, protective teddy bear," she whispered.

"I've been called many things in my lifetime, but never that."

"What? A teddy bear? I grew up with the one my mom gave me when I was born. Pooh, my bear, slept with me every night. I never went anywhere without him."

He smiled a little, gazing around the cave, needing to remain alert. "So, you see me as a Pooh bear?"

She managed a little laugh and moved her hand across his chest, smoothing the wrinkles of the damp t-shirt that lay against his skin. "You're not a Pooh bear, that's for sure. More like a snarly old grizzly. Dangerous. Unpredictable."

Mace combed his fingers gently through her hair, luxuriating in the intimacy building so naturally between them. Sierra was rallying with being in his arms, but he also knew she was terribly vulnerable right now with that concussion. And she wasn't remembering everything. In time, it would all come back. "Is that how you see me?" he wondered, resting his jaw against her hair, careful not to put pressure on her skull.

Opening her hand, Sierra murmured drowsily, "Sometimes... but other times... like now... you make me feel safe..."

Mace felt her body sag fully against him, her hand sliding a few inches down toward his belly as she dropped off into unconsciousness once again. A concussion could do that to a person. He leaned back against the wall of the cave with Sierra in his arms. Closing his own eyes, feeling deep exhaustion pulling at him, Mace wished they were anywhere but in this green hell. He felt Kushnir and his team out there, searching for them.

Hours earlier, out on his scouting excursion from their waterfall cave, he'd connected with Cale and Nate via their sat phones. The rest of his team was still moving toward the rally point deep in the jungle. They hadn't made contact with the Russians, either. Mace had told them about Sierra's condition. Nate had gotten on the sat phone and they'd discussed her head injury. He'd advised they stay where they were for at least another twenty-four hours, if possible. Sierra's dizziness, he'd told Mace, was a level-two symptom and, if they could hole up and wait, it would be best for her condition.

Mace had no problem staying here. He'd never found any other military boot prints anywhere near this waterfall, but that didn't mean the Russians didn't know about this place. Sierra might feel safe in his arms, but there was no safety anywhere else around them. His mind and heart strayed back to Sierra. He felt the slow rise and fall of her breasts against his chest. She trusted him. It was such a pulverizing realization. Ana Beth had never trusted him wholly with her life. But Sierra, who lay like a sick child, so trusting in his arms right now, cleaved open Mace's closed heart in a way that made him deeply aware of just how much he liked her. His mind skipped around the word love.

No way. He *couldn't* fall in love again. If he did... No! Sierra lived just as dangerous a life as he did. And Mace knew with a clarity that few people had experienced, that nothing was guaranteed in life. To allow himself to fall in love with this brave woman would place him in an untenable position.

Mace knew he couldn't remain an operator if he allowed himself to fall in love with Sierra. It just wouldn't work. And he wasn't about to ask her to give up her own career. That's not how it worked. A ragged sigh tore from him as he held Sierra close. The music of the waterfall was soothing to him, like wispy droplets splashing through his exhausted mind.

Mace closed his eyes, wanting desperately to sleep deeply. But he couldn't. He had to remain alert. Take cat naps only. They were being actively hunted by Kushnir. Mace could feel it.

Still, he kissed Sierra's temple, tipping his head against the rock wall, holding her safe against him. If but for a little while.

CHAPTER 13

S IERRA AWOKE SLOWLY. She lay on her side, face against her ruck sack. The waterfall sound was soothing. Her headache had reduced, and she felt better. Probably because Mace had given her an IV to replenish the badly needed liquids she'd lost. Grimacing, she opened her eyes and saw that everything was bright, the cave wall staring at her. Her mind slowly put the pieces back together, where she was at and what had happened to her. At least as much as she could remember.

She heard a slight sound and rolled over on her back. Mace was standing above her, watching her, his baseball cap tipped back on his head. His face was darkened by stubble, and she saw exhaustion in his gray eyes. His M-4 lay across his shoulder. He was still in his olive-green t-shirt and cammies, his knife in a sheath around his waist and his .45 drop holster on his thick right leg.

"How you feeling?" he asked, kneeling down, setting the rifle on the floor to his left.

"Better, I think," Sierra muttered thickly. Pushing up into a sitting position, her hair fell around her face. She pushed the heavy strands away, feeling a keen need for Mace. Carefully touching her skull, she felt the huge bump on it. There was also some dried blood around the area where the rock had struck her. "The headache is much less."

Mace nodded. "You slept well." He glanced at the watch on his wrist. "It's 1500. Midafternoon."

"Not surprised," she said slowly, her mind still shorting out. Slowly looking around, she wanted to memorize the small cave where the light shafted down through the hole above it. "Are things quiet?" and Sierra lifted her head, worried. She knew the Russians could be looking for them.

"So far," he admitted, sitting down, crossing his legs, his elbows resting on his knees. "I just got back from making a swing around the area. I talked to Cale about an hour ago by sat phone and they said Kushnir's team was trying to track them. Right now, they're leading them off on a wild goose chase, doubling back on their heading, and using a stream to hide their tracks to throw the hunters off even more."

She scowled, touching her brow. She was damp and sweaty. "Do you think Kushnir split his force? The rest looking for us? Or all of them chose one trail?" and she searched his dark, pensive eyes. Mace was a big man with shoulders that seemed to go on forever. Sierra remembered falling asleep on that powerful chest of his, inhaling his male scent, her palm against the fabric, feeling the slow beat of his magnificent, brave heart. Did he realize how courageous he really was? Sierra felt her heart open wide with her need for Mace on every level. He was a hard man, molded by the military, had suffered such great, heartrending losses and yet, here he was. With her. His gray gaze warmed as he held hers. Feeling that deep longing she always did whenever he was nearby, Sierra swallowed, her throat tightening. The risk of falling in love with Mace was tempting her as nothing else ever had. And yet, Sierra knew it wouldn't work. A part of her wept inwardly because no man had ever rocked her world, not even Jeb, as much as Mace was doing right now with his mere, quiet, stoic presence.

"That's what I think. Kushnir's men know how to track. I'm sure he saw two sets of prints veering off on two different trails and decided to take all his men onto Cale and Nate's trail to hunt us down." Mace gave her a one-cornered half smile. "We've been a thorn in his side since Belov took over the drug team. He'd like us off his back. Now that you took Belov out, Kushnir is the leader."

"Have you come close to killing him before?"

"Yes, but every time, the situation didn't develop fully enough for us to get him." He reached out, touching the back of the hand of hers that rested on her thigh. "That's why our CIA handler called you in."

Turning her hand over, she tangled her long fingers between his scarred, calloused ones. "And Belov is gone, now."

"You've only been out here two weeks, Sierra, and you've taken him down." He tightened his fingers around hers, his voice dropping with concern. "And with this concussion? I'm worried for you. We need to get you to a hospital for examination."

Alarmed, she stared at him. "Just give me a good night's sleep! I'll be fine, Mace." Her heart beat harder when she realized what he was saying. Now that she'd completed her mission, it was time to leave. But she didn't want to, despite her injury. No! Mace would be left in this hellish jungle to play a cat-and-mouse game; trying to hunt down the Russian team before they found his first.

Lifting her hand to his mouth, he brushed a kiss against the back of it. Then, he released it for her to reclaim. "It's a wait-and-see, Sierra. You got hit hard on the head. It wasn't your fault. Things happen in firefights. No one's blaming you."

Giving him a frustrated look, the flesh of her hand tingling in the wake of his mouth pressing a kiss to the back of it, Sierra fought the ache to pull Mace to her and explore his mouth. "I'll be fine," she said defiantly. But she also knew that, right now, she was a liability. Her dizziness was getting better, but she remembered how intense it had been as they'd ran down the trail, fleeing from the Russians. She saw Mace give her a nod.

"Nate's our medic. I've been in touch with him. He says you're either a level two or three concussion and he's not sure which. If your dizziness recedes by tomorrow morning, then it's probably a two."

"And I can stay a bit longer?" Sierra held her breath, not wanting to leave for so many reasons. She saw him become concerned, his chiseled mouth thinning.

"I don't know yet. We're not out of the woods until we can get out of this area and to a safer one. Then I can call command and find out about your status with us."

"Dammit!" she muttered. "A stupid rock!"

"We were lucky we didn't suffer more casualties from that RPG they threw at us. Lucky that it wasn't the concussion waves that got you. It was just a rock." Shrugging, he said, "Don't fret about it right now, Sierra. I want to get some food in you if you're up to it. We'll spend the night here unless Kushnir starts snooping around."

"If he does? Is there an alternative exit point to this cave? Or is there only one way in and out?"

"No, there's another exit that way," and he pointed behind her. "And I'm taking walk-arounds every thirty minutes, keeping guard."

She gave him an apologetic look. "You're exhausted, Mace."

"Yeah, nothing new, Sweetheart." He unwound and walked over to his ruck and brought out another bottle of water, opening it and placing it in her outstretched hand. "Drink it. Do you feel like eating?"

"My stomach is rolling. Water sounds good but the idea of food," and she wrinkled her nose, "not so much. At least… not right now."

Mace nodded. "Okay. We'll try again later because if we have to make a run for it, if Kushnir gets too close, we have to make tracks."

Sierra felt like a complete liability. She remembered weaving around like a drunk when the dizziness had assailed her. "Maybe if I get up, go pee, and then get cleaned up, I'll feel better."

Mace smiled a little and leaned down, picking up his rifle. "Good idea. There's a washcloth and some unscented soap in my ruck. Plus, a dry towel. Why don't you do that while I make another circuit around the area?"

Sierra nodded. "Be careful…" She saw his eyes change, an emotion in them, but she couldn't decipher it. Mace left quietly, moving down through the cave toward its second exit point. He disappeared into shadows, swallowed up by the darkness. Feeling frustrated, she got to her hands and knees. The dizziness didn't assail her, and she was relieved. And then she pushed to her feet, scraping them wide apart just in case the dizziness hit her. It didn't. More relief poured through Sierra.

Slowly turning, she took small, concerted steps across the smooth rock surface toward Mace's opened ruck. Sierra didn't want to leave the team yet even though she'd completed her mission that she'd come here in the first place. Her status within the team would change dramatically, and she knew it.

Sighing, she thought that maybe if she washed her hair, cleaned up, and got into some fresh clothes, it might help.

Mace returned about an hour later. He made sure Sierra knew he was coming so his arrival wouldn't startle her. He tried to stifle his reaction to her, sitting as she was on the blanket, combing her damp hair, all the mud removed, and in a clean set of cammos and an olive-green sleeveless t-shirt. But his gaze moved to her breasts anyway, out of his control. She wasn't wearing a bra under her t-shirt, and damned if he didn't feel an instant reaction through his lower body. Worse, as he approached her, he saw her nipples were thrust up against the tautness of its hanging folds, the lush curves of her breasts outlined by the fabric. She was barefoot, legs crossed, looking so much better than before. Swallowing hard, he came over and sat down opposite her, leaving more room than he wanted between them.

"You look a helluva lot better."

Sierra smiled a little, gathering her combed hair behind her shoulders. "I feel better. A shower does wonders," and she gestured toward the falls. "It was great. The water is warm."

Mace found himself wishing he could have been the one to soap her body down. "Your eyes look clearer. How are you feeling?"

"A little dizziness, but nothing like earlier. I managed to walk a straight line," and she grinned a little, "from here to the falls and back, instead of weaving around like I did before."

Mace hungered to curve his mouth across her smiling lips. There was life back in her eyes, no question. "The headache?"

"Still there but reduced."

"You should take some Ibuprofen."

"Is it allowed in a concussion?"

"Nate suggested it."

"Okay," she said. Putting the comb aside, she asked, "Anything out there?"

"Not yet. It's quiet. Birds are singing. Monkeys are still doing their thing. When they don't, that's when I get worried."

"Could you lay down for a while, Mace? Sleep? I can stand guard."

It was a tempting offer. Mace had visions of sleeping WITH Sierra, not apart from her. She looked so natural and beautiful; her hair glinting highlights from the hole above where the light lanced in throughout the cave. Her arms were firm and well-muscled as she pulled one of her knees to her body, wrapping them around it. An ache so deep that it startled him, rose through Mace, settling in his chest. For a split second, he could see her in her cabin, smiling, hiking, loving the outdoors. And him at her side. The whole scene flashed through his mind, unbidden, and drew in a deep, shaky breath. What the hell! Every cell in his body felt a soul-deep loneliness that only went away when he was around Sierra. She fulfilled him on every level. Yearning to say as much to her, knowing it was the wrong place and time, all he could do was remain silent. The last thing he wanted to do with this woman who was like life to him. Mace didn't lie to himself: Sierra being wounded and having almost died in that firefight, had serrated his heart like nothing he'd ever felt before. And he could say nothing.

The radio he wore clicked three times.

Instantly, he was on his feet, grabbing his rifle.

"What?" Sierra said in a hushed voice, reaching for her pistol beside her ruck.

"Stay still," he growled, turning toward the underside of the cascading water. "It's Pavlov. He's a friendly. Don't move…"

Mace swiftly covered the distance to the waterfall entrance. He hesitated, hidden from the outside by wet rocks and the fine spray, peering out into the jungle. Clicking his radio back three times, he waited, M-4 at the ready. His heart thudded hard in his chest as he saw the Russian medic who ran with Kushnir's team, fade out of the line of trees. He had his AK-47 in hand, and was wearing a floppy hat and Spetsnaz cammos, his ruck on his shoulders.

"Three o'clock," Mace rasped into the mic near his mouth.

The Russian halted and immediately turned toward the waterfall.

Mace saw the tension in the man's oval face. Sacha was nearly six feet tall and lean like a starving wolf. His shoulders were broad and tensed but, even more so, it was his pale-blue eyes, narrowed, that betrayed the pressure he was under. Mace drew back. He had caught the medic's glance, and then retreated beneath the waterfall, waiting for him. His mind whirled. If Pavlov was here, it could mean that some others of the men from Kushnir's team were nearby.

Turning, he gave Sierra, who was tense, pistol in hand, a signal that everything was all right. He saw the sudden relief come to her face, and she lowered the weapon.

Pavlov slipped like a silent fog between the waterfall and the wet rocks, his back to the wall, AK-47 barrel pointed downward. He nodded to Mace, who he knew well from their various meetings over the last year.

Mace signaled him to follow. He saw Sierra's face tense up all over again. She'd recognized the Spetsnaz uniform.

"It's all right," he told her as he drew near. "This is Sacha Pavlov, their combat medic." He turned to the Russian. "My partner, Sierra Chastain."

Pavlov nodded to her. And then he pinned Mace with a dark look. "Kushnir has sent four men, plus myself, down this trail. They lost you when you went into the stream."

"How close?" Mace demanded.

"A mile." A tight smile leaked out of the line of the Russian's wide mouth. "He sent me this direction. He knows there's a waterfall down here. I told him I'd check it out and get back to him."

"Good to know." Mace held out his hand to the Russian. "Good to see you, too. How are things going?"

Pavlov gripped his hand, shook it firmly and then released it. "Dangerous. As always."

"We appreciate everything you do," Mace told him. "Are you about ready to jump ship and leave them?"

"Not yet," Sacha said, glancing down at Sierra. "But it's getting closer. Belov is dead and Kushnir took over. He doesn't trust anyone. He's going to keep a tight watch on me."

Taking off his floppy camouflage hat, the medic wiped his sweaty brow with the back of his sleeve. "After Belov was killed, they knew the general direction of the shot."

Mace clapped him on the shoulder. "Don't worry about it. Do you have any time? Sierra has a concussion. A rock hit her head when the RPG blew up."

Sacha walked over to Sierra and introduced himself. His English was stilted, but he held out his hand and gently shook hers. In minutes, he had his medical ruck open and was checking her out. Mace walked over, saying nothing, looking worried. The medic studied her, taking a small flashlight and moving it slowly back and forth across her eyes. "Your pupils are not equal."

Sierra sat quietly for the exam. It was Pavlov's large, intelligent eyes, those pale-blue iris surrounded by their black rims, that gave him a startlingly alert look. She felt as if he was looking right through her. In so many ways, he reminded her of Nik Morozov and Alex Kazak, two other combat medics. Two of her best friends.

"My pupils aren't equal?" she asked Sacha. Worried, she saw the medic frown. "What does that mean?"

He knelt next to her, rifling through his medical ruck, looking for something. "Let me check you out thoroughly and then we will talk." He hesitated for a moment, searching her face. "Are you comfortable with me examining you?"

"Sure." And then she added more softly, gasping slightly only once as he hurriedly pressed a cold stethoscope against her skin, "I know Alex Kazak. He's spoken passionately about you, Sacha. He worries for you."

A grin suddenly split Pavlov's lean face as he pulled out a blood pressure cuff. "Alex! How is he? I miss my good friend." With quick efficiency, he wrapped the cuff around her upper arm. Lifting the chilly metal head of his stethoscope off from below her left collarbone with a nod, he simultaneously inflated the cuff and watched the dial as he released a small bit of air from it.

Sierra started to talk again about Alex but the medic frowned and said, "Sorry I asked. Forget about Alex. Such talk must wait. I need you to be quiet and calm while I take this reading."

She did as she was asked. The man was lean, and she felt not only his controlled strength, but his gentleness with her as well.

"Good," he murmured, putting the stethoscope back in his ruck.

Sierra sat still. She was aware of Mace standing over them and she could see worry in his eyes. Concerned herself, she turned, watching Pavlov's glistening face. His hair was military-short and black. His eyebrows lay straight across those piercing blue eyes of his. He was good-looking and she could see a number of small scars here and there on his face and lean, hard jaw.

"You are a good patient," and he smiled a little, removing the cuff. He stowed all the blood-pressure apparatus away in his ruck and then took her pulse, his two index fingers gently on her inner wrist.

She saw him frown a little.

Sacha retrieved a small note pad and pen from his ruck, quickly writing down a bunch of scrawled notations. He grabbed a pair of latex gloves and snapped them on. "Now, I must examine your wound on your head?"

"Sure," she murmured, "go ahead." He was incredibly careful in his examination of her huge bump. He dripped some lidocaine into the area so that she would feel no pain from his examination. And when he discovered the crusted blood and a small cut, he quickly cleaned it up with gauze. He removed some stubborn stone fragments from beneath her scalp painlessly with a pair of tiny tweezers, deftly wielded. Amazed at his quickness, gentleness and skill, Sierra said, "You should be a doctor, Sacha."

"I try not to hurt anyone," he said, giving her a quick smile. Sitting back on his heels, he looked at her, becoming serious. "You are a level-three concussion patient, Sierra. What that means is that you have sustained a very serious blow to your head." He twisted a look up at Mace, his voice heavier. "You need to medevac her out of here."

"What?" Sierra stared at the Russian, stunned by his diagnosis. "But... I'm fine! I feel better! I'm not so dizzy anymore—"

"Sierra," the medic said gently, gripping her hand and squeezing it tenderly, "your pupils are not equal. That is a sign of possible brain damage. It could be the rock created a blood clot where you were struck. Just because you are feeling better doesn't mean you won't crash. And that is what worries me." His brow fell and he dug into her widening eyes. "You must receive help at a hospital, preferably with a neurologist who can assess your injury far better than I can. They can give you tests to confirm or deny a blood clot you might have received from that rock striking you."

Panic seized Sierra. She did NOT want to leave Mace and his team this soon! "But—"

"No," Sacha said firmly but gently, holding up his hand. He gave her a concerned look. "It is no accident I arrived here just now. If Mace allowed you to get up tomorrow and start trotting through that jungle again, you could do life-threatening harm yourself, Sierra. You need immediate medical assistance. I'm sorry, I know you're disappointed, but it's best you be taken out of this area as soon as Mace can arrange it."

Mace knelt. "This isn't up for discussion, Sierra."

She sat back, staring at them, disappointment clearly written in her expression.

"Sacha, do you know what Kushnir is planning to do next?" Mace asked.

"He has lost the trail on your two men and has called back his team." He shrugged, looking around the cave. "I need to get back, give him a call on my radio and report nothing suspicious in this area. I think he will go back to the caves in the Highlands. We have a Russian transport helo coming in," and he looked at his watch, "at dusk, to pick up the load of cocaine. He will want to be there in plenty of time to meet it."

Scowling, Mace said, "Then, that means we can't get Sierra out of here until tomorrow morning." He rubbed his jaw. "Can she stay until then?"

"Of course. It's just that she can't be too active. No running. Not trotting. She should not be carrying extra weight. Her blood pressure is high and so is her pulse. She needs calm and rest. How far is it to where your Black Hawk can pick her up tomorrow?"

"About five miles from here. It's an easy walk so long as I know Kushnir isn't going to be around."

Sacha nodded, putting the last of his supplies into his ruck and closing it. "Kushnir is going to remain in Caverna for the next two days. You should be safe to egress tomorrow morning."

"Yeah," he said. "Is there anything else I can do for Sierra until then?"

The medic smiled a little. "If she can eat, that would be good, but I suspect nausea comes and goes with her. Give her lots of fluids. And walk her out of here. You get to carry her ruck."

Sierra started to protest but Sacha shook his head and then smiled as he rose to his feet. "Sierra, you must tell Alex I miss him greatly. It is not the same without him down here in the Petrie Dish. Will you tell him that? That I look forward, someday, to seeing him again in person?" He pulled on his ruck, strapping it up.

"I will," Sierra promised, suddenly emotional. "Thank you, Sacha. I don't like your diagnosis, but I respect it."

He leaned down and placed a swift kiss on her creased brow. "Be safe, Sierra. Maybe someday, we will meet again." He turned, gripping Mace's offered hand. "YOU stay safe, too, eh?"

"Yeah, goes for both of us. Thanks for everything, Sacha."

Mace watched the Russian move swiftly toward the waterfall. In moments, he'd disappeared out of the cave and was gone. Mace turned and knelt by Sierra. He could see the disappointment in her eyes. And damned if Sacha wasn't right: her pupils were slightly unequal, one smaller than the other. "How are you doing?" he asked, reaching out, grazing her set jaw, seeing the rebellion in her green eyes.

"Pissed. I don't want it to end like this, Mace," and she choked back a sob.

Forcing himself to stop touching her, he said, "I'm glad as hell you're leaving, Sierra. I won't lie about it." He saw her eyes widen with surprise.

She said, "I was hoping we'd get a few more days together before I had to ship out."

He saw her wan cheeks flush with pink. Mace gave her a gentle look. "There's something between us, dammit. And I'd sure as hell like to find the time and space to explore it with you. But not here. Not now. You need medical help, and we'll get it for you in Cusco."

CHAPTER 14

S IERRA WANTED TO cry. Not a very professional thing to do under the circumstances.

Still hurting from the barbed sting of Mace's gruff admittance, she was struggling to stuff all the bitter disappointment back down inside herself. He'd gotten up and brought over another bottle of water for her to drink. Sitting down, he handed it to her, less than a foot from where she sat.

"You have nothing to be ashamed of, Sierra. People get injured out in the field all the time. It doesn't mean they were screw ups or did something wrong. You took out the HVT and completed your mission." He shook his head. "We're lucky more of us weren't wounded when that RPG went off."

She slaked her thirst and capped the bottle, holding it between her hands. "It's just a downer," she admitted quietly. "I guess I just didn't want it to end this way... so soon..."

"Welcome to the Green Hell. It eats up people for breakfast, Sierra. Things operate on the fly down here. The Russians and the Latin drug lords are as flexible and mobile as we are. It's always a game of who can catch the other first. You fulfilled your order with us. You helped us in a big way."

She twisted the bottle between her fingers, the beads of condensation on it cooling as they ran. "Thank God you have Sacha as an inside contact."

"He's been our best asset," Mace agreed. "He's a man of his word and he's playing a damned dangerous game now, with Kushnir."

"Sacha is so kind," she murmured, "like Alex and Nik are."

"Combat medic's personality," Mace agreed. He leaned down, catching her downcast gaze. "Do you feel like getting something into your stomach?"

"I can try. I know we have five miles to hump tomorrow morning."

"What I'm blown away by is the fact you made it from the top of that trail to here with that injury." He reached out, caressing her cheek. "You're one tough lady."

Sierra didn't feel tough at all. It felt as if someone had pulled the plug out from the bottom on her energy reservoir. She felt like a hollow puppet filled with sawdust instead of muscle and bone. He got up again. She watched him move away with that jaguar grace of his. She felt as if she were in free fall and that Mace's solid presence steadied her.

Solid. Steady. Blunt. A man of his word. And never had she felt his protection as fiercely as when she'd fallen asleep in his arms. Sierra remembered how safe, how loved, she'd felt within his embrace.

Love. There was that word again. And she wanted to cry because she knew Mace wasn't going to leave Peru. A man like him, once he gave his word, would have to die not to keep it. And it left her heart feeling empty and aching for him. He came back and sat down, an MRE in his hands.

"I thought you might be able to at least keep down the spiced apples from my Southwest beef and bean MRE." He looked up. "Interested?"

Touched by his thoughtfulness, she nodded. "Sounds good." She watched him start to pull the MRE apart, laying it out and choosing the packet of apples. "You're such a mother hen, Mace," and she gave him a soft smile as he met her gaze.

"You'd do the same for me if I was in the hurt locker."

"You're right," she admitted, hungrily sponging him in as he worked. Sierra felt a lump growing in her throat. She pushed the hair off her shoulder and blinked several times, trying to get her emotions under control. "Mace?"

"Yeah?" His head was down as he opened the packet of apples.

"Do you know when you might come stateside again?"

"Six months. I'll be back in June." He frowned, staring at her. "Why?"

"Where do you live?"

"North Carolina, near the base."

"Would you consider coming to visit me? Providing I'm home at that time?" She touched her head. "I don't know how long it's going to take to heal from this."

He scowled, his hands stilling over the packet. "Is that what you want?"

"Yes."

"I'm out here for nine months out of every year, Sierra."

"I got that." She opened her hand, sliding her fingers down the wet side of the water bottle. "Don't you feel it?"

"What?"

"Whatever's between us? Neither of us is blind, deaf or dumb. We're old enough to know if we're interested in the other person." She was afraid of rejection, but Sierra cared too much for him to remain silent. His face grew thoughtful. The hardness in his eyes softened as he regarded her. She felt her heart opening so wide that she wanted to draw in a deep, deep breath. If she didn't tell him now…

"I can't promise you anything, Sierra. You're not a woman who's into a few nights in a bed."

And that was all he was offering her after all this! Pain stabbed through her. Tearing her gaze from his, she stared down at the bottle. "I know you are not promising me anything." The words came out low, almost painful. She felt her heart collapse with anguish.

Mace opened the heated-up packet of stewed apples. He stuck the spoon in it and held it toward her. "Try and eat these?"

Tears stung her eyes, but she forced them back. The moment their fingers touched, she wanted to throw her arms around Mace and never let him go. There was something good and honest between them. "Thanks," she said, taking the container from him and picking up her utensil.

"Tell me about your cabin," he urged.

She spooned a bit of the apples spiced with cinnamon and sugar into her mouth. They tasted good. Her stomach growled in appreciation. Swallowing them, she said, "It's a two bedroom, two story cabin."

"What's it made out of?"

Glancing over, she saw Mace looked sad. She felt the same way. "Pine. It sits up on a hill surrounded with mostly oak, beech and other hardwood kinds of trees, plus a few Douglas fir. Since I bought it two years ago, I try to do some little things about the place, in between missions."

"Like what?"

"I want to build flower boxes beneath the windows on either side of the front door. The first year, I built a picket fence around it. And I put in a garden, but stupidly, I didn't enclose it in a high enough wire fence and the deer came in and ate everything." She saw him smile a little, a glitter in his gray eyes she couldn't translate. The ache in her heart was widening. If only... If only Mace wanted some other kind of life for himself apart from this one. Sierra didn't try and fool herself. He wasn't a man who could be tamed by a woman.

Even after marrying Ana Beth, he'd gone off to war. It was a part of him. She secretly wished that his need of home and hearth was stronger than the call of the military. There were men like him. She'd seen them often enough. The family came second. *Always*.

Why did it hurt her so much, then? She wasn't an idealist. She was a solid realist. Even with Jeb, she'd known what she'd been getting into. But they had dared to dream together and look what had happened.

She spooned more warm apples into her mouth. The tartness tasted good along with the sweetness.

"Yeah, deer will tear up a garden in a helluva hurry," Mace murmured, smiling a little. He folded his hands, watching her. "Did you build the cabin or was it there already?"

"No, I bought it. It was a shell. Some of the guys and girls from Shield Security helped me finish the inside of it. Some knew how to do dry wall, others wanted to paint, a couple of the guys were great at electric and plumbing."

"What does it look like inside, Sierra?"

His low voice vibrated through her, as if stroking her.

She licked her lips and finished off the apples. "Old fashioned." And then she gave him a half shrug. "Like me, I guess." Her words sounded so hollow to her. She wanted to cry.

Swallowing, she added, "It's like stepping back into the early-1900s. I've always loved that era. The lights are hurricane lamps. Only now, they have electric bulbs instead of kerosene in them. And I have red calico curtains at the front windows above the double sinks. I close them at night. I have an oak rocker I love to rock in. It's in the living room. There's an old-fashion couch made of dark-green velvet and mahogany. In fact, Lauren Parker, my friend, and sister sniper, found it at an old antique place in Alexandria." She smiled a little and forced herself to look over at Mace. The change in his expression was startling. There was no longer that hardness in the planes of his face. His mouth was relaxed, a faint smile tipping its corners. In that moment, he didn't look like a Special Forces warrior. He looked like a man who was happy.

"Do you have a claw foot tub in the bathroom?" he wondered.

"I do. A huge one. It's my favorite place. I love to soak in a hot tub of water when I get off an assignment. I have lacy white curtains with small white velvet polka dots on them over the large window. It's a big room, and there's a white sheepskin rug on the floor. I have a large shower in there as well. But I love my long soaks in the tub."

"Do you have a guest bedroom?"

"Yes. It has a queen-sized bed in it with a beautiful old quilt I bought from this amazing woman." She smiled a little, her voice becoming more animated. "You should see it, Mace. It's all velvet squares of different colors. I just love it so much. I had a pair of dark-blue velvet drapes made for the two windows in that room. I love to go in there and just run my hands across that fabric. It feels so luxurious."

"I think you're a haus frau at heart," he said, smiling a little with her.

"Home has always been important to me," she said, holding his gaze. "I love going home to visit my mom and dad."

"Is your mom's house old-fashion-looking too?"

She grinned. "Yeah. We're a little alike, aren't we?" She saw him shrug a little. There was warmth and something else in Mace's eyes now. As if... as if talking about her cabin, her home, meant something special to him. How could it? He had no home, really. Sierra wondered if he was cursed to wander the rest of his life, going from one op to another, never really setting down roots ever again. He'd lost everything. And so had she.

He nodded and reached over, taking the emptied packet from her fingers. "We are a bit alike, but there's nothing wrong with that. How're the apples sitting?"

A little amazed, she touched her stomach briefly. "Better, really. I feel a little stronger now."

"Well, let's see how they sit for a bit and if they stay down, then let's move you on to something more substantial?"

"I need to get my energy back," she agreed.

"Did you ever paint that picket fence around your house?"

Shaken, she blinked. "What? Oh, my fence and gate? Yes, I painted some of them white. Why?"

He slowly unwound and got to his feet. "Thought it might be white. It suits you, Sierra. I can see those flower boxes full of red, pink and white geraniums, too."

She watched him move to his ruck and tuck her emptied apple packet into a plastic bag and then close it. An ache grew into her throat. Sierra swore she saw longing, real need, in Mace's gray eyes. He'd mellowed out as she had talked about her cabin in the woods. The more she'd described it, the more the haunted look on his face had intensified, with sadness mixed in with what? Hope? Was it hope? For what? Sierra knew he wouldn't give her anything permanent. But she was willing to settle for what Mace might give her if it worked out. So many ifs. No promises. Nothing for sure. Just... possibilities.

Mace made the call to his CIA handler in Washington, D.C.

Tad Jorgensen sounded bummed out by the news that Sierra had been wounded, but ecstatic that she'd taken out the HVT. Tad said he would initiate a further call to Jack Driscoll at Shield Security. He went on to say that he would also contact the Night Stalker pilots at Cusco airport and get a helicopter up there for Sierra's medical condition ASAP. They had no official medevac helos in Peru. The country lacked the funds for such things. At times, Mace chaffed at third world countries, especially when it came to his people being wounded and in need of quick extraction.

He bitched to Jorgensen, leaned on him hard until, finally, the handler he knew as 'Tad' said he'd call the Air Force and get a C-130 Hercules transport cut loose to land at Cusco tomorrow by noon.

Well before that time, Sierra should already have been flown out of the Highlands on the upcoming helo and down to the hospital for examination.

The next sat phone call Mace made was to his two men. He filled them in and heard the real worry in their voices. Particularly Nate's, who insisted he be allowed to fly with Sierra on the Black Hawk, making sure she was taken to the Cusco hospital for a round of tests, including a vital MRI, well before she ever even boarded the C-130 that would be waiting at the airport for her. Nate would then release her to leave Peru.

Mace wanted to be the one who was with Sierra on the flight to Cusco. But he was the leader of the A-team, and he couldn't just leave his men behind.

By the time he got done with all the calls, the sun was setting over the jungle canopy in the west. He stood outside, near the other exfil point from the cave, the area deep and hidden. Although his informant Sacha had told him Kushnir was leaving the area, he never took anything for granted. Re-entering the cave, he looked forward to sitting down with Sierra once more. He saw that she was leaning against the rock wall, guzzling down water, which was a good sign to his medically trained eyes.

"What did you find out?" she asked, finishing off the water. She reached up as Mace handed her another bottle.

"It's all set," he told her. Sitting down on the blanket, leaving a few feet between them, he told her the schedule and pickup times. Her face glowed with hope when he said that Nate would be her big, bad guard dog. That he'd remain at her side at all times during the medical examinations and tests locked in to take place at the Cusco hospital.

"That's so nice of Nate," she murmured, touched.

Mace said, "Medics are like that. Fierce guard dogs, but very human. Even emotional at times."

"Like being emotional is a disease?" she replied with a bit of attitude evident.

He gave her a sour grin. "Sometimes…"

Sierra looked around the cave. "I don't want to go so soon. Not because of the mission and all that stuff. But because I've gotten to know the three of you."

"We'll miss you bugging us about playing Scrabble games with you," he teased, seeing laughter come to her green eyes. Sierra was perking up and Mace drew in an inner breath of relief. He didn't know if her concussion was serious or deadly. Pavlov had treated it seriously. She was so alive, so full of life that he felt like a beggar taking little bits from her when she wasn't looking. Mace wished he could give back to Sierra even a portion of what he was receiving from her.

She laughed softly. "Well, I know one thing for sure: I'll never bet when I play Scrabble with you," and she met his gaze.

His heart sprung open over the sight of that lush mouth of hers drawing into a full smile, her eyes sparkling. Sierra wore absolutely no makeup. Her natural beauty outshone any possible cosmetics she might use. "If I end up knocking on that cabin door of yours someday, are you going to *play me a game or two of Scrabble* with me, Chastain?"

"No way."

"Way."

Sierra chuckled. "You're not only a man of few words, but even when you speak them, there's a lot more behind them than most people would ever suspect."

"I warned you I had played Scrabble. Remember?"

"Yes, yes, you did, Kilmer. I guess I was very arrogant about my own Scrabble abilities and thought I could easily win a game against you. That's on me."

Mace rubbed his jaw, the stubble thick, soon to become an actual beard. After three months spent in the jungle, he looked more like a Neanderthal than a civilized man upon emerging out of the Green Hell.

All three of the crew looked rough and tumble when they arrived back in Cusco for their two weeks of R&R.

He said, "I like that you aren't too proud to admit you made a mistake."

"Oh," Sierra murmured wryly, "my parents believed in supporting me, building my confidence, but they had an invisible ax, and when I got too smart for my own good, they chopped me down to size in a hurry. Not in a mean way, but showing me that we all make mistakes, big and small." Tilting her head, she studied him. "Was your father a lot like you? Did you take after him?"

He tied his boot lace. "I suppose you could say that. My Dad is a dirt farmer. His own dad was before him. I grew up with a plow in my hands, the leather reins over around my shoulders, and two big-assed mules hauling me around that hundred-acre patch of red clay dirt," and Mace's expression softened as he remembered those times with fondness. "He was a man of few words, just like me."

"So that's why you laughed when I told you about the deer eating my garden like it was nature's buffet specifically grown for them?" she replied.

Mace met her warm smile. "Yeah, for sure."

"Maybe I can give you some pointers on what kind of fence you might want to think about putting up around your garden." he said.

Through a grin she couldn't help, Sierra said, "I'd like that."

"I'm hungry," he said, getting up. "Feel like trying a little more food?"

She nodded. The light was shifting in the cave. And the temperature was dropping. Every once in a while, she heard the rumbles of distant thunder booming somewhere over the jungle. Her heart wouldn't stop aching. She didn't want to leave Mace. She wanted to keep peeling away the ever deeper and deeper layers of him; how he thought and how he viewed the world. Rubbing her aching head, Sierra knew that, after she ate, she would tumble fast into badly needed sleep. This would be the last night she'd be able to spend with Mace. The last…

Sierra moaned.

Mace was lying on the blanket beside her, his rifle within a hand's reach next to his ruck. He insisted on sleeping next to Sierra for a lot of reasons. One of them, purely selfish. He'd given her the space age blanket, its shiny side down so as to radiate the heat of her body back into itself. He'd slept in his t-shirt and cammos, always leaving his boots on. Not sure of the time, he lifted the flap on his watch dial. It was 0200. Outside, he heard thunder crashing down nearby, overwhelming even the sound of the noisy but somehow musical waterfall. Sierra was restless. He was a light sleeper, came with the job, and every time she'd made a soft noise, any distressing sound, he'd snapped awake.

Turning over, she pushed the blanket off her. Flashes of lightning above the cave lit up its interior for brief, stuttering moments, refracted through the waterfall's turbulent curtain. She was sweaty, mumbling something, her arms tight around her belly, legs drawn up. A nightmare? More than likely.

Just as Mace was about to reach out and slide his hand across her shoulders to try and calm her, he saw the tears running down her cheeks. What the hell? Worried it might be a side effect of her head injury, he propped himself up on one elbow, reaching out, settling a hand on her shoulder. She sobbed, tucking her head downward, chin against her chest, almost rolling into a ball. WTF?!

"Sierra?" Mace called, his voice low, urgent. He gave her a slight shake.

"No!" she screamed.

Jerking upright, Mace froze, hearing her cry echo around the cave. His heart banged once to underscore the utter grief her heard in her voice. Afraid she'd scream again, not knowing who might be around to hear it, he moved closer to her, both hands on her shoulders. He stopped her rocking motion. Was she having a stroke? Hell, he didn't know. Now, Mace wished Nate or Sacha were here. They would know if it was her head injury doing this or not.

"Sierra!" he whispered near her ear. "Wake up!" and he gave her a strong-enough shake, but not so much as to damage her neck or injure her more than she already was. He heard her give a low, keening cry, like an animal that had been mortally wounded. And then, she stiffened.

"It's all right," he soothed roughly, "it's all right. Are you in pain? Is it your head?"

A partial sob caught in her throat, and she struggled upright. "Oh, God... oh, God..." she whimpered. Sierra pushed the loose hair away from her face, tears streaming down it. "Not now... not now... I'm so sorry, Mace..."

"Are you all right?" he gripped her shoulders. Another flash of lightning illuminated her face. It was frozen with grief, her eyes dark and large, tears spilling from them down over her cheeks. "It is your head?" he demanded, panic eating at him.

"N-no," she choked out, placing her hand against her mouth, knowing sound carried.

"Then what?" Mace asked thickly, his emotions unravelling. What the hell had scared her this badly? His heart was pounding with an unaccustomed urgency. He heard her moan and she crawled into his arms, seeking, finding him in the darkness. Surprised, his arms automatically swept her up against him. Her sobs drowned in his t-shirt, her fingers digging into his chest as she shook.

Confused, Mace didn't know what to do or say. He did the only thing he knew and that was to run his trembling hand across her shoulders and lightly caress her thick hair. As he skimmed her shoulders and upper back, her sobs lessened, and she began to relax. She felt good against him. For a moment, Mace closed his eyes, picturing them on that velvet quilt over her bed, holding her, kissing her, stretching her out beside him to love her.

All he wanted to do was kiss Sierra. Kiss her and feel how her lips felt beneath his mouth. She burrowed into him, between his legs, pressing herself against him, brow against his jaw. Mace could feel her warm tears wetting the material of his t-shirt, could hear her wincing inwardly with every soft hitch as she struggled not to cry. He knew all too well that, for the wounded, the nightmares often came.

She'd led a dangerous life as a sniper. PTSD came in many forms but, whatever its format, it was trauma and grief expressing itself in their sleeping world, making them revisit and relive the same thing over and over again. He wondered obliquely what her own trauma was about. He thought it might have to do with Jeb. It would make sense that it was.

Her scent, part sweat and part soap, entered his nostrils. He felt her lift her head away and he looked down. "Are you alright?" he asked, his voice low and filled with emotion. The next thing Mace knew, he was pressing small kisses across her hairline, along her temple, then tasting the salt of the tears on her smooth, high cheeks. He felt his control dissolving, his hunger surging for her. And then, the unthinkable happened.

She kissed him.

Mace groaned as her soft, wet lips slid hungrily against his. For a second, he froze. His whole body exploded with all the need he'd been forcing down deep within himself. Her mouth was opening, coaxing him to reciprocate, her breath ragged, tears tasted between their lips. Automatically, he held her more firmly, feeling her breasts fully against him. He curved his mouth gently against hers, not wanting to hurt Sierra, not wanting to scare the hell out of her with the animal need screaming through him. The last thing he wanted to do was drive her away. Frighten her. He felt her sob, the sound caught between their clinging mouths. He absorbed it, deepening his gradual exploration of her, feeling her go soft in his arms, feeling a quiver race through her as he cupped her face with his large hands, angling her to taste him even deeper. Wanting more. Asking for more.

CHAPTER 15

S IERRA DROWNED IN Mace's mouth as he caressed her lips. The nightmare that had held her in its grief-ridden depths dissolved beneath the slow exploration and building heat of his mouth worshipping hers. All her senses were honed in on Mace. She could feel his heart thudding against her own, crushed against him, glorying in the strength of his arms around her, holding her, responding to her need for physical connection with him. Her nostrils flared, drawing in his scent, the sweat and scent that was only him. His mouth skimmed her lips, tasting her. There was nothing urgent about his kisses. They were tender, asking her to participate as much or little as she wanted. Her tears stopped as she felt wrapped in the cocoon of his male strength and gentleness.

Never had she been kissed like this before! Closing her eyes, she sank fully into Mace, entrusting him with her life, entrusting him with her heart that was so torn and bleeding right now.

If she'd ever doubted Mace's intentions toward her, Sierra knew, without him even saying anything, that he was serious about her. His breath was moist and warm against her cheek, his mouth deepening their kiss, her own opening more to his request. A new ache took root in her heart. Everything about Mace was the opposite of Jeb. This man was boarded up, holding on to so much grief himself. But so was she. And when he carefully threaded his fingers through a few strands of her hair, she moaned softly, clinging to his lips, wanting more of him. Every touch he bestowed upon her was galvanizing, her body aching with its own special hunger and needs.

Reluctantly, Mace withdrew from her wet lips. She slowly opened her eyes, looking up at him. As more of the lightning strikes flashed nearby, she saw his eyes were hooded, piercing, as they watched her. Sierra saw heat and arousal in them, knew he wanted her. She desperately wanted him back. And she saw something else that shook her to her soul: there was love for her in his gleaming gray gaze. For her alone. Swallowing through her tightened throat, she reached up, sliding her fingertips against the hard line of his jaw. Sierra could feel Mace holding himself in check, felt the tension vibrating powerfully through him. Knew he wanted to love her. Here and now. It was such a wrong time for everything between them.

"Talk to me," Mace rasped, continuing to smooth her hair away from her face and shoulder. "What was that nightmare about?"

Her chest tightened. Sierra felt more tears gather in her eyes as she stared helplessly up at his dark, shadowed face. "I-I, Mace, I'm sorry. I didn't mean to wake you—"

"Hush," he growled, leaning down, kissing her brow. "Just talk to me, Sierra. What was it all about?"

An inner tremble went through her. Her lips tingled in the wake of his kiss. How badly she wanted more of this man who had turned out to be so amazingly gentle and understanding with her. Just to look at him, he seemed cold, hard and tough. No one would ever suspect Mace was a man with a tender heart in his chest. But he had one, and it gave Sierra the courage to speak about something she'd never given voice to before.

"W-when Jeb died in my arms on the MH-47 Night Stalker helo that picked us up, I must have screamed and cried for the hour it took us to fly into Bagram." She wiped her cheek with a trembling hand, grief serrating her. "I went with him as they wheeled him into the morgue. I was going to tell him good-bye there." She glanced up at Mace. His face was set, his gaze never leaving hers, his eyes alive with raw emotions. "I held him. I cried on his chest for so long. I don't remember how long. Finally, one of the women doctors who was there, gathered me up and walked me out. I-I was hysterical. I had lost Jeb. His blood was all over my hands. All over my chest and arms, but I didn't care... I didn't care..." and her voice grew hoarse.

"You loved him," Mace said in a low tone, cupping her jaw, looking deeply into her tearful eyes. "You were in shock. Anyone would be, Sweetheart."

His words flowed like healing hands through Sierra. She couldn't explain it, the catch in his deep voice, the softened look in his eyes. Mace felt her pain. Understood it as few ever would. "It wasn't over," she admitted in a strained voice.

"What do you mean?"

She closed her eyes and sank against his shoulder, her fingers curving around his thick neck. When his hand came to rest against the back of her head, she sobbed once. Tears squeezed from her eyes. "I-I've never told anyone about what happened except my folks. Only they know."

"Know what, Sierra? Talk to me. I'm here. I care. You know that."

Yes, she did she know that. Just the scent of him, his hand lightly caressing, following the waterfall-like cascade of hair that flowed down her back, gave her the courage she needed.

She said, "The forensic's doctor was walking me down the hall, toward the entrance doors. I-I had to go over to the Marine Corps headquarters there at Bagram and fill out a sit rep, situation report, on what happened. I was in shock; I couldn't see where I was going. She had her arm around my shoulders, guiding me, trying to help me."

She sniffed, wiping her eyes. Then she lay her head against his shoulder. Her voice became scratchy with tears that refused to stop.

"I was almost to the doors when suddenly, I had such horrible, painful cramps that I bent over and nearly fell. I gripped my arms to my belly and screamed in pain. I didn't know what was going on, only that I had stopped in the middle of the hall, bent double, feeling suddenly faint. If the doctor hadn't held me up, I'd have collapsed on the floor, Mace." More tears fell and she nuzzled into his shoulder, brow against his jaw. "I felt this hot rush of blood between my legs. At first, I thought I had been wounded and didn't know it. But then, as it gushed out of me, I realized I had been pregnant." Her voice lowered with grief. "And I didn't even know it. I didn't know it until I miscarried right there on the spot." She felt Mace groan and hold her a little tighter, his chin resting against her brow.

Sierra had to get it out of her. It was like a living thing twisting and roiling through her. It had always felt like that, but tonight, right now, it was worse. Painful. Filled with such grief and loss. "I-I remember collapsing to the floor. The w-woman doctor was shouting for help. She prevented me from face-planting, but then, the pain was so bad, I fainted. It was the last thing I remembered."

"I'm so sorry," was all Mace could utter. He held her tightly against him, his eyes shut.

"I woke up two hours later. They'd gotten an ambulance and taken me to Bagram ER. There was a woman ob-gyn who was there and took care of me. I lost a lot of blood and had to have a transfusion. I had a D and C. I woke up in such pain. She gave me pain meds through the IV and told me that I'd been three months along, that I'd been pregnant. With Jeb's baby..." and her voice trailed off. "In one night, I lost him and our baby. Even worse, I'd never known I was pregnant. Three months earlier, we'd been back for R&R in the states. Jeb always used a condom. I guess... I guess it broke..."

"I'm so sorry, Sweetheart," he rumbled near her ear. "So damn sorry for you..." and he pressed a kiss to her hair, holding her gently against him. "What happened then?"

It felt like the balloon of grief that always been within her had suddenly been punctured and deflated as she shared the story with Mace. Sierra had no explanation for it. Being in his arms, being cradled and held safe, held with love and care, must have given her the necessary courage to finally give the loss of her baby a voice. *Finally.* Mace, of all people, would understand.

Sierra sniffed and tried to wipe the tears away from her eyes. "I-I cried some more. I was a mess, Mace. The doctor gave me some anti-anxiety medication because I was hysterical. I remember very little after that. Just… blips… pieces. I got sent home on a C-5 two days after I was stabilized. I went back to Camp Pendleton, to the hospital there, got checked out and told I was fine. That my lab tests were normal, that I would be given a sick chit for two weeks in order to recover. In the meantime, Jeb's body was flown back on another C-5 to Joint Base Andrews. I called his parents. They knew how much we loved one another. I-I told them what h-happened, but not all the gory details. They wanted him buried at Arlington, so I met them there for the funeral. It—it was such a sad time for all of us, Mace."

"Did you ever tell them you were pregnant?"

"No… I couldn't. Why compound their grief, Mace? They were such a tight, loving family. We'd spent time with them every year. We'd come in for a visit to their farm in Tennessee. I knew them well. I just… couldn't… tell them."

He grunted and kissed her temple. "Some secrets will be buried with us."

Wasn't that the truth? Sierra whispered, "My nightmare was about the attack on our hide, Mace. I relived the whole shooting, Jeb dying in my arms on that helo racing to Bagram to try and save him, all over again. My miscarriage…"

"I understand. You've been through a lot in the last twenty-four hours, Sierra. When shit happens like this, the nightmares from our past get stirred up, too. The damned things rise to the surface. It sucks."

She managed a slender smile, nestled into his arms, never wanting to leave. Wanting to love him fully. But she couldn't. Not here. And she had a concussion and who knows what might happen if she *did* try to love him. Blood pressure went up, she knew that. And her brain was fragile at this point. Wanting to love Mace would have to wait.

"Even worse," she admitted thickly, "was that I didn't even know I was pregnant. So often, because of the stress of the job, I wouldn't have a period monthly. I'd sometimes skip months before having another one. So, I didn't think anything of it when one didn't come along on our last mission together. I'd never been pregnant before and I didn't know the signs…" and she shook her head, closing her eyes, absorbing Mace's strength, his care.

"Don't blame yourself," he growled. "You didn't know."

"Looking back on it," Sierra whispered, "I did have signs. I was more emotional than usual. Moody. And I felt different. But I was so focused on our mission… I just blew it all off. I didn't put it together." She dragged in a ragged sigh. "To this day, I wonder if I had put it together, if I'd realized I was pregnant, that I would have left the field immediately. I'd have gone stateside. Jeb might have had another partner. Or they might have moved him out of that area to a safer one—"

"Don't go there," Mace warned her heavily, stroking her hair and shoulders. "Don't do that to yourself, Sierra. You have to stay with what happened. All it does is continually tear you up at moments like this when the nightmare returns."

A violently harsh crack of thunder reverberated in through the cave entrance, beams from the momentary flash of its brilliant bolt painting waterfall shadows of tears down both their faces, mingling with the real ones. And then they were back in merciful darkness once again.

"You know the drill," she admitted, voice low with grief. "You understand."

"Yeah, I do. I can't tell you how many times I replayed Ana Beth's situation. In her case, she knew she was pregnant. The night's I spent wondering why the hell she didn't tell me…"

Squeezing her eyes shut, Sierra slid her arm around his shoulders, trying to hold him with her woman's strength, feeling his deep grief. "That had to be so hard on you, Mace."

"If I'd have known, I would have immediately pulled out of the field. I'd have come home to take care of her and the baby. She didn't even give me that choice."

Sierra heard the raw, unresolved grief in his voice, the tremble of emotions behind it, barely contained. Desperately, she wanted to ease his pain, but the two of them were so caught up in their own separate pain, that neither of them was likely to have happy endings. It had no kind of ending written at all. Their futures together just dangled out there, swaying back and forth in front of both of them from frayed threads.

"You can't go there either, Mace. You know that." Sierra said.

"Yeah," he breathed, "I know. But my heart, my emotions, don't. I just keep reliving it from different perspectives and angles. Asking myself how I could have made it different." He caressed her cheek. "She never trusted me. Not fully. I could never figure out why, Sierra. I never did anything to show Ana Beth that I wasn't loyal and totally in love with her. I was crazy in love with her for all those years. I never stopped feeling my love for her…"

Pain drifted through Sierra. Pain for Mace. For the unanswerable confusion she heard in his voice. She caressed his neck and shoulder. "Well, I trust you. Obviously," and she leaned back to look up into his rugged, hard face. His eyes glittered. Alive with raw emotions. Hers felt equally raw. "At least, Mace," she said quietly, holding his gaze, "I trusted you. You know things about me no one else ever will. That means something, doesn't it?" and she searched his eyes. They were filled with grief, with loss, with what might have been. As he swallowed hard and then gazed down at her, she saw the turmoil in his face recede and something else, something warming to her heart, take its place.

"Yeah, you trust me," he said, fingers moving across her brow, smoothing out the wrinkles. "You're fearless in that department, Sweetheart." His voice grew low. "Thank you for sharing that with me. I know you didn't have to," and he looked deep into her eyes.

Her throat stung with her tears for Mace. "I wanted to. I knew, somehow, if I ever told you, that of all the people on this earth, you'd understand." She saw him nod, close his eyes, and she felt wrapped in an intense, unnamable emotion as he gently squeezed her. She was torn-up, her head beginning to ache again, probably from all the tears she'd shed on Mace's t-shirt. Easing out of his arms, she touched the damp shirt stretched across his massive chest.

"I got you so wet."

He smiled a little, moving the thick strands of her hair back across her shoulder. "You can cry on me any time you want, Sweetheart. Any time. I'm here for you…"

Sierra forced herself not to cry the next morning as the Black Hawk came down. She gave Cale a quick hug of good-bye. And then she walked over to Mace, who stood so tall and rugged, alert for the enemy as the helo landed. The gusts of the rotor wash slapped at them. Nate had picked up her ruck and sniper rifle, already carrying them toward the opening door of the Hawk. She threw her arms around Mace's shoulder, kissing his bearded cheek.

"Come home to me," she whispered unsteadily, near his ear. "Any time…"

Mace hugged her tightly for a moment, and then released her.

Sierra stepped out of his arms, seeing a glitter of tears in his eyes. And then, in a blink, the tears were gone. That hard, unreadable game face of his was back in place. Would he come visit her six months down the line? Or not? Unsure of anything, she lifted her hand in farewell and turned, bowing her head to protect it from the debris kicked up by the blades. She was going home without the man that she'd fallen so helplessly in love with. It had just *happened*. She'd been committed to her life as a security contractor. Now… everything had changed.

Nate guided her into the helo. The physician was sitting in one of the two jump seats. He was a Peruvian medical doctor with short, black hair and brown eyes. He smiled a hello to Sierra as she came in with Nate's hand on her elbow, guiding her to the other seat bolted to the deck of the vibrating Hawk. The crew chief slid the door shut and locked it. Before Nate even got her harnessed into the seat, the two Army Night Stalker pilots had lifted the bird off and made a wide, swooping bank, heading back down the rocky cliffs, heading for Cusco.

Sierra caught one last glimpse of Mace out through the helo's narrow window. He stood, M-4 over one shoulder, his gaze following the bird as it banked and turned. Her heart thrashed wildly in her chest. An ache embraced her, and she closed her eyes, fighting back her emotions, fighting back the tears that wanted to fall.

Mace would stay behind in that green hell. He would find the next HVT on his team's hit-list. Despite the growing distance between them under the thundering rotors, she still saw the look in Mace's gray eyes that told her so, saw the undeniable commitment. And Kushnir could kill him... Nate and Cale, too, on any given day when the cards on the table turned against them. Now, she knew the dangerous dance they all played against one another. She pressed a hand to her heart. She couldn't even put on a helmet to protect her hearing because of the huge swollen bump on her head. Instead, Nate retrieved her a pair of safety earphones that fit easily over her head. They would guard her eardrums from the cacophony that was the shaking, roaring helicopter. Reaching out, she gripped Nate's hand.

He sat on the floor next to her. Close by. A guardian. And he looked up at her, his eyes so serious as he squeezed her hand in return, as if to silently tell her everything was going to be all right.

These A-teams that hunted in the jungles of Peru were brave men on a mission that no one back in the States would ever find out about. All heroes. All in such a deadly, daily game. Swallowing against a lump, Sierra closed her eyes. Six months. Six long, torturous months until Mace would be finished in this jungle. Would he and his men make it out or not? There was no way for Sierra to know. Now, she was scared for them. Scared because she cared for the whole bunch of them. Nate and Cal had become like brothers to her.

She worried about them, not herself. Soon enough, she'd be at the Cusco hospital. There, Nate would remain at her side at all times. He was a highly trained 18 Delta corpsman. He knew the tests, the procedures and, more importantly, he knew how to read the lab reports. Even better, he could talk medicalese with her doctors and then break it down into bite-sized chunks for her to understand. What lay ahead for her? Sierra found herself not concerned one way or another. Her heart was centered on Mace. On her worry for Nate and Cale. The only other time she'd felt this much out of control was when Jeb had died in her arms. And when she'd she miscarried. Those were special hells.

Lauren Parker-Kazak and her husband Alex Kazak met Sierra at Reagan International Airport. They waited outside the security area, hugging and holding her when she appeared. And she'd cried unashamedly as they bracketed her and walked her toward the trains that would take them to the baggage pickup area. Sierra was wearing light civilian clothes: jeans, a sweater, and her denim jacket. But in late January, the snow lay like a white blanket across the airport. Alex carried her gear as they walked out of the Baggage Claim. Lauren had brought a winter coat from Sierra's cabin. And a set of mittens and a bright-red knit hat for her head. Sierra was grateful for her friends doing so much for her as she put all the cold-weather gear on. They cared. The family atmosphere at Shield Security was one of the big reasons she'd gone with them instead of some other security company.

In the SUV, Sierra sat in the passenger seat while Lauren drove the car over recently plowed roads. The sun was shining overhead, the black asphalt gleaming with shimmering rivulets from the melting snow. It felt good to be home. But she ached for Mace. For his face. For his low, growling voice. For that wry smile that would sometimes tip up that corner of his mouth. And especially to see the hardness leave his eyes, see them turn warm with yearning—for her.

Alex leaned forward, his hand resting gently on Sierra's shoulder. "Tell us how you are doing?"

"I'm okay," she said. Touching her head briefly, she added, "There's a small blood clot in my brain. I don't really feel it. I feel fine. The Peruvian neurologist said that, in time, it would dissolve and go away on its own. I asked him how long and he just shrugged his shoulders. He said he didn't know. Sometimes, it takes up to a year or more."

Alex nodded. "Yes, that is true." He gave her a gentle look. "So, that means you are grounded, Sierra. No more ops for you. Too much activity, too high a blood pressure and it could influence that clot. You know that. Yes?"

Sierra loved the Ukrainian combat medic. She smiled a little. "I got it, believe me."

Lauren reached out and patted her thigh. "Jack is assigning you a desk job, Sierra. The guy is expanding so rapidly that he's hurting for in-house people who know the business. I know he's going to ask you to work in the mission planning section, with Cal Sinclaire. Do you think you'd be okay with that?" and she gave her a quick, concerned look.

"It sounds good," she said. "The neurologist said as long as I led a somewhat unexciting life for at least six months, that I could go to work and do normal things. Just not a lot of violent exercise or exertion, is all."

"He is correct," Alex said, patting her shoulder. "You must allow us to help you, Sierra. We live five miles from one another. If you need anything, you will call on us?"

"Yeah," Lauren said, giving Sierra a one-eyebrow-raised look as she drove. "No heavy lifting. You hear us? Ryan is already in touch with the best neurologist in our area. He's got a list waiting for you of do's and don't's. And you had BETTER ask for help. Okay?"

Sierra felt warmth fill her chest. "I promise, I'll be good. And yes, you're the closest to where I live. I'll ask for help. I promise."

"Even in grocery shopping," Alex reminded her with a scowl. "No lifting of sacks of groceries, Sierra. You will take me or Lauren with you. We will be your pack animals until you are well."

Tears burned in Sierra's eyes. She had always loved the people who worked at Shield. Sky and Cal, Alex and Lauren, were her closest friends. And she knew they would be there for her. "I'm all yours, guys," she teased, giving them a broken smile. "I'll behave, I promise."

Alex said, "Jack has an appointment set for you with Dr. Janice Ardmore tomorrow afternoon. He's giving me time off to drive you into downtown Alexandria, to make it. Are you okay with that?"

"I am, thank you." Sierra longed to be back at her cabin. Longed to have Mace there, waiting for her. But it wasn't to be. Already, she was fighting angst and worry for him and his team. Where was he at? How was he feeling? Was he missing her as much as she missed him? How safe were they? Was Kashnir hunting them down? The anxiety over their situation haunted her as nothing else ever had.

She folded her hands in her lap, feeling tiredness sweep through her. All she wanted right now was her warm cabin filled with her beloved antiques from the mid-eighteenth century. To lay down on that soft velvet quilt across her bed. And to sleep. And dream. Dream of Mace kissing her, his mouth so strong and yet so incredibly life-giving and gentle as it skimmed her lips. Her heart ached. Her soul cried out for him to be in her life.

As she opened her eyes, watching the snow-covered landscape, the snaking freeway heading toward the rural area outside of Alexandria in the distance, Sierra felt so torn. Would Mace even try to contact her? In three months, he'd have two weeks of R&R in Cusco. Would he try to email her? Skype or Zoom her? How badly she wanted all of that.

Even though Mace had a satellite phone, she knew it was for CIA and military use only. Yes, he had her cell phone number. But that meant nothing. Sierra expected not to hear from him until at least three months from now. Sometime in early April, if even then. She couldn't protect herself from her own heart where Mace was concerned. No longer did Sierra try to hide from what she already knew. She had fallen artlessly in love with Mace Kilmer, and there was no backing out of it. Now, all Sierra could do was wait. And hope.

CHAPTER 16

"WHY SO GLUM?" Lauren asked, coming into Sierra's small office at Shield Security. She had just come from the firing range, put her weapons in the armory and was about to go to lunch with her husband, Alex.

Raising her head, Sierra looked up from the paperwork spread across her maple desk. "Hi, Lauren. How'd range shooting go with the new women? With such springlike weather in March? They should have had some good shooting scores."

"You're right, the day is wonderful. Spring is here, but in Virginia, it comes early like this," she said, leaning against the doorframe, arms across her green sweater. "These gals are from three different countries, but damn, they do know how to shoot." She glanced out the door and down the hall. "Alex and I were going to eat down in the cafeteria." She looked at her watch. It was noon. "Aren't you hungry?"

Grimacing, Sierra said, "No... not really."

"You're pining away for Mace. Aren't you?"

Sierra could never keep much of anything from Lauren. She was the head of the sniper school here at Shield, and at times, she swore she could read minds. "Yeah, I am. I know it's stupid..."

"You love the guy," Lauren said, giving her a soft look.

"He never said the words. And neither did I."

"Wimps."

Grinning a little, Sierra always liked being in Lauren's brusque, non-diplomatic world. "We are." But there were reasons, and she wouldn't share them with anyone. Mace had entrusted her with his deepest wounds, and she would never give them away. It was a treasure he'd given her. And she was the safe it was locked away in.

"Come on," Lauren urged. "Oh, here's Alex." She gestured for Sierra to stand up. "You're going to eat, Girl. You've lost at least fifteen pounds in the last three months. What are you doing? Endlessly eating soup and crackers? Today, you're going to eat for real. Let's go..."

With a protesting groan, Sierra got up. She saw Alex's tall form at the door.

He was as tall as Mace, equally broad shouldered. She smiled to herself as Alex leaned down, kissing his wife on the temple, resting his hands on her shoulders. She pictured Mace doing the same with her. The ache in her heart never went away; just a quiet longing for him that was never fulfilled.

"Have you heard from Mace yet?" Alex asked.

Shaking her head, Sierra followed them out into the hall and locked the door behind her. "No. Not yet."

Lauren said, "Isn't he supposed to get R&R soon?"

"Yes."

"Don't worry," she soothed, patting Sierra's shoulder, "He'll call you from Cusco."

Sierra wished she was that sure. But she'd heard nothing. She hadn't expected to. Mace was chasing Kashnir and his team.

Following her pair of besties down the stairs to the small thirty-table cafeteria, she saw that the majority of Shield personnel were there, most already chowing down, some stragglers sliding their trays along the stainless-steel serving counter.

"Hmmm," Alex said, "I think I smell borscht soup! Perhaps our chef finally took pity upon me?" and he grinned wickedly at them.

Sierra knew Alex was a terror on Sandy the chef to expand the menu because at least a third of Shield employees came from all around the world. He knew how to sweet talk a woman, no question. Lauren picked out several items and set them on her tray as they walked their way down the line.

"And you're eating every last one of 'em, Chastain. No argument, "she said, pinning her with a dark look.

"I'll try."

Lauren snorted. Alex followed the two women as Lauren chose a table in the corner by a window. Outside, the sun was shining brightly. The level of noise was low as people ate with one another. Lauren had chosen a bowl of borscht, beet soup with cream, a beef sandwich filled with veggies, and a small dessert of chocolate pudding. Sierra knew she should eat more. During her three months inactivity, unable to go exercise, even jog on the indoor rubber course at Shield's extensive gym complex whenever the weather turned inclement, if felt as if she wasn't into living very much. Her heart, if she were honest, remained down in Peru. Mace still held it in his scarred hands.

"He'll call you," Lauren said, confident as she nibbled on some French fries.

Alex sat down between them. "If there is anything between you," he said, "Mace will be in contact with you as soon as he can. You know that, Sierra."

Yeah, she knew that, forcing herself to sip the delicious-tasting borscht. "I jump every time my phone rings at home."

Lauren gave her a sympathetic look. "If Mace is half the man you've described to us, he'll be in touch, Sierra. You have to have faith."

It was a Friday night and Sierra was depressed. As she sat in her rocker, a bowl of popcorn in her lap, watching one of her favorite TV programs, she had to force herself to keep nibbling at them... Lauren had now made it her mission in life to put the weight she'd lost back on, come hell or high water.

The first week of April had passed and there'd still been no call from Mace. She worried. All the time. It was hell being out of touch with someone she cared for. Who she loved. Sierra knew their R&R timing hinged on whatever was going on in the jungle. If Mace and his team were engaged, those two weeks of downtime were put off until later. Her mind chaffing, she munched on the salty, buttery popcorn. Lauren was weighing her, every Monday at work. And if she didn't at least inch up a pound weekly, Lauren wouldn't let her out of her sight in the cafeteria. She was constantly choosing the most fattening foods for Sierra now. Still, she loved her sniper sister dearly. Lauren cared.

The phone rang.

Sierra almost dropped the bowl of popcorn from her lap. Heart pounding, she picked the receiver up from the small wooden table next to her rocker.

"Hello?" She sounded breathless. Anxious.

"It's Mace. How are you doing?"

Sierra nearly laughed. He sounded like he was biting out the words, his gruff, usual self. "Mace! Are you alright? I'm fine." Her heart wouldn't stop pounding and she felt tears jam into her eyes. Choking them back, she asked, "Where are you? Cusco?"

"Yeah, we're here. Just got in last night."

"You sound so tired."

"The usual," he grunted. "How is your head? That blood clot? Is it going away?"

She smiled and closed her eyes, hanging onto his deep, rumbling voice. "I just saw the neurologist yesterday. She said it's ninety percent dissolved. Another couple of weeks, and it should be gone."

"That's good to hear. What have you been doing since I last saw you?"

She could hear the warmth in his voice, the relief that she was healing. Her heart amped up with silent hope. How badly she wanted to tell him that she loved him. Her fingers tightened around the receiver. Quickly, she filled him in.

"So, how do you like riding a desk?" he teased.

Smiling a little, she said, "It's okay. Better than I thought it would be. I'm good at mission planning, and with my extensive ops background and experience, I can add what I know to the mix. Make the missions safer for our people. It's a worthy goal."

"You sound happy."

Closing her eyes, Sierra's throat closed. "I'm... okay..." There was a long silence. She couldn't hear any noise in the background. Mace might be in a hotel in Cusco, away from downtown traffic.

"Are you taking care of yourself, Sierra?"

Wincing inwardly, she compressed her lips. "Well, it's been a huge change in my life. Lauren Parker, my girlfriend who works at Shield, Alex Kazak's wife, is harping on me to gain back the lost weight. She's now taken me on as a mission," and she forced a laugh she didn't feel. "What about you, Mace? Are you, Cale and Nate, okay?" She knew that what he did was top secret, and she was now out of the loop. He wouldn't be able to tell her much and Sierra knew it. Still, just little things made a difference to her, however. Mace must have heard the strain in her tone.

"Yeah, we're all fine. Nate got some foot rot, which pissed him off to no end. He's the medic and you'd think he'd be more watchful about keeping a dry pair of socks around and changing them more often, but he didn't."

"Poor Nate. Probably hurt his 18 Delta feelings. Huh?" and she smiled, feeling a little lighter. When Mace laughed, her heart swelled with love for him. He rarely laughed.

"Yeah, he's in his room here at the hotel drying out his white, wrinkled feet as I speak."

"And Cale? How is he?"

"Fine. So am I."

"Has it been hard since I left? I mean, trying to hunt down Kashnir?" She could feel Mace wrestling with what to tell her.

"We're still chasing the bastard."

"I hope Sacha is okay? Do you know if he is or not?"

"I saw him last week. He's good. He asked about you and I told him what Nate had said about your injury."

How badly Sierra wanted to speak of serious, personal things. "What are you calling on? A throw-away cell phone?" Because he couldn't use the sat phone for personal calls like this.

"Yeah, bought one in the pharmacy here in the hotel."

There was silence. Sierra felt like her chest was going to explode with so many things she wanted to share with Mace. "I was wondering about something. You said you would go back to North Carolina when your deployment was up. Do you have a house there? An apartment?"

"Nothing. When I return, I stay at the NCO barracks."

Her heart squeezed with pain. Mace had no home. Was that why he was so interested in her cabin? Her home? Setting the bowl of popcorn on the table, she said, "Since I'm limited to what I can do by my doctor, I asked her if I could do some wood working. Jack has an incredible carpentry area at Shield. When my doctor said I could do some hammering, sawing and nailing, I got hold of one of the security contractors who knows a lot about making things. I asked if he'd help teach me how to make flower boxes for my two front windows. You'd be proud of me, Mace. I not only cut my own planks, but I nailed them together. And I sanded them, stained them and now, they're ready to go once we get Spring around here."

"Sounds good. What kind of flowers are you going to put in them?"

She heard his voice relax. As if... as if sharing something so insignificant as flower boxes was a tiny piece of a home he no longer had. Mace was rootless. Aimless. There was nothing for him to come back to here in the States. "Well, I figure if you come visit me in June, you can help suggest the best kinds to put in them." Her heart thudded once to underscore her fear, that he was going to tell her he wasn't going to come for a visit. That whatever they had, was over. Again, there was a long, drawn-out silence.

Sierra swore she was still connected with Mace, could feel him, his moods, even though he rarely gave them words. She felt him now... felt him wrestling with all the unspoken emotions he was feeling. Why, oh why, couldn't he just be personal? Intimate? They had been on that level before. They'd shared their worst secrets back and forth between them.

"I'd like that, Sierra. I'm kind of a geranium guy. My mother loved them, had them planted everywhere when I was a kid."

She heard such yearning in his low voice. For what? A home? Someplace to go? Someplace where he was welcomed? To someone who wanted to see him? Throw their arms around his shoulders? It was painful to swallow, the tension thrumming through her. "Mace...I, this is so hard for me."

"What?"

Closing her eyes, Sierra whispered, "I miss you so much I ache. I can't think two thoughts without thinking of you. I worry its one-sided, that it's just me. I used to think I was a realistic person, logical and with a lot of common sense. But now..., now I feel like I've turned into some romantic idealist who is a dreamer, and my reality has shot out the window."

She held her breath, knowing she was blurting out how she really felt about him. How would Mace react? She feared it was one-sided. Her side only. That she had fallen in love with him, not the other way around. But his kiss... his kiss had been warm, life-infusing, breathing his breath into her lungs, lifting her, making her feel cherished. And loved.

A hand moving to her throat in worry, she could hear her heart beating in her ears, as if adrenaline were starting to flow into her bloodstream. She was that fearful. Threatened by harsh truth. Mace had to answer. He wouldn't avoid it, she knew that. Now, Sierra found herself anxious and sorry she'd said anything. It was impossible for her to keep up the social patter, to walk around the elephant in the room.

"A lot has happened in the last three months, and I don't want to talk about it over a phone, Sierra," he said gruffly.

Her terror amped up. "All right," she whispered, an ache in her voice. "I understand." But she didn't. She could feel Mace waffling over something important. Big. But what was it?

"Have you done anything else to your cabin since you returned?"

Her heart squeezed with such longing for him. If only Mace would give her even just a single breadcrumb of hope. One word. Just—something. But he was talking as if her honesty had been set on a shelf somewhere. Rubbing her brow, she said tonelessly, "I'm starting to get the guest bedroom fixed up. I chose a light lavender paint for it. Lauren and I went to an antique store in the city, and I found an old oak dresser that will go perfect in that room."

"What about curtains?"

She felt a trickle of warmth go through her heart. "I haven't figured that out yet. I have the velvet quilt in my master bedroom. I took it off the guest bedroom one because I love it so much, I love the wonderful texture of it, that I did it. I'm not sure what I want in the guest bedroom yet."

"What about something lacy and frilly? Wasn't lace a big thing mid-1800s?"

She was amazed at his knowledge. "Why… yes, I was thinking that direction. I have a Sears catalog from that era and I was looking at it the other day. Lauren knows a seamstress and she was saying the woman could choose the material I'd like and she could make a set for me based upon the illustrations from the catalog."

"Lauren sounds like a go-to woman. I'm glad she's your friend, Sierra."

Tears burned in her eyes. Mace couldn't know how much she was affected by being separated from him. He didn't want to talk serious stuff. Just keep it light. It was the last thing she wanted to do but Sierra knew operators couldn't go there. Especially since he was going back into that green hell in two weeks. Mace had to stay focused. Not worried about her. She tried to sound upbeat. "I think I'll drag Laura to a fabric store. They always have all kinds of lace there. Maybe I could somewhat match the lace to the illustration."

"There's a lot of lace made by the Q'ero Indians down here. Too bad we didn't think about that when you were with the team. The ladies sell it on the plazas of Cusco. Good stuff. All handmade."

Her heart rose with hope. "Why don't you snoop around for me? You have a computer at your disposal. Just Google that catalog and you'll see the lace." And then she teased, "That is, if you want to be seen buying lace," and she forced another laugh she didn't feel. Mace's laughter, however, was warm and deep. And she desperately needed that sound, needed him. If she could reach through the phone to touch him, she would have.

"That's a good idea. Think I'll drag Cale along with me. His mother's a helluva seamstress. He might know a little more about lace than I do."

Hope infused her. Mace wouldn't say something like that if he wasn't going to do it. "I'd like that—a lot." Her voice dropped. "Thank you, Mace."

"I wish I could do more for you, Sweetheart, but I can't."

Hope exploded through her. Every time he called her by that endearment, her heart flooded with such love for him it nearly made her speechless. Swallowing, she whispered, "I know…"

"Just keep getting better, Sierra. Okay? Listen to Lauren. Get your weight back. Eat."

A smile tugged at her mouth. "Now you're sounding like the mother hen you are, Kilmer."

"I want you a hundred percent healthy, Chastain. Got it?"

Her heart started thundering at the sudden emotion she heard barely withheld in his growling tone. "Yes, sir, Sergeant. I got it."

Mace sat in the chair of his hotel room, the burner phone in his hand. His brows moved downward as he wrestled with so many damned escaping emotions. Sierra's breathy laughter, her smoky voice, the feelings on her every word, made him ache for her in every possible way. Getting up, he turned the phone off. Dropping it on the carpet, he smashed it with the heel of his boot. They could never use a landline for any personal calls. Only these kinds of burner phones were available. And only one call. One time. He wanted to call Sierra back. Just to hear her talk. He could care less what she spoke about, he just needed that voice of hers, that rich tapestry of emotion that was a part of her, to come over the airwaves to feed him. He was starving without her.

Rubbing his chest, he leaned down, scooped up the pieces of the broken phone and put them in a plastic bag, stuffing it into his opened ruck on the bed. For the first time in three years, he wanted the hell out of here. He wanted to be with Sierra. To finish what they'd started. Running his fingers through his neck-length, recently washed hair, Mace scowled around the quiet room. His mind felt like a rabid animal running around inside his skull. If Sierra thought she couldn't think two thoughts without thinking of him, that meant she was always inside his head. The woman was like fog, stealing through his mind.

Mace saw her everywhere. Anywhere. He'd see something in the jungle and then instantly recall a conversation they'd had. And his mind was like a trap; he remembered everything.

Prowling around the room, he felt restless and unsettled. Before he'd met Sierra, coming to Cusco consisted of hot showers, a helluva lot of sleep, getting drunk on pisco sours, chowing down on the best Peruvian food they could find. And then the cycle repeated itself every day, without any changes.

It was so damned easy for him to close his eyes, and picture holding Sierra, feeling her soft breasts pressed to his chest, the smell of her, the texture of her hair, the velvet warmth of her flesh. Shaking his head, Mace wondered if he was going crazy. Maybe he had been down here too long. Been too far away from civilization. From things like lace curtains. Or Sierra's lean, beautiful body stretched out naked on that velvet quilt of hers. If she knew how many times a day he lapsed back into their short time together, she'd be shocked. But only when things were safe out in the jungle, did he allow those memories, those heart photographs he'd taken of her, to rise in front of him, to be cherished. To be loved.

Pacing, he felt alternately wanting to leap on a plane and head stateside to her, to wanting to run the exact opposite direction. He was scared in a way he never had been before and that was a mystery to Mace. What he felt terrified him. Hell, Kashnir terrified him. But he'd grown so used to that kind of fear it no longer had a hold over him, didn't stop him from doing his job out in the jungle.

Sierra… even her name was like the sweet whisper of a breeze through him. She was like her namesake mountains in California: tall, tough, beautiful, ever-changing with light and seasons. He sat on the edge of the bed, wondering what she was wearing right now. He'd wanted to ask her. To describe it in detail, so hungry to see her again. Any small piece of information he could build a visual on of her was like gold to Mace. His heart twinged as he replayed her sobbing against him, gripping his t-shirt, as if she was going to be swept away from him. Or maybe she was clinging to him because he was an oak in her storm, solid and steady. She had come to him; he hadn't pulled her into his arms.

Damn, the woman had a bigger set of balls on her than he did. She'd had the courage to crawl into his arms without asking. Because she'd known. Sierra had known he'd hold her, care for her, love her.

Hell.

Mace couldn't name a time when he felt so damned agitated inwardly, as if his heart was about to rip out of his chest if he couldn't at least hear Sierra's low, timbered voice. Just the tone of it tamed him, soothed him and he'd never told her that. He hadn't told her hardly anything. Except his heartache. And she'd sat there, her huge cypress-green eyes wide and glistening with unspilled tears as he'd told her everything. Sierra was unable to put on a game face. It wasn't in her. What you saw, you got. Mace could read her so damned easily. He'd seen her compassion, saw it in the way her lips had parted, heard it in her softened voice. He'd never told anyone about that time in his life. A few of his team members knew, but they were men and it got buried with them. No one knew the grief. The amount he carried.

Until Sierra had dropped into his life. She just had some magical way of loosening up every last, miserable, grief-stricken experience he'd ever had. That's all she knew about him though. The bad stuff. Nothing about his growing-up years, the fun things he and his brothers had done together. Or anything about his parents, who had doted upon them. Not once had he ever talked to her about something good that had happened in his life. And damn, he wanted to share that part of him with her, too.

Mace was miserable. He thought he knew what depression was. What grief was. But this pain in his chest had started the morning Sierra had left his arms and walked onto that Black Hawk bound for the Cusco hospital. He'd thought he had led a decent life. One that made a difference. But this sensation of loneliness cut so deep into him that he felt like he was invisibly hemorrhaging from the loss of her in his life. Sierra had lifted him. Had made him smile, which wasn't something he did often. She'd made him laugh, and he rarely found anything in his hard life to laugh about.

Sierra had struggled while she was with him. And he had too. He was still struggling. Somehow, she'd made peace with her past, or at least, it seemed so. She had openly admitted she wanted a relationship with him. What the hell could he give her? Three months of incredible, sheer joy? And then leave for nine months? Her not knowing if he would ever return? Leave her a widow? Cause her more pain and suffering. She'd suffered enough already with the loss of Jeb and their baby. Wasn't that enough?

A new kind of gutting sadness filtered through Mace as he sat there, mulling over his feelings about Sierra. When he'd called earlier, it was out of guilt. He'd already made up his mind to not visit her. Not leave her dangling, giving her false hope. Just walk away. Not give her more pain. More worry. Mace did not want to hurt this woman. She was special. She was artless, honest and didn't play games. And the moment he heard her voice on the phone, his prior decision to brush her off had exploded. What the hell was he going to do? What could he honestly offer her?

He'd made a promise to his dead brother, Caleb, so long ago, to take down those fucking drug murderers. He'd gone after the head of the snake: going into drug cartel country, their own back yard, and had killed his fair share of them over the years. It had given him brute satisfaction. Just one more bastard in the dirt who wasn't going to kill another innocent young person like his brother.

Somehow, Mace had to get his shit together, call Sierra back, and tell her he wasn't coming. That he couldn't. That he didn't DARE. Because he knew himself well enough to know that Sierra gently held his heart as no other woman ever had or would. And he'd want to stay with her forever. She didn't deserve to be hurt like that.

What did that make him? A damn coward, that's what. Mace could feel his heart tearing open, the pain of the almost literal feeling so profound that he placed his hand against his chest. Worse, he wanted to cry for what he could never have. Cry for Sierra because she was priceless to him and all he could ever give her was pain, grief and anxiety. Even if they were married, she'd end up a widow eventually. Mace was a realist. In his line of duty, he'd lasted longer than most. But his number would come up. Sooner or later, it would. He knew Sierra was falling in love with him and he wasn't going to put her through that trauma again. He'd suffered through it himself. And so had she. Mace wouldn't drag her through it a second time.

CHAPTER 17

M ACE COULDN'T DO it. He'd bought a burner phone the last day of their R&R in Cusco. Walking through the city in the morning, paying no attention to the tourists crowding every plaza, his heart was at war with his mind. Nate and Cale had both bitched that he was turning into a moody bastard on this trip. *No shit.* For the first time in his life, he was torn in making a decision that wasn't black or white. Sierra was a gray area. A no-mans'-land that he was completely unfamiliar with.

Every time he'd thought of calling her, he knew it would mean losing her. The very thought of that weight of loss felt like a sixteen-pound sledgehammer walloping him in the chest so hard that he could barely catch his breath. The anguish that came after the blow was overwhelming. Sierra made him want to live, dammit. Made him want to dream of other things. Like a house. A real home. A wife. Children. He was thirty years old. And he was only thinking within these parameters now?!

Plus, he didn't want to hurt her, dammit. She'd been honest with him every step of the way. He was the one pulling his punch. The one who was lying. Not telling her the whole truth, always hiding in a maze of partial truths. Mace had only felt this miserable once before: the day Ana Beth and their baby had died. In Cusco he had even gone into the local Catholic church for noontime mass, sitting in the back pew, just staring at the black Christ hanging on the cross at the front of the packed church. He felt a little like Him; pulled between two worlds. He'd borne his own fair share of crosses in his life. First, for his father, after his mother died of cancer when Mace was fourteen. And then another when Joseph ran away to Charleston at sixteen and got drawn into drug dealing. Sitting there, listening to the priest drone on in Latin, Mace felt the weight of the world pressing down on his shoulders. He'd grown up as a kid who'd been turned into a workhorse back in the times long before he could even remember. That's all he knew how to do: Carry burdens for others.

But he'd promised his father he'd avenge Caleb's death. Make a difference by drilling a hole in the hull of the drug shipments being smuggled into the USA. And he had, ever since the age of eighteen. Mace was tired. He could feel it seeping through every cell in his body. When Sierra had been with him, he'd felt alive for the first time since he could even remember. His love for Ana Beth had been a teenager's puppy-love. What he felt for Sierra was far more mature, much more intense, making him feel open to consider other branches of work.

That was a murky quicksand at best. He could become a security contractor, which is where most operators went after leaving the military. And he'd be right back into danger. And Sierra would worry. She'd become a widow, sure as hell.

Rubbing his face, Mace saw no way out. Only that he wanted out, but there was no clear path. No clean, down-and-dirty answer. Everything was... well... gray. As he got up in the middle of the church mass and walked out, he finally made his decision. He wouldn't call Sierra. Needing more time, Mace headed down the long flight of stairs from the building's arched doorway. Tomorrow morning, he and his team were going back into the jungle. And he had three more months to slog through on his deployment before he could do anything. Maybe, in the next three months, things would become clearer. He hoped so. He couldn't stand being stretched like this, feeling like he was being drawn and quartered. Emotionally, he was exhausted and there was no one he could talk to about any of this. His men needed to keep their focus on their quarry: Kushnir.

"Look out!"

Nate's sharp warning came too late for Mace to react. They were preparing to cross a stream around midday, up near the Highlands. He caught a flash of a six-foot-long snake, a Fer-de-lance, right by where his boot was coming down on the bank. The pit viper, one of the deadliest in both Central and South America, lunged at him, mouth wide open. He tried to twist away but the lightning strike of the venomous reptile's fangs sank deep into Mace's right boot. He felt the flash of pain as they pierced through the thick, wet leather and into his foot. *Son-of-a-bitch!*

Cale pulled his pistol, saw the snake coil away from Mace's boot, its attack done, and shot.

The Fer-de-lance's head separated from its twisting, writhing body.

Mace hit the ground hard, rolling. He heard Nate cursing. Heard him running toward him. Swiftly, Mace sat up, jerking off his ruck. Each of the men carried a vial of antivenin for Fer-de-lance bites on them at all times. The viper was everywhere down here and none of the A-teams went anywhere without those life-saving vials.

Cale cursed richly, racing to Mace's side. Time was of the essence. If they couldn't get the antivenin into him within the first twenty minutes, he could outright die. Cale hauled off his ruck, dug around in it for his vial, then thrust it into Mace's hand.

Nate dropped by his side, his medical ruck already open. He ripped his knife from its sheath, cutting through the laces of Mace's boot, hauling it off, then stripped his soggy sock off as well, throwing it aside.

Mace steadied his breathing. "I've got two doses of antivenins ready," he told Nate, watching the man's hands fly between his bleeding foot and his ruck. "Cale? Get that elastic wrap? I need it now." Standard operating procedure was for Nate to make crosswise slices into the two fang marks that were bleeding on the side of Mace's foot. He saw the medic draw a scalpel and tensed, knowing he'd feel the pain of the cuts. Nate worked fast and in moments, the cuts were bleeding. Hoping like hell the Fer-de-lance had already used its venom on some other animal, Mace sat up. His heart had to be above the venom bite, or he would go into shock and maybe into cardiac arrest. His two men were working fast, speaking low, knowing what was at stake here.

"Wrap him," Nate quietly told Cale. Nate grabbed the sat phone out of his ruck, making a call to the Night Stalkers in Lima. They were going to have to scramble *now*, and haul ass getting that Black Hawk up here. He told the sergeant at the other end what had happened in a low, calm voice. He knew it would do no good to go hysterical. That would only raise Mace's blood pressure and push the deadly venom through his bloodstream that much faster.

Cale wrapped the elastic bandage tightly just below Mace's knee, as a tourniquet. It would slow the venom's march through his body. Nate's brow knit as he concentrated.

"Cale," Nate said, only his equally furrowed brow betraying the calm in his voice, "get that antivenin into Mace's main artery at the bend in his elbow. Get the IV in first, and then stick the needle into the port after you have it going. Okay?

"Roger that." Cale got up, moving hurriedly around Mace.

Mace felt his foot swelling. He couldn't see it, but he sure as hell could feel it. The two huge fang marks were big ones, blood was running freely off his foot. He knew how much trouble he was in. Judging from the tension in his men's faces, they knew too. The Fer-De-Lance was the deadliest of all the jungle vipers down here. Most people died because they were caught too far out to get to a hospital in time.

"One antivenin shot into the port?" Cale snapped to Nate.

"Both! That's a fuckin' mother of a snake. Over six feet long! It has more venom than the smaller ones."

Mace knew that he was going to probably lose consciousness at some point soon. He also understood the effects of the viper's bite. It would destroy his red blood cells, dissolve the platelets which were key in clotting his blood and stopping him from hemorrhaging to death. And this huge viper's venom would surely do its job faster than usual.

"How you doing Mace?"

"Okay. Not going into shock yet. My foot feels like its swelling though."

Nate nodded, looking quickly at his watch. "You're gonna walk away from this."

"I'm not going anywhere." came back Mace's fading mutter.

Cale chuckled. "You're too fuckin' mean to die, Kilmer."

"Cale, get that IV going. Find my morphine. And an antibiotic," Nate told him in a low tone.

Mace knew what was coming. The first effect of the poison would be hellacious, mind-blowing pain. Nate would give him just enough morphine to take the edge off it so he could remain conscious and talk to him. The swelling no one could do anything about. Cale was digging like a madman through Nate's huge medical ruck. He hauled out the IV and attached it to a bag of saline. Every Special Forces operator knew basic EMT skills, and they all knew how to push an IV.

Cale knelt, pulling on fresh latex gloves. His hands trembled a little.

"Steady," Mace told him quietly. "It's all right." It wasn't. His mind was whirling with so many thoughts. Mostly of Sierra. Of the fact he might not ever see he again. He felt pain in his heart, and it wasn't a symptom of the venom. It was grief. Raw and hurting.

Cale slowed down, rubbed an alcohol swab over the hollow in the crook of Mace's elbow and quickly inserted the IV needle, taping it into place. He attached the bag of saline to the branch of a nearby bush above Mace's head. Grabbing the two antivenins, he stuck one and then the other syringe into the port. "How fast the drip, Nate?"

"Full bore. Open it all the way up. Get that antibiotic into him, too."

"Got it," Cale said, dropping syringes wherever they fell once finished with them.

"Any symptoms yet, Mace?" Nate asked.

"No." He saw the worry in Nate's sweaty face. Mace knew that it could take fifteen or more vials of antivenin to save someone who had been bitten by a Fer-de-lance. They only had three. His gut told him that wasn't going to be nearly enough. He needed a hospital now. Not two hours from now. And that was about how long it was going to take the Black Hawk to get up here. Worse, he worried about Kushnir and his team. Were they nearby? No one knew.

"How much morphine?" Cale demanded, holding up the bottle and poking a fresh syringe into it.

Nate told him, continuing his work.

Mace began to feel a little woozy and knew it was the morphine kicking in. Soon, his head would clear. He sat with his hands flat on the muddy earth behind him.

"Want me to make a sat phone call to the hospital in Cusco?" Mace asked the medic.

"No, I'll do it." Nate glanced over at Cale. "Take his blood pressure and pulse. Also, get the pulse oximeter out of my ruck. Stick it on his index finger. Read me what his oxygen level says?"

Cale got up, went around Mace, digging into the ruck some more. He put the small oxcimeter on Mace's large index finger. "Your fingers are dirty, Mace."

"You think?" he asked dryly, grinning over at Cale. The pulse-ox beeped, and Cale removed it. His brows went down. "Eighty five percent."

"Okay, he's starting to slide," Nate told him. "Get his blood pressure. And pulse."

Mace didn't feel anything yet. But he knew it was coming. And once the venom swam freely through his bloodstream, he knew it was going to be bad.

"190 over 60," Cale told the medic. "Pulse is bounding at 120 like cannonballs."

"Shit," Nate muttered, giving Mace a quick glance. "You look fine to me."

"I feel fine," Mace said calmly.

"It's going to hit you like a freight train," Cale growled, throwing the loops of the stethoscope back around his neck. "What else can I do, Nate?"

"Not all that much… Well, you could grab me the sat phone."

Cale instantly got to his feet and handed the phone over to Nate.

There wasn't much for Mace to do except stay calm and still. The more he bought into the hysteria that he was going to die of the venom, the quicker it would flood his body. He knew from the stats he had studied, that the venom was acting swiftly. But no surprise there. He listened to Nate call the nearest hospital, the one in Cusco, and heard him talking to the head of their ER, giving back all the information.

Nate was making sure they had enough antivenin on hand when they arrived by the Nightstalker helo. Mace was grateful that these men were his comrades in arms. They were damn well trained. They were focused, not panicking. They knew their business.

Mace started to feel his foot swell in earnest. He knew the venom took thirty minutes and they were at the twenty-minute mark. Yep, his foot was beginning to blow up like a balloon. Nate signed off on the sat phone. Mace wasn't one to ask favors from some deity, but he did find himself praying that the snake hadn't bitten into a major artery. If it had, he knew he'd die. He'd never make it to Cusco in time.

"Okay," Nate murmured, leaning over Cale, "I'll take over from here. You call the Army at the Lima airport. Get an ETA on that Hawk for me?"

"Hey," Mace said, "how's the shelf life on the antivenin? It's only good for ninety days."

"We're within limits," Nate told him. He put on yet another pair of latex gloves and quickly cleaned up the bloody area. "You're going to be fine, Mace. We've done everything in time. I just need you to stay relaxed."

Standard medical pablum, Mace knew, but he nodded and let Nate pretend it kept him calmer. Medics were funny people. Someone could be dying on them, but they would tell them they were fine. And Mace knew he wasn't fine.

Cale turned and said, "Fifty-five minutes ETA," to Nate.

Mace saw Nate's face tense, but he said nothing as he quickly wrapped Mace's swelling foot in loose gauze to protect it from further infection from the jungle Petrie dish. The longer it took to get him to a hospital, the less likely it was that he'd make it. This was the last thing Mace remembered.

Sierra had just finished her first cup of Saturday morning coffee when the phone rang. It was only six a.m. Who was calling at this hour? As she rushed to the phone on the wall of her kitchen, the late May sunrise was coloring the eastern sky a lush pink color outside. There was a Shield Security Memorial Day picnic on roster for this afternoon at a nearby park and she'd just been getting ready to make deviled eggs for all the staff who would be there. The sky was clear, and Spring had definitely sprung.

"Hello?"

"Sierra? This is Nate. I'm calling from Cusco."

"Nate?" she gasped. "What's wrong?" Her heartbeat tripled, her fingers closing tightly around the phone. Sierra stared blindly out the kitchen windows, not even seeing the deepening color of sunrise.

"Mace got bit by a Fer-de-lance viper in the jungle. I'm here at the Cusco hospital with him. Look, I'm sorry to land this on your doorstep, but he's in bad shape."

"Oh, God.... no...," and Sierra gripped the counter. Of all things that could have happened, it was a viper that had gotten to him. Not a bullet. "H-how is he?"

"Critical," Nate admitted heavily. "Listen, Cale and I are here with him. We're doing everything medically and humanly possible for him. The docs here know how to treat this viper's venom, but he got a shitload of it in his foot. The snake bit clean through his leather boot."

"What can I do?" she asked, her voice wobbling with terror. Mace could

NOT die! She felt pain gut her.

Nate said, "He told me before you left, that if anything happened to him? On his personal papers, you're his point of contact. Did you know he put you down as his POA, power of attorney?"

"What?"

"Yeah, right here. I'm looking at the papers right now because Cale and I have to set up an Air Force C-130 to pick him up and take him to the nearest hospital to where you live. That would be Joint Base Andrews, right?"

She heard the stress in Nate's voice. Blinking, stunned by the news, she stammered, "Yes... Andrews. Nate? When did this POA thing happen?" and she choked, emotion welling up through her.

"I don't know, Sierra. I mean... well, hell, Cale and I knew there was something between the two of you. You'd have to be blind not to see it. Mace never said anything about it, though. Neither of us knew he'd put you down as his POA until he told me to give you these papers if anything ever happened to him down here. I promised I'd let you know..."

Touching her brow, her heart tearing with anguish, Sierra whispered, "I didn't know about this at all, Nate... I'm sorry. Oh, God..." and tears jammed into her eyes, running down her drawn cheeks.

"I'm so sorry to drop all this on you," he apologized, his voice cracking with raw emotion. "But Mace has you down as next of kin and his POA. That means you're to make all decisions for him if he's incapacitated. From the military's view, you're his legal guardian if he can't make decisions for himself. And believe me, he can't make any of them right now. They have him in ICU right now and he's unconscious. They're afraid he's going to nosedive into a coma... and that's the worst sign possible... I'm so sorry..."

Urgency thrummed through her. "Then, what do I need to do?"

"There's a Colonel Jackson who's his commander out of the base in North Carolina where we're stationed whenever we're back stateside. He's going to be calling you to verify you are his POA. Just go along with him, Sierra. Tell him that yes, you're Mace's legal guardian, that you know you're his POA."

"But, what about his father? Hank Kilmer?"

"Mace doesn't have him on this contact form, Sierra. Only you. Are you up to this? I'm sorry I can't be up there to help you or explain this in more detail. I-I'm not sure he's going to pull through. You need to know that. He... uh... he became conscious for a few minutes in ER after we got him flown in here, and he asked for you. Said to contact you and I was to give you this info."

Staggered, Sierra forced her emotions away. "Should I fly into Cusco? To be with him?"

"No. We're going to know by the end of the next twenty-four hours whether he's going to pull through or not. They've already given him a platelet transfusion. He took a shitload of venom into him. The docs here are wanting to amputate his foot from the ankle down because of the severe tissue damage from the viper bite. I've been fighting with them on it all morning to stop it from happening. What I need from you is to talk to his primary physician here at the hospital. Tell him you do NOT authorize the amputation. I'm going to give you the doctor's fax number and you send him a copy of the POA, so he knows it's legal and he'll abide by your decision. Mace is tough. If anyone's going to pull through, he will. And he'll be damn well good and pissed off if they cut off his foot in his unconscious state. You can stop that now."

Shaken, Sierra tried to think coherently. She grabbed the small pad and pen she had hanging beneath the wall phone. "Can you have the doctor call me so I can talk with him and tell him I'm faxing the POA legal document?"

"Yeah, here's his name and numbers. I'm going to hunt the bastard down right now. In the meantime, take down my and Cale's cell phone numbers as well. These aren't burners, they're our personal phones. One of us will be in contact with you the minute anything changes. What I need from you is to know that if he stabilizes and gets out of ICU, they're flying him into Joint Base Andrews."

She was writing as fast as she could. "Okay, I got it. Do you know Alex Kazak? The ex-Spetsnaz combat medic? Mace knows him."

"Sure, we saved the guy's life."

"He lives five miles away from where I live. Alex was in Peru for years with Alexandrov's drug team. He knows tropical medicine, Nate. Should I call him? Get his help and guidance on this? I can call Jack Driscoll, owner of Shield Security. He can pull strings and make things happen where very few other people can."

"Get your ducks in a row up there," Nate advised. "Alex is perfect for this. A lot of doctors who don't know tropical medicine will screw Mace up if he survives this. Alex can be your medical advocate and can speak for you because you're the POA. Alex can be your eyes and ears on it, and he can interface with doctors directly who may not know Fer-De-Lance venom and what it does to a human being or how to properly treat it. He can actually help educate them. It will go better for Mace, if Alex is in the breach between the docs and him and yourself."

"Good," she whispered, closing her eyes. "I want to be there right now with him, Nate."

"I know. I'm sorry, but you can't. This happened so fast. No one was expecting it."

"Has his dad been called?"

"Yes, I talked to him earlier. He's fine with you taking care of Mace. I think, relieved, because he's got arthritis and can't move around much like he used to. Plus, he lives alone and doesn't know anything about medicine."

Nodding, her heart pounding, she said, "Then it's good that I'll take the responsibility for him. Give me his phone number?"

Nate gave it to her. He sounded exhausted and Sierra felt the full pressure on the 18 Delta medic through the strained, emotional tone of his voice. Thank God, Nate was there. If Mace made it out of this alive, it would be due to Nate's abilities as a medic. She said, "Listen, you need to rest, too. Call me the minute there is any change in Mace's condition?"

"You know I will."

Sierra hung up the phone, completely immune to the beauty of the sky turning gold and pink as the sun edged further up over the eastern horizon. She rested her hips against the kitchen counter, trying to think. Her love for Mace overwhelmed her. What had he done? What was he planning? He'd changed all his personnel records to say she was his POA? Had he been coming home in June to… What? To let her know? Wiping her face, she shook off all her wonderings over the possibilities. Right now, she had to wake up Lauren and Alex. It was six-thirty a.m. Her mind whirled with who to contact after talking with Alex. She knew Jack Driscoll had power behind-the-scenes, that he could move mountains via the CIA when necessary. He would be key in getting Mace transferred here as soon as humanly possible.

IF Mace made it. What if he didn't? Sierra pressed her hand against her chest above the light-green tee she wore, the pain almost too much to bear. She loved him. He had never said those words to her. Think! She had to think! She felt sorry for Nate and Cale. It must have been hell for them to see Mace get bit and go down. She knew they were like brothers to one another. Tight. Inseparable.

With shaking hands, she put all the new phone numbers in her cell phone's address book. Some relief shot through her as she picked up the wall phone to call the doctor in Cusco and stop them from wanting to amputate Mace's foot. As she waited for the phone to be picked up at the other end, she knew Alex had training in tropical medicine and venom protocols and drugs. He would be indispensable. Wiping her face, brushing the tears out of her eyes, Sierra fought to get herself together. She wasn't going to be able to help Mace if she broke down sobbing in terror.

CHAPTER 18

THE CALL FROM Nate came in the next morning to Sierra. Mace had passed the crisis point and he was going to live. She'd cried unashamedly on the phone, blubbering out her thanks to Nate, who sounded close to tears himself. Mace was still groggy, Nate told her. He tried to keep the medicalese to a minimum so that she would understand. Basically, the venom had taken down nearly all his platelets, which left him open to his whole-body hemorrhaging and bleeding out. The Cusco hospital had quickly demanded more platelet transfusion IVs flown in from Lima, and that had been the lifesaver. Sierra slid to the kitchen floor, her back against the cabinets, clutching her phone, sobbing. If Nate had any doubt she loved Mace, it was gone now. She couldn't talk directly to Mace because he was still in the ICU. He was sliding in and out of semi-consciousness, mumbling a lot, calling her name, Nate told her. Sierra cried harder, relief sweeping through her.

After that, things seemed to move at the speed of light. Sierra was so grateful for Alex and Lauren's support throughout the next two days. And somehow, Jack Driscoll had gotten Mace transferred to a nearby civilian hospital in Arlington, known for its tropical medicine department. Much to her relief, Sierra didn't ask who he'd called, what favors he'd pulled in, but Mace would be flown by C-130 into Joint Air Base Andrews and then a civilian ambulance would take him to the hospital.

Andrews was only a thirty-minute drive from her cabin. Alex rubbed his hands together, grinning like a fool, ecstatic over the developments. He had already been in touch with the doctors at the tropical unit and knew they had received Mace's lab reports from the Cusco hospital. Everyone was waiting for Mace to arrive.

Sierra could barely think at this point, sleep deprived, anxious and worried for him. The last call from Nate had come in as Mace was being moved from the Cusco hospital to the airport where the Air Force C-130 was waiting to fly him stateside. He would be monitored by an RN and paramedic.

The early June morning was crisp and clear as Sierra walked with Lauren and Alex into the red brick hospital rising eight stories high above them. Alex knew the medical system and had already found out where Mace would be taken. He would be assigned to the sixth floor where the tropical unit was located. He was getting a private room. Jack Driscoll had paid out some ungodly sum, Sierra knew, to make this all happen. All of Mace's medical bills would be covered by Shield Security. Not by the military, who would never authorize a civilian hospital for their own personnel. Sierra had never felt as grateful in her life as she was to the men and women of Shield. Mace wasn't one of them, but she was. And it was well known that Jack took care of his own. As he'd told Sierra many times before, they were a family. And family sticks together. Now, she was seeing the truth behind his words.

How badly Sierra wanted to meet Mace at the ER entrance as the ambulance drove in, but Alex cautioned her to remain in the waiting room on the sixth floor. He told her Mace would be exhausted from the flight. Maybe semiconscious. The doctors would want time with him once he arrived. There would be examinations, lab tests, blood pulled to assess his updated condition. And until his medical team felt he was stable, no one would be allowed in to see him. The waiting was excruciating for Sierra. She sat tensely in the 6th floor lounge, her hands gripped together in her lap, her heart running wild. How badly she wanted to see Mace. Touch him. Kiss him. Hold him. He'd nearly died. She'd nearly lost him before they'd even had a chance at any kind of relationship. Even now, she wasn't sure there even WAS a relationship. Just because Mace had put her down as his POA, didn't mean anything. It was always wait-and-see with him.

Mace was barely able to think or speak. The last nurse and doctor had left his private room. Late-afternoon sunlight shone in slats through the venetian blinds over the room's window. They had transferred him to this pale-blue room, gotten him into a clean gown, checked out his snake bite puncture, and created a tent over his feet to keep the sheets off it.

For Mace, it was good to hear English instead of Spanish. Given his condition, his mind still swimming in venom, he had a tough time translating Spanish to English. Nate had been there, standing guard dog duty for him. No one was going to cut off his foot. And after the team of U.S. doctors examined it, they agreed that the swollen appendage could be saved. But it was going to be a long road back, they warned him. Mace was fine with that. He would go through anything to keep his foot. They hooked him up to an IV, giving him the medications to continue to thwart the venom still inside his system.

His mind was still fogged, and he wasn't at all sure why he was at a civilian facility instead of a military hospital. Nate had talked urgently to him, but Mace had been groggy, unable to retain or remember much of anything. The only person he wanted to see was Sierra. Nate had promised when he arrived stateside, she would be there to see him. The doctor had told him that she and Alex and Lauren Kazak were in the visitors' lounge, anxious to see him. He was sitting up, his foot aching, but the pain was tolerable thanks to the morphine they could give him just enough of. Nate had told him how close he'd come to dying.

The door slowly opened. He looked up, seeing Sierra move quietly into his room. His heart thudded once to underscore his need for her. She had her hair down loose, a black, shining cloak over the cap sleeves of her light-green t-shirt. She looked anxious, her cypress-colored eyes wide with anxiety. Mace could see the exhaustion and strain in her face and understood the stress she too had been under. Sierra shut the door behind her. She looked good to him in a set of forest-green slacks that shouted of her long, long legs. If Mace had any doubts about whether he loved this woman, they were erased the moment she gave him that soft, tentative smile as she walked over to his bedside.

He was weak and had to force himself to lift his hand to hers. "Helluva way to meet up again," he rumbled, his voice still rough from the aftermath of the intubation tube they'd stuck down his throat back in Peru to keep him breathing. Sierra's fingers felt warm, woman-strong, as they curved gently around his, as if to protect him from the world he lived within.

Sierra nodded, her throat aching with the tears she didn't dare allow fall. She touched his shoulder, holding his gaze. "You're home, Mace...," and she leaned over him, placing her lips against the hard-set line of his mouth.

Every cell that was still alive in his ruptured body, every cell that hadn't been torn apart by the viper's venom, responded to her warm lips suddenly covering his. Mace groaned, weakly lifted his free hand, and settled it on her shoulder, his fingers tangling through her thick, clean hair. She smelled so good to him, a hint of fresh pine from her skin mixed with the orange scent lingering in her hair. The way her lush mouth covered his, the sweetness of her hello kiss, totaled Mace. He felt himself suddenly responding, coming to life once again. Sierra fed him a powerful sense of wanting to live, to believe in hope. Her hand sliding against his shoulder, his skin tightening, welcoming him home to her.

Home. How long had he not had one? Mace kissed her with all the strength he could muster, which was damn little. His body wasn't coordinated yet, nor was his shorting-out mind, both still in the throes of healing from the venom that had nearly killed him. Mace slid his fingers across the nape of Sierra's neck, angling her, wanting more of her mouth against his, wanting to love her with his body. It was nowhere near that point of recovery right now. But his heart was, and Mace felt such incredible gratitude toward Sierra for never giving up on him. Always there. Always someone he could count on, no matter what. As she gently drew away, her palm remaining pressed to his stubbled jaw, he saw the tears and the grief and worry for him in her eyes. And that once again punctuated why he felt so conflicted, so torn asunder over his want for Sierra. His want for what he knew could be so good between them. If they were together, she would look like this every time he left, never sure he would return. His fingers sliding through her clean hair as he did so, Mace released her. "You look beautiful," he rasped thickly, smiling weakly. "I'm glad you're here… thank you…"

Sierra sat on the edge of the bed, her hip against his, facing him, absorbing his roughened voice. "How are you doing?" She reached for his large hand, enclosing it with her smaller ones.

"Better now." Mace saw the angst reflected in her green eyes, saw the unsureness within them. How he wanted to tell her he loved her. The words almost tore out of his raw, burning throat. But what kind of life could he offer her? "I'm sorry to put you through this, Sierra." And he was. More than she would ever know.

"I'm so glad Nate called me from the hospital. Listen, you need to rest. You look so tired."

He heard the tremble in her smoky voice, saw the hurt he caused her. It took him down hard. "I've never felt this weak," Mace admitted gravely as he searched Sierra's strained expression.

"You look like hell warmed over." Sierra managed a thin smile. "All I want to do is get you to my cabin where I can cook for you, care for you, and help you regain your health, Mace. I just need to get the doctors here to release you sooner, not later."

Her grit stunned Mace. There might be tears in Sierra's eyes, she might be hurt by his inability to make a decision about them, but she had a steel-like stubborn streak inside her he was just beginning to fully see. "That sounds pretty damn good to me, Sweetheart. You don't have to do this, though. You do know that?" and he searched her darkening eyes. Even in his present state, Mace could feel the grief and joy entwined within Sierra. He knew she loved him. It was right out there in plain sight. And she too, was fighting back the words, the admittance. He'd given her no hope. He'd not given her a commitment. He couldn't, as much as he wanted to. Another kind of misery flooded him. Sierra had opened her heart to him and was now opening her home to him as well. Willing to sacrifice her time to help him through this.

"I WANT to do this for you, Mace. Look, you need to rest. Alex and Lauren wanted to see you. Are you okay with that? Or do you want them to visit at another time?"

"I'm not operational yet. Maybe later? Thank them for coming, though."

He held the green gaze of her eyes, saw love shining in them, gold in their depths, and felt his heart opening wide to her. "I guess you already know I put you down as my POA?"

"Nate told me," Sierra offered quietly. "It's all right, Mace." She reached out, sliding her hand down his hard jaw. "Right now, you need to rest. All I want is any part of you that you'll share with me. And I'm fine with however much or little that is. That's what this time apart from you has taught me." She swallowed, her eyes darkening.

Mace felt tears burning in his eyes. Ever since he had regained consciousness; he'd been so damned emotional. He'd nearly died. Exhaustion was stalking him. The plane flight had been stressful, taking him further down. His eyes started to droop closed even as he fought to keep them open, wanting to talk further with Sierra. Just to hear her voice. Like the starving beggar he was, he absorbed her every light, warm touch. He wanted so much more. He wanted to love her. But it wasn't going to happen.

Sierra slipped off the bed and pulled the covers up to his waist, smoothed out a few wrinkles in the blue gown across his broad shoulders. "You need to sleep, Mace. I'll let Alex and Lauren know. They'll understand." She pulled a cell phone from her purse and placed it on the bed stand so he could reach it. "This is a cell phone for you. I put all our phone numbers in there. If you need anything, call one of us?"

Mace felt the massive weight bearing down on his eyelids. He fought to stay awake, to absorb Sierra's face, those eyes that shined with so much hope for both of them. "Will you come back?"

"That's a promise, Kilmer. You're not getting rid of me anymore. Those days are over."

Sierra collapsed just outside the door. Pressing her palms against her face, she felt Lauren's hand slide across her shoulder. Looking up, Sierra saw her tall friend looking down, giving her a concerned look.

"Is he okay? Are you?"

Nodding jerkily, she whispered, "He looks awful, Lauren. Like death…," and she choked, pressing a hand against her mouth, trying not to cry.

"Come on," Lauren urged, effortlessly easing Sierra to her feet, and tucking her under her arm. "Let's go back to the lounge. Alex is waiting there for us." She patted Sierra's arm as they walked. "Mace is alive. And that's all that matters right now. Things will sort themselves out over time," she soothed.

Alex stood when they walked into the lounge. He opened his arms to Sierra, seeing the devastated look on her face, the shock. "Come here," he murmured. "You need to be held for a moment."

It was as if the world had been holding its breath and now the blast of its exhale suddenly avalanched down upon Sierra. The moment Alex's large, strong arms enclosed her, drawing her gently against his giant body, she released the backlog of tears she'd fought not to reveal to Mace. She hadn't cried until now, not since Nate had called her that morning to tell her Mace had been bitten. Alex spoke to her in awkward English, patting her back as if she were a scared child. Wasn't she? Yes. Scared of losing Mace. Scared of their unsure future. Loving him so much it hurt. Not knowing what he was going to do in the future. The last time in her life Sierra had felt so pulverized by so many disparate emotions was when Jeb had died in her arms.

Lauren offered her some tissues, gently placing them in her hand as Alex led her over to the red plastic couch where the couple sat down, seating Sierra between them.

Sierra shakily wiped her eyes, sniffling, and blowing her nose with the wads of tissues that Lauren continuously provided. Clutching another sodden bunch in her hand, her voice trembling, she told Alex, "He looks terrible. It scared me so much."

"Yes," Alex said, sympathetic, his arm around her shoulders, "his hematocrit is low, and he's had several platelet transfusions. He has gone through a special hell, Sierra. And Mace knows he could have died several times in the last five days. I am sure he is feeling as unsteady as you are feeling right now. But that will pass. While you were in with Mace, I got the lead doctor to give me his latest lab readings. His platelet count is now stabilizing, so the worst is over." Alex stroked her hair gently. "He is going to make it, Sierra. I promise you that."

"G-good, because he scared the hell out of me. He was so pale. Alex, his skin is almost translucent. His eyes looked so dark. He's so tired..."

Lauren sat close, her hand on Sierra's thigh, patting it, giving her comfort. "Alex said that viper is the worst of all of them. He said Mace has a long recovery in front of him. At least he'll be with you, Sierra. He won't be alone. He has a home with you."

Nodding, Sierra blew her nose again. "He said he'd come home with me. I have so many things to talk with him about, about us, what he wants, what I want... But he's so groggy. I'll table it all until he's better."

"That is wise," Alex offered. He smiled a little. "You need to make Borscht. Did you know red beets help build red blood cells in the body? You should make a big pot, have some sour cream on hand—"

"Alex," Lauren warned him gently, giving him a pleading look. "Sierra's in overwhelm. Not right now, okay?"

Contrite, Alex gave Sierra an apologetic look. "I will make Borscht for Mace. In fact, I have several strong, fortifying Ukrainian soups I will make for him, and we will drive them over to you. Is that all right?"

Grateful, Sierra nodded. "Thank you, Alex. I'd love that. You're such a life saver." And she gave them a warm look. "Both of you. I couldn't get through this without either of you."

"Mace will revive now," Alex predicted proudly. "He loves you. And you love him. A man in his shape just needs his woman around him. She infuses him with laughter, a smile, a touch, and he will get well much sooner than being anywhere else."

"You're a hopeless romantic, Alex," Sierra joked softly, loving the big medic. She was so glad Lauren and he had fallen in love. Lauren deserved someone as kind and good-hearted as Alex was.

"I know," he said, grinning broadly. "Just call me your teddy bear. Everyone needs one. I will bring you hearty, strong, good-tasting soups for the next several weeks until you tell me to stop. Mace will thrive on them. We can also cook for *you* if you would like?"

"No, I can cook. Jack's letting me work from home, which is nice, so I can be there for Mace."

"He needs you," Alex agreed somberly. "He is a man who has been alone for too long, he has thick walls he has hidden behind for far too long. But you will draw him out because you love him. And he will respond, Sierra. You are the best medicine he could have whether he knows it or not right now."

"I'm not so sure he loves me, Alex." Sierra gave them a sorrowful look. "It's the elephant in the room. Neither of us has said it to one another." She pressed her hand against her aching heart. "I just feel so much pain, so much unsureness."

Lauren nodded. "Listen, when Alex tried to get me to understand he loved me, I ran from him, Sierra. I was afraid of him for so many reasons. But he just kept being there for me in small, unthreatening ways. He was so patient with me." She looked over at her husband, love in her eyes for him. "Alex just tolerated my snarly moods, my harshness toward him and just took it."

"Because," Alex said, reaching across Sierra to caress his wife's cheek, "I loved you. I knew you were the woman I had been dreaming of all my life. You were the one." He smiled a little. "And when I finally realized why you were frightened of me, why you did not want me around, then I loved you even more. Because I knew I could love you as you deserved."

Lauren smiled softly at Alex. She looked at Sierra and held her tear-filled eyes. "Don't give up on Mace. Just be there for him. Even if he pushes you away, or gets snarly, or withdraws, just be there for him. Alex can be your sounding board on this. He went through it with me."

Sierra gave Alex a warm, grateful look. "I can use all the help I can get. I just feel like I'm on such thin ice with Mace. He's so locked-up. He won't talk to me. Won't tell me what's in his heart, how he really feels about me. I don't know how to get him to talk with me, Alex."

"It will take time," he soothed, patting her shoulder. "And I will tell you, as bad as his foot is, he is not going anywhere for six months. He is pretty much housebound. So, you will have him beneath your roof for a long time. And once he gets used to you being in his life on a daily basis, he will know what he has, Sierra. He will know the good feelings, your care, your love in large and small ways. Over time, you will dissolve those walls he has built. And the person it will be hard on is you." He patted her shoulder again. "But you have Lauren and I. We will be your witnesses. We will hold you when you want to cry. We will listen with our hearts. You will get through this. I know Mace might be locked up, but he is no fool. There is no man who can walk away from a woman he loves."

Miserably, Sierra whispered, "I hope you're right. I really do, Alex."

Lauren stood. "Come on, you two. Let's go home. Alex? You need to start making those fortifying soups for Mace. And I need to get a load of laundry in the washer."

Sierra rose and threw her arms around Lauren. "Thank you," she whispered. "For everything."

Alex came over and smiled down at them. "It is a beautiful summer day. We need to celebrate the good of what has happened." He rubbed his hands together and grinned. "Let us go home. I need to get that soup made for Mace. Borscht first. He needs all the iron from plants he can get so he can once more urge his body to build strong, healthy red blood cells."

Sierra followed them to the bank of elevators across from the nurses' desk. She paused, and then went over to thank the women behind it. They would be the ones caring for Mace. They knew she was his POA and seemed grateful when she gave them the two phone numbers she could be reached at if anything came up.

Outside, the sun was warm, the sky a deep blue with fluffy white clouds drifting across it above the city of Arlington. Hope filled her heart as she walked to the parking lot in back of the hospital. Mace was alive. He'd survived. Sierra was pretty sure she was still a bit in shock over the events that had tumbled wildly out of her control over the last five days.

Alex had his arm around his wife, kissing the top of her head. Sierra wanted so badly that Mace would have that same look of love in his face that Alex had in that moment for Lauren. They were so deeply in love with one another. Every time she saw them together, their love seemed even more profound than before. How Sierra wanted that same thing between Mace and herself.

But would he finally be honest with her? Would he let down, let her into his head? His thoughts? How he really felt toward her? Alex's words and calm buoyed her. She knew that he and Lauren had also endured a long haul with one another. Yet, he'd allowed his love for her to fuel his patience long enough to wait until she could realize his true feelings.

Would Mace be able to do that? Or not?

CHAPTER 19

S IERRA SAW THE discomfort in Mace's eyes as Cal Sinclaire ratchetted him in his wheelchair side to side up the steps to her cabin door. The June morning was warming up, the sky a pale blue above her as she waited patiently on the porch while Cal did the heavy lifting. He had visited Mace last week in the hospital, along with Sky. And today, because he was only slated to sit in on a mission planning at Shield Security later in the afternoon, Cal had volunteered to help her bring Mace out of the hospital. He'd stabilized enough and Sierra wasn't sure who was happier about it: her or Mace. Over the last seven days he'd been getting more and more restless as his strength had begun to return. He'd turned grumpy and short with her, but she understood he'd felt like a caged jaguar in that sterile hospital room, unable to get out and stalk around.

Now, his foot had healed sufficiently to be put in a soft cast up to just below his knee. What he didn't like at all was the fact he was going to have to rely on a walker for a vague number of weeks, depending upon how fast he healed. A man like him, a Special Forces operator, just did not want to be seen hobbling around with the help of a walker. Sierra was glad Alex would be coming by later today to check on Mace's foot. She had been diligently schooled by a nurse on how to clean his foot three times daily, the main worry being that the open fang wounds would invite in bacteria or virus, either of which could gain a foothold and prove deadly to Mace.

For the last two days, she'd been the one cleaning out his wounds beneath the nurse's guidance. She felt comfortable enough with the task but having Alex's eyes on the wound once a day for the next week, made her feel some relief, too. She didn't want to accidentally make Mace's injury worse.

Stepping inside, Sierra pointed back to the right side of the hall where the guest bedroom was located. The room was fully decorated, although she had no curtains up on the two windows yet, wanting lace of some sort, but hadn't had the time to look for just the right type. Luckily, they had venetian blinds over them. She carried Mace's new walker which folded up nicely for transport. Her heart opened as she saw his reaction upon entering her cabin. Maybe a little bit of wonder? It was very mid-1800s. And she thought she sensed some appreciation in Mace's roaming gaze as Cal wheeled him through the living room and down the hall.

Shutting the front door, Sierra put her purse and car keys on a desk nearby. She took off her baseball cap and hung it on a wooden peg above. Taking off her lightweight denim jacket, she smoothed out the sleeveless red muscle shirt she wore beneath. Jeans clad her legs. They were the daily wardrobe in the house because she was still doing so much work outside, getting the garden fence installed.

Walking into the guest bedroom, she watched as Mace hobbled out of the wheelchair on his good foot, keeping the other one in the air as he sat down on the edge of the queen-sized bed. Cal pushed the lightweight wheelchair over to an empty corner.

"Here's your new wheels," Sierra said, opening the walker and placing it where Mace could get a hold of it.

"Thanks," Mace grumped, glaring over at the wheelchair. "If I don't ever have to use that thing in the corner again, I'll be happy."

Cal Sinclaire wandered over, nodding. "Yeah, kinda hurts an operator's feelings to be reduced to a set of wheels and not his own two feet." He touched Mace on the shoulder of his dark blue t-shirt. "Give yourself some slack and keep pampering that foot. You'll get mobile sooner if you do, partner."

Sierra came over, bringing several pillows with her, placing a couple so that Mace could lean comfortably against the headboard, and sliding two more in beneath his knees. She stacked the last two at the end of the bed where he could prop up the injured foot so that it wasn't resting lower than his heart. Gravity always drew bodily fluids to the lowest point. Unless his foot were elevated, his blood would pool in it and it would swell up once more and Mace would go back through a hell of throbbing pain as a result. Getting the foot propped up was important. "Feel like resting a bit?" she asked him, keeping her voice light.

"Not really," Mace said, looking around. "I need to move."

Cal chuckled. "Spoken like a true operator. Can't sit still more than ten minutes in any given place." He looked over at Sierra. "Let Sky and I know if you need any help?"

Sierra hugged Cal. "I will. Thanks so much for helping us."

"Any time." Cal left the room and saw his way out.

Hearing the front door close, Sierra stood at the foot of the bed, sensing Mace's mood. "Feel good being out of that hospital?" she asked.

"Better believe it." He rested his back against the headboard and dutifully placed his foot up on the pillows.

"Any pain in the foot?"

"There's always pain." And then scowled. "I'm okay, Sierra. I don't want any pain pills."

"Your foot is looking a little red," she noted. "Probably because of all the movement."

"Well, it had better get used to it," Mace growled. "I'm through being bedbound. I'd give anything to be able to walk into a hot shower."

Her heart went out to him. All Mace could have was a nurse washing him down every day. She wanted to do it for him, finding her secret pleasure in touching him. Mace looked incredibly fit, the dark blue t-shirt almost looking too small for him, its fabric gripping his contours.

"Oh," she murmured, "Alex brought your duffle bag in," and she pointed to it in the corner of the room near the wheelchair. "It finally arrived yesterday."

Mace perked up. "Good." He sat up, looking at it intently. "I was wondering when the Army was going to get its act together and send it to me."

"Does the bed feel okay to you?" she wondered. It was a very firm mattress.

"Yeah, feels good, thank you."

Already, she could see Mace was in a better space and mood, no longer tied to that hospital bed. "What would you like? Are you hungry?"

"A real, homemade cup of coffee sounds damn good." He looked at the walker. "And I'd like to be able to check out your home. After you described your two-story cabin to me, I was looking forward to being out here."

"Well," she said wryly, pointing at the curtainless windows, "as you can see, I'm still not done with decorating this room."

He stared at the windows for a moment. "You never found that old-timey lace for them yet?"

Shaking her head, she said, "No, just didn't get the time to research it. Every time Lauren and I tried to get our schedules to agree, one of us wasn't available." She shrugged a little, holding his clear gray gaze. A sharply defined shadow accented his jawline. This morning, Mace had not allowed the nurse to shave him. He'd wanted to do it himself once he got to her cabin.

Sierra said, "I wasn't really in a hurry until all this happened to you. I'll try and find some curtains in the next week. I hate that the windows look naked without something around them."

"Well," he said, "don't worry about it."

"Coffee coming up. Do you want to try out your walker? Meet me out at the kitchen table?" Sierra knew how important it was to Mace to have some control over his life once again. When he looked up at her and she saw his eyes grow a little stormy, Sierra knew he was feeling a lot of unspoken emotions. Mace rarely, hardly ever, showed any of them. Except his irritability and frustration at being trussed up like a goose ready for a baking dish in that hospital bed. Even then, he had never lashed out at her. It spoke to his character.

"Yeah," he said, placing his large hand over one handle of the walker and pulling it closer. "No reason to feel like I'm stuck anymore."

She smiled and left the room, heading for the kitchen.

Mace hated the walker. But at least he was walking, hopping along on his good foot, keeping most of the weight off the other one. He liked the warmth of the large kitchen and the U-shaped counters surrounding it. The kitchen table was a small square affair at one end. Something twisted in his chest as he saw Sierra, her hair in a ponytail, making coffee. It was a common enough sight, but it still sent a powerful emotional wave through him. He had a plastic bag in one hand, and it kept slapping against his walker as he slowly made his way past her. Once at the table, he pulled out a chair. Placing the bag on the table, he sat down, hungrily sponging her in. She'd already positioned another chair for him with a pillow on it within strategic leg-length. He quickly lifted his bad foot with a grunt which turned quickly to a sigh as he lowered it gratefully onto the pillow.

"You have a nice place," he said. Mace saw her tip her gaze in his direction. Sierra wore no makeup. His gaze settled momentarily on her softly curved mouth, and it sent a sheet of unexpected heat down through his body. For the last seven days, climbing out of that venom haze, he hadn't felt sexual at all. Today, it was different; seeing her lean, proud torso encased in that red muscle shirt, showcasing her breasts, and those jeans outlining her flared hips and long legs, Mace felt his lower body awakening.

"Thanks," she murmured. "What's in the bag?" She poured them both coffee into two bright yellow ceramic mugs.

"Something I picked up for you in Peru," he said, taking the cup. It meant so much to Mace to have his strength returning. Now, he could even sip coffee, his hand solid and steady once more. Every day, he saw small but hopeful signs of his tough, hardened body coming back online. He watched her sit down at his elbow, bringing over the sugar bowl and spooning a couple of teaspoons into her own coffee. There was a small silver pitcher of cream and she poured some in.

He, however, liked his coffee strong, hot and black. As he sipped it, he gave her a satisfied growl. "Now, this is coffee," he muttered. "That shit they had in the hospital was anemic. They don't know how to make good coffee there."

Sierra smiled and stirred the sugar and cream into swirls in her black brew. "You like military coffee, Mace. It's so strong a spoon like this would stand at attention in the center of it."

Chuckling, he felt the tension begin to bleed out of him. He'd had some trepidation about coming to Sierra's home but now that he was here, he wondered why he had felt that way. The cabin was alight with morning sunshine through the many large, well-placed windows. He saw the red curtains she'd told him of, framing the large, wide windows on two sides of the kitchen. "You're right," he said. "Still, it's good coffee."

"That's a relief," she teased, sharing a warm smile with him.

"Are you working at home today?" he wondered.

"Yes. For the next week or two at least, until you get oriented around here. Know where the food is at and can start cooking for yourself."

Mace felt grateful. Her face was free of stress, her cypress-green eyes large and so damned readable. He ached for Sierra. There hadn't been a night that went by in the hospital where he didn't dream of her being at his side, embraced by him, her long, sleek body against his. "You might not have to spend a week babysitting me. I intend to be mobile. I'm not sitting in that guest bedroom all day."

She sipped her coffee. "I didn't think you would. But until those fang holes close up, you know you have to stay inside. Don't you dare go outside and get bacteria in them."

"I saw the red rocker swing you have on the porch," he noted, gesturing in that direction. "I'm sure the doc wouldn't mind if I go out there? What do you think? At least, I'll be outside."

Mace didn't like being housebound. Sierra couldn't blame him. Since age eighteen, he'd challenged the elements and weather. "Give it a couple of days?"

He grimaced. "For you, I will." He reached for the green plastic sack. "Here, I was going to bring these to you when I left the field in June. I hope you like them."

Touched that he'd bought her something, she set her coffee aside. Pulling the sack over, she opened it up. Inside there was a largish bundle wrapped in brown paper and string. Pulling it out, she asked, "What did you get me?" She saw amusement and eagerness in Mace's eyes.

"Hey, you're talking to an operator," he teased. "I'm not telling. Go ahead, open it up." His pulse sped up. Would Sierra like the gift? Mace found himself worried she wouldn't. She delicately untied the string and pulled it off the large, bulky package. He wanted to please her. Make her happy. He had hurt her a lot of ways in the past and now, maybe this gift would be a small token of how much he cared for her. He held his breath momentarily as she carefully opened the brown paper wrapping. Mace saw her eyes widen with surprise.

"Oh, my, Mace!" she whispered excitedly, "my lace curtains!"

He felt heat tunnel through him as color rushed to her cheeks, her green eyes shining with such joy as she lifted one of the handmade curtains up to view it more closely.

"I found that lace pattern online," he told her, his voice suddenly tight. The look of joy on Sierra's face was one he wanted to photograph forever in his heart. She was completely surprised.

"I knew an old Q'ero woman who makes lace and sells it on one of Cusco's main plazas," he admitted sheepishly. "I took the pattern to her and asked her to make two sets of curtains for you." He felt a lump in his throat as he saw her face crumple with gratitude. "Do you like them? Do you think they'll be okay for that room?"

Making a soft sound, Sierra placed the curtain aside, rose and slid her arms around his shoulders, giving him a hug. "Oh, thank you, Mace! This is so thoughtful... I mean," she gushed, releasing him and touching the lace curtains, "...you are so incredibly thoughtful...," and she sniffed, wiping tears from her eyes.

Her tears tore him up and the skin across his shoulders still sizzled from her unexpected hug. How he'd wanted to turn and meet her mouth. Kiss her senseless. Take her to his bed. Love her. Hear soft, satisfied sounds in her slender throat as he pleased her. All of it had been there, hanging before him. It was surely not possible. His gut tightened. Yet, making Sierra happy even just this once stripped him of another thin layer of doubt. Just seeing the sparkle dancing in her eyes, her excitement as she lifted the curtains, making small sounds of awe and pleasure as she turned them over and ran her fingers lightly across the fine lace. It made Mace smile.

"I haven't done much to make you very happy," he admitted, his voice apologetic with barely held emotions. "When you told me about those curtains over that phone call, the excitement in your voice, I wanted to do something special for you, Sierra." The soft look she gave him damn near totaled him. It was filled with such love for him, and for him alone. He felt like such a coward in comparison to Sierra. She was laying it out in front of him. Never saying the words. But he saw her heart in her eyes, in the sudden grateful expression she shared with him. Her fingers were never still, touching the lace delicately, admiring it, murmuring as she smoothed her hand along its surface. How Mace wished she would do that to him. But then, it was him that had placed the wall between them, wasn't it?

"I-this is so...," she choked, giving him a warm look as she quickly brushed the tears from her eyes, "...so wonderful, Mace. They're perfect! The woman who did this is amazing! I'm just at a loss for words..."

His heart swelled with love for this woman who bravely wore her emotions without apology. Sierra knew no other way and he was like a seedy little beggar in the radiance of her happiness, lapping up her joy, starved for it. Starved for her.

"You think they'll do?" he managed, his voice low and tight with all the feelings that wanted to escape.

"Oh, yes," Sierra laughed. "They're just perfect! I'd hate to think of the cost, though. The lacework on these curtains is just incredible, Mace."

"You're worth it," he said gruffly, unable to hold the luminosity in her green eyes. He knew, somehow, that Sierra would come to him if he let her. If he opened his arms to her, she would walk into them. If he wanted to kiss her, he knew she would eagerly kiss him in return. To say he felt like the worst of men was an understatement. Why couldn't he just spend the time here with her? Bed her? Love her? And then walk away? Mace didn't have those answers yet. Maybe because Sierra was so artless, so damned emotionally honest with him, that he sought ways not to hurt her further. And hurt her, he had. Unable to give her what she really wanted. Maybe he was better off in the hospital. It wouldn't remind him of all the things that couldn't be. Rubbing his gut, he felt like there was a nest of snakes writhing in there every time he saw the hidden pain in Sierra's eyes. The longing she had for him. The yearning for something they both wanted.

But he stood in the way. The promise he'd given his devastated father after Caleb had died at age twelve had changed the trajectory of his life. And then, his mother had suddenly died when he was fourteen. The dual losses had buckled his father. Had broken him under their weight. And the only thing that had ever seemed to bring his father back to him, through all those years of hardship and grief, was his promise to go into the Army and seek revenge for his family's sake.

And he'd done that for fourteen years now. Looking at Sierra, watching her graceful hands fly lovingly across the lace, he had never felt so desperate, so unhappy and alone. All Mace really wanted was to ask Sierra to live with him forever. But, closing his eyes for a moment, Mace couldn't see a way to make that happen. He just couldn't, not matter how desperately he wanted it to be so.

"I'm going to hang these up in your bedroom right now!" she said, standing. Gathering them up in her arms, she smiled over at him. "I already have the curtain rods. I HAVE to see these hanging up, Mace! I'll be back in a few minutes."

Mace gave her a nod, absorbing her excitement as she rushed out of the kitchen, the lace curtains gathered carefully in her arms. The sweet sway of her hips, those long legs of hers, just made him awaken further and want her even more. Looking up, he saw the blue sky out the windows. She had cracked them open over the kitchen sinks and he could hear the calls and singing of birds outside the cabin through the gaps. He wanted to do more for her. He'd do anything to see again and again the look that had been on Sierra's face from the moment she realized he'd brought her those lace curtains. All he wanted to do was to make her happy. Hear her laugh. See that wide smile of hers. Why couldn't life be simple? Why did it have to be so damned convoluted and twisted like some Gordian Knot that he could never untie or release?

He decided to get up. Mace needed to see her put up those curtains in his bedroom. Grabbing the hated walker, he pushed upright. His injured foot had a dressing with a sock over it for protection, and then encased in soft foam boot held in place with Velcro straps. Making his way a lot slower than he wanted, he finally arrived at the door to the bedroom. Sierra was just finishing up. The glow on her face made heat flash directly down to his lower body. She turned, realizing he was standing there.

"Look!" she said, laughing. "Look how beautiful they are, Mace!" She climbed down off the wooden chair and set it back in the corner.

"They look really nice," he murmured, thinking that the curtains really did make the room complete its mid-1800s feel. Sierra had an unerring eye for what went well design-wise, there was no question. But she was a sniper and possessed an eye for detail few people would ever have. He saw her smiling as she walked quickly toward him. Mace was completely unprepared when she halted in front of his walker, threw her arms around him and pressed herself against him, her lips finding his.

His whole world exploded as her mouth slid warmly against his. He hadn't been expecting this: the lush heat of her skimming and rocking his lips open, cajoling him, wanting him to kiss her as eagerly in return as she was kissing him. All his walls dissolved in an instant and he slid his arm around her shoulders, drawing her against him, the walker standing as one last barrier between them. Mace sank into the welcome heat of her mouth, her soft curves bending against the wedges of his hard, unforgiving male body.

His nostrils flared as he took in the faint scent of oranges in her sleek, silky hair brushing against his jaw and temple. Mace was surprised by Sierra's boldness as she opened her mouth more, her tongue slowly moving across his lower lip. Groaning, his arm automatically tightened around her. And all he heard was her sigh of satisfaction as she teased his tongue in return. His whole lower body roared to life and a throbbing ache gripped his hard erection. She couldn't press herself against him, the metal walker in the way, but he felt her sinuous heat, anyway. There was nothing but radiant life in his woman he held in his free arm. As her tongue moved more deeply, inviting his to meet hers, he felt the rapid beat of his heart. There was no way she didn't know how much he wanted her.

His breath was rough and ragged as he slid his hand up her spine, gripping her around the back of her neck, adjusting her mouth to his so they fit even better together. He wished like hell he had two hands free, but he had to lean against the walker, keep his balance, keep most of his weight off his injured, throbbing foot. He heard a soft, vibrating sound in Sierra's throat as she kissed him deeply. She wanted him as bad as he wanted her. Mace cursed his wound because, under any other circumstance, he'd have picked Sierra up, taken her to his bed and stripped her of her clothes and they'd have become as one with all the urgency of two animals ensnared in mating heat.

Her long, slender fingers framed his face, moving across his scalp, feeling him, memorizing him. Her hands were restless, touching him, his flesh heating wherever they skimmed his neck and shoulders. And then, when her hand drifted down the side of his ribs, caressing his hip and moving provocatively against his erection, Mace gave a low warning growl. His body grew hot and hungry. He was losing his control beneath her soft, curious exploration of him. The sounds she made told him how pleased she was with him, regardless of his wound. Regardless of how hampered he was right now. There was nothing wrong with him sexually, that was for damn sure. Sierra's heat could resurrect a rock. Her fingers tantalized his erection, teasing him. She was silently asking him to take her, love her. Right now. And how Mace wanted it even more. He could only explore her with his one free hand, and it frustrated the hell out of him. The walker remained a wall between them. He wanted to experience her sinuous movements, that soft sway of her hips against his, inflaming him to a point where he was damn near mindless. As her hand slid across the nape of his neck, she nipped his lower lip, opening her eyes, a hungry gleam in them.

"I'm going to love you, Mace," she whispered, her voice low and smoky. And she tilted her head, studying him, strong and unwavering in her request.

He was too far gone. Wanting Sierra for too long. Giving a jerky nod, he released her.

"My bedroom," she urged him softly, stepping aside. "I've been dreaming of loving you on my beautiful velvet patchwork quilt for so long…"

CHAPTER 20

M ACE HAD ALWAYS been the alpha male when it came to sex, but now he felt he may just become the weaker participant. As Sierra guided him into her room, he was taken by the dreamy quality of it. He was aching for her, having had still but a bare taste of her, and now she was guiding him to sit on the bed, kneeling down, removing his sneaker and pulling off the sock under it. Her black hair glinted with reddish highlights under the muted western light pouring into her bedroom. Mesmerized by the gracefulness of her fingers as she untied the laces, Mace felt his whole body ratchet up one more painful knot for her. How long had he dreamed of being with Sierra? Feeling her warmth? Her arms holding him, her body moving in sync with him? He swallowed hard, seeing so much.

He slid his hands beneath her jaw, lifting it so their eyes met. He saw arousal in them, and it spurred his appetite for her even more. There was a fearlessness in them, the look of a woman clearly wanting her man and not taking no for an answer. And yet, Mace didn't feel weaker than she was. For the first time in his life, he realized he was meeting a woman who was fully his equal in every possible way. And Sierra was furlongs ahead of him when it came to being emotionally courageous. To be risky enough to love him despite the nothingness he'd given back. He dug into her wide, lustrous eyes. "Are you SURE, Sierra?" He watched her lips lift into a smile.

"Never more so, Mace." she slid her hands across his knees, searching his face, his eyes.

His throat tightened. "I can't offer you anything, Sierra. You know that."

As she shrugged, her fingers busy with the snap of his jeans, then pulling down his zipper she said, "I'll take whatever you'll give me Mace." She stood, reaching out, caressing his hair. "I don't have any condoms around here. It's been almost two years so I'm a little rusty. And in case you want to know, I'm disease-free."

Such courage. She stood there like the warrior queen she was. Mace held her confident gaze, drowning in the fire he saw in her eyes, that arousal dissolving any hesitation. "No condom either," he admitted. "No diseases. I've always used a condom in the past. What time of the month are you?" Because Mace sure as hell didn't want to get her pregnant. He found himself holding his breath, wanting to love her even if the timing might be off. He felt shaken by her like he never had been before. Her hips were wide, her belly softly rounded. She could carry a baby no problem at all. And Sierra would be one hell of a mother, a natural, able to give her love openly and freely, unequivocally. The look in her eyes grew amused.

"I guess neither one of us were prepared to make love. I just finished my period last week, so I'm in the clear."

Before he could say anything else, she leaned over, slid her fingers beneath the edges of his t-shirt, drawing it over his arms and head. She dropped it over the rocker that sat at the end of the king-sized bed. Stepping back, she pushed her shoes off with her heels and shimmied out of her jeans and top. All of them went on the rocker. Smiling, she said, "I'm not a very shy person, Mace, as you can tell."

Hell, it was a great view. He sat stunned, drinking in the smooth, curving lines of her strong, fit body. She still had on only a plain white cotton bra and a set of slender briefs that only enhanced her pretty belly and those goddamn fetching hips, making him itch to slide his hands around them, draw her into him. "Help me get out of my jeans?" he rasped.

Holding out her hand, Sierra helped him stand. He leaned on her shoulder to steady himself as she quickly and carefully pulled off his soft boot and then his jeans one leg at a time. He had to concentrate on his balance hard as she did so, kneeling in front of him, the view down her cleavage making his legs clumsy as he tottered with each gentle movement. Mace had been right: she had small, beautiful breasts, the kind a man could hold in just the palms of his hands, feel their weight, feel their heat and promise. Finally getting his jeans off, she smiled up at him and stood.

"Boxers have to go."

"I've always undressed the woman first," he griped, standing, absorbing the joy in her face. She wanted to love him as much as he wanted to love her. Nothing had ever felt so right to Mace as this one single moment with Sierra.

"You're a man who resists changes, Mace," she murmured, sliding her fingers around within the elastic band of his boxers, moving them provocatively, watching his face change, watching it grow tight with lust. Very slowly, she slid them down, pleased with how strong his erection was. Lifting the material away from it, she added, "Change is a good thing. Don't you think?" and she pulled his boxers off, rising, her fingers trailing lightly up the insides of his legs, up to his thighs as she stood. And when her fingers wrapped warmly around him, Mace groaned, his hand gripping her shoulder tightly, his eyes squinching shut.

"I'll explode," he rasped. "I'm close, Sierra. I don't want to come yet. I want to please you, too."

She released him and urged him to sit down on the bed. "We'll please one another. I'm not keeping count on who's first or second," she said huskily, moving him so that his legs were on her bed. Getting two pillows, Sierra placed one beneath his knee and another beneath the heel of his injured foot. "Now," she said firmly, straightening, her hands on her hips, giving him a dark look, "you CANNOT be squirming and moving around. You need to keep that foot rested and you can't be using your legs or hips in any way." He tapped his shoulder smartly. "You're on your back for this round. Okay?"

He grinned. "Helluva position to be in. Reverse missionary."

"Yeah, well, get over it, Kilmer," and she pulled off her bra, revealing her breasts.

He damn near swallowed his tongue, more than ready to lay on his back and be pleasured by this woman with that hunter's gleam in her eyes. When Sierra pulled off her panties and stood naked before him, absolutely unapologetic, he grinned. "You're a woman on a mission."

Sierra knelt carefully bringing her leg across his hips, settling carefully upon his erection, always aware of his injured foot. She saw his eyes shutter closed, a groan emitting from him. Spreading her hands, she laid them on his slab-hard belly, slowly sliding them upward, holding his narrowing gaze. "I'm Cherokee, Kilmer. In our matriarchal society, women are equals. I'm your equal. And I'll bet," she whispered, peering down a satisfied look, "you've never made love with a woman who was."

She got that right, but Mace relaxed, closing his eyes, his mind imprinting the aching pleasure of the feel of her cool, long fingers gliding cross his stomach, memorizing him slowly. Her fingers raked through the dark hair across his chest. His hands reached out, under their own volition, as she stretched across him, her breasts so close. He had to feel her. As he stroked his hands down from her shoulders and his fingers followed the curves of her breasts, he heard the swift intake of her breath. And as he cupped both of them within his palms, he felt like a man who had died and gone to Nirvana. Sierra might be the aggressor here, but he was no wimp either when it came to knowing how to bring a woman to her knees with sheer physical pleasure. As he moved his thumbs languidly across her nipples, he heard a moan vibrate in her throat, her hands stilling upon his broad chest, her entire body freezing for moment. Opening his eyes, he saw her own closed, her lips slightly parted, gratification in her face. Yeah, she liked that. And she was exquisitely sensitive he was discovering as he pulled her forward, leaning up, capturing one of those pleading nipples and drawing it into the heat of his mouth.

Sierra cried out softly. Her fingers dug spasmodically into his broad shoulders as he suckled her. Her breath suddenly grew ragged as he teased the other nipple between his thumb and index finger. She quivered almost violently, and he would bet his life she was sopping wet between her thighs. Hungry to shove the both of them together, he was no longer the weakling he'd been a week ago. He had his full strength back. He released that beautiful, hard nipple and guided her firmly down beside him. And then Mace turned the tables on Sierra, smiling down into her eyes, seeing them become druzy with heavy arousal.

"You're mine, Sweetheart," he growled, sliding his calloused hand downward, following the delicious curve of her belly, his fingers moving between her thighs, urging her open. "I want to see how wet you are…," and he eased his fingers down between her moist folds. Instantly, she moaned with pleasure, her hips lifting automatically. Mace smiled up at her, his fingers moving slowly inside her, watching her face, watching the hunger spring to life in her eyes. Oh, no question, she was as much a sexual hunter as he was, and that discovery pleased him. She was honey-sweet, the fluids thick, and he eased one finger more deeply into her, testing her. A low, keening sound tore from her as she arched into him, begging for more. No question, she was his equal. He liked her responsiveness. There were no inhibitions. Laying on his side, he had full, unfettered access to her lush, sinuous body. She was so damn tight. She was right: she hadn't had sex in a long time. And Mace knew he wasn't average size. He had to be careful not to hurt her. He had to keep his lust reigned in because right now, he wanted to do nothing less than plunge hard into her depths and take her rough and wild. But that would have to wait. As he eased his fingers out and began to stroke that swollen knot so close to her entrance with them instead, she moved restlessly, her fingernails digging into his arms, nearly sobbing. Yeah, she was hot and she was so close.

Mace didn't want to hurt her so he eased away enough to lay on his back, and hauled her up and over him, her curved, strong thighs gripping either side of his narrow hips once more. Sierra was panting, her eyes blown, caught up in the heat and burning pleasure of being brought to the verge of orgasm. Mace knew the signs. He cupped her face, trying to make eye contact with her, but she was so far gone, so ready and hot. "Listen to me," he growled, "you take as much or as little of me as you want? Do you hear me, Sierra?" His fingers tightened around her. "I DON'T want to hurt you. Do you understand?" and he dug into her druzy, heated eyes.

With a bare nod, unable to speak, Sierra lifted away from his hands. She lowered herself across his erection, closing her eyes, a hum of satisfaction vibrating within her as she stroked her wet core slowly up and down along the length of his thick, hard member.

Mace damn near lost it. He gripped her hips, his teeth clenched as the honey fluids of her body bathed him. She was so close, her head tipped back, her lips parted, her entire body quivering. He wanted to give her pleasure first, knowing it was going to slow her down because she was tight, and he was large.

The moment he began to move against her, sliding her slowly back and forth across his hardness, she started to come loose in his hands. Mace felt her contract, felt a rush of hot fluids bathing him, heard her cry out, her back arched, gripping his forearms, lost in the explosive orgasm that was carrying her away on its river of intense pleasure. He couldn't tear his gaze from her. She was arched, her breasts thrust forward, those nipples taut, begging. A pink flush began at her belly and flowed upward, telling him she was in the throes of the long, hungry orgasm that had stolen her mind. Now, she was a pure, primal animal and he grunted, prolonging the orgasm for her, thrusting upward, bringing more of her weight down upon him, not allowing her orgasm to end. He milked it until, finally, he felt her begin to weaken.

Mace released her hips. Sierra collapsed and laid against his sweaty body, her brow nestling against his jaw, her arms curved weakly around his neck, sobbing for breath, quivering, and feeling so damned alive. His heart flooding with such a fierce love for this courageous woman, Mace closed his eyes, simply absorbing her warmth against him and the sweat they shared between them. Her breasts felt delicious against him and he ran his fingers from her shoulders all the way down her damp back to her hips, cupping her cheeks, holding her tight against him, savoring her in every possible way.

Tangling his fingers through her black hair, he eased the strands away from her face. He pulled back just enough to see the flush across her features, hear her torn, ragged breath, feel its moistness against his face, her lips pulled into such a satisfied smile that it made Mace feel like an actual man for the first time in what felt like forever. Nothing ever felt as good to him as fulfilling the woman at his side. Sierra deserved this. She deserved to be happy, that look of pleasure reflected in her eyes, those thick, black lashes sweeping against her flushed cheeks.

He loved her.

For the space of a single heartbeat, Mace felt his way through that massive realization. He'd known it in his head, and a little in his heart. But now, sharing Sierra in the most intimate of ways, her courage combined with what he was willing to give her, shattered him in ways he'd never been before. Mace lay there with her in his arms, their bodies pressed hotly against one another, the slickness of perspiration between them, each breath shared between them a delicious, ongoing dessert.

As Sierra slowly opened her eyes, Mace smiled into them. Those cypress-colored eyes of hers were filled with sunlight-gold flecks dancing in their depths, telling him just how good she felt. How much pleasure he'd given her. He felt her lift her hand, weakly resting it against his jaw.

"Wow," she uttered. "Wow...."

He chuckled and took her hand, kissing each fingertip in succession. "I think you had a couple years of stored-up orgasms in you," he teased. "I've never seen a woman's last as long as yours did."

Wrinkling her nose, she laughed. "I really needed that. It felt so good, Mace." Her voice grew husky. "I wanted to please you first."

Shrugging a little, he gave her an amused look. "You can when you feel like it. Right now, I like you right where you're at. You need to rest and revive. Then, you can please me all you want, Sweetheart."

Love infused Sierra. If she'd ever doubted Mace was the right man for her, that feeling was now gone. He'd placed his own needs aside for hers. Few men ever did that. It was all about honoring one's partner, truly treating them as an equal. But now, it was her turn to care for and love him back. She had felt his warm hardness against her core, felt it so thick and strong. There was nothing anywhere on Mace's body or within his mind that she could term weak.

As she moved slowly, sitting up across his girth once again, sinuously sliding herself along his length, he gripped her hips hard, teeth clenched. He was so close himself. Intuitively, Sierra knew it had been a long time for him, too. Not as long as for her, but the way he reacted as she slowly stroked him with her thick fluids and core, he would have to hope her body would accommodate him. And if it didn't completely, all was not lost. And Mace would understand. Still, Sierra knew she could give this valiant, harden warrior the pleasure which he so richly deserved.

As she lifted her hips, pressing her breasts into his awaiting palms, she smiled down at him. Sierra saw the animal in him, and it excited her. Even now, without ever having drawn him inside her, he was there. A passion flowed through her as she placed her core against the tip of his erection. Instantly, Mace tensed, his fingers digging into her hips, his breath a sudden, sharp intake. His eyes shut tightly and as she began to slowly introduce her body to him, she felt her muscles stretching, burning. Easing out a little, her body already preparing for another orgasm, she felt the liquid warmth coat her and she eased down again.

Mace growled, trying to control his reaction. Sierra knew he wanted so badly to lift his hips and thrust deeply into her. But her body, while trying to accommodate him, was much slower to react than his. Taking his mouth as he brushed her nipples, heat bolted down from her breasts to her core. Just that act of triggering the pleasure in her nipples made her surge down upon him. His mouth was strong against hers, bold, his tongue moving and teasing hers, emulating the rhythm of copulation. The burning, the momentary stretching and pain, dissolved as her body increased its fluids from his stimulation. She rocked slowly, loving the feel of his warm, steel strength within her, heightening her sensitivity, stroking her sweet spot until she moaned.

And then, when she had taken half of him into her, he lifted her, capturing one of her nipples. And instantly, she cried out softly, the riveting fire skittering downward. He lifted his hips slowly and she tore her mouth from his, eyes shut tightly, lost in the power and heat suddenly building deep within her. As he lavished her nipples, her whole lower body began to bubble like a cauldron ready to boil over. His hips slowly thrusting upward, stretching her, going deeper within her, stroking the swollen knot at her entrance, Sierra keened, rising, her hands flat against his tense torso as she fully seated him into her. The low burnings dissolved and ran into the hottest fire she'd ever felt within her. It built up, making her mindless. Sierra loved the animal side of herself, a very necessary and beautiful part of every human being. But with Mace, who had been primal to begin with, she'd barely be able to scratch the surface of the animal passion flooding out from deep inside him. As she felt him begin a slow, easy rhythm in and out of her, every nerve of Sierra's body began to ripple with pleasure with each thrust.

And when he settled his large hands around her hips, holding her in place, increasing his pace, she rocked against him, lost in the swirling, inferno building within her. "I'm so close," she cried out, breathless, wanting him to come with her.

Mace grunted, pumped deep into her, angling her slightly, finding, trapping that knot of nerves higher up in her channel, making every push even more pleasurable for her. Her world suddenly started dismantling, his size and girth triggering reactions within her that had never been stimulated before. The volcanic contraction of her orgasm made her cry out his name, her fingers taut against his chest, frozen with such incredible, raw pleasure and heat rifling through her in ever-widening circles that all she could do was gasp and cry out with every pulse into her. And then, she felt him surge, stiffen and grunt, his hands taut against her hips. Sierra knew he was climaxing, and she fought her own euphoria to prolong his release by sliding quickly and hearing his groaning sound like an animal snarling. Her spirit soared. Her heart broke open with such a powerful love for Mace that Sierra was swept away on their tide of light, explosions, and waves of intense, violent, shared animal pleasure.

Sierra had no idea where time had gone, or how she was once more collapsed against Mace's powerful body. His fingers were lightly stroking her damp shoulders and following her spine downward, as if to sooth her after such an untamed and wonderful ride. Her body ached and felt sore in its ultra-sensitive places. Mace must have somehow known because he murmured her name and gently eased out of her. She moaned and kept her eyes closed, continuing to feel the delicious rivulets of heat still expanding deep within her afterward. The next thing she knew, he had settled her on his left side, rolled toward her and then tucked her in against him, holding her tightly, as if he never wanted to let her go again.

The euphoria was like a leaf twirling lazily on a soft breeze within Sierra. She absorbed Mace's arm around her shoulders, his other hand lightly soothing her, every touch like a feather teasing her flesh that skittered with tiny shocks of even more pleasure. Nuzzling beneath his jaw, she placed a kiss against the strong column of his neck, inhaling his male scent, dragging it deeply into her lungs. As she slowly smoothed her palm against his damp chest hair, she smiled weakly. "I don't want this to ever end, Mace... it's so... wonderful... beautiful... *you're* beautiful." And he was. He was perfect for her in every way. She felt him chuckle, feeling more than hearing it through her palm resting against his chest.

"I'm with you, Sweetheart." He caressed her hair, nudging thick strands across her shoulder. "You are incredible. Your body... you rock in my world, Woman."

His voice was low and gravely. It vibrated through Sierra. She hungrily absorbed this moment with Mace. But in the back of her mind, however unwillingly they came, Sierra heard the familiar voices telling her that moments like this would not be forever. Her heart quelled and she lay there, her body pressed fully along his, trying to find a way to get him to realize that what they shared was rare. That it was worth perusing. Worth cultivating. If only... If only he could see it. What was holding Mace a prisoner?

He never talked, never shared, and, more than anything, Sierra was being driven to the point where she had to get past Mace's walls and find out what it was that entrapped and imprisoned him, that didn't allow him to embrace her fully and forever.

"You're like a wild, female Jaguar," he rasped against her ear, feeling her make a happy sound in her throat. Threading his fingers through her clean, sleek hair, he marveled at the light caught in its strands, reflected by beams of the deepening orange color from the western window.

Lifting her head enough to catch his hooded, stormy-gray gaze, she whispered, "You're my jaguar mate, then."

Mace nodded, feeling his throat tighten as she put her head down once more, closing her eyes, content to lay limply against him. *Mate.* Yes, she was. So much more than that. He had found the other missing part of himself. He'd never met a woman quite like Sierra. She was bold, bone-honest, and unafraid to go where mere mortals feared to tread. Mace had to remind himself she was military trained. A vaunted sniper. There was no room in Sierra's world for fear to rule. And she was just as fearless in letting him know how much she wanted him. He liked her assertiveness. It was a complete turn on for him. And she was his match, no question. He'd never experienced as deep and intense a climax as he'd had with her. She milked him dry, turned him inside out, and he felt like the most loved person in the universe right now.

His brow fell. Unconsciously, his arm tightened a little more around her shoulders, holding her closer, if that was even possible. Sierra loved him with all her womanly fierceness. He'd felt it with each touch of skin on skin, through her mouth, and within her guileless, loving heart. Mace had never felt loved like this before. His body still vibrated, still swam in the pool of pleasure that continued to simmer within him. She'd fully brought out his primal side, but she was equally primal, too. Neither of them was close to being civilized, he realized with a newfound joy. There was a time and place to be an animal. And sex was definitely one of those arenas. But sex with Sierra had turned into more than primal mating. It had evolved and entwined his heart, making him feel things he'd never felt before. And it all added up to an experience with her that he couldn't even begin to put words to. All he could do was touch her, kiss her, drown in her beautiful, radiant gaze, and be swallowed whole by that winsome smile of hers.

Mace lay there, realizing the depth of his love for Sierra. How damned deep it really ran. And getting deeper by the day. He didn't know when it had happened. Only that it had. He placed one arm over his eyes, allowing himself to dream. It wasn't something he allowed himself to do very often. To dream was to want changes. And he'd given his word. And when a man gave his word, he didn't break it.

To dream meant he was railing against the promise he'd made to his father so long ago. To dream meant Mace wanted to change, just as Sierra had said. Those changes he'd gone through with her were the most beautiful moments he'd spent in his entire life. She was morphing him into something else, he realized. Just by her being herself. It wasn't that she was manipulating him. Mace knew the difference.

No. As he began to allow himself to dream, he dreamed of them. Together. Of waking up with Sierra in his arms, her warmth against his in this very bed. Dreams of living a normal life. Settling down. Marrying her. Wanting to give her children because he knew she loved them. And so did he. Children had always held a special place in his heart. He went so far as to dream of what their children would look like, their faces, the color of their eyes and hair. And at some point, Mace dropped off into a dreamless sleep, with the woman he loved with his life in his arms.

CHAPTER 21

I T WAS LATE June and Sierra was glad to be out between the furrows of her garden, weeding. Cal, Lauren and Alex Kazak, had been out often to help her put the deer fence around it. Mace hadn't been able to help out much, limited by his walker a lot of the time.

But now, he was graduating to utilizing a cane and she glanced over her shoulder on this Saturday morning to see him with a can of paint out at the front gate to the cabin. She smiled to herself, continuing down the row on her hands and knees, picking out every last little weed that thought it was going to take root.

She'd put up the picket fence around the cabin herself but had never gotten around to fully painting it. Now, over the last week since Mace's swollen foot had reduced in size by half and the fang holes had closed, he was outside every chance he got. Her heart warmed just thinking of him. Nights were special to her. On nearly every one, they made hungry, passionate love, as if they couldn't get enough of one another.

The morning was cool and the sky cloudless. She sat back on her heels, gloved hands resting on her jeans as she surveyed her plot of two hundred square feet. She had tomatoes of three different varieties, green beans, Hubbard squash, a row of different pot herbs, sweet potatoes, and scallions. Mace had helped her pick out the seeds, suggesting certain veggies for this land and altitude. He couldn't help her with their planting, but he always brought out a chair and sat there keeping her company. Her heart warmed but she drew in a deep sigh. Mace was going to leave her. She sensed it.

Sometimes, usually at night, when she was in her rocking chair watching TV, she would look up and he'd be on the couch, staring at her. It didn't unsettle her, but he looked so damned torn, as if undecided. And in bed, especially after making love to one another, she would try to get through those walls of his. He would gently turn her questions aside, avoiding her and 'it'. Whatever 'it' was. They all carried an 'it' of personal trauma. She did. He did. How she wished she knew what his was.

Sierra felt like she was battling an invisible enemy who she could neither see nor define. What was Mace hiding? Who had stoved him up like this? She knew from long experience that operators were pretty well emotionally suppressed to the nth degree. And it was tough for them to open up. And if they ever even slightly pried the lid off, they feared their own personal 'it' could escape, and they might never get it back in that box they all kept buried deep within themselves.

Was that in Mace's box?

What was so terrible in there that whenever he started opening up to her, he feared the lid would rip off from its hinges and had to slam it shut again? Sierra suspected that he thought, if that ever happened, it would interfere with his job as an operator, a major distraction that could get him, or worse in his mind, members of his team killed. She felt as if she were on thin ice with him all the time, that nothing between them was stable or reliable. He still had not told her he loved her. But in all honestly, Sierra hadn't mentioned her own admission of love since that one time she'd blurted it out back in Peru. She was pulling her own punch, too. Sometimes, she was so weary from the dance they did around one another, that she'd take a walk into the woods and cry to release her heartache.

Getting up, brushing her knees off, she wanted to go help Mace paint the picket fence. She washed her hands under a faucet just outside the gate, then wiped them dry on the thighs of her jeans. Mace was so alone. So often, she felt an aching loneliness within him. Was he still grieving about Ana Beth? About their baby? Surely, he was but Sierra didn't know if that was the big bad that lurked inside his box or not. She plopped down beside him, throwing him a smile. He wore his dark green baseball cap, a bright red t-shirt that showed off his gorgeous masculine body, and jeans that emphasized his long, powerful legs.

"Like some company?"

"I always like your company," he said. "What do you think?"

She peered at the painted picket his brush had just gotten done with. Days ago, Mace had patiently sanded down every last one by hand before bringing out the paint and brush. He was a stickler for doing a job right or not at all. "Looks good. Would you like some help? Have another paintbrush? Maybe I can paint one side and you do the other?" She drowned in his light-gray eyes. Sierra was getting to know the nuances of tone of his eyes, whether light or dark. They were an indicator of his mood. When they were light like this, it meant he was happy. Indeed, he was relaxed, sitting on the tarp that covered the grass so it wouldn't get splattered with paint.

"Sure," he said, handing her a small brush. "If you go on the other side, we can share the same can of paint."

"I like the way you think," she murmured. Sierra caught her hair up in a twist on top of her head and anchored it, not wanting any paint to get in the strands. She felt Mace watching her. It almost felt like an invisible, loving embrace.

Sitting down, she reached between two slats, dipped her brush in the can of paint and began to lay it on the other side of the next picket he was working on. "Tell me about your father, Hank?" Sierra looked across at Mace. "I got to talk to him once, calling him about your condition right after you arrived here."

"Yeah, he said you did." Mace took a deep breath. "My father has always been a hardworking man, Sierra. He is a quiet man of his word, and he never went back on a promise."

"He sounded pretty gruff," she admitted.

"What? Like me?" and Mace grinned a little.

"Are you two a lot alike?" she wondered.

"Probably are."

"You were the oldest. Right?"

"Yes."

"What happened to your father when Caleb died of his..." and she paused, her brow furrowing in sympathy as she continued, "...of his drug overdose?" Sierra watched the pain come to his darkening gray eyes. She hated snooping into his family history, but she had to because she felt whatever was just under the lid was there.

"It took my father down," Mace admitted heavily. "He never saw it coming. I didn't see it, either. My mother, Hannah, did. She always worried about all us boys at school with so many drugs around."

"How did your mom take it?"

"Hard."

The word came out flat. Filled with grief. Sierra reached through the fence, gently touching his hand. "I'm so sorry, Mace."

He shook his head. "Two years later, she died of cancer of the pancreas. I always thought the shock and loss of Caleb did it. It took her down in a different way."

"Is that when Joseph ran away? To Charleston?" She saw his mouth turn into a slash.

"Yeah. My father needed us by his side, but Joseph ran away."

"Was Joseph like you?"

"No, nothing like me. He was lazy. My father and he got into constant battles with one another. My mother was always defending Joe."

"Sounds like a pretty stressful family situation."

Mace looked up at her. "I guess it was, but you know? At the time, I never realized it. I do now. I know enough guys in Special Forces, and they all talk from time to time about their families. I realized later that our family had a lot of dysfunction going on."

"A lot of emotions, too?" Sierra asked softly, watching him. Mace's eyes grew darker, and she knew it was a sign of his feelings rising. He never gave voice to them. Not yet.

"Yeah. Caleb was sweet, like mom. I took after dad. Joe was a rebel. Always was. Still is…" Mace replied, his voice rich with bitterness.

She continued to paint, glancing up at him every now and then. "And, where is Joe now? Do you know?"

"Last I heard from Dad, he was in jail. The ATF did a drug dragnet in Charleston, where he's at, and he got caught up in it, and arrested and charged."

"Does Joe talk to you? Or your dad?" She saw Mace look angry for just a moment, and then it was gone.

"No. My dad found out about it because Joe wanted bail money and the bail bondsman called him to ask for it. My dad refused. I was glad he did."

"Have you ever talked with Joseph since?"

"Never."

The word was snapped out like a trap shutting. The hurt, the tears, the confusion was in Mace's expression. Sierra was slowly beginning to see him trust her with other parts of himself. He didn't try to hide from her as much. "You said your dad was sick?"

"Yeah, rheumatoid arthritis. He got it ten years ago. Had to sell the family farm and moved into Charleston." Shrugging, Mace said in a low tone, "Ever since that happened, I've been sending half my monthly paycheck to pay for rent on a small apartment for him. I didn't want him to become homeless."

"The medical bills ate up the price he got for your farm?"

Mace shook his head, his voice hard. "Damned medical doctors took advantage of him. He's a simple man, Sierra. You probably found that out when you talked to him."

"Yes, but he was very respectful to me. He really appreciated me calling him and telling him how you were. I thought he was going to cry… I mean, it was obvious how much he loves you."

"He's a good man, Sierra. I love him with my life."

Her heart felt so much sympathy for Mace. It was the first time he'd said something emotional about his father. Mace seemed to step around emotions as if they were landmines planted to kill him. "I know his son," she offered gently, giving him a kind look. "He's an incredible man, a hero, and a good person." She saw ruddiness come to Mace's cheeks as he avoided her gaze, pushing his brush around in the paint can. Reaching out to his forearm, she moved her fingers up and down his skin, feeling the ropy muscles beneath respond. She watched his mouth begin to relax. He calmed whenever she made contact with him. She'd seen it in Peru. And here, as well.

"You were fourteen when Caleb suddenly died. It must have left you spinning, Mace."

Shrugging, he muttered, "I blamed myself. I was the oldest. I should have been watching him more closely. I was responsible for him."

"But I thought when you got home from school, you had to go out into the field with your dad and plow?"

"I did," Mace said. He shifted over on his butt to the next picket. "I wanted to do both things, but I couldn't."

Sierra finished up painting her side and moved over opposite him again, dipping her brush in the can. "Then how could you have been more responsible for Caleb than you were? He was in grade school. You were in junior high at the time. You weren't at the same school, were you?"

"No, opposite sides of town."

"Then how can you blame yourself?" she asked quietly, holding his pain-filled gaze.

Shaking his head, he muttered, "I was a kid then, Sierra. I just felt responsible. I felt bad. My father was crying. My mother was hysterical. Joe ran to the barn because he couldn't take it. I felt it was my duty to stay and help."

"But you did? You stayed? You tried to be of help in some way?" The sudden weariness in his eyes told her everything.

"Nothing I did to support Joe made a difference," he admitted tiredly.

Reaching out, Sierra laid her hand on his knee. "You were just a child, Mace. Only fourteen. Who took care of you in all of this?"

"What do you mean?"

She heard the defensiveness in his voice. "You were a child. They were adults. They were supposed to give you comfort, protection and support, not the other way around."

"Comfort?" His voice rose with disgust. "There wasn't anyone in our family who comforted anyone, Sierra. We were all torn apart. My father was blaming me..." and then he snapped his mouth shut, looking away for moment.

Sierra jerked in a breath, her eyes widening. A muscle in Mace's jaw leaped. He was clenching his teeth. "Why did he blame you?"

"I don't know," Mace said irritably. "I was the oldest. I grew up being told by my parents that I was responsible for Caleb and Joe." He rubbed his furrowed brow. "I did a shitty job of it."

Her heart broke for Mace. Sierra could see him as a tall, skinny fourteen-year-old, carrying so much on his shoulders that he had no control over. "It wasn't your load to carry in the first place, Mace. It belonged to your parents. Not you."

"Yeah, well that sure as hell didn't work, did it?" He jammed the paint-brush down into the can, slopping some of the white paint out and onto the tarp.

Sierra wanted to press him. She felt Mace trusted her more than anyone else in his life. They had shared an intimacy so deep and beautiful that he was allowing her inside those walls of his. "The death of a child often breaks up a marriage," she said gently. "You were a child yourself, Mace. No one can blame you for anything. You were the innocent in this dysfunctional drama."

He closed his eyes, his mouth thinning. "I'm hardly innocent." And he opened his eyes, staring at her.

"At fourteen, you were," she insisted. "When your mom got ill, did every-thing fall on your shoulders again?" She saw his shoulders sag, as if still carrying all those ancient loads.

"Mom got sick with cancer a year after Caleb died. My Dad had to farm. I started to cut classes to come home early to take care of her."

Sierra couldn't imagine a young boy like Mace being the primary caregiver. "It must have been so hard on you."

"Joe was never home," Mace said bitterly. "He was always running with a gang at school. He got into drugs and began selling them. He was cutting classes. The teachers were calling my dad about his drug dealing, but he was so screwed by work and his wife dying in front of his eyes that he couldn't handle one more tragedy."

"And so, it all fell on you?" She spoke the words quietly and watched his eyes grow dark with anguish, feeling how many tears he still carried inside him over those grim days of his family's struggling life.

Mace stopped painting, looking off in the distance. His voice was tight with his unshed tears. "It had nowhere else to go, Sierra. Things got worse after mom died. Joe lost it, accused my father that it was all his fault she died. And then he ran away to Charleston, never to be heard from again."

"Awful," Sierra whispered, her voice trembling. "That must have been so terrible…"

Mace set his brush in a can of water and then picked up a cloth and wiped his hands. "My father broke right in front of my eyes. I'd never seen him cry, but he was sobbing. His whole life had been ripped out from under him."

"What did you do?"

Mace sighed and looked over at her. "I wanted to do something… anything… to get my dad back. I went over and held him, and I promised him I'd go after the drug dealers in South America who were sending that shit up to the States. The same shit that killed Caleb. That turned Joe into a druggie." His mouth turned into a slash. "My Dad just clung to me, sobbing. He couldn't stop. Later, when he stopped crying, he told me to go kill those sons-of-bitches for him and for my mother and for Caleb." He paused and then said grimly, "I promised him I would."

Promised. Sierra sat very still. She knew what a promise meant in Mace's world. Swallowing hard, her voice unsteady, she said, "Then, you joined the Army at eighteen with that goal in mind. Right?"

"Yes." He looked down at his paint-splotched hands. "A promise is a promise."

"You've done it for fourteen years, Mace. Isn't that enough?" She couldn't keep the tears out of her eyes or out of her voice. He slowly looked over at her and her heart shrank with such pain that she couldn't breathe for a moment.

"Does a promise have a time limit, Sierra?"

The pain in her heart increased and she wanted to cry for Mace. He had never been kept protected. He was the oldest of the children and had grown up strong and forced to mature way too early. She could see how, during what should have been his innocent childhood years, the dysfunction of his family had shifted suddenly onto his shoulders, his father no longer able to carry the load.

"I don't know," she answered quietly. "I do know you're an honorable man. And that your word is your bond, Mace. You don't give it lightly but when you do, people can count on you to carry through with it." She saw him give her a sad, remorseful look for a moment.

"Yeah, someone will scratch that into my tombstone someday," he said in disgust.

Getting up, Sierra couldn't stand to feel that terrible aloneness that had always cloaked Mace. She stepped her long legs over the fence that separated them and knelt by his side.

"Come here," she whispered, sliding her arms around his broad, slumped shoulders. "Let ME hold you. Okay?" And she drew him into her arms, pulled his head against her shoulder and held him within her feminine strength. At first, Mace resisted, but she wouldn't give in, holding him tightly against herself. Finally, he relaxed, face pressed against her neck and jaw, his arms sliding around her, drawing her even closer to him.

"You're good for me," he said gruffly, pressing a kiss into her shoulder.

Battling back tears, not wanting Mace to see them falling, she said nothing, and only squeezed him more tightly. Mace surrendered over to her fully and she knelt there holding this tall, proud man who so desperately needed care for and love himself. He'd had so much taken from him at such a young age. Tears broke over the dams of her lower eyelids and leaked down her cheeks and, inwardly, Sierra groaned. They plopped down on Mace. He pulled back, staring at her, his expression concerned.

"What's this?" he demanded, using his thumbs to wipe the tears off her cheeks.

His face blurred in front of her and she struggled. "I'm crying for *you*, Mace. You had no one to hold you. To help you through your own grief and loss." She reached up, cupping his jaw, holding his dark-gray eyes so filled with pain and awareness. "You were just a little boy. No one should have put those responsibilities on you. Joe shouldn't have gone off like he did. It wasn't your dad's fault. Caleb was too young. You were all innocent. Your parents did the best they could. No one is blaming anyone here. I just hurt so much for you because you're still carrying around all your family's baggage on your shoulders. I ache for you…," and she crushed him against her, holding him hard, sobbing into his shoulder as he held her.

Mace felt like hell. Early evening had arrived, and he'd only gotten half of the fence painted. His knees were stiff as he slowly got up. All day, he'd run Sierra's words, her questions, and his answers, around in his head. His emotions were in turmoil. He'd damn near cried along with Sierra earlier in the morning himself. He was feeling more and more how much she was understanding his suffering. She had a big heart, and she was compassionate to the bone. If he were honest with himself, he still wanted to cry, but he was afraid to. If he started, Mace wasn't sure he could stop. His love for Sierra was growing stronger and deeper in his heart by the day. She was sensitive, caring, loving and so open with her feelings, good or bad. He'd never been around anyone like her before.

He heard Sierra call from the porch that it was dinner time. She had taken a shower and changed clothes. She wore a soft-pink sleeveless blouse, a set of white shorts, and sandals. Picking up the paint-splattered tarp, he folded it up, put the lid on the paint can and took everything to the small shed on the side of the cabin.

Wanting to make love to her, driven to have her in his arms, he went in the house and washed up in the bathroom. Coming out to the kitchen, the smells of food wonderful, he walked over to where she was making a salad on the counter.

"Hey," he murmured, sliding his arms around her waist, kissing the exposed nape of her neck, "come here?"

Sierra put the paring knife down on the wooden board, wiped her hands dry on a towel and turned around in his arms. "How are you doing?" she asked, sliding her arms around his waist, studying him tenderly.

Instantly, Mace felt tears sting the back of his eyes. He cleared his throat and said, "Can dinner wait? I want to make love with you right now." He'd never done this before, but the need pushing him was going to eat him alive if he didn't bury himself into Sierra's warm, womanly depths. He needed a safe harbor. Needed her so damn badly.

"Sure," she murmured, releasing him. "Let me turn off the stove?"

He moved away, feeling shaky inside, never having felt like this before. "I'll meet you in the bedroom," he said gruffly.

A sensation reminiscent of what he'd felt at age sixteen when his mother died, and Joe ran away haunted him like a predator that was going to eat him alive.

Sierra sensed what was going on inside him as she turned off the oven. Her opening up of Mace's past had created an emotional deluge within him. She could see his confusion. She felt so many powerful, conflicting emotions in his vulnerable face, saw he needed her in a desperate kind of way that crumpled her heart. Mace needed to cry. He needed to be held. She could do those things for him. Unsure of how it would unfold, she quickly untied her apron and set it on the counter, walking through the living room to their bedroom.

Mace was sitting on the edge of the bed, thighs open, elbows on them, hands clasped, head down. His shoulders were slumped. Everything in his pose spoke of defeat. Of giving up. And maybe this had to happen in order for him to move on. To have a life just for himself instead of still carrying all his family's weight around that was dragging him down like a millstone he might never be free of. Her heart was so heavy for him. She loved him and it hurt her to her soul to see the suffering in his eyes as he raised them when she quietly came and knelt in front of him, her hands on his upper arms. His whole body was so tense it felt as if he was going to shatter apart any moment into a million pieces. Moving her hands gently up and down his upper arms, she whispered, "Talk to me?" and she searched his charcoal-colored eyes, saw the raw pain in them.

"I don't know," he whispered, reaching out, pulling her into his arms, situating her between his thighs. Sliding his fingers through the cascade of hair she'd released earlier from its ties, pressing his face into its clean strands, he trembled, his arms tightening even more around her.

She rubbed his shoulders that were so hunched over. Mace didn't know how to cry. All he could feel was the twisting emotions roaring through him and they had no outlet. Nowhere to go. "I love you, Mace," she whispered against his ear. "You're hurting... let me help?" and she felt tears flood her eyes. Lifting her head away, she tilted it and caught his misery-ladened gaze. "Let me help you..." She saw him look up, stare at her, transfixed, as tears rolled down her cheeks. And then his face twisted, as if trying to battle back some unseen opponent. Sierra leaned forward, her hands framing his face, her mouth softly touching the hardened line of his. Her tears flowed into the corners of her mouth as she pressed and ask him entrance, his lips opening beneath hers. Sierra heard a sob choke out of Mace. She lifted her mouth away from his and wrapped her arms around him, holding him as he pressed his face against her neck and shoulder. "It's all right," she soothed unsteadily, caressing his hair, "it's all right, Mace, just let it go. Give me your tears. I'll just hold you..."

CHAPTER 22

M ACE FOUND HIMSELF lying on the bed, holding on to Sierra like she was a life raft and, if he let go, he knew he'd drown. The sounds twisting out of his throat sounded other-worldly even to himself as he clung to her softly curved body, his head buried against her shoulder. He sounded like a trapped animal, shrieking out in pain and panic. The sobs kept tearing out of him and he could no longer control or stop them. Just the gentle touch of her hand on his head, on his shaking shoulders, helped him to stop fighting back. The tears that rolled out of his burning eyes felt acrid. All he could feel was a glut of pain rolling up through him, in wave after torturous wave. And throughout his wrenching, tearing sobs ripping out of his contorted mouth, Sierra was there with her low, husky voice, soothing him, telling him she loved him and would be there for him.

Her arms were so damn strong. And he was a big man. She was half his size and yet, her strength kept him grounded, allowed him to weep just as he'd seen his father do so many years before. They were terrible sounds, filled with such heartbreak and loss. Mace felt all his suppressed emotions vomiting out of him and he knew no way to stop them. Nor did he try.

Having no idea how long he'd wept, Mace felt Sierra shift, pushing him gently onto his back. She lay beside him, her face soft with sympathy as she tenderly dried his cheeks off with her fingers. Reaching up, Mace realized she had cried as well, but he had been unaware of her tears, too lost in his own emotional storm.

"Come here," he said thickly, bringing her down to kiss her. He put his lips against hers, tasting the salt across them, felt her tremble, knew she was no less affected by this weeping than he was. Because Sierra loved him. She'd spoken the words he said in his head so often. It had done something powerful within him as if some key to unlock the steel cage around his heart had released him. Mace couldn't explain it, only feel it. Sierra's mouth was warm, opening to him, giving back to him, filling him with her love and he readily accepted it. Because now that he felt freed at such a deep level, it was impossible to put it into coherent words. Now that his walls had finally dissolved, he could give back equally to her what she was offering him. Sierra's hair slipped across her shoulders, cool and silky against his heated skin, pooling across his damp t-shirt.

Easing her away from him so he could look into her eyes, he rasped, "I love you, Sierra. Just know that…"

Sierra smiled brokenly, reaching out, grazing his cheek. "You've loved me for a long time, Mace Kilmer. But it sure is nice to hear you say those words."

Groaning, Mace shook his head, his voice filled with apology. "I knew. I knew a long time ago, Sweetheart. I was just…" and he took a serrating breath, "I needed to try and figure everything out that was going on inside of me."

"I realized that." Sierra gave him an understanding look, moving a few strands of hair off his broad brow. "Your family, their demands on you, had you tied up in knots inside yourself, Mace. Your parents made you the strong one. They both looked to you when they were feeling weak and out of control. But you didn't realize that. How could you? You were just fourteen years old."

Shaking her head, Sierra leaned down, kissing his brow, his cheeks and finally, his mouth. Lingering against his lips, she whispered, "You are so honorable, Mace. So damned strong. And you more than carried out your promise to your father to hunt down those drug lord bastards." Lifting her head, Sierra gave him a warm look. "You're allowed to have a life of your own, now. You're allowed to fall in love with me, Mace. And we're allowed to have a life together if that's what you want."

He felt amazingly calm inside, given that, half an hour ago, he'd felt like there was a wild animal loose within his guts, clawing him apart from the inside out. "How the hell did you get to be so smart? That's what I want to know," and a faint smile touched his mouth.

"Luck of the lottery draw," she admitted wryly. "I just know your child-hood was taken away from you at a very early age, Mace. All you know is work, responsibility and honor. Those aren't bad things, but ever since you put the family yoke on your shoulders to carry as well, you've suffered. A lot." Sierra skimmed his cheek. "And more than anything, I want you to be happy, Mace. I want to hear you laugh. See you smile. To wake up happy every morning, looking forward to the day with me. Not seeing the day ahead of you as some old, old promise that shouldn't ever have been agreed to in the first place. Your dad was too filled with grief and guilt. He was so wrapped up in his own pain that he had no energy, no room emotionally left within him, to help you through yours, Maee. And, because you were so strong, they all unconsciously leaned on you, instead. And you just took it because you could. You were too young to understand any of it."

He dragged in a long, ragged breath, memorizing her beautiful face, those sad green but so understanding eyes of hers, the wetness of her lips, the passion in her low voice, the love she held for him. "You're a fierce damn warrior," he muttered. "Do you know that?"

"I'm fiercely in love with you," Sierra admitted brokenly. "I want so much for you to stay with me, Mace. To stop going back down to Peru. Stop all of it. I want you here with me. You DESERVE your own life, dammit. And I'm selfish enough to ask you to stay with me and find out. Live with me. Love me. Laugh and cry with me. But don't... God... don't go back down there to Peru again. Please..."

Her pleading ripped his vulnerable heart wide open even more. He was feeling emotions so cleanly and brightly, no longer fearing them. The tears glittering in Sierra's eyes, her quavering voice, made Mace wince. It was the reaction to the pain he'd put her through for all the months since they'd parted. Easing her onto her back, smoothing the tears from her cheeks, he said gruffly, "I'm going nowhere but to you, Sierra. You need to hear that from me. I was wrong in not telling you sooner. I hurt you and I'm so damned sorry for it. You've been nothing but honest and clear with me from the day we met. And yes, you pushed me into feeling like I was up against a wall I couldn't climb or get around. But it forced me to admit I wanted you. I remembered my promise to my father. I was torn, Sweetheart. Torn up inside. I knew I couldn't do both. I had to make a choice." His voice lowered with anguish. "Right now, I feel rotten for the way I've treated you. I never lied to you, though. And I didn't lead you on. I made no promises to you I couldn't keep, Sierra."

"I know you didn't." She caught his hand, holding it against her breast, drowning in his light-gray eyes. "You were a man of honor every step of the way, Mace. And I never blamed you. I was just trying to figure out why. I knew you loved me. I saw it in your face so many times when you didn't think I was watching you. I felt it, Darling. I felt your love, your protection. And that night we kissed in the waterfall cave, I knew. I knew in my heart and soul, that you loved me."

Nodding, Mace drew her hand to his, kissing the back of it. "I've been pretty damned blind."

"No, you weren't blind. You were set up to take the fall for your entire family. There's a huge difference, Mace." Sierra's voice grew low with pleading. "And don't feel bad that you didn't see it. No child of fourteen ever could. You couldn't."

"I see it now." Mace kissed her lips, tasting them, the salt of her tears, the sweetness of her mouth. "When you started poking around in my family, asking all those questions this morning, I felt like you were popping rivets apart inside of me, opening me up in a way to see what was going on, but from a different perspective. Maybe an overview. I don't know. But it helped me see the pattern you were trying to help me out of."

"Everything is a pattern," Sierra agreed softly, "there's healthy ones and then there's unhealthy ones. You being trapped in your unhealthy family pattern was causing you to surrender your entire life to a promise that your father should never have allowed you to make. He shouldn't have agreed to it. I think spending fourteen years of your life fulfilling that promise is enough. Don't you?"

Mace drew in a breath. "I see it now, Sierra. I don't know what I'm going to do, though. My enlistment is up in two months. I'll need to find a civilian job."

"Then don't re-up," she said, "because Jack Driscoll is desperate to hire military men like yourself who can set up mission plans. You can stay here in Alexandria. You can make a salary of over a hundred-and-fifty thousand dollars a year doing something that would come so easily to you. Jack needs men with experience like you, Mace." Sierra moved her hand down his strong, lean arm. "And you can live here with me."

Mace smiled a little, studying her in the dying gold and orange rays of the sun through the windows of the bedroom. "One thing I know for sure, Sweetheart, is that I'm going to stay here, make you happy, love you and we'll be a team, together."

Sierra sighed and closed her eyes, rolling over into Mace's awaiting arms. He held her gently, kissing her hair, sliding his hand down her back and over her hip. "I love you so much, Mace," she quavered, "so much…"

A flood of tenderness flowed through Mace as he slowly undressed Sierra, taking his time, kissing her here and there, along her slender neck, feeling her react, those wonderful sounds that came from within her as he unbuttoned her pink, sleeveless blouse, laying it open, exposing her white cotton bra. The swell of her breasts beckoned, and he placed a wet kiss between them. Fumbling with the release, he saw her smile and sit up and help him, her breasts exposed as she pulled it off. His entire lower body hummed with hunger and need for this woman.

"Let me help you with the rest," she said a little breathlessly, easing out of his arms and standing by the bed. In no time, Sierra was out of her white shorts, had kicked off her sandals and pulled off her white cotton panties. She smiled, seeing the look in Mace's eyes. He was already shedding his clothes and, by the time she was standing naked by the bed, he'd come over, pulling her back down onto it and into his arms.

Mace groaned as she slid her lush body against his, their hips melded, his erection pressing against her belly. He cradled her in his arms, sliding her black hair aside, taking her mouth. There was a new urgency in him to claim Sierra now that their love had been admitted mutually. As his hand curved slowly around her breast, he watched her lashes shutter closed, her well-kissed lips parting, her hips insistent against his.

He liked her assertiveness, liked her boldness and wildness that was such a natural part of her. She wasn't laying still, her hands skimming his body, cupping his hips, fingers trailing down the outside of his strong thighs. Every touch was lighting more fires across his body. They were good in bed together. Every time it became better, deeper in its intimacy, taking him far beyond anything he had ever experienced with another woman.

As he leaned over, capturing her tight, peaked nipple between his lips, she eased away just enough to slide him into her. The movement caught him off guard and he groaned, suckling her, feeling her cry out. Mace wanted to hear her, feel her, and he released her nipple, giving her an intense look. Her half-closed eyes were glistening with arousal. Easing her onto her back, her thighs sliding apart to allow him deeper into herself, he smiled down at her. Framing her face with his large hands, he thrust slowly into her. All the way. Feeling her wet, slick body expanding, accepting him like a tight glove surrounding him. He saw her eyes change, widen and then pleasure gleam in them. She lifted her hips, teasing him. Mace could barely think as she established a rhythm designed to suck him dry.

Her breath was becoming ragged as he thrust into her, feeling her heat, feeling her getting close to orgasm. He'd never been with another woman as passionate as Sierra. One who enjoyed the act with him as much as she did. There was such pleasure in stroking slowly, deeply, into her, watching her eyes shift and change, her lips parted, those sounds of satisfaction caught in her exposed throat. Mace wanted to please her fully, slowly, let her know just how much he loved her. Taking her mouth, he slid his lips against hers, absorbing her softness, wetness and taste. Sliding his hand beneath her hip, he knew just the precise angle to lift her at to tease that swollen knot at her entrance. He felt her stiffen, a whimper filling his mouth as he teased her unmercifully, asking her to allow him to guide them this time. And she did, relaxing fully against Mace, allowing him to set the pace.

There was nothing he wanted to do quickly with Sierra this time. It was true, they had a hunger for one another that bordered on the voracious. And there was hardly a night that went by that they didn't make hungry, wild love with one another. And every time was like the first time.

But this time now, Mace wanted to worship Sierra, wanted to nip, lick and kiss every inch of her golden, damp, quivering body. He couldn't get enough of her. He'd never been addicted to anything, but he was addicted to her. And, as he slowed their pace, feeling her utterly surrender herself in every way to him, allowing him to cherish every single inch of her sinuous body, Mace knew how to tease her until she would begin to sob and beg him to allow her to orgasm. It wasn't even about teasing this time as he suckled first one pink, hardened nipple and then the other. It was about giving back to her in every possible way he knew how.

Her fingers were busy sliding through his short hair. She was hungrily taking his mouth, her tongue dancing with his. It made Mace groan. She knew how to unravel him so quickly and he broke their kiss, giving her a wry look. "This time," he growled, "is for you, Sweetheart…" She smiled up into his eyes and sent her fingers trailing across his chest, sending sparks of fire along his tightening flesh.

Mace knew, if he remained in her, she'd tease him into coming. And right now, he wanted to simply worship her body from head to toe. If she was disappointed as he removed himself, she didn't say anything. He moved down to her delicate feet. And he kissed each perfect toe, and then the slender arch and slowly moved up her long, sculpted legs. She was restless beneath his slow onslaught, her fingers digging into his shoulders as he began to lave his tongue along the inside of her right thigh. Mace knew she was needing him to touch her, the sounds urgent in her throat, her fingers gripping his shoulders, telling him.

As he licked her inner thigh, feeling her tense, inhaling the scent of her sex fragrance, Mace wanted to give her some relief. He slid one finger just inside her wet entrance, and Sierra suddenly whimpered, her hips thrusting up, wanting more of him. He began to stroke her hard, swollen knot. It told him she was so ready, so ripe. Slipping his hand beneath the small of her back, he captured her, held her so that all Sierra could do was pant, call his name, one hand gripping his upper arm in need. Mace didn't disappoint her as he felt her walls contract tightly. She cried out, her hips bucking against his hand as her body imploded inwardly. Satisfaction soared through Mace as he rocked her, milking her body, feeling her move into that dazed universe of burning heat and rippling pleasure that glowed throughout her lower body. His heart widened even more as he felt all the emotions tunneling through him as she sobbed out his name.

This was all so new to Mace. Before, he'd held his emotions in tight check, never allowing them to see the light of day. Yet, this willful, strong, and feminine locksmith Sierra, had picked open the unbreakable lock of his heart in a way that had never happened before. As he eased his finger from within her, he covered her, smiling down into her dazed green eyes, seeing the deep satisfaction the orgasm had given her. Appreciating her expression, he eased himself into her hot, sweet body and saw her eyes shutter closed, a moan rising in her throat as he filled her.

Mace knew she was sensitive, so he laid gently over her, taking most of the weight off her on his elbows planted on either side of her shoulders. He kissed her tenderly, feeling her respond, his body aching for release. There was something powerful in waiting for her to move through those magical levels of gratification. He could feel her gripping him tightly, the slick warmth of his body building its tension within himself. There was no need to rush his climax. Mace was satisfied in waiting, being one with Sierra, watching the corners of her mouth lifting, feeling her hands resting against his back. No longer was she restless, caught instead in the magical web of the orgasms. It boarded on the mystical, as if both their spirits were in complete and loving union with one another.

"You feel good in me," she whispered, settling her hands around his hips, slowly lifting her own, holding his gray, stormy gaze.

Inhaling a swift breath as she captured him, twisting teasingly, Mace groaned. Her hips swayed, turned, capturing him tightly and he gripped the velvet quilt of the bed between his fists, hissing. Resting his brow against hers, he rasped, "I want you to come with me…"

She laughed huskily, thrusting her hips against his. "Oh, I'm already there, Mace… Let go… It's all right…" and she slipped her legs around his hips, arching, taking him fully into her.

Grunting, trying to hold back until he felt Sierra become ready, hearing her give a small cry, his name tearing from her parted lips, only then, did Mace allow himself to surge forward, pumping swiftly into her, taking her, claiming her as he felt the hammering fire roar down his spine, through his tightened muscles and spilling hotly into her awaiting, sweet body. It felt as if his head had melted, and he was unable to think or even move. Mace groaned, tensing, his fists gripped within the quilt, teeth clenched as the intense pleasure roared through his paralyzed body.

It felt as if his release went on forever, longer than he could ever recall, his heart thudding heavily in his chest. He felt Sierra's slender hands stroking his dampened shoulders, heard her calling his name, telling him she loved him. He loved her, and he released his hands from the quilt, sliding them around her face, taking her mouth tenderly, breathing his breath into her, exchanging his own with hers. He lay upon her, feeling her lush curves, the way they surrendered to his angular, more muscular frame.

In the end, as Mace lifted his mouth from hers, drowning in the green and gold of Sierra's half-closed eyes, he felt like a man reborn.

It had been her steadfast love for him, her stubbornness in knowing they were right for one another, her courage to always keep reaching out to him, letting him know she was the one. And was she, forever. And, best of all, as Mace slowly eased out of her, taking Sierra into his arms, and rolling onto his side, he knew he loved her. Fully. Completely. For the first time in Mace's life, he knew what real love was. It was throbbing like sunlight through his chest, chasing away so much of the old, scarred, heavy grief that had come before it. Now, all that would be in the past.

As he pulled Sierra against him, her head on his shoulder, her slender arm spanning his chest, Mace closed his eyes and smiled. Really smiled. Because he was free from the past. All he needed now in the present, and in the future, was the woman in his arms, his warrioress. So brave. So strong. As Mace lay there, he felt that final surrender slip out through him. Through his heart; for the first time in forever, allowing this new joy full passage.

The emotions he felt right now were so damned intense, uplifting and filled with hope, that he couldn't speak.

Shifting his fingers through her long, thick hair, Mace was already planning a life with Sierra. His mind wasn't fully functioning, but he didn't care, all his senses were oriented on her and them. The scent of sex, the pounding of her heart against his chest, the light stroking of her fingertips brushing along his ribcage, the moist warmth of her breath spilling lightly along his neck, all conspired to take Mace into a deep, healing sleep with Sierra at his side. Tomorrow was a new day for both of them…

"I got the job at Shield," Mace told Sierra as he walked into the cabin two days later. She was at the counter, making them a lunch of grilled cheese sandwiches with sweet pickles on the side.

"I'm not surprised," she said, smiling over at him, "I knew Jack would snap you up in a heartbeat."

Mace shut the door. "It was a three-hour interview. Pretty intense, but Driscoll knows what he's after and what he wants," he said, throwing his baseball cap on the wooden hook. He walked into the kitchen where she was working. Sierra looked girlish in her bare feet, those loose, red shorts covering her mid-thigh, and a white tee with capped sleeves emphasizing her golden skin. Best of all, she wore her hair down, which he liked so much. The black cloak of it moved across her shoulders and back. He slid his hand beneath those strands, moving them aside to place a small nip against the back of her neck, lick and kiss it, feeling her react pleasurably.

"Mmmm," she said, putting the cheese and bread aside, turning around, sliding her hands around his waist, "I love the way you love me, Mace Kilmer."

He drowned in her upturned face, love written clearly across every aspect of her expression. Taking her into his arms, their hips meeting, Mace said,

"You look beautiful, Sierra. Must be all that lovemaking we do every night?" and he grinned, giving her a quick kiss across her smiling mouth. She was incredibly willful, unafraid to express her emotions with him. Mace drowned in her cypress-colored eyes, seeing nothing but love in them for him.

"Yes, and we're rather sleep-deprived the last two months, Kilmer," she teased with a laugh.

Shrugging, he turned her so his hips were against the counter, and she could lean her own against him. "Are you complaining?"

"No way," she murmured, sliding her hand across his shaven jaw. "So? When do you start? I bet Jack wanted you yesterday."

Nodding, Mace slid his fingers through her hair, watching her eyes begin to close. She loved her scalp gently massaged and he began to do so, watching her lips part. They couldn't touch one another without taking it to the next level and then they'd always end up on the velvet quilt. "He knows I have a week to go on my Army career. After that, he wants me to go to work for Shield."

"I'll bet Cal is happy to have you on board. He was overwhelmed with work."

"Yeah, I met him and talked with him and Alex Kazak, who's working in the mission section as well. We had a good, long-range talk in one of the conference rooms with Jack. You know it's not easy finding men like us. People with heavy experience in foreign countries pulling black ops."

"I do know," Sierra said, giving him a proud look. Mace had put on a charcoal-striped business suit for the interview, and he looked handsome, powerful, a man of the world. He wore a conservative blue tie, a crisp white college shirt beneath it. The change in clothing looked polar to her. He no longer looked anything like the gruff, hardened, Special Forces A team leader she'd first met down in Peru.

Instead, over these last two months, Mace had softened, his hardness replaced with more smiles and laughter. How Sierra loved to hear Mace laugh. It was a deep, rolling sound that moved her and always flung open the doors of her heart.

"He's giving me one-hundred and eighty thousand dollars a year. He said his people get six-month upgrades, depending upon their duties. He feels mission planning is the most important aspect of Shield, and I have a sense that, within a year, I'll be making over two-hundred thousand dollars."

"I knew he would value you," Sierra murmured. "Jack had to be impressed with your background and experience, but this is amazing, Mace. It will stop you from worrying about finances now."

"It means I can get my father into a better apartment that has more services for him and his condition."

Sierra knew how important that was to Mace. "It's a win-win for both of you." She knew Mace worried about his father. There were some things in Mace that would never change. One of those was being a responsible son.

He had made a quick trip back to see his father, Hank Kilmer, and Sierra had seen Mace return, and heard that many of the bridges between them were now healing.

Speaking of healing… Mace's foot after the second month since being bit by the Fer-De-Lance, had finally healed. He could wear his own shoe size now and was beginning a daily morning regimen walking along the dirt road by where they lived, walking a mile even before breakfast. He was returning to his peak physical condition and Sierra knew how important that was to Mace.

"Come in the living room for a minute?" he asked, releasing her. Mace shrugged out of his business suit coat, draping it over a chair. As they walked into the living room, he tugged apart the knot of his tie and discarded it to one side. Opening the top button on his collar, he grasped Sierra's hand and led her to the couch, drawing her down beside him. "I've got a little something for you," he said, reaching into his pants pocket.

Sierra gave him a quizzical look and watched him draw out a red velvet box. Mace opened it. She stared down at the rings for a moment and then back up at him.

"Marry me, Sierra?" he asked her, holding her gaze. "I can't think of a life without you in it. And I don't want to wait any longer to ask you… to make this official."

Tears burned in her eyes as she lightly touched the bands. The gems in her engagement ring was the color of her eyes. They were three-channel-cut rectangular stones. Lifting her gaze, she whispered, "You know I'll marry you, Kilmer. There was never any question on my end of that," and she leaned forward, framing his face with her palms, kissing him long and deep.

Once they stepped away from the kiss, holding the ring box in her hands, his arm around her shoulders, holding her close, Sierra asked, "When did you get these?"

"Long story," he murmured wryly, kissing her hair. "Cal knew a good jeweler in San Diego. I had told him I didn't want the usual wedding ring set… that I wanted something special. I wanted to get gemstones that were the color of your eyes. So, it took a while and quite a few phone calls. They are green tourmaline, from Brazil." He gave her a concerned look. "Do you really like it? Or maybe you'd rather have diamonds instead?"

"I love them," Sierra assured him gently, touching his cheek, smiling into his light-gray eyes. "This is so thoughtful of you, Mace. You constantly surprise me." She pulled out the engagement ring, handed it to him and said, "Slip this on my finger? Make this official?"

He grinned and nodded as she offered her slender hand to him. "Now, if it fits, I can stop worrying," he joked. The gold ring slid easily onto her finger. Holding her hand, he leaned down and kissed her smiling mouth. "I love you, Sierra Chastain. Now, all we need to do is figure out a wedding date."

Throwing her arms round his shoulders, she kissed him warmly and whispered, "Sooner, not later. Okay, Kilmer?"

"Suits me," he agreed, tucking her beneath his arm. He moved his hand across her belly, studying her. "I know you want children. So do I." His hand stilled over her rounded abdomen. "It's up to you, Sierra. I'll be happy with whatever you want." He saw her face soften and grow tender. She placed her hand over his.

"I'm ready when you are. I keep imagining two or three kids here, in our cabin."

Mace chuckled. "Then I'd best get to work in my off time from Shield and build three more rooms onto this cabin." Their house sat on a five-acre parcel. Mace could expand the pine cabin any way they wanted. He saw Sierra smile and nod.

"And I'll help you build those rooms. I'm handy with a hammer and nails." she said.

"And paint and dry wall," he added, feeling powerful surges of love tunnel through him. "We'll do it together, like we do everything else."

Sierra kept his large, wide hand against her belly. "We have a whole, wonderful life that we're building together, Mace. And I'm so happy…"

END

Don't miss Lindsay McKenna's next Shadow Team series novel, *Shadow Target.*

Available from Lindsay McKenna and Blue Turtle Publishing and wherever you buy eBooks.

Excerpt from Shadow Target

T AL'S LIPS THINNED. "Remember? I told you there was a curve ball to this assignment?"

Shep Porter held her somber look. He sat in a Mission room at Delos, a global charity organization. There were eight people, all from Planning, at the oval maple table. "You did. What is it?"

Gesturing to the screen on the wall to his left, she said, "The PIC, Pilot In Command, and her co-pilot both work for Shield Security out of Bahir Dar. Willow Chamberlin is the PIC. Your ex-wife."

The pit of Shep's stomach clenched into a painful fist. He stared at Tal, who was leading the planning of this mission, feeling shock race through him. He had very little connection with Willow. Shep never asked where she was or what she was doing. They kept their few emails brief, breezy and impersonal. He always looked forward to them, no matter how brief or blasé they were. Knowing he'd hurt Willow badly, Shep knew she was protecting herself from his earlier immature actions. She was a Feminist, and he had overreacted to her all the time. And because they were both confident and very sure of themselves, neither gave or considered compromised to keep their budding relationship viable. It was death spiral for their marriage, no matter how well they got along in bed. That was three years ago, and now, it seemed like another lifetime.

Tal studied him as silence cloaked the room. She put another photo on the screen of the wall of the Planning room.

Shep turned, his gaze on Willow. She was wearing a dark green one-piece flight suit with the Delos patch of red and yellow rising sun above her left breast pocket with her name, Chamberlin, W. below it. On her left arm was an American flag. On the right, as part of her undercover status, in big yellow embroidered letters was Delos Charities with her name below it.

His throat tightened, unable to tear his gaze from her oval, unsmiling face. She wore an olive-green baseball cap with the Delos logo on the front of it. She had bright carrot red hair gathered in a ponytail. It was her green eyes, large, intelligent and and taking no prisoners look in them. Willow was standing next to her Otter twin engine aircraft, her hands on her hips, looking confident. He knew that look. After all? She'd been a badass combat pilot, hurling destruction below her to keep Americans safe on the ever-changing battlefield called Afghanistan years earlier.

"Willow and her co-pilot, Dev, are both Shield Security employees, and they are undercover as Delo's employees, and they have been at Bahir Dar for two years. Her job as PIC was to take all the supplies Delos ships in monthly, to all the villages that you see on that map in front of you. Her copilot is Dev Mitchell, another ex-USAF transport pilot and they fly into each of the dirt strips next to the village to deliver the goods and supplies to the Delos charity that supports its people."

Shep noticed the black nylon drop holster around Willow's right thigh and the .45 pistol in it. "So nowhere in Africa is safe?" he asked, turning to Cav, the expert in that part of the world for this planning session.

"Not really," the ex-SEAL said. "Some places are safer than others. Some hire security guards to keep it that way. With domestic or foreign terrorism, no place in the world is safe anymore, Shep. It isn't just Africa." Cav pointed toward the screen. "As I understand it, Willow and Dev are in constant potential danger because they're operating in outlying, rural villages. We know that Tefere David, a known terrorist in the Middle East, who is a real ongoing threat, has his soldiers rove these areas, looking for ways to rob Delos IF they can get inside the fence to get to the plunder in the school or medical buildings. The only reason they haven't is due to a back door agreement with Ethiopian Army General Hakym. He's placed a squad of ten soldiers at each Delos charity. Those men live in those villages, and it has detoured a number of attacks by Tefere David on them, as a result. But it's not foolproof."

"And," Wyatt, the manager on this mission, said, "that's ending once we get our new security measures in place via Shield Security employees we've just hired. We may also have to place a permanent security team at each one of these villages until Tefere David can be caught and brought to justice or killed by one of General Hakym's hunter-killer teams who are out always looking for him. They are actively seeking him and his men, but the Middle East is a big area and he doesn't have unlimited resources to find that bastard."

"I see." Shep tried to settle his thudding heart as he kept his gaze trained on Willow's face. Her nose was red from being outdoors too long. She was typical redhead in that her skin was very susceptible to too much sunlight. That was why she always wore a baseball cap at Bagram Army-air base in Afghanistan where she had been stationed in Afghanistan. The sleeves on her uniform were rolled up to just below her elbows and he saw the aviators watch on her slender right wrist. Willow was five foot seven inches tall, around a hundred and forty pounds. She was built lean like a greyhound, with small breasts and slender hips. But that look did not reveal her assertive, Type A personality in the least. To an outsider, no one would guess she'd been a combat pilot. He smiled to himself, knowing she was a like a Belgian malinois war trained dog who took no prisoners. It didn't show up except when she was sitting in the cockpit of her F-15 Eagle, taking out the bad guys to protect Americans below where she flew.

"Well?" Tal pressed gently, holding his gaze. "Are you still in this assignment or not? You will be interfacing with Willow all the time. She and her copilot will be constantly flying in and out of the villages where you'll be working to put the security fencing in place for that particular charity."

He shrugged. "I'm okay with it." He saw Tal's eyes narrow speculatively on him, almost feeling her energy in his mind, as if trying to read his real thoughts.

Wyatt added, "Look, Willow and Dev have worked two years for Delos out in that area of the world. They're good at what they do. Both are savvy ex-military trained pilots and they know the lay of the land. You need to realize that they both have experiences and observations that is going to help the new Shield security team you'll have, and your Delos people, so you need to listen to them, Shep. Is that going to be a problem between you and Willow?"

Shep knew his faults. Just like Willow, but he had accused her headstrong and bullheaded. When one put two pieces of titanium steel in the same room with one another, there was not much give or flexibility accorded to the other. Rubbing his bearded jaw, he said, "Not a problem. I value my people's protection. I'll listen to Willow and Dev's experience and counsel. Just because Willow and I couldn't make the marriage work doesn't mean I can't work with her on a professional level." Shep saw the question in Wyatt's eyes, but the Texan said nothing except to give him a brief nod.

"Okay, everyone can leave except Tal, Alex, Matt, Shep and myself," Wyatt told the employees at the table. Within a few minutes, the room was cleared out, the door shut, and silence returned to it.

Alexa said, "Shep? This is personal between the four of us. We're shutting off the recording equipment because it needs to stay within our circle. I know Willow personally. I've worked with her closely in the past. Because I was an Air Force officer and flew a combat jet like she did." She opened her hands. "You might say we're sisters of a sort because of the background and experiences as combat pilots that we share."

"Okay," Shep said, "what are you trying to say, Alexa?"

Moving uncomfortably, Alexa said, "I've never lost contact with her. We've always remained good friends. From time to time, Willow would open up to me about her marriage to you. It sounded more like a dog and cat in a fight. You two butted heads constantly. Neither of you, from the sounds of it, could make a compromise. You were both right. Neither was ever wrong. It was like putting two Type A's into a room to figure out a compromise on something and it never worked." She tilted her head. "Am I wrong about this analysis?"

Shep could feel the tension rise in the silence of the room. Women talked; he knew that. So, he wasn't surprised that Willow and Alexa were tighter than thieves because of their mutual military background. Clearing his throat, he said, "No, your observations are correct."

"Okay," Alexa pressed, "if that's so? What makes you think that you'll be able to get along now for the sake of the assignment?"

It was a fair question and Shep knew it. He ruffled inwardly, his pride hurt. But then, he knew he had too much pride and wasn't able to admit when he was wrong about something. It was a bad habit; one he had worked on constantly to be honest since Willow walked out on him. "Maturity? Time? We've been divorced three years. I hope I've matured since then." And then he grimaced. "I know where my faults are at, Alexa. And I'm working on them every day. I have changed but Willow is going to have to find that out once we meet up."

Wyatt cleared his throat. "Shep, with all due respect, I've looked at the reports from your people when researching your field reports. You are considered an able manager, you listen well, you ask for the employees' thoughts and ideas. That's very different than what we're hearing what happened between you and Willow. You seemed to be able to respect and hear your employees and that's praise coming from them. Am I correct about that?"

Shep felt their collective concern at the table. Another legitimate question and he knew the Delos people were trying to ensure this would be a successful outcome to their mission. He could feel their confusion and if he could honestly carry off the assignment successfully, given his behavior toward Willow. Folding his hands over the manual in front of him, he gave them all a serious look. "You're right. I'm fine working with employees. With Willow? It was different and I'm not going to throw blame around. I'll make this mission work because we aren't married any longer. To me? She's an employee from another company. I'm a professional hired by Delos. I'll slip into my management harness, and we'll get along fine, and I'll make it work." He saw relief in their expressions. They needed assurance that he would do his level best to keep it a peaceful venture, not a contentious one like their marriage had been for those stormy years.

Tal sat back, a pleased look on her face. "Okay, good enough, Shep. Wyatt is going to send Willow an encrypted file that is going to give her info about the up-and-coming mission, plus info on the large Shield Security team coming in under cover as Delos employees. You have a construction team to manage as well. Our next step is to find out whether she can work with YOU."

Available from
Lindsay McKenna

Blue Turtle Publishing

SHADOW TEAM SERIES
Last Stand
Collateral Damage
No Quarter
Unforgettable
Hostile Territory

NON-SERIES BOOKS
Down Range (Reprint)
Dangerous Prey (Reprint)
Love Me Before Dawn (Reprint)
Point of Departure (Reprint)
Touch the Heavens (Reprint)

WOMEN OF GLORY SERIES
No Quarter Given (Reprint)
The Gauntlet (Reprint)
Under Fire (Reprint)

LOVE & GLORY SERIES
A Question of Honor, Book 1 (Reprint)
No Surrender, Book 2 (Reprint)
Return of a Hero, Book 3 (Reprint)
Dawn of Valor, Book 4 (Reprint)

LOVE & DANGER SERIES
Morgan's Son, Book 5 (Reprint)
Morgan's Wife, Book 6 (Reprint)
Morgan's Rescue, Book 7 (Reprint)
Morgan's Marriage, Book 8 (Reprint)

WARRIORS FOR THE LIGHT
Unforgiven, Book 1 (Reprint)
Dark Truth, Book 2 (Reprint)
The Quest, Book 3 (Reprint)
Reunion, Book 4 (Reprint)
The Adversary, Book 5 (Reprint)

Guardian, Book 6 (Reprint)

DELOS

Last Chance, prologue novella to Nowhere to Hide
Nowhere to Hide, Book 1
Tangled Pursuit, Book 2
Forged in Fire, Book 3
Broken Dreams, Book 4
Blind Sided, BN2
Secret Dream, B1B novella, epilogue to Nowhere to Hide
Hold On, Book 5
Hold Me, 5B1, sequel to Hold On
Unbound Pursuit, 2B1 novella, epilogue to Tangled Pursuit
Secrets, 2B2 novella, sequel to Unbound Pursuit, 2B1
Snowflake's Gift, Book 6
Never Enough, 3B1, novella, sequel to Forged in Fire
Dream of Me, 4B1, novella, sequel to Broken Dreams
Trapped, Book 7
Taking a Chance 7B1, novella, sequel to Trapped
The Hidden Heart, 7B2, novella, sequel to Taking A Chance
Boxcar Christmas, Book 8
Sanctuary, Book 9
Dangerous, Book 10
Redemption, 10B1, novella, sequel to Dangerous

Kensington

SILVER CREEK SERIES

Silver Creek Fire
Courage Under Fire

WIND RIVER VALLEY SERIES

Wind River Wrangler
Wind River Rancher
Wind River Cowboy
Christmas with my Cowboy
Wrangler's Challenge
Lone Rider
Wind River Lawman
Kassie's Cowboy
Home to Wind River
Western Weddings: Wind River Wedding
Wind River Protector
Wind River Undercover

Everything Lindsay McKenna

My website is dedicated to all my series. There are articles on characters, my publishing schedule, and information about each book written by me. You can also learn more about my newsletter, which covers my upcoming books, publishing schedule, giveaways, exclusive cover peeks and more.

lindsaymckenna.com

Made in United States
Orlando, FL
13 March 2024

44736542R00128